I0761689

FLOODLINES

ALSO BY

SALEEM HADDAD

Guapa

Saleem Haddad

FLOODLINES

Europa Editions
27 Union Square West, Suite 302
New York NY 10003
www.europaeditions.com
info@europaeditions.com

This book is a work of fiction. Any references to historical events, real people, or real locales are used fictitiously.

First Publication 2026 by Europa Editions

Library of Congress Cataloging in Publication Data is available
ISBN 979-8-88966-165-8

Haddad, Saleem
Floodlines

Cover design by Ginevra Rapisardi

Cover image: *Untitled*, 1974 by Nazar Selim. Courtesy of Ramzi and Saeda Dalloul Art Foundation (DAF), Beirut

Prepress by Grafica Punto Print – Rome

Printed in the USA

CONTENTS

For Adam (habs)

People are trapped in history
and history is trapped in them.
—James Baldwin

FLOODLINES

Part I

Archive Fever

"Nothing sorts out memories from ordinary moments.
Later on they do claim remembrance
when they show their scars."
—*La Jettée*

Nizar

July 2014

"I need you to visit Ishtar."

His mother's voice was clear. Nizar asked her to repeat herself anyway.

"I need you to get the family story out of her."

Nizar looked down from the edge of his balcony. Three floors below, the concrete felt welcoming in its hardness.

"I want nothing to do with her."

"Nizar, I have no one else to turn to. I'd like to arrange this exhibition while your grandmother is still with us, and I don't know how much time—" Nizar heard the flick of his mother's lighter at the other end of the line. "Look, I'm just asking for this one thing. Get her to tell you the family history and write it down for me."

"Why don't you just pay her to do it?"

Zainab sighed. "Because I know my sister. She'll take the money, find some way to say that it's morally reprehensible to force her to narrativise or to simplify, and then not do it."

"I haven't spoken to her since that dinner," he said, resenting how easily his mother forced him to unpack memories he had long ago sealed off.

"I suspect she's in a fragile state."

"She's *always* in a fragile state."

"This ISIS stuff has really . . ." Zainab interrupted herself and took a deep drag of her cigarette. "Anyway. Do you have any upcoming work trips, habibi?"

He looked over to the flats across the canal. In one, an old man in a bathrobe typed steadily at his desk. "I don't do that kind of work anymore."

"What do you mean?"

He considered how to explain this decision to his mother. How to tell her that after moving out of the flat with Alfie he had been walking around his new neighbourhood in Hackney when he noticed a CrossFit gym under one of the station arches. How he had found himself entranced by the young, hard-bodied trainers with garish tattoos, how they strutted through the white powdered chalk hanging in the air, slapping each other's backs. How in the past he had scoffed at those who invested hours sculpting a body that would inevitably decay, but in that moment realised his long-held belief—that an investment in the mind was forever—now struck him as naïve. How he had paid a membership fee and began to go every day. How he found the anti-intellectualism to be a reprieve, because there was no chance for the mind to wander during a work-out; he could only focus on his form, his breath, his weights. How he powered through sets of gruelling circuits named after American soldiers who died in Iraq and Afghanistan, and how after each class he collapsed on the floor of the gym, his muscles sore for days, a satisfying pain. How his shoulders broadened, his thighs thickened, and his pecs swelled. How muscles he never knew existed emerged underneath his skin. How disciplining his body brought control in a collapsing world, and how when the instructors yelled *FEEL THE BURN* he thought not of the searing flesh from the explosion but of the lactic acid burning through his muscles. How when he began to follow men on social media who demonstrated workout routines and discussed the virtues of bone broth, his algorithm interspersed half-naked men with brutalised Palestinian bodies and shell-shocked Syrian boys, their body parts like cuts of meat. Here: a thigh. There: a torso. How he was no longer sure if the photos were there to arouse or enrage. How his new body brought a different kind of attention, and in the spring while scrolling through endless torsos on Grindr, a message appeared that caught his eye: 90 quid to suck ur cock. How when the man came over, heavyset, in his fifties, he gave Nizar the money and all he had to do was unzip his trousers. It was so damn easy, and a few days later he did it again, and again, and as the bodies piled up and the atrocities multiplied, he recoiled at those who touted the virtues of journalism, who defended the media as heroes in pursuit of the truth. Whose truth? With the right spin, a government could push news of a massacre off the headlines. How could he tell his mother that it was more moral to sell his body than to sell his soul for some bullshit idea of the truth? He no longer believed that journalists were truth-seekers. They were carriers of the apocalypse, scavengers for a story: desperate for clicks, exposing global misery to pad their pockets, leading the masses down whirlpools of clickbait, the curators of an assembly line of death that floated down social media feeds and quickly disappeared until everyone forgot what it was they were so angry about, only that they had a fireball of rage inside of them, throbbing and ready to explode. He saw it in his own feed, the way news drifted down his timeline like the flow of a river: death, fires, war, floods, famine, sex. Malnourished children in Yarmouk, malnourished women in Beverly Hills. Swiping left, swiping right, chat rooms, saunas, jerking off to a sea of changing faces, sucking off one man, fisting another. What else to do in this ungovernable world but master control over his body? What an achievement! The glaciers were melting, but he completed fifty double-unders without breaking form. Palestine was being disappeared, but he doubled the weight of his snatches in a month. The Islamic State dissolved the concepts of Syria and Iraq, but his quads were indestructible. The Assad regime was starving hundreds of thousands, but if he ate nothing but boiled chicken for three days he could glimpse the outline of his abs under the right lighting. How could he tell her that sex was salvation?

That they could colonise his hole, but they would never colonise his mind. That he had sex because the world was getting warmer, hotter, so hot, baby. That he could do nothing about the oil drilling but yeah mate, drill deep. How afterwards he would lie on an unfamiliar bed in a euphoric calm that lasted a few minutes, and then the world would encroach and he would have to find another, would have to keep moving, because to connect was to be shackled, to love was to be enslaved. Better to pass the bodies down the assembly line, moving along until suddenly and without warning he would be walking down the street one summer and a twink would yell out 'Hey Daddy!' and he would turn around and realise that the twink was talking to *him*, that time had moved on, persistently, relentlessly, and he would have to clench his jaw to stop from screaming.

"I haven't done any war reporting all year," he said. "I thought I told you."

He looked out towards the horizon. "I've got to go. I'm in the middle of something."

"Wait," Zainab said. "The main reason I called, and this is the third time, by the way, is to wish you a happy birthday."

"Right. Thanks. You too."

"What do you mean?"

"I don't know. It's the day you birthed me, so I guess it's your day too."

"Is that how these things work?"

Silence fell through the cracks of the conversation.

"Thirty-two?"

"Thirty-three."

"If you *do* get the chance to speak to Ishtar . . ."

"I'm not getting involved in your family squabbles. Please don't call me about this again."

Nizar hung up and stepped down from the railing. Dark clouds hung low in the sky and imprisoned the moisture and heat in the air, just like the day he had met Alfie five years earlier. It was the summer of 2009, and he'd been standing on a different ledge. The northbound Victoria line platform at King's Cross. Gazing down at the filthy tracks, the promise of death flashed in his mind.

He looked up at the orange numbers. One minute until the train arrived. Or was it more? He recalled something a friend had told him once, how the time displayed wasn't really accurate, that a minute stretched out longer—ninety seconds, maybe more. It was a trick to calm the nerves of anxious commuters, to give the illusion that the next train was just that bit closer.

A low rumble vibrated through the soles of his shoes. He imagined the train's approach, the burst of stale air it would bring with it, the twin beams piercing the darkness, growing larger, closer. He imagined his body: limbs twisted, bones shattered, blood mixing with the oil and grime of the tracks. Would it be quick? A flash of pain and then nothing? Or would it linger, his consciousness trapped in a broken body as the world spun above him? He closed his eyes and was back in Baghdad, among the strewn bodies, the contorted limbs, the furnace of heat. He took a breath, his lungs filling with damp, metallic air. The smell of charred flesh and rubber was suffocating. He felt the blood drip down his cheek, the terrifying silence that preceded the screams—

A hand on the back of his neck. Uninitiated skin-on-skin contact, a cataclysmic subversion of the unspoken rules of the metropolitan transport system. In another situation Nizar might have smacked aside the stranger's hand, but an intimacy in the touch stopped him. The hand pulled him back, rooted him in the present. He opened his eyes as the train thundered by, a blur of white and blue. A gust of wind whipped at his clothes. The disquiet retreated, a wave drawing back into the sea.

"You alright?"

Nizar nodded and followed the crowds inside the carriage. The stranger took a seat beside him. He looked down at the hand that had been on the back of his neck. The fingers were pale and wrinkled; the hands of an old man. Nizar looked at the darkened window across from him. In the reflection, the owner of the hand appeared younger than he expected. Late twenties, no more than a couple of years older than himself. The man had a dark beard and cradled a tote bag on his lap. Tattoos ran down each of his arms. He caught Nizar's gaze in the reflection.

At the next stop, the man stood up and left the tube, moving through the crowd without looking back. Nizar followed, weaving through a group of teenagers with large Zara shopping bags. Catching up with the stranger on the platform, Nizar tapped his shoulder.

The man turned around. He had brown eyes, warm and unassuming. Laughter lines at the corners of his eyes suggested a history of happiness.

"Thank you," Nizar said. The stranger brushed off his gratitude with a faint smile, his eyes dropping to the floor.

"I'm Nizar."

"Alfie."

The name seemed perfectly suited. He was tall and conventionally handsome, like an Alfred, but a charming dishevelment to his appearance made 'Alfie' more apt. His beard was scruffy and he had a silver hoop earring in one ear. The tattoos along his left arm consisted of various lines and circles that looked almost child-like, and along his right was an intricate arrangement of flowers emerging from water, with tiny gold and pink fish swimming between the leaves. His t-shirt was old, the sleeves haphazardly cut off. On the front in large block letters were the words 'Made in England. Destroyed in Magaluf.'

"It's ironic," Alfie explained, glancing down at his shirt.

They shuffled out of the underground and turned onto Upper Street. Alfie explained he was on his way to meet a friend at Ottolenghi. Nizar held himself back from commenting on the problematics of Ottolenghi's liberal Zionism.

"I'm heading to Waterstones," Nizar said, nodding vaguely up the street. A lie. He didn't want to scare him off by disclosing that he'd only gotten off the tube to follow him.

"So what is it you do?" Nizar asked, trying to keep his voice light as they walked.

"I'm a DJ. And a songwriter of sorts." Alfie added the second part quickly, an afterthought he seemed embarrassed to admit.

Nizar told him that he was a journalist.

"What kind of journalism?"

"Like war stuff," he said dismissively.

Alfie stopped and turned to him with mock gravity. "So we're both braving the worst of humanity in some of the most desperate and dangerous places in the world."

Nizar glanced at their reflection in the furniture shop window. Standing side-by-side, they looked, he couldn't help but think, good together. There was an easy alignment to their bodies, like they belonged to the same photograph. As he looked past their reflection into the softly lit showroom—minimalist table lamps, a sprawling mustard sofa—he saw something else: a glimpse of himself living alongside someone. The thought was startling. In the blur of glass and overpriced furniture, the vision of them building a life together took shape in his mind with exhilarating potential, like the beginnings of a creative project.

"That was a joke," Alfie said, studying Nizar's face for hints of offence.

Nizar smiled to ease his concerns, grabbing his arm as they carried on down the road.

"In any case, have you been to Soho on a Saturday night? It's basically Mogadishu."

"I'll take your word for it." He was self-conscious about the fact he felt more comfortable being interrogated by an armed militia than standing amongst a group of shirtless men at a club.

"Why not come see it for yourself?" Alfie asked, as Ottolenghi's red awning came into view. "I'll be DJing at *Heaven* tonight. I start at ten, but it doesn't pick up until later."

And so, he did. Drink in hand, he scanned the room until he saw Alfie standing behind a booth in the corner, his headphones held to one ear, his eyes closed in concentration as garish electro-pop blasted through the speakers. Beside him stood a muscular, shirtless man, and a pink-haired drag queen. Nizar watched as the shirtless man tapped Alfie on the shoulder, one hand gripping Alfie's neck and the other pulling him closer at the waist. Alfie smiled politely at whatever the man said and returned his focus to the laptop, gently loosening the young man's grip on him. All at once, Nizar was overcome with a fear that Alfie would not remember him, or—worse—treat him with the same polite disregard as he had the shirtless man. Just as he considered turning around, Alfie saw him and smiled.

"I suppose you're here to report on the latest crisis engulfing the Republic of Soho?" Alfie shouted over the music.

"Something like that."

He patted the area next to him in the booth. "Better view from up here."

The shirtless man begrudgingly made space for him and Nizar climbed onto the platform, relieved to be insulated from the dance floor's drunken unpredictability. He stood awkwardly while Alfie mixed one song into another. Each time Nizar considered leaving, Alfie turned to him and grinned, or else pointed something out to keep him within reach. Between changing tracks, Alfie entertained him by mimicking different people's dancing, rolling his eyes at song requests, and dramatically refusing to play the Black-Eyed Peas. During a ten-minute mix of Kylie Minogue's 'Slow', Alfie provided running commentary on the dance floor in a surprisingly impressive David Attenborough impression:

"To your right you can see a gaggle of hens at one of their parties. This is part of the heterosexual mating ritual, a chaotic celebration prior to their captivity. Be warned. In an hour or so when they are truly drunk they get quite savage, preying on vulnerable twinks in their vicinity. Oh, here we go, one of them is approaching now. She looks like a Britney fan." Alfie paused and grabbed him by the neck, pulling him closer. "Britney fans are one of the most dangerous brigades out there." Alfie's fingers playfully weaved through the curls on the back of Nizar's head.

The woman, in her late twenties with platinum blonde hair and glittery eye shadow, stumbled towards the booth. She leaned over the deck, spilling some of her drink on the turntable.

"Oi, watch the equipment!" Alfie growled with surprising roughness.

The girl turned to Nizar. "You his boyfriend, hun?"

Nizar was about to shake his head when Alfie responded.

"Yeah, he is. What do you want?"

"Can you play 'Toxic'?"

After Alfie's set, they left the club and headed to Old Compton Street. In front of Cafe Nero, Alfie stopped and kissed him.

"Come home with me," he said. And Nizar did.

Alfie did not mention the scar until after they arrived at the flat, until after they had ripped off each other's clothes and had drunken sex on the mattress in the corner of his room, until after they had both come and were lying down beside each other, staring into each other's eyes. It was only then that Alfie ran his thumb along the jagged stretch of skin that ran down Nizar's cheek.

"How did you get this?"

There was no escaping the memory burned into his flesh.

Nizar began to shiver. He tried to tell the story, but the blast and the limbs and the blood glistening on the asphalt overwhelmed him. Alfie held him tightly, the warmth of his body keeping the memories at bay, and Nizar believed this to be a sign that the worst was over.

He missed Alfie so much. As he stood on the balcony, a flood of tears threatened to burst from him, but he held them back.

To get out of the house, Nizar decided to treat himself to an expensive dinner. He made a reservation at the restaurant Alfie had taken him to for his last birthday, and in a cruel twist the waitress led him to the exact table he and Alfie had dined at the year before. Sitting across from the now-empty chair, Nizar recalled the conversation they'd had that night. Alfie had mentioned buying a van and traveling around Europe.

"Sounds a tad cliché," he'd remarked. At the time, he could only see Alfie as someone entirely unserious, liberated from the shackles of human suffering in which Nizar found himself drowning.

"Who cares? It would feel so free to just pack up and run away."

"I've spent my entire life running away."

Alfie had looked at Nizar then, with a clarity so piercing that even in the midst of his Valium-induced fog he saw himself through Alfie's eyes: as someone who'd seen a lot, who'd grown as a person because of it, but who was also deeply unhappy, and unable—even unwilling—to extract himself from his despair. Their eyes locked in a shared moment of savage honesty, until Alfie looked away.

Now, Nizar ordered a large glass of Syrah, the baked aubergine, and the third most expensive steak on the menu. He considered how their relationship had involved a balancing act between the person they thought they were and the person their lover perceived them to be. Perhaps, unknowingly, he had morphed into Alfie's worst perceptions of him.

The aubergine was sweet and smoky, its fleshy insides dissolving in his mouth. There was a certain liberation in eating alone, he realised, a sense of possibility wrapped around a hard ball of shame. He considered his mother's plea to get in touch with Ishtar.

No, there was no reason to get in touch with her again.

When the steak arrived his fork pierced the flesh, unleashing a mixture of oil and blood that oozed onto the plate. Nizar thought of his grandmother. She must be in her eighties, and though he felt prepared for her death in a vague and indeterminate future, the urgency in his mother's voice had thrust it into the very real present. His grandmother's decay flashed vividly in his mind. He put the steak in his mouth, and as he bit down he was all at once aware that what he was eating had been alive, a sentient being endowed with consciousness and memories. Nausea came over him in waves. He put down his fork and stumbled to the bathroom. In the white porcelain toilet, he violently threw up.

His stomach empty, he stood at the sink and cupped water to his face. The conversation with his mother had fractured the dam inside him. He looked at his reflection in the mirror. Clammy skin, flushed. Hair plastered to brow. He touched a fingertip to the scar on his cheek, hooked its ridge with his nail, and drew it apart. The ridge deepened then bloomed, flowering into a red seam that oozed and threaded to the jaw. His face streaked with dirt. Eyes wide and unseeing. Shirt torn and sodden with a stranger's blood. He shut his eyes. When he opened them, only the old scar remained.

Ten Days Earlier

Zainab

June 2014

Zainab was halfway down the path when a side door to the cottage swung open. Her mother appeared, a stained rag in one hand, her butcher's apron splattered with paint. Had it only been a year since they last saw each other? Her mother's eyes were still sharp and piercing, but her face was gaunt, her normally upright posture arched. She had aged so much, or else Zainab's memory of her had somehow frozen at a convenient moment in the past.

"I heard the car," Bridget remarked. She had been working, Zainab gathered, and this realisation triggered a sudden anxiety in having interrupted her.

Zainab moved to hug her, but her mother recoiled from her embrace.

"Don't! I'm covered in paint."

Zainab took in her surroundings.

"This place is beautiful," she said. The house was nestled between a landscape of rolling green hills and forests. The property itself, two semi-attached granite structures that stood almost perpendicular to one another, was larger than she expected. "Where's Mediha?"

"She's away for the week," Bridget said, leading Zainab through the side door and into the kitchen. It smelled of paint thinner and ground coffee. "Did she not mention?"

"No."

"Oh. Well, she left a note," Bridget gestured towards an envelope on the kitchen counter. "I just need a few minutes to clean up. Ishtar should be here soon."

Inside the envelope were three typed pages. A last-minute space in a week-long meditation retreat had opened, her younger sister had written, and she would return at the weekend. The rest of the letter was a bullet-pointed manual with house rules and notes on caring for their mother. The tone was professional yet terse, as if Mediha expected her to struggle to understand anything more than simple, direct language. She couldn't help but feel the patronising tone Mediha used with her was driven by the belief that, as Zainab had stayed in the Arab world, she had somehow evaded a necessary civilising process. In lieu of a goodbye, Mediha ended the letter with: *Please, Zainab, DON'T let Mama smoke.*

"How was the flight from Dubai, Bulbul?" her mother asked, walking into the kitchen. She had removed the paint-stained apron and was wearing a light blue sweater and jeans.

"It was fine, direct to Glasgow." Zainab noticed a smudge of paint on her mother's hairline. She reached to wipe it away, then stopped herself. "I slept for most of it."

Her mother nodded and turned on the kettle. "Can I have one of your cigarettes?"

Zainab shoved Mediha's letter into her pocket and fished through her bag. She pulled out her cigarettes and knocked two out of the packet.

"Don't tell Mediha, she'll kill me."

"You and me both," Bridget stuck the cigarette in her mouth and motioned for a light.

Ishtar arrived soon after, wearing an oversized shirt and black jeans with a duffle bag slung over her shoulder. At sixty, Zainab's older sister remained a striking presence, slender and strong, with large hands and lean, muscular arms. Her dark hair contained a single streak of white that emerged from the crown of her head like a bolt of lightning. Her appearance fell somewhere between Zainab's, whose dark skin and large features looked very Arab, and Mediha's, with her more British look.

Zainab handed her the letter. "Instructions from Mediha."

"Have you read them?"

"Yeah."

Ishtar let the pages flutter to the table. "I'll follow your lead."

"I suppose I ought to give you a tour." Bridget took them into a spacious living room, its high ceilings crossed with dark wooden beams. The space was filled with an eclectic mix of furniture, vibrant patterns, and Middle Eastern handicrafts. The walls were painted a soft cream. To the right of the fireplace, a hallway extended toward the rest of the house. The old wooden floors creaked beneath their feet as they stopped at the first door, which Bridget unlocked with a heavy set of keys.

"Ishtar, you're staying in Mediha's office."

The room had a large wooden desk, and beside it a fold-out sofa-bed had been prepared. Ishtar dropped her bag with a thud and walked towards the large shelves lined with folders and books. She scanned the titles, running a finger along the spines before pulling out a book titled *Gender and Islam*. She read the back cover, flipped through the pages, then let it snap shut.

"Of course," she said dryly, putting it back in its place.

At the end of the hall was another locked door. "That's Mediha's room," Bridget explained. "She doesn't like anyone going in there," she added, herding them back into the living room and towards a door beside the pantry.

"My live-in studio," Bridget said, as they stepped into the large, airy room. "Zainab, you'll be staying here with me."

The room was vast and sleek, with polished white floorboards and brushed steel fittings that felt at odds with the rest of the cottage. Floor-to-ceiling windows looked out onto the garden with its backdrop of hills mottled with birch and pine, and flooded the space with natural light. In an alcove facing the window stood an easel and canvas surrounded by tubes of paint, stained rags, and tissue paper.

"This is nicer than expected," Ishtar said, looking at Zainab with an arch of her thick eyebrow. "Did you know the house was this nice?"

Zainab turned to her mother. "Was this room here when Mediha bought the house?"

"No, she had it built. She initially drew up the plans so that my studio faced the side-road. I had to fight her for the view. *But Mama, if you face the road, you can see who comes in and out*, she tried to tell me. I said she should face the bloody road if it entertained her so much."

Zainab chuckled.

"She'll probably hold it against you for the rest of your life," Ishtar said.

"That shouldn't be too long then . . ."

"Mashallah, Mama, don't say that."

"Don't be so superstitious, Zainab," Bridget laughed, squeezing her cheek. "There's nothing wrong with death. You just become worm food."

Zainab turned back to the large windows. On one of the distant slopes stood a single cow, perfectly still. Behind her she could hear Ishtar moving through the large room.

"How could Mediha afford all this?" Ishtar asked, coming up beside Zainab. She lifted a palette knife from the worktable and turned it over in her hand.

It was a question Zainab had also considered. Two years earlier, when the time came for their mother to be cared for, it made the most sense that the responsibility should fall to Mediha. Zainab had offered to take Bridget in, though everyone knew the heat in Dubai would be too much for a woman in her early eighties. Ishtar hadn't been considered. Despite being the eldest, she lived on a cramped houseboat in London and could barely keep herself afloat. Mediha's acceptance did not come without its fair share of resentment. She protested the injustice, accusing her older sisters of sabotaging her. When she finally relented, with some financial incentive from Zainab, she sold her one-bedroom flat in Edinburgh and purchased this property in a quaint part of the Scottish countryside a few miles outside Dunkeld. But even with Zainab's contribution, Mediha couldn't have afforded such a renovation on a lecturer's salary.

Bridget responded with vague references to Mediha's "practical nature" and ability to "make things happen", before swiftly ushering them back into the living room, where the afternoon light fell in thin, dusty slants across the mismatched furniture.

"You'll have to help me prepare the cot for Nizar," Bridget said. "We can put it in—"

"Nizar isn't coming," Zainab said. Her voice was tighter than she intended. Her mother frowned.

"That's a shame." Bridget studied Zainab's face. "Is he okay?"

"He . . . he had a sudden work trip," Zainab lied, her hand drifting to the back of her neck.

Zainab had only discovered that her son was not coming two days prior, when she'd called to ask him to bring up a few jars of her favourite moisturiser from a shop in Knightsbridge. In the weeks leading up to the family gathering he had been distant and non-committal—not unusual for him. When he finally admitted he wasn't coming, Zainab wasn't surprised. For some time now she'd sensed her son was slipping away from her, but the more she tried to pull him in, the further away he drifted.

The last time she had seen him was late last summer, where she'd arranged a dinner with Ishtar, Nizar, and his partner, Alfie, at *Daquise* in South Kensington, an old favourite of theirs. Her son walked in looking dishevelled, his mannerisms erratic and unfocused. Alfie, too, seemed unlike himself. Normally warm and affable, he sat across from her with a tense, shuttered gaze.

"Are you okay?" Zainab asked once they had settled into their seats.

Nizar glanced up from the wine list. "I'm fine."

"You don't look fine."

"Look, I just got back from Syria and I'm tired." He called for the waiter. "Can we get the Viognier?"

"It's all this war stuff," Zainab said. "It's not healthy to be exposed to so much violence and chaos. Couldn't you report on nicer things?"

Nizar looked at her as if he wasn't quite sure they had understood each other, then he sighed, not with irritation but something closer to resignation. "War isn't any more chaotic than everyday life," he said, as his hands absent-mindedly folded and unfolded his napkin. "It might seem that way from afar, but a closer look reveals quite intricate systems and patterns."

"Much like a family, I suppose," Alfie muttered.

"And what is that supposed to mean?" Nizar's voice was sharp.

"The way you describe war sounds like family relationships," Alfie said, louder and more assured. "On the surface families might seem chaotic, but there are historical patterns and dynamics that everyone plays a role in." He turned to Zainab. "Don't you think so? That a family can be like a war zone?"

Zainab sensed herself being pulled into a pre-existing argument and quickly changed the subject. She told them about her visit to the Tate Modern that afternoon, how she'd been surprised to see a piece by an Egyptian modernist painter who had used a combination of silver leaf, aluminium, tar, and oil paint. She'd recognised something familiar in the painting, a kind of sticky sadness. Alfie pressed for details, but she couldn't find the words to say more.

Ishtar arrived, frenetic and mercurial. Dressed in black, her hair was pulled into a tight ponytail which added to the severity of her features. A pair of triangular earrings hung from her ears, the gold glistening in the soft glow of the table lamp.

"Sorry I'm late," she addressed the table, before turning to her nephew. "Nizar, I never see you. You wouldn't think we live in the same city."

"Have you met my sister Ishtar before?" Zainab asked Alfie. "She's an artist, too. A real artist though, not like me."

"Don't sell yourself short." Ishtar slid into her seat and poured herself a glass of wine. "Your work is beautiful, Bulbul."

A flush rose to Zainab's cheeks, a combination of the wine and the rare compliment from her sister. "I just do handicrafts . . . there's no deeper meaning in it."

"I wouldn't say your weakness is the depth of meaning so much as your tendency to indulge in nostalgia and aestheticize the past into pretty trinkets." Ishtar turned to Nizar. "Ever since we were kids, your mother has always been taught to beautify, to make pretty all manner of ugliness. Me, I've never been one to muzzle myself to be 'agreeable' or 'nice'."

"Did you know that Nizar sketches?" Alfie said to Zainab.

"Does he?" It stung that Nizar had never mentioned this to her, but she masked it with a smile. She could feel her son studying her with a curious expression.

"He's very talented. It's not a surprise, of course, given your family. But the sketches . . . they're so haunting."

The starters arrived, giving Zainab time to swallow her hurt. When the waiter left, she turned to Nizar. "You used to sketch a lot when you were younger."

"You're upset," Nizar said, dipping a piece of bread in his soup.

"I'm not upset," Zainab blinked, caught off guard by how easily he had read her. "I'm just—"

"This is why I don't tell her," Nizar turned to Alfie.

"Why *wouldn't* you tell me?" Zainab looked down, her spoon tracing the swirls of sour cream on the surface of her borscht. "It makes me sad."

"Mama, look at me," Nizar reached across the table, his fingers brushing her wrist.

She looked into his eyes, which were dark and impenetrable. "Am I not allowed to be hurt that you're hiding things from me?"

"Stop turning everything into a weapon, I beg you."

"Niz, that's not fair," Alfie interjected.

"This doesn't concern you," Nizar snapped.

"Nizar used to shit himself," Zainab said. The words tumbled out of her abruptly.

Ishtar spat the dumpling out of her mouth. The table fell silent.

"It started when we moved to Jordan, so he must have been about nine or ten. Poor thing. I'd beg him, you know. 'Let's go make kaka before we leave the house.' And he would say he had no kaka but then when we'd be out, the smell would just suffuse the—"

"Zainab, darling," Ishtar said. "We're eating."

Zainab looked at Alfie. "Go on," he nodded, putting a hand on Nizar's shoulder. "I want to hear it."

"I had to act like it was completely normal. If people were around, I blamed the smell on a fart or some leaky sewage from somewhere. If there was a dog around, we'd blame the poor thing." Zainab laughed, then softened her tone. "But it was hard for him. We moved around a lot. It was hard for the both of us, of course, but especially for Nizar. When you're young and the ground keeps shifting underneath you . . ." She turned to Nizar, who was watching her with a clenched jaw. "I think your body just reacted in its own way. Maybe you were trying to control whatever you could, and your bowel movements were something you had a bit of control over, to keep it all in . . . until you couldn't anymore."

"You've got to be kidding me," Nizar muttered, running a hand through his curly hair, but none of that mattered because Zainab perceived a subtle understanding in Alfie's eyes. She had communicated to Alfie that Nizar was a complex person, a person who had experienced deep upheaval. She was trying to equip her son's lover with the tools he might need to deal with him.

"He did tell me you moved around a lot," Alfie said. "But why did you leave Baghdad?"

Zainab caught Ishtar's eye, before quickly looking away. "It's a long story. I don't even remember it all myself. It's been over thirty years now."

"Do you still consider it home? Or is Dubai home?"

"I'm not sure . . ." Zainab's voice trailed off. "I don't even know what home should feel like. There's this quote by Naguib Mahfouz, an Egyptian novelist, that home is where all our attempts to escape cease."

Alfie smiled. "That's beautiful."

"A load of straight male nonsense if you ask me," Ishtar said, jabbing her fork in the air for emphasis. "Completely ignores the reality that home can quickly become unsafe, and you have no choice but to flee."

Zainab sighed. "I sometimes feel like I've spent my whole life running away."

Nizar looked up from his plate. Zainab could tell he was still angry, but in that moment he also understood exactly what she was trying to say.

"Enough about the past," Zainab said, pouring herself more wine. "Nizar, tell us about Syria."

Ishtar's eyes narrowed. "You were in Syria?"

"I was reporting on the chemical attack."

"Oh dear," Ishtar muttered to herself. "First the British boyfriend, now he's talking of chemical attacks . . ."

Nizar's eyes widened. "Isn't your girlfriend *Irish*?"

"Ex-girlfriend. And in any case, Irish isn't the same as British—"

"Your *mother* is British!"

"And that's why I'm so familiar with their divide-and-conquer tactics," Ishtar wiped her mouth with the napkin.

"Anyway, I'm not saying there *wasn't* a chemical attack, but I'd expect more of a critical eye—"

"Ishtar," Zainab pleaded, "let's just agree to disagree." She foresaw the trajectory of the conversation: Ishtar and Nizar would toss micro-aggressions at each other, eroding all nuance as they pushed one another to extreme positions, until they erupted into a fiery battle where they picked apart each other's philosophy and character, climaxing in harsh judgements that would leave them fuming on opposite sides of an irreparable fissure.

"That's *not* how this is going to end," Ishtar said, pulling out a pouch of tobacco from her bag and starting to roll a cigarette. "This liberal 'let's-agree-to-disagree' shite."

Nizar leaned across the table, his voice tightening. "So the thousands I saw suffering neurotoxic symptoms—"

"War-mongering propaganda!"

"Hundreds of dead. Women and children and—"

"It was journalists like yourself—"

"Five-year-olds convulsing in front of my eyes—"

"Who midwifed the narratives—"

"Frothing at the *fucking mouth*—"

"That Bush and Blair used to destroy Iraq—"

"Enough," Zainab snapped.

"They want to do to Syria what they did to Iraq," Ishtar licked the edge of the paper, sealing her cigarette. "Chemical attacks. Doesn't that sound familiar?"

"You're heartless." Nizar shot to his feet, knocking the table in the process. Zainab's bowl wobbled, splashing red across the tablecloth.

"And you, my dear nephew, are naïve." Ishtar struck a match and lit the cigarette. She inhaled deeply, then tilted her head back slightly as she exhaled, letting the smoke curl up around her face like a crown. "Your job is to tell the truth, yet you peddle in lies and fake news."

"Ishtar, you're not just a failed artist," Nizar slung his leather messenger bag over his shoulder in a swift, furious motion. "You're also a failed person."

* * *

After a light supper they sat in the garden. Surrounded by wildflowers, they drank whiskey and watched the sun begin its slow, mid-summer descent, bathing the sky in hues of pink and gold. There was a chill in the air; a delightful reprieve to the long Dubai summer. It was a beautiful, tranquil moment. It was the right time to share her news.

Six months earlier, Zainab's husband Mohammad had woken up complaining of indigestion. Half an hour later, he began to vomit blood. At the hospital, doctors discovered a tumour the size of a fist in his upper stomach. The next morning, her husband of fourteen years was dead. Zainab became a widow, a title she could finally claim after having falsely used it for decades.

All this, her family knew. But there was one detail she had left out.

"I've been wanting to tell you something," Zainab announced. "I was going to wait until Mediha was here, but I think it's better to discuss it with the both of you first."

Bridget raised an eyebrow. "Sounds ominous."

"When Mohammad died, he left his estate in my name."

"What does that mean?" Ishtar asked.

"It means I've got a lot of money."

Bridget turned to look at her. "What do you mean by 'a lot'?"

"I don't know the exact amount. It's in different assets, and—"

"How do you not know?" Ishtar scoffed.

"Because I'm shit at maths and there's someone who manages it. I guess somewhere in the range of fifteen million dollars?"

"Fuck me," Ishtar whistled, leaning back on her chair. "I guess marrying a Gulfie worked out after all."

Bridget frowned. "Have you given some thought as to what you'll do with it?"

Zainab adjusted the blanket on her lap and took a deep breath. "That's what I wanted to talk to you about."

"I'd better see some of it," Ishtar said. She followed this with a laugh, but Zainab knew she wasn't joking. Her older sister had been 'borrowing' money from her—money Zainab never saw again—since they were teenagers. The discovery of Zainab's newfound wealth would entrench this dynamic within the folds of their relationship for the rest of their lives.

Zainab poured herself more whiskey and lit a cigarette. "Mama, didn't you say that many of Baba's sculptures and paintings in Iraq were lost during the war?"

Her mother was quiet for some time. "Yes," she finally said. "During the *wars*, not just the last one. Things were left behind in the Baghdad house with your aunt Rajiha, and she sold a bunch of them without the necessary paperwork . . . you know how mad that woman was. Anyway, the Americans invaded and then it was a free-for-all . . ." She turned to Zainab, who was nodding along enthusiastically. "But yes, most of the artwork is gone."

Hearing the loss in her mother's voice, Zainab was desperate to resurrect the glimmer of hope that the past three decades had extinguished. She reached over and squeezed her mother's leg.

"I was thinking that with this money we might be able to track all of the artworks down. We can hire some people in Iraq to look for them." She paused, but neither her mother nor her sister responded. "I know several curators in Dubai who would love the idea of exhibiting the works. Maybe even a permanent collection!"

Bridget's face did not light up as Zainab had expected. In fact, she appeared unnerved.

"Mama, what's wrong?"

Bridget pressed her lips together. "Nothing's wrong—"

"You look upset."

"I'm just thinking."

"We could tell *your* story, Mama. The story of all the things you and Baba did." Unable to contain her excitement, she turned now to Ishtar. "Imagine this: an exhibition that brings together Mama and Baba's lost works. An East-Meets-West love story of a British woman and an Iraqi man who fell in love in post-war London and moved to Baghdad in the fifties to start one of the most influential art movements in modern Iraqi history!"

"That seems a tad off, politically," Ishtar said, plucking a dead fly from her drink.

"Whatever. My point is—"

"Not whatever," Ishtar cut in sharply. She closed her eyes, steepling the long, slender fingers of her hands to emphasize her point. "To hold such an exhibition and to frame it as this harmonious East-Meets-West love story, when the British have just pillaged our country. *And* to hold the exhibition in the Gulf, which is laundering its image with all these so-called festivals of culture. It's a bit tone-deaf, don't you think? Surely you don't want to put forward the idea that our family is somehow aligned with British interests in Iraq . . . or Gulf interests, for that matter."

"I don't think that's how it would be perceived. We won't be making a statement on anything but the past."

Ishtar shook her head. "The political mood won't allow for such a reparative reading."

"OK fine, then you can come up with better framing. That's why I want everyone involved. You've got the knowledge, Mama has the history, Mediha has the organisational skills, and I've got the money and contacts." Zainab turned to her mother, who had been silent during all this. "What do you think?"

"Have you started any of this yet?"

The tone of her mother's question struck an interesting note.

"Why?"

"I'm just curious." Bridget paused. "It's a nice idea . . . but I'm an old fart and your father died a long time ago. I don't have it in me to dredge up old memories."

"What do you mean?"

Bridget sighed. "What I mean is that it's best to let the past stay in the past. There are better things you could do with the money."

"Mama has a point," Ishtar said. "We should be focusing on the present, on the future. Why not create a fund for contemporary Iraqi artists?"

Zainab stubbed out her cigarette, the burning ember hissing as it kissed the shallow pool of water at the bottom of the ashtray. This was not the response she had expected. "I thought it would be a nice way to honour Baba's legacy. He was the most famous artist in Iraq . . ."

"And he's still well known," Bridget said.

"Yeah, but it's not the same."

"I mean, we're all artists here," Ishtar said. "Baba had so much support back in the day. He had the whole Iraqi state behind him. Couldn't this money be used to support Iraqi artists working today who don't have that kind of privilege?"

Zainab looked up at the sky, which like her mood had darkened. Bridget reached over and patted her leg.

"I wouldn't mention anything to Mediha just yet, Bulbul. Let's leave this between the three of us for now."

* * *

A setback, certainly. But after the first night, the week unspooled in a soft, reassuring calm, coaxing Zainab inside a prison of hope. Mediha's instructions long forgotten, Ishtar and Zainab indulged their mother with long breakfasts like they used to have in Baghdad, where they spent hours grazing upon a vast spread of fruit, cheese, and meats as they smoked cigarettes, drank countless cups of coffee, and reminisced over old friendships and memories. At times Zainab found herself exiled from the conversation, as Ishtar and Bridget talked about their creative preoccupations, debated the work of contemporary artists, and critiqued each other's projects, often returning to conversations they had started years before. There was an ease to their exchange, a rhythm Zainab admired and envied. What she remembered most clearly was not what was said but the way Bridget looked at Ishtar, head slightly tilted, eyes soft with a kind of quiet reverence, and it struck her—not for the first time—how their mother regarded Ishtar as the creative one, the one with vision. Just as she saw Zainab as the beautiful one. The recognition of this wasn't exactly painful, though Zainab felt, as she often did around them, a slight sense of being left out of a higher plane of intimacy. And yet, watching them so immersed in their world of ideas, she found a space of quiet amusement at how deeply familiar this dynamic felt.

One day, Zainab and Ishtar baked oatmeal cookies. As they ate them in the garden, Zainab took a photograph of her mother who was smiling broadly with a half-eaten cookie in her hand. It was a beautiful photo. Their mother looked happy and content, surrounded by the wildflowers in a riot of colour. Zainab posted the photo on Facebook with the caption: *Cozy afternoons with Mama*. Within an hour, the post garnered nearly seventy likes. The photograph delivered to Zainab what she had wanted: bringing her to the attention of old Baghdad friends and family, who commented adoringly about how healthy Bridget looked, how much they missed 'the old times in Baghdad'. Zainab relished every comment, responding to each with a carefully selected recollection of her own, until she felt herself floating on a cloud of joyous memories.

Most afternoons, while Bridget painted or napped, Ishtar and Zainab went for long woodland walks, where Ishtar spoke about her ideas, her projects and visions. Though she knew Ishtar's long soliloquies were merely pitches for a slice of Mohammad's inheritance, Zainab received them like offerings—smiling, nodding, occasionally asking a question. She enjoyed hearing her older sister speak. Ishtar's mind had a way of casting old ideas in a new light that changed her perspective on the world.

On days when it rained, Zainab stayed at home and snooped. She walked through the cottage, examining trinkets in drawers, trying to get inside the skin of Mediha and Bridget's daily life. She felt a spark of longing when a particular smell or object triggered a memory: a holiday in London, the dry winters of Baghdad, a long-forgotten friend, and she found herself chasing the dizzying feeling of almost stepping into a past life that shimmered out of reach.

Two days before Mediha's return, Zainab came across the letter. She had been looking through a stack of mail in a kitchen drawer when a cream-coloured envelope branded with the Sotheby's logo caught her eye. Her heart raced as she pulled out the letter.

> Dear Mediha,
>
> We have reviewed the remaining artworks by your late father, Haydar Mathloum, and are thrilled to confirm that the collection has been accepted for auction at Sotheby's.

Zainab's hands trembled as she scanned the letter. The auction date was set for early next year, and a list of the paintings was attached. She recognised many of the artworks that had supposedly been lost in the wars. The letter also made reference to a scheduled meeting with Mediha in their London office on the 27th June. Today was the 27th June.

For years, Mediha and Bridget had sworn not to have any of Baba's works. They had been lost in Baghdad, abandoned in the old family home, or looted in the chaos of the invasion. They had lied. Her shock was eclipsed by a stronger, more righteous emotion: rage, running like a river through her body. She pocketed the letter and steadied herself against the cabinet. She had been so naïve, so silly to believe them, to try in earnest to rally them around the cause of recovering the paintings. Mediha had hidden them for years and was now selling them off. And for what? Money, leverage, the thrill of control? They were more than just artworks; each held a piece of Baba's soul.

* * *

"Shall we share the lasagne?" Ishtar asked, studying the large chalkboard above the bar. Their mother had retired for her afternoon nap, and Zainab had suggested they drive to the local pub for a drink. She needed to get Ishtar alone to tell her what she had found.

"I'm not hungry, but—"

"Maybe we should have the lamb . . . or is that too heavy?" Ishtar tapped her chin as she considered the options. She asked the bartender about the lamb, then about the roast chicken. The bartender answered dutifully, the card machine hanging from her limp wrist as the line behind them grew longer.

"Fuck it. One roast lamb, and two plates of chips." She turned to Zainab, who gave the bartender her credit card.

"I've been thinking about boats," Ishtar said once they had settled in a corner of the pub.

"OK, but before that . . ." Zainab began, but her sister was not listening.

"About our history and myths and what they can teach us about our present. And that's how I got the idea of an expedition down the Tigris."

Zainab cradled her glass of wine. "An expedition? Now?"

"It won't be easy, of course, given the situation, but this inheritance money is our chance to really take our work to the next level. Male artists of our generation have risen to fame for amateurish scribblings, and these days, to be a successful Arab woman artist you have to pander, and I'm certainly not going to pander. I'm not going to frame my work within the 'plight of the Iraqi woman' bollocks, not when the plight of Iraqi women has become a Trojan horse for wars and occupations." Ishtar moved her beer to the side and pulled out her laptop from her bag, placing it on the table between them. "Mediha makes that kind of art. With her gender degree and her belief that the plight of Arab women needs to be screamed from the rooftops. Poor girl, all rage and no taste."

"Speaking of Mediha . . ."

"Remember how Baba came across the Sumerian artefacts during his Iraqi Museum apprenticeship in the forties? That was a key breakthrough for him. He saw how the past could help his generation understand the challenges of their present. In many ways, my project would be doing the same."

There was no way she would get Ishtar's attention until her sister had said what she wanted to say. "So what exactly are you proposing?"

"An expedition down the Tigris," Ishtar clicked on a file and turned the screen to show a map of Iraq. "From the north of Iraq all the way down to Shat al-Arab. On an ark. Well, actually we should start further up . . . in Hasankeyf. Southeastern Turkey. Did you know that Hasankeyf is one of the oldest continuously inhabited settlements in the world?"

"Hang on, did you say an ark? Like Noah's ark?"

"Exactly," Ishtar said, her brown eyes glinting with resolute exhilaration. "Though what you're probably picturing now is some giant ark from a Hollywood film. That's a very Eurocentric design. What I'm proposing is an ark that would resemble the *real* Noah's ark. One constructed from a composite of traditional Mesopotamian boats."

The food arrived, and Ishtar shoved a forkful of lamb into her mouth. Zainab watched her movements with growing unease. Ishtar's mood had changed since discovering the news of Mohammad's inheritance. She had become restless, the tide of her mania swelling dangerously. She closed her eyes as she chewed, nodding her head slightly in feigned ecstasy. She opened her eyes suddenly, as if remembering something.

"You see, the story of Noah's ark was told long before the Bible," she said, the lamb half-chewed in her mouth. "Various ancient Mesopotamian civilisations have references to a Great Flood so presumably this Flood, the one people associate with Noah, must have happened in Mesopotamia. And, according to the Epic of Gilgamesh, the Mesopotamian Noah is a man named Utnapishtim."

According to the myth, Ishtar explained, the earth had been inhabited by too many people, and their noise disrupted the sleep of the gods. In response, the gods sent plagues and droughts to reduce the numbers of people, and when that wasn't enough, they unleashed a great flood to destroy humanity. But Enki, the god of water, was fond of Utnapishtim and revealed to him the gods' plan.

"Ishtar," Zainab interrupted. "I really need to—"

Ishtar raised a chip to silence her. "Let's say that you are Utnapishtim, and Enki comes to you and says: 'Utnapishtim, mate, I'm going to flood this place.' What would you do?"

Zainab thought for a moment. "I guess I'd build a boat."

"No shit you'd built a boat." Ishtar dropped the chip into her mouth. "But would you build a giant boat from scratch?"

Ishtar paused, waiting for Zainab's answer.

"I guess not?"

"You *guess* not? Of course you wouldn't," Ishtar's voice rose sharply. A man at the table beside them turned in their direction. "You wouldn't have time to build an enormous boat from scratch. You'd cobble together whatever material you had and create something from that. That's what Utnapishtim did. He built his ark using the three traditional boats present in Mesopotamia, and that's exactly what I plan to do."

Zainab leaned back in her chair and closed her eyes. "I suppose you want me to fund this?"

"Don't you want to support Iraqi heritage?" Ishtar leaned in, her tone suddenly earnest. "Even if we weren't sisters, wouldn't you want to be part of something like this? Something forward-thinking and hopeful? So much of contemporary Iraqi art is a reaction to the devastation of the last thirty years. I simply cannot sit in another fucking exhibition hall in London, drinking wine and talking about Iraqi suffering without even a shred of irony."

Zainab seized her moment. "Speaking of the art world," she pulled the Sotheby's letter from her bag and handed it to Ishtar. Ishtar read the letter slowly. When she was finished, she folded the letter and handed it back.

"I can't believe Mediha would do something like this," Ishtar said, shaking her head.

"It's right there in front of you. She's doing it behind our backs. The paintings belong to all three of us, not just her. It's not right."

Ishtar considered her words carefully. "It *isn't* right. But what would her motivation be? If it was about the money, then this could all be easily resolved."

"Exactly. And I *do* wire Mama money. I've always contributed more than my fair share." Zainab paused, but Ishtar offered nothing. "She's a liar and a thief," Zainab added, trying to radicalise her older sister. "Doesn't that bother you? Are you just going to let her sell them?"

"I—" Ishtar stopped herself, shook her head. "It's not like *you* need the money."

"It's not about the bloody money! We can't let the paintings get scattered around the world. Baba's entire body of work will be lost. When Mediha comes tomorrow you must have my back on this. I can't do it alone."

Ishtar's gaze hardened. "I'm not getting in the middle of your feud."

Of course she wasn't. Ishtar always placed a convenient distance between herself and the family problems, knowing exactly how to keep her hands clean while getting others to do the dirty work. But as Zainab watched her sister push her plate back slightly, the congealed lamb glistening under the dim light, she realised the news had stripped Ishtar of her appetite. For now, this was a victory Zainab could claim.

* * *

Across the lavish spread of olive-oil drizzled labneh, wedges of white cheese dusted with za'atar, platters of dates and figs alongside buttered toast, marmalade, and soft-boiled eggs, Zainab slid the letter toward Bridget. Her mother played dumb.

"What does it say?" Bridget said, a half-eaten piece of toast in her hand. "I can't read without my glasses Bulbul . . ."

"It's about auctioning off Baba's work! Let me read it to you: 'Given the success we've had with your father's sculpture in 2007, we feel we are well-placed to find the right home for his paintings.' *Surely* you must be aware of this?"

Bridget unravelled into a mess of stammers and aborted sentences. "You and your sister . . . all this fighting . . . leave me out of it! I don't . . . what did I do to cause these problems between you?"

They heard the jangling of keys as the front door opened.

"I'm back," Mediha called out from the living room. "Where is everyone?"

Ishtar caught Zainab's eye and motioned to the Sotheby's

letter, which she quickly stuffed in her bag. Seconds later, Mediha walked into the kitchen, to which Bridget responded with a loud, rolling burp. Mediha winced, as if physically pained by the sound.

"What a lovely welcome." Mediha turned to the breakfast spread, studying the food on the table with disapproval. Her eyes landed on the marmalade. "I hope you're not letting her eat sugar."

Zainab stood up. "Have a seat Mediha, we prepared this for you."

"Is that why you're all nearly done?" Mediha dropped her handbag on the kitchen counter. "I'll just have some tea, I'm fasting."

An uneasy silence descended. Zainab began to put away the spread while Mediha prepared a thermos of tea.

"Why is everyone so quiet?" Mediha leaned back on the counter. She was wearing weather-beaten hiking trousers tucked into thick socks. Her stringy auburn hair was scraped into a ponytail, her face scrubbed bare of any make-up. "Catch me up on the news."

"Zainab's a multi-millionaire," Ishtar said as she rinsed a plate in the sink.

Zainab turned towards Mediha, mining her sister's face for a flicker of surprise or envy, even amusement. But apart from a subtle tightening around her mouth, her expression was impossible to decipher.

"Inheritance?"

"Yes."

"Congratulations," she responded cooly. "What do you plan to do with it?"

"At the very least, I want to set Nizar up so he doesn't have to do any more war reporting." His close call in Baghdad had terrified her. "I don't want him traveling to dangerous places anymore."

"And what's the alternative?" Ishtar asked. "To just look away while people suffer?"

"Yes," Zainab snapped, still irritated that Ishtar had revealed her news. "Exactly that."

"Oh, Zainab," Mediha said, pushing herself off the counter. "It's so Iraqi of you to think that if you just turn a blind eye, you can brush everything under the surface."

"What does that mean?"

Mediha didn't explain. Instead, she grabbed her thermos of tea and turned to the others. "Let me unpack and do some gardening, and we can catch up properly over lunch."

Later, as Mediha tended the vegetable patch, Zainab told her of the plan to find the family's lost artworks. Mediha was silent as Zainab spoke, her fingers working deep into the soil.

"It's an interesting idea," she said, squinting with the sun in her face. "But the Gulf, really? Wouldn't this be better handled by a European institution?"

"What's wrong with the Gulf?"

"I just wouldn't trust them to handle the works."

"I disagree, but what do you think about the plan itself?"

Mediha stood up and wiped her hands on her hiking trousers. "I mean, sure. It's your project Zainab. I wouldn't want to interfere."

Zainab's gaze drifted past Mediha to the far edge of the vegetable patch, where a pumpkin lay sunken in the dirt, its blackening flesh furred with mould. She wondered how long it had been rotting, and why no one had noticed.

* * *

Zainab woke the following morning to the soft murmur of the television in the next room. She got out of bed and put on her sweater. It was colder today, the view outside enveloped within a comforting grey fog.

They were all in the living room. On the television, bulldozers tore through the borders of Syria and Iraq. Iraqi flags were brought down, replaced by the black banners of the Caliphate. *The end of Sykes-Picot*, a journalist declared, parroting the militants' words.

For a long time no one spoke. Finally, Mediha said, "They want to erase hundreds of years of history. As if Iraq never existed."

Ishtar reached for the remote and turned off the screen. She looked up at Mediha, who was perched beside her on the edge of the sofa.

"Where did you get the money for the renovations?"

Mediha blinked. "What do you mean?"

"Surely your salary as a lecturer—"

"Senior lecturer, but go on . . ."

"Who paid for the renovations?"

Mediha placed her cup of tea on the side table with exaggerated care. "That's a bit of a loaded question."

"It's an important question," Zainab said, remaining at a safe distance by the door to her mother's studio.

Mediha stood up and began to collect the empty mugs around them. "I sold some of my own paintings. The collection I exhibited a few years ago, the one I invited you to, Ishtar, but you were too busy, even though it was just a few stops from your place in London—"

Ishtar threw her hands in the air. "Here we go!"

"As it turns out, my art isn't half bad," Mediha continued, heading towards the kitchen door. "If there's one good thing that has come out of the war, it's the interest in Iraqi art . . ."

"You could have asked me for help," Zainab said.

Mediha turned around. "Are you saying my art isn't good?"

"I'm saying I would have chipped in more."

"We wouldn't want to perpetuate old patterns now, would we?" Mediha turned back towards the kitchen. "Now, if your curiosity has been adequately satiated, I'm going to do the dishes and then finish up some work."

While Mediha worked in her bedroom, Zainab and Ishtar busied themselves with building a fire. Bridget looked on in silence as Ishtar brought some chopped wood from the shed, and Zainab found a box of matches in the kitchen. The news coming out of Iraq had added an unexpected urgency to her plan. She had hoped that by telling Mediha about her idea for the exhibition she would rattle her enough to confess. But her sister had remained tight-lipped. The only way to get to the truth of the matter, she realised, was to address the issue head on.

The living room had warmed up nicely by the time Mediha emerged from the bedroom, laptop in hand, her face hardened like a fist.

"Mediha," Zainab began. "I've got a bone to pick with you."

"You've got a bone to pick with *me*?" Mediha's tone was so ferocious, so unexpected, that the confrontation Zainab had spent the last two hours preparing fell apart. "What did my list say about sugar? I was *so* clear. No sugar. *No sugar*. And what did you do?"

"We didn't—"

"I just saw the fucking cookie on Facebook."

Mediha shoved her laptop in Zainab's face.

Ishtar peered over her shoulder. "You seriously uploaded it on Facebook?"

"If you're going to lie, Zainab, at least don't be dumb enough to post a photo on social media. You come here and exhaust her and mess up her schedule—"

"I'm standing right here—"

"—and then you leave, and *I* have to deal with the consequences. Are you trying to kill her?" Mediha pointed her finger at them. "Is that your plan?"

"You're a horrible woman," Zainab said, pulling on her coat.

"Following rules makes me horrible? Keeping our mother *alive* makes me—"

"A truly horrible woman. With an ugly soul."

"Ugly? You called me ugly—"

"I said your soul was ugly—"

"Did you hear that, Mum? She called me ugly!"

"You know what, Mediha?" Zainab turned around and walked back towards her. "You *are* ugly. And a thief too. I saw the letter from Sotheby's."

Mediha's eyes narrowed.

"I feel so stupid," Zainab said, her voice quivering. "Here I am trying to do something good with what I've got, to restore Baba's legacy—"

"Again with the bloody legacy!" Ishtar exclaimed. "What motivates you in all of this, really?"

Zainab turned to her older sister. "Don't you care about Baba's work?"

"The entire country has been annihilated, Zainab This isn't about some altruistic desire, this is about *your* image. You're so consumed by appearances—"

"By what people think of you—" Mediha jumped in.

"—and this kind of thing just pushes you up a notch on some imagined social hierarchy. You're not much better, Mediha," Ishtar quipped, casually tossing a grenade in the other direction. "I've read your artist bio, piggybacking off Baba's success: 'daughter of renowned artist Haydar Mathloum'—"

"Can you all, please, calm down," Bridget called out from the sofa, though her voice seemed miles away.

"You think you're so much better than us, Ishtar," Zainab snapped. "But what have you done except live off my hard work?"

Ishtar laughed. "The hard work of prostituting yourself to a rich Gulfie and waiting for him to die . . ."

Bridget slammed her hand on the coffee table. "That's enough!"

Zainab turned to her mother. "*Now* you're stepping in? Does it take them to say something so . . . *vulgar* for you to finally intervene?"

"Bulbul, calm down." Bridget stood up and walked towards them. "You're over-reacting."

"But she's selling the family paintings! Unless . . ." Zainab paused. "You knew about this too?"

The three sisters looked at their mother, waiting for her to explain. To take responsibility for the oatmeal cookies, the cigarettes, the paintings. The silence between them stretched like a tear across the room. Finally, Bridget burst into tears.

"Why is this happening?" She covered her face in her hands. "What have I done as a mother to make you treat each other like this? Is this my fault?"

"Yes!" Zainab screamed, opening the front door and stepping out into the rain. "Everything, all of this, is your fault!"

Nizar

July 2014

Though he had never been there, Nizar dreamt he was in his mother's family home in Baghdad. Water poured through the ceiling and down the walls in ribbons, pooling across the floor like a mirror. Broken furniture was tossed across the room. The family paintings lay in wreckage underwater, their pigments feathering into iridescent slicks at the surface. River fish—large and golden—swam in circles around his shins, nipping at his heels until the pain made him lurch backwards. He shouted for help and the water answered, gushing into his mouth and nose, brackish and metallic.

Nizar woke, suddenly and in fear. He hadn't had such a vivid nightmare in at least a year, and back then they'd revolved around his work: dreams of being chased by militias and armed groups, of explosions, kidnappings, and mutilated corpses. This time, the battlefield was his mother's family, and the prize—their family legacy—had been destroyed amidst the fighting.

He reached for his laptop and searched his aunt's name on Facebook. He clicked on the message icon. Underneath the last link she'd sent him, an article titled 'The West's REAL objective in Syria', Nizar typed:

Are you in London? It would be good to see you . . .

His aunt replied ten minutes later, at 4:17 A.M..

I am. Come down to the houseboat anytime.

The next day he made his way to Ishtar's narrowboat, which was docked in Regent's Canal. The front door was ajar, but a wooden sculpture of a bull obscured his view inside.

"Ishtar?" Nizar called out, stepping onto the wheelhouse. A black cat emerged from inside and circled his feet.

He dropped his bag by the door and took off his shoes. The belly of the boat was larger than he expected. Plants and sculptures adorned every surface. There were leaning towers of books, piles of raw materials—wood, metal, canvas. The walls were covered with maps and masks and newspaper clippings.

She sat in an armchair in the midst of all this, staring at her laptop. She wore jeans and an oversized shirt, a keffiyeh draped across her shoulders. Her cheeks were wet with tears. Nizar had been prepared to see his aunt in low spirits, but there was something in her face—in the shadows under her eyes and the shallow depth of her vision—that rattled him.

"Khala, are you okay?"

"No." The word emerged like a puff of smoke.

He walked towards her cautiously and crouched beside her. "What are you watching?"

The screen displayed an article from the *Wall Street Journal* about the Islamic State's destruction of holy sites in Iraq. Ishtar clicked on the video. The footage showed an urban Iraqi horizon, low-rise sandy buildings and a single mosque in the distance, its minaret reflecting the morning light. The mosque exploded in a flash of orange, sending clouds of dust mushrooming in all directions. A voice behind the lens said: 'Oh God, keep filming Abu Ahmed.'

"Your grandfather was studying art in Paris when the war broke out," Ishtar said quietly. "He moved to Rome but had no choice but to return to Iraq when it spread. He had lived amongst so much beauty in Europe, then in the blink of an eye it was all gone, and he found himself back in dusty old Baghdad."

She talked about how, upon his return, he began working in the antiquities department at the Iraqi Museum, where he came across old Sumerian artefacts. He discovered the richness of Iraqi history, the ability of art to survive long after massacres crumbled the civilisations that created them. Ishtar's chest heaved as more tears began to fall.

Nizar placed his hand on her shoulder. He had always seen Ishtar as rooted, a sharp contrast with himself. In the end, they'd arrived at the same rock bottom.

"They're not just destroying artefacts and holy sites, Nizar. It's the very *idea* of Iraq that they intend to annihilate." She wiped her face with the edge of her keffiyeh. "To conquer a civilisation you must destroy their culture, their history, their past, wipe out their memory of themselves and fill the empty spaces with new narratives. The Americans did this, erecting military bases on archaeological sites, all the looting, no accountability or reckoning. Maliki and his thugs have been a nightmare for so long, but this is just . . ."

Her voice trailed off. Nizar grasped for something to staunch his aunt's grief. A hug? Some tears of his own? He knew that whatever tears he shed would not emerge from sadness. He *wanted* to feel the loss of the holy sites, to empathise with the pain sculpted on Ishtar's face, but the truth of the matter, the shameful truth Nizar only realised in that moment, was that he felt relief. As he'd watched the video of the explosion, he felt a weight lift from his soul. He too wanted to obliterate the past biting at his life, to release the world from the weight of history.

He took away Ishtar's laptop and set it aside.

"Let's get you some tea."

Ishtar nodded, wiping her eyes. Growing up, Nizar had revered her. She had achieved a degree of credibility in the art world and was not afraid to wield this success as a sword against anyone who dared question her. Looking at his aunt now, Nizar saw her in a new light: as a vulnerable woman, an artist who had held herself and others to unachievable standards, even when this left her isolated and alone.

As he waited for the kettle to boil, Nizar explored the kitchen. On the table was an old copy of *The Times*, dated

8th May. He ran his finger over the headline: 'British Special Forces Join Hunt for Kidnapped Girls'. Underneath was a picture of Malala, solemnly holding up a sign that read #BringBackOurGirls. Above the photograph, Ishtar had scribbled: *WHO and WHAT designates which girls are worth saving?*

He poured the boiling water into the mugs and returned to where Ishtar was sitting, handing her the tea before taking a seat on the leather sofa across from her. The black cat jumped off the windowsill and crawled onto Ishtar's lap. Her hands, calloused from decades of painting and sculpting, wrapped themselves around its belly as she picked up the small creature pawing gently at her wrist.

"This is Gilgamesh."

They sat in silence, watching the steam rise from their mugs. Nizar expected her to ask why he got in touch after a year of estrangement, but his aunt appeared neither curious nor surprised, and did not inquire about his reason. His eyes drifted to the bookshelf beside them, and a chalkboard with its scribbled to-do list:

- Neuter Gilgamesh
- Eggs
- Mooring licence
- NHS forms
- Firewood

"My anchor," Ishtar said, following Nizar's gaze.

"So have you neutered Gilgamesh?"

"Not yet. He's probably impregnating the other cats on the canal. The last thing I need is for people to start claiming some kind of . . . parental feline support. He's getting a bit violent, too. Maybe it's the hormones." Ishtar took in a deep breath. "I just feel bad for the poor guy, chopping his balls off like that."

The image of Gilgamesh's testicles sat with them for a

moment. The young cat, none the wiser, pawed at the frayed edges of Ishtar's keffiyeh.

Nizar stood and examined the bookshelf more closely. There were old editions of Arab and Islamic folktales, their spines sun-faded and creased. His aunt must have brought these with her when she left Baghdad in the eighties. There were volumes on Iraqi art, books on coastal navigations, several more on the War on Terror, and a self-published manuscript entitled *Rivers of Fire: A Mythic Cartography of the Fertile Crescent*. Next to the manuscript was a set of paper boats arranged like a miniature flotilla, each constructed from torn pages of an old London A-to-Z. Ishtar had used the pages of the neighbourhoods surrounding the Thames, so that the boats had the blue of the river snaking through them.

Nizar picked up a boat and traced his finger down the blue line. "Is this something you're working on now?"

"One of the things."

Nizar looked at her quizzically. "The Thames . . . ?"

"No, not the Thames. But rivers. Arteries of the land . . ."

He turned back to the shelf. "It's good that you're working."

Suddenly Ishtar was behind him.

"Did your mother send you?" Her eyes flashed like the blade of a knife.

"No," Nizar lied.

"Then why are you here?" She was so close he could smell the nicotine on her breath.

"Never mind," he placed the boat back on the shelf. "I'll leave. Thanks for the tea."

He walked to the door and began to put on his shoes.

"I just crashed," Ishtar said. The words caught in her throat.

Nizar looked up. She was back in the armchair, her face half-concealed in shadow.

"A month ago I planned to sail down the Tigris, and now I can barely get to the corner-shop to buy cigarettes. I saw the complete fragmentation of my country and I just . . . my brain just . . . *KAPOW*," she mimicked an explosion with her hands.

Nizar was tempted to put on his shoes, grab his bag, and walk out the door, but a specific memory came to him, a cold night in February two months after he and Alfie had moved in together, when Nizar was at Alfie's set and a handsome actor pushed him aside to speak to Alfie. This ignited a foul mood in him that shape-shifted throughout the evening, turning into anger at the rain, frustration at having to chase freelance payments, hopelessness at having missed the last bus home, and simmering rage at the drone wars in Pakistan. As they walked down Tottenham Court Road, Alfie had grabbed Nizar's hand and began to skip down the pavement. Nizar had no choice but to follow, his legs falling into the same rhythm, until they were both skipping, hand-in-hand, and laughing hysterically at the absurdity of it.

"We look insane!" Nizar had said, his stomach cramping from laughter.

"We're just two poofs skipping in the rain."

Alfie's face flashed in his mind. Tender, generous, hopeful. Kind to a fault, always eager to help.

Nizar turned to Ishtar. "Do you want to talk?"

"My mind is not with me."

"We can go at your own pace."

Ishtar sighed. "I wanted to build an ark. Remember the story of The Flood, the great catastrophe to hit Mesopotamia? Well, we are now living through another catastrophe." Ishtar paused, then emphatically shook her head to rearrange her thoughts. "We must start from the beginning. You know the story of Gilgamesh?"

"Yes, Gilgamesh is on a quest to be neutered."

Ishtar smiled. "Maybe that's the problem. It's the *idea* of castrating Gilgamesh that weighs heavy on me. I should have called the bloody cat Bob. Perhaps I'd feel less guilty about cutting his balls off. Or better yet, I'd call him Tony Blair. But then I'd take a cruel joy in his castration . . ."

"So, the beginning is Gilgamesh?"

"Yes. On the surface, it's about one man's quest for immortality. But I see Gilgamesh's search not to be about immortality, per se, but rather hope. Hope in the face of our inevitable mortality. When I think of our family, each of us, throughout the generations, has been on a quest for hope. Of course, everyone knows your grandfather. To him, art was a way to reassert Iraq's self-esteem, something that seems laughable in the current environment. But his father was also a pioneer. He helped develop Iraq's national curriculum on fine arts."

"You're continuing in this tradition too," he said, picking up a book Ishtar had contributed to on diasporic Iraqi art.

"I'm just chronicling the country's destruction," Ishtar scoffed. "The complete annihilation of the land, climate, people, society, ecology . . ."

Ishtar drained the last of her tea and motioned for Nizar to turn the kettle back on. When a fresh cup was made, she continued.

"The story actually begins with my grandmother."

Ishtar eased herself up from the chair and walked towards a cupboard in the corner of the room. She rummaged through a tower of clothes before returning with a large wool blanket. Red, orange, and yellow, it was woven with symmetrical patterns.

"This was created by your great-grandmother. It's one of the only things we have from her." Ishtar ran her fingers along the pattern that framed the edges. "You see these? They're snowflakes. Funny, no? It's a very Iraqi design, yet there are snowflakes."

It was the winter of 1925, Ishtar explained. The Ottoman Empire had crumbled, making way for British and French forces to carve up southwest Asia into mandates of control.

Ishtar's grandfather, Haj Akram, was thirty-one years old. He had been a former officer of the empire, part of a generation of young officers who joined the Arab resistance. For his role in securing safe passage for Armenians escaping the killings in Turkey, he had been captured and imprisoned by the Atatürk government.

"My grandfather had been in prison for a year or so when news of his upcoming execution was announced. His wife, Fatima, was desperate. She was just a seamstress, already struggling to raise their three children herself. One night, she heard that Atatürk was travelling from Istanbul to Ankara. She asked around, studied the route his procession was meant to take, and calculated where she might be able to intercept him . . ."

It was snowing. Fatima wrapped herself in a thick shawl and took her three children with her. Kuteiba was nine, Haydar was six, and the youngest, Rajiha, just two years old. She brought her husband's best works, paintings of bridges and landscapes from his time serving in Turkey and Iraq, and they waited behind a bush by the side of the road. The children huddled around her for warmth. After hours of waiting, the earth began to shake. Fatima heard the faint sound of hooves cutting through the snow. The procession had arrived.

Fatima had to get her timing right. If she jumped into the path too late, she risked being trampled. But if she jumped too soon, the procession would simply veer around her. The sounds grew louder, and soon the silhouetted shape of horses appeared, storming down the path at a ferocious speed.

Fatima pushed her children into the bush and darted across the snowy path. She waved her arms and yelled at the carriage to stop. The procession kept moving and the horses raced towards her, their muscular legs cutting through the air. Fatima threw herself on the ground in the centre of the path. Kuteiba and Haydar ran towards her, Kuteiba carrying Rajiha in his arms. She tried to push them away from the carriage's path, but they wrapped themselves around her body. Defeated, she lay her head against the snow and stared up at the sky, waiting for the hooves to pierce them.

"That's when the snowflake floated into her field of vision," Ishtar said. She lit a cigarette. The skin around her lips creased as she drew in a mouthful of smoke.

Fatima watched the snowflake descend. She marvelled at its intricate composition, studying the edges where crystallised water met the air around it. A sense of calm cut through the anguish that had gripped her body. She had cast her fate in the same way the snowflake had. As the hooves thundered closer she felt the snowflake touch her cheek, until the boundary between them dissolved.

The carriage screeched to a halt, inches from Fatima and her children. She felt the heat from the horses on her skin. Angry voices ordered her to stand up.

Her husband's paintings were scattered along the path and she picked them up, stowing them in her bag. A guard marched towards her and grabbed her arm, yet she refused to move, demanding to see Atatürk. Suddenly, the door to the carriage opened. A man stepped out, wearing leather gloves and a heavy brown coat. He had a tidy moustache and a piercing gaze. She knew exactly who he was.

Fatima bowed her head, then introduced herself as the wife of a prisoner. She told Atatürk that her husband had been a loyal lieutenant of the Ottoman Army, that he had helped to build the Hindiyah Barrage on the Euphrates and had lived and worked in Ankara for many years.

'He's an artist too,' Fatima said. She handed over her husband's paintings. She explained that he had studied in Constantinople and had a large body of work documenting the changing landscape

of the Ottoman Empire. 'If you won't spare his life for his children, then please, spare it for his art'.

Atatürk studied the paintings. One of the Hindiyah Barrage, which her husband had painted upon completion, another of a riverbank, with water buffalos grazing on the meadows while canoes floated lazily in the water. Finally, he looked up at her.

Ishtar stubbed out her cigarette as she finished the story.

"Atatürk only said one thing to my grandmother: 'Tell your husband it was his art that saved his life.'"

The statement hung between them. Ishtar closed her eyes and ran her hands absent-mindedly over the blanket.

"How much of that story is true?" Nizar asked.

Ishtar smiled. "Does it matter? What matters is the meaning behind it. From the very beginning, it was our art that saved us."

Nizar contemplated this. It was his mother's phone call, her fervent desire to showcase the family's artworks, that had pulled him back from the edge.

"In that case," he said, resting a hand on her leg, "let's make this boat project happen."

Zainab
July 2014

Date: July 10, 2014, 3:46 P.M.
From: Mediha
To: Zainab
Subject: Paintings

Zainab,

I've had three people e-mail me in the last week asking about Baba's paintings. This is exactly why I did NOT tell you about them. Don't you realise the artworks were rescued from Baghdad after the invasion? Let's just say that I don't recall either you or Ishtar risking your lives to return to Baghdad to do it . . .

Smuggling national treasures out of a country is VERY ILLEGAL and could land someone in a LOT of trouble. I'm working closely with Sotheby's to ensure that we deal sensitively with this information. Please understand that this is a serious matter and not fodder for your Dubai housewives gossip circles.

Delete this e-mail once you've received it.

Reading the email in her workroom, Zainab's anger flared. How dare Mediha talk to her in this way, as if she were stupid—oh, but she must remain calm. Must resist the urge to reply immediately. She would be the adult, would keep her tone even and use this to get to the bottom of things. Besides, she had something on her sister now: an admission of guilt, a panicked confession.

She spent the evening carefully drafting her response and copied in Ishtar and Nizar. She needed back-up. She could not—*should not*—be dealing with this on her own. The next morning, she re-read her drafted response. Was the line about stealing too much? Before she could second-guess it, she hit send.

Date: July 11, 2014, 9:14 A.M.
From: Zainab
To: Mediha
Cc: Ishtar; Nizar
Subject: Re: Paintings

Dear Mediha,

I am copying in Ishtar because I feel all three of us, as Haydar's daughters, should be involved in these discussions. Whatever happens to those paintings should be decided by all of us. I'm also copying in Nizar, because he is part of the family and might have some ideas about how we can move forward with the family's works.

I don't quite know how to describe all of the emotions I've been feeling after discovering that Baba's paintings—which you and Mama told me had been lost in Baghdad—are in fact locked away in your house. I feel both elated and betrayed. Why did you keep this a secret for so long? Can't you understand how this makes us suspicious of your intentions? You've effectively stolen from the family!

I have asked others about the paintings because you have not been forthright about the situation. You've lied and deflected, and have made no effort to contact me to explain yourself or apologise.

But, since you've reached out, I'm giving you the chance to answer my questions:

1) What paintings do you have?

2) How and when did you acquire them?
3) What are you selling and why are you selling them?
4) What is happening with the money?
5) Who in the family was aware of this?

If you cannot give me answers, then I'll have no choice but to continue searching for them myself.

Yours,
Zainab

The response came thirty minutes later.

Date: July 11, 2014, 09:43 A.M.
From: Mediha
To: Zainab
Cc: Ishtar; Nizar
Subject: Re: Paintings

Zainab, the ONE thing I asked you to do was delete my email given the sensitive information inside it, and instead you reply copying in OTHER people, including your son, who is A JOURNALIST (to clarify, this entire conversation is COMPLETELY OFF THE RECORD and if ANYONE QUOTES, USES, OR ATTRIBUTES anything I say you will be hearing from my lawyer).

First of all, I have nothing to apologise for. You were being aggressive with me in my own home, and I was simply trying to protect myself.

Second of all, I will not be answering your questions. I'm not naïve enough to fall for such entrapment. Just to be clear, so that you can stop claiming I am withholding information: I have spent the last several years archiving the various sketches, paintings, and sculptures that I effectively rescued from Iraq. I don't suppose either you or Ishtar would have been willing or even able to undertake this job. All of this in addition to taking care of Mama and teaching FOUR courses per semester.

Mama has entrusted me to oversee the sale of the artworks. There is no point in holding on to them at this stage, and we (Mama and I) believe it is best to use the money from the paintings to make sure Mama's life is as comfortable as possible. And yes, that did include selling some of Baba's work to build Mama's studio here in Dunkeld. As Mama's primary carer it is my duty to honour her wishes. The question is, for once in your life, Zainab, will you?

M.

Zainab stared at her screen. What a performance. *Rescued from Iraq!* What is this insane language? Her sister spoke of Iraq like it were the seventh circle of hell. She was a deeply unwell woman, her brain poisoned with all that self-righteous Western piety and superiority. While Zainab stewed, her inbox chimed again.

Date: July 11, 2014, 10:17 A.M.
From: Nizar
To: Zainab
Cc: Ishtar; Mediha
Subject: Re: Paintings

Mediha—I have zero interest in writing about you or the paintings.

Mum—please remove me from this conversation.

Zainab sighed and sat back in her chair. Where was Ishtar? She called her older sister. The line rang and rang, then clicked to automated voicemail.

"Ishtar," she pleaded. "Please check your emails and call me back ASAP." She hung up and decided to text, just in case.

Have you seen M's emails? Why haven't you said anything? Your voice is crucial, not just as an artist but as the eldest daughter! Can you reply with something?!

She returned to Nizar's email and clicked 'Reply', furiously tapping on the keys. She had to keep the tone cool, had to maintain reason.

Date: July 11, 2014, 10:49 A.M.
From: Zainab
To: Mediha
Cc: Ishtar; Nizar
Subject: Re: Paintings

If selling the paintings is REALLY about securing money for Mama, then this whole thing is a non-issue. I am very happy to pay whatever is needed for Mama's care and support. Somehow, I don't think selling the paintings is about that. I know you have always been keen to rid yourself of your Iraqiness, but please leave the family paintings out of this purifying cleanse.

My preference is, and has always been, that we hold an exhibition in the region to celebrate Baba's works, rather than just selling them off under the cover of darkness. You and Mama will see not a penny from me unless this is agreed upon. And if we can't reach a decision, the paintings should be divided equally among all of us according to inheritance laws.

Finally, I kindly ask that you don't speak to me like I am stupid and don't know how things work.

The emails now came in rapid succession.

Date: July 11, 2014, 11:03 A.M.
From: Mediha

To: Zainab
Subject: Re: Paintings

What are you talking about? As much as you might want to impose some sort of sharia law, please accept that Mama lives in the UK, and here in the UK—where civil law prevails—we have our own inheritance laws which we abide by. Mama has entrusted me to oversee the works and one thing I will NOT do is send the paintings back to the region after I have done everything in my power to rescue them from there.

Date: July 11, 2014, 11:06 A.M.
From: Zainab
To: Mediha
Cc: Ishtar; Nizar
Subject: Re: Paintings

Mediha, focus. I'm not talking about sending the paintings to Iraq. I'm talking about an exhibition here in Dubai where there is both willingness and expertise to organise a formal exhibition, which would properly contextualise Baba's work. What do you think?

Eighteen days passed in silence. She feared this would be the end of it when, at a dinner party, an art collector—unaware of who she was—mentioned his admiration for her father's work. She introduced herself and they spoke for hours. The next morning, she reopened the conversation.

Date: July 30, 2014, 12:59 P.M.
From: Zainab
To: Mediha; Ishtar
Subject: Re: Paintings

Dear Mediha and Ishtar,

It's been a while now with no response to my last email. I am writing to inform you both—in the spirit of transparency—that yesterday evening I met Sheikh Mansour Al-Qubaiti, who is an Emirati and an avid collector of modern Arab art. He is a big fan of Mama and Baba's work and was surprised to hear that their work is going to be auctioned off in Sotheby's. He feels (and I agree) that to auction off the works like this, without giving them the public exhibition they deserve, would not be in the interest of Baba's legacy.

Excitingly, he has also offered to hold an exhibition here in Dubai. Given that Baba's profile has not been prominent over the last decade or so, such an exhibition would bring his works back into the public eye, and would restore Baba to his rightful place in contemporary Arab art.

Yours,

Zainab

Zainab was in the supermarket when she received Mediha's response. She abandoned her shopping cart, walked out of the store, and sat in her car in the parking lot for thirty minutes, trying to control her breathing.

Date: July 30, 2014, 03:30 P.M.
From: Mediha
To: Zainab
Subject: Re: Paintings

The paintings will not be sent to the Middle East. Get this idea out of your dumb head. Baba's works will remain in the UK where they can be kept secure. I don't trust the Gulf's ability to preserve and archive.

Your concern over Baba's 'legacy' is laughable. What is driving all this sudden love and adoration? We all know that after he died, you were a traitor to Baba's legacy, to our family, and to the country in EVERY sense of the word.

You were a traitor.

Mediha knew exactly how to destroy her. Somehow, she drove herself home. There, she drew the bedroom curtains, swallowed the diazepam pills Nizar had left her on his last visit, and wept under the covers until she fell asleep.

The following morning, Zainab woke with a new emotion. Her first instinct upon reading Mediha's email had been to run away, but this self-imposed powerlessness, a protective armour she had utilised all her life, had done her more harm than good. She hadn't been raised with wealth, and didn't possess the skill of turning money into power. But she had money now. She needed to stand her ground. Not fear her sisters, nor endlessly search for common ground. As she lay in bed, the only thing Zainab felt was steely determination. She was going to get her hands on the family paintings.

Nizar

July 2014

From a young age, Nizar had learnt to scan the edges. Cockroaches loved edges, and the mere thought of them set his skin crawling. Their dark lacquered shells that brought to mind decay and disease, their spindly antennae writhing in the air. The brittle crunch they made when crushed, the ooze that emerged from their bodies which promised more eggs. A single cockroach meant it was too late—an infestation had already occurred, millions of roaches traveling the hidden corridors of pipes and plaster. Much like a sudden outbreak of violence is indicative of buried fissures that have been simmering for years, the sight of a cockroach signals its hidden ecosystem underneath houses and cities. What appears on the surface has been breeding in the dark for a long time.

Nizar's anxiety appeared to him as a large cockroach, popping up when he least expected it. When he woke the morning after meeting Ishtar, he was unsurprised to find the cockroach curled on his chest. It had become his companion ever since he'd moved out of the home he'd shared with Alfie.

As he made his way to the kitchen to brew some coffee, the cockroach scuttled behind him. Pregnant clouds hung low in the sky, allowing only slivers of silver light to cut through. Nothing seemed to cast a shadow.

He put on some shorts, an old t-shirt, and his running shoes. Running had always been his sanctuary, his way to—if not stop the thoughts racing through his mind—at least give them a linear direction of travel. The air was warm as he sprinted down

Brick Lane, dodging pools of vomit outside vintage clothes shops. As long as he kept moving, as long as he didn't look back, he could keep a safe distance from the past.

We must start from the beginning. His aunt's voice appeared in his mind as he ran through Aldgate, a ghost town without the weekday office workers. He crossed the river over Tower Bridge and tried to recall when things had started to fall apart. It was like pulling on an endless piece of string. He remembered how a month after meeting, he and Alfie had been lying in bed when Alfie reached over and grabbed Nizar's phone from the bedside table. Kneeling above him, his thighs on either side of his torso, he pointed the phone at Nizar's face and began to film. He pushed two fingers into his mouth, then three, then four. Nizar took them in to the knuckles, breathing through his gag reflex. The fingers explored the inside of his mouth with cold curiosity, and when Nizar retched Alfie pulled them out. He pressed his thumb against Nizar's chin and drew his jaw down, gathering saliva on the edge of his tongue. He let it fall from his pursed lips, dripping into Nizar's open mouth. He leaned over and kissed him, then pushed his head down towards his cock. Nizar sucked him ferociously, and it was only afterwards that he looked up and saw he was still being filmed.

Later, Nizar had watched the video on his phone. The expression on his face was all lust and no shame; he had never seen himself so uninhibited before. His instincts warned him to delete the video, but the idea of the footage being gone forever filled him with a strange sadness.

That evening, Alfie suggested Naples.

"We can drive down the Amalfi coast. I want to see Vesuvius."

"But why?"

"A holiday."

Nizar considered this. "I don't think I've ever been on holiday before."

"Your mum never took you?"

"We moved around too much," Nizar said. The words snagged on something unexpected.

"Did you move because of your mother's job?"

"We moved because of my mother's life."

Alfie laughed. This was early on, when such remarks still charmed him, and he ran his hand through Nizar's curls and down his face. When his fingers stopped on Nizar's scar, his smile disappeared.

"Don't feel sorry for me—"

"I'm not—"

"—just because I've never been on some bourgeois holiday."

They booked the Amalfi coast for late September, a few days after Nizar was due to return from Yemen. He'd been commissioned to write about the war in the northern governorate of Sa'ada. It was the Ramadan of 2009 and the Saudi government was waging a brutal bombing campaign in the north of Yemen, a festival of pain.

In Sana'a airport, he purchased a cheap blue Nokia as a back-up burner phone. For the first three days he met with UN bureaucrats, NGO workers, weapons dealers, government officials, and militia contacts. His calls to the Saudi embassy were met with polite requests to call back another time.

NGOs assigned codenames to the different warring groups. The Houthis were 'the Beach Boys', the Saudi government 'Abba', and the Yemeni government were 'the Spice Girls'. Foreign doctors returned from hospitals in the worst hit areas, their faces gaunt and ashen, spilling memories of families annihilated with a single missile. Propaganda wars raged. The Beach Boys filmed the atrocities, ignoring pleas from medical staff not to film the dead. Abba blocked aid trucks, and convoys stalled at the border under the relentless desert heat. Medicines threatened to spoil under the sun.

The Ramadan tradition of turning the day on its head amplified the chaos. The powerful didn't work until after dark: orders to kill were made in the dead of night, black skies buzzed with jet planes heading north.

Nizar went to bed at dawn and woke three hours later. He sat on the rooftop of his hotel in the old city, watching the jets soar through the sky as he planned the day's meetings, confirmed appointments, called contacts, revised interview questions, and checked the websites of militias to get a feel for the war's momentum.

Security updates flashed on his phone alongside Alfie's holiday tips, infusing his two worlds. We should take a boat to Ischia one day because *THE SPICE GIRLS HAVE BLOCKED THE MAIN ROAD FROM SA'ADA TO SANA'A.* There's this pizzeria in Naples where *A BOMB KILLED A FAMILY OF TWENTY-SIX. THE BEACH BOYS THREATEN TO RETALIATE WITH* ten things you MUST do in the Amalfi coast.

On the fourth day, Nizar headed north with Abdallah, a chain-smoking driver Nizar had worked with on a previous trip.

Much of Sa'ada city had been levelled by air strikes, and Nizar stopped to take photos of the rubble with his camera phone. Abdallah was nervous and looked up at the skies, muttering that it was too dangerous to be outside for long. They stayed in a UN compound, and on the first evening visited a bunkered hospital supported by Médecins Sans Frontières. Civilians were wheeled in with torn limbs and gashes in their flesh. Corridors were crowded with patients on gurneys, IVs punched into their veins. A surgeon with blood-stained scrubs scolded a teary-eyed African nurse who wiped her face with wads of tissue paper.

"Don't ask about their family or their personal lives," the surgeon said in a Dutch accent. "You cannot humanise them. You will go mad."

The surgeon turned to Nizar, and her eyes dropped to the notebook in his hand. She sighed.

"I'm very busy."

Nizar fought the nausea he felt, intruding on these moments of life and death. "Just a few questions."

The surgeon led him to a courtyard where anxious family members paced.

"Our teams have been under shelling, performing complex surgeries that come in five at a time. No sleep, electricity blackouts. Children come in with small fragment injuries, but when you open them up you discover these tiny fragments destroyed their internal organs. Our staff are overwhelmed. They've threatened to walk out and close the hospital . . ."

A hand gripped his arm. Nizar turned around and came face to face with a young man holding a Kalashnikov, his eyes crimson with grief.

"Hey!" The surgeon yelled. "No weapons in the hospital!"

The man grabbed Nizar's shoulder. "You're a journalist?" he asked in Arabic. "Come take photos of my mother's corpse. Show the world what they are doing."

Nizar began to follow him, but the surgeon grabbed his arm.

"No," she said in English, then again in broken Arabic. "*La'. Mush mumkin*. You cannot take photographs without the patient's consent."

"But the patient is dead," Nizar said. His phone buzzed in his pocket.

Are you reading that book about Pompeii? Can't wait to see the remains . . .

Abdallah had been waiting. As they walked out, Nizar's eyes landed on a child of about ten, standing alone in the corner of the room. The boy's face was devoid of expression, his pupils large and unfocused.

"He just came in with his mother," Abdallah whispered. "She was missing half her head."

They drove to a displacement camp outside the city, where Nizar interviewed the inhabitants. He wrote their stories down and took photographs of the makeshift tents, of clothes hanging on flimsy wires, of aid distribution trucks emptied of supplies. He thought of Naples, imagined a pizza emerging from a clay oven.

On their return to Sana'a, Abdallah drove in silence. Nizar looked out the window: at the edge of the city, a bombed building. Two tribal militiamen guarded the rubble. A large poster of a Houthi leader hung from a pole. As they drove by, Nizar grabbed his phone and took a quick picture.

Seconds later, gunshots. In the rearview mirror, Nizar saw the militiamen running towards the car, shouting. Abdallah pressed on the gas, his hands clenching the wheel. A hundred meters ahead, he stomped on the brakes. Two different men with guns had blocked the road, their rifles pointing towards them.

"You took a photo?" Abdallah whispered as the men approached the car.

"Yes."

"You idiot!"

Abdallah rolled down the window. The man pointed his gun towards Nizar.

"He took a photo on his phone."

"We are with the UN," Abdallah lied.

"Give me the phone," the man demanded, gesturing with his hand.

Nizar reached for his pocket, then remembered the video Alfie had taken earlier that summer: Alfie's fingers exploring his mouth, his own face—bisected by Alfie's cock—staring up in lust. He experienced an otherworldly lightheadedness as he recalled the footage, his wilful and liberating emasculation, indulging his desires without shame or guilt. He was all at once overcome with the dissociative terror of being inside the tribal militiamen's minds as they watched the video for the first time.

"There are no photos," Nizar said.

The other man tapped on the passenger window with the butt of his rifle. They were in no rush.

Nizar rummaged through his backpack to distract them. He pulled his phone out of his pocket and slid it under the seat, then removed the Nokia from his bag and handed it to the men.

"There are no photos," Nizar repeated, steelier now. "I was just pointing out the destruction to my friend."

The man looked through the burner phone, then handed it back to Nizar before waving them through. It was clear they didn't believe him, but decided they were neither important enough to detain, nor interesting enough to toy with.

When the men disappeared from the horizon, Nizar turned to Abdallah.

"Why did you lie? What if they asked to see our UN papers?"

"Why did *I* lie?" Abdallah was indignant. "Why did *you* take a photo?" He stuck a cigarette in his mouth. The car swerved as he fumbled with the lighter. "Everyone's a liar in this war. To survive, you have to learn to lie."

Nizar arrived back at the hotel in Sana'a just as the day's fast broke. He watched the sun set from his window, taking large swigs from the bottle of whiskey he'd smuggled in with him. He tried to weave the week's information into a story, a coherent narrative to make sense of the violence. He wanted to maintain a grip on the truth, but it liquified in his hands. It was difficult to feel he was doing anything more than continuing the endless narratives of reporters who had come before him.

By midnight he was drunk and delirious. A night's worth of sleep rationed over an entire week had taken its toll. He ignored Alfie's enthusiastic messages, resenting him for the video, for how close he had come to being exposed.

Instead, he drunkenly wandered the narrow streets of the old city, the Ramadan crowds seemingly unaffected by the massacres a short drive away. For a few hours, Nizar lost himself in the city's energy. It reminded him why he'd fallen in love with Yemen on his first trip two years earlier: the children who joked and yelled for their photo to be taken, the playfulness of the people, how quick everyone was to smile.

He took a kebab from a street vendor back to the rooftop of his hotel. The Burj al-Salam was the tallest building in the old city, looking out over the gingerbread-like buildings and the rugged mountains. Suddenly, the electricity cut out. The city was shrouded in darkness, except for the large mosque on the horizon, blinking like a lighthouse in the sky.

* * *

He was outside the Tate when the sky finally broke. Warm sheets of rain descended upon the crowds, and a woman in a white sundress ran towards the entrance, followed by a man using a newspaper as a cover. Nizar moved through a large group of tourists and stood at the top of the Turbine Hall, listening to the echoes of footsteps in that vast, industrial cathedral. He let himself be carried forward, drenched and drifting toward the escalators like debris caught in the undertow. He felt something drawing him in, a force he could not understand, until he found himself standing in front of a dark and abstract painting in one of the upper galleries.

'Mahzoum'. *Defeat.* The caption explained that the painting was completed in 1963. The artist, Hamed Abdalla, had relocated from Egypt to Copenhagen a few years earlier, and then later lived in exile in Paris. *Defeat* was Abdalla's reflection on political failure and the after-effects of violence. It was the painting his mother had mentioned the night they met for dinner last summer.

Nizar observed the painting for a long time. Abdalla had wrapped silver leaf with aluminium and used a blowtorch to scorch parts of the canvas. The effect was to give the painting the appearance of having survived an explosion. Nizar's eyes were drawn to the bottom left corner, where tar pooled across the canvas like an oil spill. Towards the top of the piece, bird-like scratches appeared to fly away from the painting, as if trying to escape the suffocating darkness. He understood what his mother had meant, that feeling of familiar sadness.

It was not just Yemen, but what followed. If he had jumped into another war zone he would have remained insulated, but only a few days after returning from Sana'a Nizar found himself in a boutique hotel around the corner from a bustling piazza. The hotel was run by a single caretaker, an older homosexual who—upon realising they were a couple—gave Nizar and Alfie the best room, with large windows and high ceilings decorated with elaborate murals.

"These are traditional windows from the late nineteenth-century," the caretaker explained as he showed off the room. Nizar noted with envy the ease with which the caretaker existed in his surroundings, how in command he was of his own history. "Just keep them shut when you're out, because it's easy for thieves to climb through."

In the morning, they had breakfast in the small communal area. At the next table, two British women with sunburned faces ate cornettis while leafing through old copies of *Heat* magazine. The television was turned to CNN, the sound muted. Nizar read the scrolling text at the bottom of the screen. A Saudi air strike on a camp for displaced persons in Yemen. Eighty people dead.

Nizar dropped his knife.

"That's where I was," he said to Alfie. "I was in that camp last week."

He stood up and walked towards the television. He studied the faces on the screen, the women crying and beating their chests, the charred remains, the aid workers in flak jackets running through the dust. He searched for the volume button. Behind him, the British women loudly planned their day trip to Capri. He turned around.

"Shut up," he snapped.

The women looked at him, their faces frozen in horror.

Alfie grabbed his hand and led him out of the room. They drove to Positano and explored the coastline, walking up and down the steep staircases between the colourful houses. They had dinner in restaurants carefully selected by Alfie, where he encouraged Nizar to savour the fresh tomato sauce on a pizza, or the almost imperceptible crunch of the pasta. On the beach, Alfie dozed on his side, a single headphone blasting music into his ear. Nizar could only make out the deep bass as he lay on the pebbled beach, reading a book on the philosophy of travel. Around him, holiday-goers—he was one of them now, he realised—played on the beach or splashed in the turquoise water. He looked down at the boarding pass he had absent-mindedly used as a bookmark. Emirates Airlines, Sana'a to Dubai. Economy class. It had only been a week, but the trip felt like a distant nightmare. Here in Italy, relaxing on the beach, he was not the same person he was ten days ago.

He buried the boarding pass under some pebbles and replaced it with a receipt for the gelato they'd bought earlier that day. He stood and walked along the seaweed-strewn beach, making his way to the water.

Later, swimming back to shore, Nizar realised the tide had pulled him away from their spot. He scanned the beach until he finally spotted Alfie and the light blue towel he was sleeping on. Behind him, a teenage boy carried a large rock. The boy lifted it above his head, and before Nizar realised what was happening, he dropped it on Alfie, smashing his face into the ground.

Nizar heard himself scream. He ran through the shallow water. On the beach, he stopped. Blinked. Alfie was sitting up and staring at him. It had been a trick of perspective. The boy had dropped the rock six feet from where Alfie was sleeping, using it as a wedge to keep his umbrella from tipping over.

Alfie was running towards him now.

“What’s going on?” he panted, meeting Nizar halfway down the beach.

“I thought . . .” Nizar hesitated. “I think the sun is getting to me.”

“You’re bleeding.”

Nizar looked down. His big toe had split open. Blood ribboned through the backwash over the pebbled beach.

“It’s fine. It doesn’t hurt.” His heart was beating fast, his breath shallow.

“It looks deep.” Alfie bent down and held Nizar’s toe. “Let’s get it cleaned up.”

Back at the hotel, Alfie showered. Nizar lay on the bed and stared at the ceiling. In his periphery, something moved. He turned his head to see a large brown cockroach scuttle from behind the curtain. He swore and jumped up on the bed.

“What is it?” Alfie emerged naked from the bathroom. Nizar pointed to the bug, which scrambled under the bed. Alfie reached for it with a rolled-up magazine. There was a loud crunch. He swept the dead cockroach towards Nizar to show him the carcass.

“You’ve just spent ten days in a warzone, and you’re squealing because there’s a cockroach in the room?”

Nizar did not remember the photograph he had taken, of the two militiamen standing guard by the half-destroyed building, until later that afternoon, as he sat on the balcony and watched the sun set over the coast. He picked up his phone and found it. There was something haunting about the two emaciated bodies guarding a river of destroyed concrete. He pulled out his sketchbook and began to draw the image. He worked for forty-five minutes before Alfie came up behind him with a glass of wine.

“Whatcha doing?”

Nizar closed the sketchbook.

“Were you drawing?”

"They're just scribbles."

"Let me see!" Alfie placed his glass on the table and picked up the sketchbook. He flipped through the pages, examining the various sketches. Destroyed buildings, rubble, half-collapsed bridges. Faces of child soldiers, militiamen, young protesters, border patrol officers.

"Scribbles I make while waiting for planes."

"Do you do these from memory or from photographs?"

"A bit of both."

Alfie sat down. "And this stuff is real? Stuff you've seen?"

Nizar nodded. "I guess it helps me visualise the story . . . gives the writing some texture."

Alfie stopped at the page where Nizar had sketched a crater on the road, based on a photograph he had taken in the southern suburbs of Beirut after the Israeli bombardment. "I love your use of watercolour in this one."

"I like watercolours. Everything sort of bleeds into everything else."

Alfie closed the book and placed it on the table. He kissed Nizar's cheek. "I didn't know I was dating an artist."

"I'm not an artist."

"But you have artists in your family."

"I'm not an artist, Alfie." He was surprised by the force of his words.

Alfie grabbed him by the hand and pulled him back into the bedroom. In the large mirror propped against the wall, Nizar watched with detachment as their bodies pushed against one another. He thought of the displacement camp. He wondered which of the people he interviewed were now dead. How could he be here while the bodies of innocent children were pulverised by bombs?

Afterwards, the two of them dozed with the windows open. Alfie's leg was draped over his own, anchoring Nizar to his body, to the bed, to the holiday, while his mind escaped somewhere darker. He was overcome with a strange vertigo. It had been easier—or at least more familiar—to live in a world of darkness, no matter how violent and brutal, than to acknowledge that the world could be both breathtakingly beautiful and heartbreakingly cruel. Alfie had brought this juxtaposition to him, and the contrast was so evident, so clear, that Nizar almost resented him for bringing it into his life.

Alfie woke, rolled on top of him, and looked him in the eyes. He smelled of sex and sleep.

"I love you," he whispered, touching Nizar's nose with his own.

It was the first time the words were directed at him with such ease and conviction.

"I love you too." He kissed him gently on the lips, willing himself to remain in the moment, not to leave his body and float up into the darkness.

Zainab

August 2014

Sitting in her workroom, Zainab re-read the email she had just sent.

Date: August 1, 2014, 10:05 A.M.
From: Mathloum, Zainab
To: Al-Qubaiti, Mansour
Subject: Family Artwork Exhibition in Dubai

Dear Sheikh Mansour,

It was a pleasure meeting you the other evening. I'm writing with good news: the family artworks will no longer be auctioned; I am in the process of acquiring them. You expressed interest in presenting a retrospective of my parents' work in Dubai—could we schedule a time to discuss? With thanks and best regards,

Zainab

She closed her laptop and took a deep breath. Around her, floor-to-ceiling shelves housed paints and brushes, rolls of fabric, trinkets she collected from the markets in Satwa (clay figurines, masks, jewels, and evil eye amulets), alongside the junk and debris she found in the street (feathers and barbed wire, pieces of wood in unusual shapes, animal bones, dried flowers, scraps of metal, rubber and plastic). Zainab used these objects in her 'handicrafts', the dismissive word Ishtar once used to refer to Zainab's artwork, and that she had since appropriated for herself.

With the email sent, Zainab returned to her work. Over the last several months, she had developed an interest in metal-work: copper and silver sheets that she shaped into bookmarks, tablecloth holders, coffee cups and trays, and onto which she embossed palm trees, traditional Baghdadi minarets, water buffalos, and faces with large Sumerian eyes. Working on her Mesopotamian-inspired crafts joyously reconnected her to Iraq, to her memories, to her father.

Her artisanal work, which traded on nostalgia and turath, was popular with the wealthy Iraqi community in Dubai, and she was often busy with orders. Her friends encouraged her to hire an assistant who could do the brunt of the manual labour, but Zainab did all the work herself. She spent ten or twelve gruelling hours a day in this small room, an enclave of the kitchen, embossing metal and dyeing cloth and carving prints on wooden blocks until her neck throbbed and her shoulders spasmed and her back seized from the pain.

She had an order to finish before tomorrow—a set of embossed candleholders—but her shoulders still ached from the previous day's work and she needed a break.

Walking down the hall towards the living room, Zainab admired all the work she had done to build her home. At fifty-six, she finally owned her own furniture. Every piece in her Jumeirah villa belonged to her and no one before her. When she married Mohammed and moved to Dubai fifteen years ago, she had transplanted herself into his furnished existence. In the wake of her husband's death, Zainab embraced the existential opportunity to refurnish. She filled each room in her new villa with chairs and rugs and tables and beds and lighting fixtures and mirrors and ottomans and shelves made from mango wood and Indian silks in rich, warm shades of red and brown and gold. All of it, every piece, carefully selected by her.

She sat on her sofa and looked at the paintings adorning the walls. Some were painted by her father, others by her aunt

Rajiha. She also had a couple of pieces by her mother and a few by Ishtar. *This* was how paintings should be, celebrated and proudly displayed, not forgotten in some closet in the middle of nowhere.

If her family knew how much she valued her furniture they would think her shallow, but these possessions held a deeper meaning. For so long she had struggled to plant roots. Was it guilt at the thought of doing so in a soil that wasn't Iraq? Or fear that any roots she planted would be snatched away, as they had been before? How ironic that after decades, Zainab had anchored herself in Dubai, a city built upon shifting sands. Dubai's transience was an opioid for her, a pleasantly numbing type of freedom, and just as she thought this, she heard Janis Joplin's gravelly voice in her mind: *Freedom's just another word for nothing left to lose.*

Her phone rang, breaking the chain of memories.

"Zainab, it's Mansour."

"Sheikh Mansour! I just emailed you."

"I was thrilled to receive it. I had to call immediately."

A once abstract idea was now taking shape, crystallising. "Are you in Dubai?"

"New York. It's two A.M. here but I'm still working. I'm trying to set up exhibitions of modern Arab art at a few museums in the States and . . . well, it's been a struggle. Why can't the Americans think beyond their own political frames? If the art doesn't fit their own narrative of our region, they aren't interested."

He yawned, and Zainab heard the buzz of an espresso machine.

"Just yesterday I was telling MoMA about your father's work, so when I got your email, I knew it had to be a sign. I'm so happy to hear you're no longer auctioning the works. Please don't take this the wrong way, but Iraq is no longer as sexy for the Western art market. They're looking at Syria now. The Arab

Spring. Iraq, especially mid-twentieth century Iraqi art, is old news." He paused. "Can I ask why your family wanted to sell the works?"

Zainab hesitated. She didn't fully understand her sister's reasons. Perhaps Mediha simply wanted to be rid of them, of anything that tied her to Iraq. "I never believed auctioning the works was a good idea," she replied carefully. "That was my sister's initiative, and she really doesn't know that much about art . . ."

"Even if your family do decide to sell, it makes financial sense to raise your father's profile first. He was too important a figure for his art to be sold for peanuts. I'm assuming you have an estate for your father's work?"

"An estate?"

"Yes, someone who is in charge of the artworks."

"I don't know."

"Well that's the first step to think about. It just makes it easier if there's some person—or entity—that curators can directly engage with."

Zainab's heart sunk. She'd hoped the process would be easy.

"Zainab, I just want to repeat that it would be a dream to hold an exhibition for your parents in the Emirates. I've got a strong team there. They can curate and archive and contextualise. We would tell the story of how your parents bridged elements from ancient Mesopotamian and Islamic art with modern European schools. Do you have the paintings now?"

"I'm . . . in the process of acquiring them."

"If it's easier I can speak directly to your sister—"

"No," Zainab said, too harshly. Realising her tone had startled him, she softened it. "I'd prefer to be the main point of contact for now. If we can't exhibit the paintings in Baghdad, Dubai would be the next best thing."

They set a date to meet for coffee, and Zainab returned to the sofa. She had been pacing throughout the call and felt breathless. She thought of the time, thirty years earlier, when she had left Baghdad for Kuwait, that tiny country carved out of a fold in Iraq and Saudi Arabia. When she'd first arrived there, four months pregnant, she had rented a furnished studio apartment in Salmiyah. She told herself it was only temporary, yet it was a stepping-stone on which she spent eight blissful years. She hadn't thought she could find happiness within the fog of grief that had followed her from Iraq. Kuwait had taken in thousands like her: exiles, rejects, outcasts. Those running away, but still yearning for some version of a middle-class Arab life. Once born, Nizar had the nursery he loved, then the American school. She had her secretarial job in a bank, not to mention all the restaurants, house parties, and deep friendships she had cultivated. There was the sense that they could make a life there, one that was safe and would remain that way for the rest of their lives . . .

But Iraq found its way to her again. When Saddam's tanks rolled through Kuwait City, Zainab made it through the darkest days with masking tape on the windows and a steady rotation of Disney films and Jane Fonda work-out videos. She squatted and lunged to the dawning realisation that she and Nizar would soon have to leave. She was Iraqi, her son was half-Palestinian—identities that had curdled in the heat of Kuwait's invasion.

For the second time in thirty years, Zainab had to abandon a burning country. Before the Americans swooped in to liberate the city, she packed two suitcases filled with clothes and a ration of luxuries: two Janis Joplin records and a Jane Fonda exercise video for her; two action figures and four books for Nizar. They jumped on a bus that deposited them in a provincial purgatory amidst the nightmarish hell-fires of its neighbours.

Amman, 1990.

A mould-stricken room in a three-star hotel on Gardens Street.

They spent six days there, sating their hunger with cheap

crisps bought from the family-run supermarket on the street corner. The smell of cigarettes clung to the furniture. By the bed, the black telephone with its sticky buttons rang constantly. She called friends to ask where she could buy Vogue cigarettes, which segued into muddled requests for money that left her feeling ashamed. Nizar seemed—at the time—blissfully content with the crisps they ate for their meals, distracted by the promise of the tiny plastic toys that sometimes appeared inside the packets.

"We'll settle soon," she told him as they cradled each other on the springy single mattress.

"Why can't we just stay here?"

"Do you want to stay because you like it here, or because I'm letting you eat all these crisps?"

He buried his head in her lap. He was desperately anchoring himself to something.

On a friend's suggestion, she bought two one-way tickets to Cyprus.

Nicosia, 1990.

Furnished apartment number one.

A boxy sofa set, upholstered in teal-blue fabric. A dining table set with chrome-legged chairs and a smoked glass table, slightly too delicate for comfort. A floor lamp with a geometric shade that cast soft pools of light in the evenings, giving the room a Scandinavian feel. An upright piano in the living room, its wood a polished deep chestnut, which quickly became Nizar's fixation. He sat on the bench for hours, savouring the different sounds each key made.

Soon after moving in, the landlord—who had kindly offered the apartment at a lower rate for two months—now wanted full rent. When Zainab couldn't pay, he told her of a one-bedroom apartment he owned in the basement of the same building.

Nicosia, 1991.

Furnished apartment number two.

A narrow window ran along the top of one wall, casting the room in a perpetual fluorescent gloom. The furniture was sparse and mismatched, second-string pieces that had made their way down from the nicer apartments upstairs. In lieu of a couch, a giant neon beanbag was slung in the centre of the living room.

Nizar walked through the flat before returning in a panic.

"There's no piano!" He looked at her with his father's eyes.

Zainab was already borrowing money from friends, purchasing food in bulk, and selling Nizar on the idea that two home-made cheese and honey sandwiches (which she had dubbed the 'Super Duper Sandwich') were enough for breakfast and lunch. A piano was a no-go.

The neon beanbag became synonymous with the theme of CNN World News. While she curled into it and watched Americans drop bombs on Baghdad, Nizar stood on the dining table and gazed out the window. The weather grew cold and frosty, and though it was his first real winter after a lifetime in the desert, he appeared tense and anxious. He watched the dark streets, as though waiting for someone to appear and take them away.

To stimulate him, she drove to the Troodos Mountains on the weekends. It was the first time either of them had seen snow. They made snowmen and trudged through the whiteness, wrapped in thick wool scarves and mittens which made them feel chic and European.

To make ends meet, Zainab took on two jobs. In the early afternoons she worked as a typist, typing up news cards for a Cypriot radio agency. She came home in time to cook Nizar a meal, help with homework, and put him to sleep, then went to her other job from midnight to five in the morning, monitoring Iraqi radio and translating the main points for a Spanish news service. She translated reports of the bombing of Baghdad and watched as her hometown turned to rubble. Her mother and aunt Rajiha were still there. When the war ended, the realisation that her father's monument in the centre of Baghdad remained intact steadied something inside of her. The city had endured.

As winter gave way to spring the trips to the mountains continued, and on a hike in late April, as they made their way around a steep bend in the cliff, Nizar stopped. He peered down, kicked a small stone off the edge. As their gaze followed the stone's long descent to the valley below, Zainab was overcome with an image of her eight-year-old son's body tumbling down and crashing against the rocks. Perhaps Nizar had a similar thought, because he turned to her with a look of terror. It was the terror of understanding that at some point they would die. Their lives would end, just as their lives in Kuwait had, suddenly and without warning.

The war wound down, and she was let go from her job at the radio station. Interest had waned. News of suffering under sanctions was no match for the awe-inspiring fireworks that had preceded it.

Zainab considered moving to the UK—she had the passport after all. Ishtar and Mediha had settled there, and their mother had just made the hard decision to follow. But Zainab needed to be in the Arab world.

"Are you *sure* you packed everything?" Nizar asked, as they checked-in to their flight to Amman that summer.

"Yes," Zainab insisted, placing a hand on her nine-year-old's head. But no sooner had she said this, she remembered a Greek recipe book in the top drawer of the kitchen cupboard, Nizar's panda schoolbag left at the back of the closet, and her last remaining Jane Fonda video. Traces of their past life, left behind like breadcrumbs.

Hailing a taxi at the airport in Amman, the driver looked her up and down as she struggled with the suitcases.

"Why don't you sit in the front?" he suggested.

She declined.

In the backseat she felt his gaze through the mirror, his eyes like mildew creeping over her neck and breasts. She clutched her handbag close to her body. Nizar sat quietly beside her.

"Where are you coming from?" the driver asked.

"Cyprus. But we used to live in Kuwait."

"So you're one of those . . ." he muttered.

At a traffic light, he reached his arm behind the seat and brushed the side of her leg. Once. Twice. She shifted closer to her son, seeking his protection while trying to ensure he remained oblivious to what was happening. She thought of her father's brother, but pushed it quickly to the recesses of her mind.

The driver stopped two blocks from the address.

"It's on the next street," she said.

"Did they not teach you how to walk in Kuwait?"

She got out of the car and dragged her heavy suitcases from the trunk, then gave the man the fare. He took the money and grabbed her, his large hand enveloping her wrist. He pulled her close to his pock-marked face and looked her dead in the eyes.

"You Kuwait families deserve everything that happened to you."

Amman, 1992.

Furnished apartment number three.

The Shmeisani apartment had belonged to the recently deceased great-aunt of a friend and smelt faintly of dust and fried onions—a scent that persisted no matter how much she cleaned. The living room was dominated by a wood-framed couch with golden tassels, its cushions stiff with age. Thick velvet curtains opened onto an iron-railed balcony that overlooked a bird garden, home to a collection of roaming peacocks, shaggy herons, and a chain-smoking caged monkey. Every morning, Zainab enjoyed her coffee on the balcony, listening to the parrots and the roosters' hoarse, echoing cries.

The place was also infested with cockroaches. Nizar screamed whenever one darted from behind the toilet or across the kitchen floor. Everything about the new apartment, about the new city, filled Nizar with loathing.

"Do you like your school?" she asked him a few weeks later.

Nizar glared at her. "Everyone's obsessed with my religion, where I'm from, where my father is . . ."

Zainab found herself comparing Nizar's childhood to her own. Yes, her childhood had had its difficulties, and she too had barely known her father. But she'd had a community. She'd had moments of joy. It was all gone now, but she had her memories. What memories were being created for her son?

Zainab spoke regularly to Amma Rajiha, her father's younger sister. She was the last remaining family member in Baghdad. On the phone Rajiha downplayed the sanctions, occasionally noting difficulties with getting paint, and some medicines, but ending every complaint with "But thanks to God we are fine. God is with us." Since when did Rajiha start speaking the language of God, Zainab wondered. That was when she felt it. The first deep pangs of estrangement.

The best thing that came from their four years in Amman was Amjad. Like her, Amjad was a drifter, a Palestinian journalist and quasi-intellectual who drank too much and smoked even more. At thirty, he had already been jailed twice. She had never been interested in politics, but felt a thrill as he railed against the government. When Israel and Jordan signed their peace treaty, he wept. He was also tender and loving, helping with errands and bureaucratic hurdles. They shared the hazy hunger of exile. She felt comforted and safe in his presence.

He was also patient with Nizar. Outings always ended in tantrums, with Nizar throwing his body to the ground and screeching at the top of his lungs. Like the rest of Zainab's family, he was too easily swept up in the tide of his emotions. She loved him, of course, loved him more than anything, but she was also terrified. Terrified of him and terrified for him.

At ten years old, he began to soil his pants. The smell followed the two of them like the musk of a wild animal.

"The boy is using his bowels to protest his exile," Amjad remarked once with a hint of admiration.

During those outbursts Zainab longed for Andre, for whatever insight Nizar's father might have. If Andre were still alive, perhaps he might have revealed that he too misbehaved as a child. This could have soothed her, could have rationalised Nizar's behaviour. Instead, she could only stand by helplessly as her son pulsed with insatiable rage.

Zainab's family sometimes passed through on their way to or from Baghdad. Amma Rajiha was the only one who visited every year. She found Nizar's tantrums delightful.

"It is a sign of brilliance," she'd said after Nizar had slammed the door so hard a vase crashed to the floor. "I was a complicated child too, you know."

Her mother visited only once. When she arrived Zainab tried to enlist her help, but her British mother had no clue what to do with Nizar's rage and would just ignore the poor boy rolling on the floor in agonised sobs.

"He's too old to be behaving like this," her mother had said. They were at the Dead Sea and Nizar had yelled so loudly that Zainab dunked her head in the salty water. "The boy is spoiled."

Spoiled? Zainab had to hold herself back from reprimanding her mother for comparing her son to a piece of rotten fruit. *The boy has never met his father, the rug has been pulled from under our feet, and we have been struggling to find a base for ourselves for years. I didn't spoil him you cold-hearted bitch.*

Ishtar passed through Amman several times on her visits to Syria, where she was having an affair with the wife of the Pakistani Ambassador. Ishtar and Nizar spent hours painting together and working on various crafts. In Ishtar's presence, Nizar settled into a strange and contented calm that lingered for weeks after her departure, before the rage inevitably returned.

Kuwait City, 1995.

Furnished apartment number four.

A short-term let in a newly built complex. Cool marble floors. Pale beige walls and recessed lighting. A brand-new leather sofa. Modern amenities—a dishwasher, a dryer, a grill. A glossy MDF entertainment unit that held a flat screen TV connected to hundreds of global channels.

There was even a communal swimming pool.

The two months there felt like an endless holiday. They had no obligations beyond plunging into the pool and watching American sitcoms while eating ice cream as the crisp air-conditioning soothed their sunburnt skin. They ate McDonalds for the first time, American chocolates and peanut butter, none of which had been available in Amman.

When the two months passed and it was time to move, Nizar presented his case for staying. There was a swimming pool, he explained. And what about the dishwasher. She liked that, didn't she?

"Nizar, we can't afford this place."

It was the piano all over again.

The move came in mid-September. An unfurnished apartment on the ground floor of a building in the neighbourhood of Salwa. No swimming pool on site, nor the promise of a nearby beach. Just endless desert along the quiet road that ended with a Sultan Shopping Centre. The apartment had a small backyard, which trapped the heat inside its concrete walls like a furnace.

"Where's all the furniture?" Nizar asked, confused.

He had never been in an unfurnished home before, Zainab realised.

"We're going to furnish it ourselves." The forced excitement in her voice ricocheted against the walls of the barren living room. "You can even pick out your own bed."

Nizar chose a black metal frame from the shop. Zainab couldn't tighten the screws properly, so the bed creaked. They also bought a television, and as soon as they arrived home she opened the box and stuck her face inside, savouring the fresh smell of new plastic.

Kuwait had changed. The warmth she remembered prior to the invasion was replaced by rampant American consumerism and a veiled hostility towards certain Arabs. Zainab learned to disguise her Iraqi accent and accentuate her Britishness. Nizar struggled to make friends. He spent his afternoons drawing alone in his room, unable to sleep. The paralysing fear of his Cypriot anxieties, which were replaced by the fury of his Jordanian rage, now made way for an insatiable Kuwaiti sadness. At night he wept for hours. She held him as he sobbed, keeping his loneliness company.

"Why do I feel like this?" he asked, his face streaked with tears.

She didn't know what to say.

After nine months in Kuwait, Zainab called Andre's mother in Beirut. She had not spoken to her dead fiancé's mother in a decade.

"We need to get out of Kuwait."

The old woman was silent for a long time. Finally, she agreed.

In June, Zainab announced they were leaving.

"Where now?" Nizar asked, unsurprised. His voice had broken. He was becoming a man.

"We're going to live with your grandmother."

"Bibi?"

"No, your other grandmother. Bernadette."

"Who the fuck is that?"

They flew to Jordan, spending the night with one of Zainab's old high school friends from Baghdad. She had just arrived from Iraq, escaping the sanctions. While Nizar slept on the sofa bed the two women stayed up on the balcony, smoking and drinking. Her friend described a Baghdad that Zainab did not recognise.

"I chopped vegetables in the dark during the electricity cuts. Because I couldn't see, I would end up chopping bits of skin from my fingers. We used to joke that at least with bits of skin in the food we were getting some protein." Her friend recited the anecdote with a rehearsed rhythm. It was clearly a story she'd repeated often, smoothing out its edges and exaggerating its tragic comedy.

The next morning, they got in a taxi and headed to the border. They spent a night in a convent in Damascus, where friendly nuns left jasmine flowers between their linen sheets. Then they were on the road again. For fifteen years the seismic shifts of political upheavals had tossed them around like confetti. Finally, they landed in the city that had killed Andre.

"We're here," Zainab announced.

Nizar looked up from his sketchbook. "What a shithole."

Beirut, 1996.

Furnished apartment number five.

A bullet-ridden apartment in Hazmieh, home to what could have been, in another lifetime, Zainab's mother-in-law. To Nizar this grandmother was a stranger, one who followed him around with a dustbin and brush, or else stared at him like he were a ghost. Now widowed, Bernadette was the last of her kind. She sat in her crumbling apartment and clutched her rosary beads, praying for death. When they threw away rotting meat from the refrigerator, on its last legs from constant power cuts, she complained of their wastefulness. She observed them suspiciously, insisted they go to church, and bribed a priest to baptise Nizar one morning while Zainab was at work. She spent her days on her balcony, amongst her dying flowers in their cracked flowerpots, playing Solitaire and weeping as the sun set on another long, drawn-out day.

"What is this life?" Bernadette sighed, in between deep drags of her thin brown menthols.

That was how they spent the next few years, until Zainab

met her future husband in a cafe in Monot: Mohammad, an Emirati on holiday in Beirut who had briefly forsaken his crisp white robe for jeans and Gucci sunglasses. They caught each other's eye. Over coffee, she told him her life story. He listened intently, and when she'd finished recounting all the furnished apartments, Mohammad only asked her one thing:

"But what is it you actually want to do with your life?"

It was the first time anyone had asked her this.

"I want to be an artist." The words tumbled out of her without shame.

"Then let me make you an artist."

"He wants me to move to Dubai," Zainab later told her son, now seventeen and about to start his first semester at the American University of Beirut. "You can come if you want . . ."

What did she hear in her own voice? Would she even admit it to herself? That each word dripped with: *No. Don't. Come.* Did he know? And was it so bad, really, that after all this time she was finally doing something for herself?

"I'll stay." He lit one of her cigarettes. "But I'm not living with that fucking psycho anymore."

Zainab nodded. "We'll find you a furnished apartment."

* * *

A low groan pressed against the windows of Zainab's Jumeirah villa, like a heavy breath dragging across the glass. The light was flat and strange, the sky a yellowed bruise. Zainab flattened a palm to the pane as swirls of dust whipped through the garden.

Another sandstorm.

She lit a cigarette and watched as the storm moved across the garden, swallowing the tiled patio and blurring the edges of the potted palms. Sheets of sand dragged across the rippling surface of the pool. There had been more storms than usual this year, as though the desert had remembered itself and was returning to reclaim what belonged to it.

Her family would forgive her. They would understand that she did not want the paintings for herself. She was protecting something greater than that. Once Mediha understood this, once they all saw what she was trying to preserve, everything would fall into place. Everyone would remember their family again, the paths they blazed for Iraqi artists. Zainab could hold her own head up, higher than before.

The storm reached the glass doors. Dust surged against the windowpanes, a tide of fists pounding to be let in.

There was much work to be done.

Nizar
August 2014

August settled over the city in a warm hush, and Nizar began to come three, sometimes four times a week. Before stepping aboard the houseboat, he'd discreetly tap 'Record' on his phone, before slipping it back in his pocket. Ishtar would be furious if she discovered the true reason for his visits. As far as she knew, Nizar was there for one reason only: to help her realise her project of building a Mesopotamian ark.

Their meetings commenced with the making of tea. He made it a habit to ask whether Ishtar had neutered Gilgamesh. His aunt would chuckle and shake her head. This question was a litmus test. If the cat had been neutered, the flood was receding. If the cat still had his testicles, the waters remained dangerously high.

Once settled, Ishtar would begin to speak. Her thoughts moved in strange and unpredictable ways. She might start with the botched restoration of the marshes in southern Iraq, then segue into an explanation of ancient Sumerian farming techniques, which might spark a passionate diatribe on the ways modernisation transformed architectural practices, somehow ending with a literary analysis of the underlying themes in the Epic of Gilgamesh and their relevance to the historical moment they were living in.

"Pay attention," she would scold, when his mind began to wander. "This is relevant."

The ark project was the epicentre of all their discussions, the nucleus around which everything revolved. For Ishtar, the ark was a symbolic reminder of the strength of uniting Iraq's disparate geographies, and the expedition a warning cry about the rivers' dying ecosystems.

One day, as they sat at her small kitchen table, she picked up a napkin and sketched out three shapes.

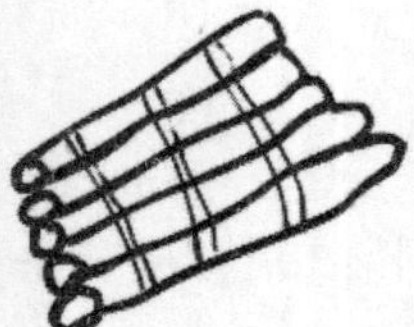

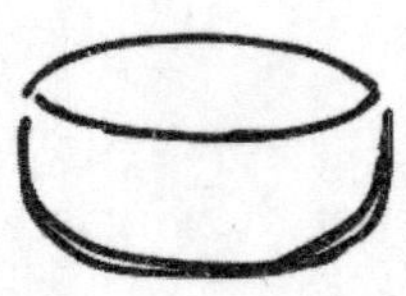

"There are three types of traditional boats," she said, pointing to the sketches. "The first is the kalak, which is a raft supported on inflated goatskins, originating in northern Mesopotamia. The second is the guffa, a circular coracle woven from reeds and leaves, usually used in the centre of Iraq. And lastly, the meshouf, which looks like a canoe and is common in the marshes of what is now southern Iraq. The structure of each is perfectly suited to the nature of the water along different parts of the river."

On the napkin, Ishtar drew a circle. "First, the guffa. You take seven of these and pull them together into a large circle—one in the centre, surrounded by six others. Looking at it from above, in Iraq we would call this image the Seba'ayoun, the seven eyes. It's a pattern you see everywhere there, in amulets, drawn on buildings, in jewellery. It's used to ward off evil."

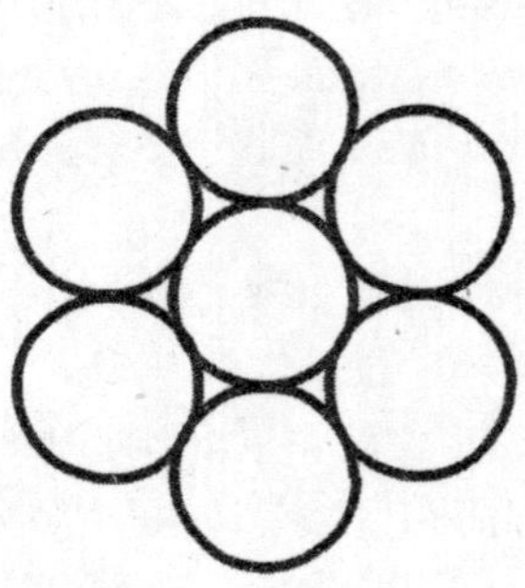

"Then, you surround this with the canoe-shaped meshouf, extending from this Seba'ayoun structure like petals on a flower." She drew six more circles between each almond-shaped petal, so that the pattern repeated itself in a hexagonal shape resembling a snowflake. "Finally, on top of this structure you place the third type of boat—the kalak, the raft common in the north of Mesopotamia." She continued to expand the pattern outwards. "The Flood tablet confirms that the ark was actually circular in nature, but what is often imagined is a giant coracle. In reality, I believe the ark was not so much one giant boat but a composite of hundreds of smaller boats. Such a design allows the vessel to be as large as you need it to be. Imagine hundreds of these boats, all tied together. You would have a giant ark that could carry anything you need."

Conversations about the ark were suffused with family memories, the gold his mother had sent him for.

"When my grandfather, Haj Akram, returned to Baghdad, painting was not common. The city had become a poverty-stricken provincial town under Ottoman rule, a brackish pond in a forgotten corner of the earth. He saw it as his duty to restore the city's cultural life, teaching painting to members of the British-appointed royal family, even helping develop a national curriculum on fine arts."

"And your own father followed in his footsteps?"

"In a sense. My grandfather saw the techniques and approaches of European art not as a threat but as a source for learning. My father went even further. He realised that the country's past, the Sumerians and Assyrians and Babylonians, could also be a source of inspiration."

In the first few meetings her sentences emerged halting and broken, like chipped cuneiform tablets. Nizar found himself filling the lacunae, imagining the missing clauses.

"You were talking about Amma Rajiha," he might say, steering her back on course.

"Yes . . . my father was the middle child of three: Kuteiba was his older brother, and Rajiha their younger sister. He was particularly close with Rajiha. When he returned from Europe during the war, he introduced her to the works of Matisse and Picasso, the sculptures of Moore and Giacometti, the engravings of Rodin and the statues of Phidias . . . In a sense, Rajiha become an artist through Haydar. They were close their entire lives."

"Is that why Rajiha and Bibi didn't get along?"

"When he met my mother in London and she followed him to Baghdad, Rajiha felt replaced. By a British woman, no less . . . Rajiha had always had a strong anti-colonial streak. The two women fought for his attention, then after he died they battled over his legacy." She raised an eyebrow. "Sound familiar?"

"What about the elder brother . . . Kuteiba?"

Ishtar's face hardened. "He didn't have a creative bone in his body. He served in the military but was forcibly retired when the Ba'athists came to power. He says it was because he refused to join the party, but I never believed that to be the whole truth."

At the end of their meetings, Ishtar often walked Nizar to the station. On one of these walks, Ishtar turned to him.

"When I was a teenager, I often sat with my aunt Rajiha on those long Friday afternoons. She told me stories about our family, about art and Iraq. She passed all these stories to me, that kooky woman."

"Poor Rajiha," Nizar said. During the four years he and his mother lived in Amman, Rajiha had visited their house once a year. Now, decades later, he could recall only the vaguest details of his great-aunt: her henna-dyed hair and large nose, the musty smell of damp clothes that lingered around her. His mother had told him that Rajiha was a kleptomaniac. But she never stole anything valuable, and when Nizar secretly dug through her bag at the end of each visit he would only find small and worthless scraps: broken pieces of chalk, old cassette tapes, some rotting fruit. Maybe a bowl.

"I always thought she was a lesbian," Ishtar said. "No one ever mentioned it, but it was just a hunch. Times were different then, I suppose."

"I guess homosexuality runs in the family."

"That's not the only thing," Ishtar laughed. "Sometimes I wonder whether she also passed her craziness on to me, through these stories." Ishtar flicked her cigarette to the ground and stepped on the embers. "I suppose I'm now passing them to you. Like a snakebite, you're sucking out my memories like venom."

* * *

There was something that returned him to Ishtar's houseboat week after week, a current deeper and more personal to him than recording the family story or helping Ishtar with her project. The houseboat conversations soothed a disquiet inside him. Making sense of the past cohered the fragmentation of the present. After their meetings, his own history came to him in waves. On his way home, he would recall the life he and Alfie had built. How, six months after meeting, they pooled their furniture together and made a home in a small one-bedroom apartment in a council estate in Bethnal Green. Though the double was a tight squeeze for two six-foot men, it was a joy to sleep wedged against each other in a bed they could call their own. He remembered how they put Alfie's old computer in the living room and called it a television, and how on a stool by the bathtub they placed a yellowing plant they rescued from Lidl. On a bookshelf in the living room, Alfie displayed his favourite childhood toys. He showed Nizar one that his mother had made: a fuzzy neon green creature with long spindly legs—something between a frog and an octopus.

"Don't you have any old toys?"

"My mother and I moved around too much. We didn't hold on to things."

Those five years with Alfie sat apart from the rest of Nizar's life. They made a routine, accrued their small mythology of memories, cultivated jokes and rituals. Since they were both born on a Thursday, they celebrated every week with a curry in Whitechapel. They shared the spiciest lamb vindaloo, thick loaves of hot Peshwari naan, and ice-cold *Tiger* beers as they plotted all the places they would go. The Perhentian Islands, Rio de Janeiro, a road trip across the Balkans.

In their first year, Nizar studied Alfie's demeanour with exotic curiosity, learning his lover's habits and routines. Alfie loved long baths. He would steep for hours, drinking peppermint tea and eating chocolates. Stock Aitken Waterman songs blasted from an old MacBook balanced on the toilet lid as he flipped through magazines, their pages curling. When he finally emerged, skin flushed red, he whistled his way through the flat, dripping water on the old carpets before plonking himself down in the centre of the living room to scroll through his phone. Nizar watched the steam rise from Alfie's back and marvelled at how a man could be so nonchalant, floating along on the bright swell of life, at ease in his own current.

There was a vulnerability to Alfie that felt both rare and unguarded. He could not tolerate abrupt noises and was often quick to cry, in joy as much as sorrow. Nizar envied his openness to the world, his refusal to flinch from feeling, unafraid of the threat of loss. Yet in darker moods, he resented how a life could proceed so delicately, untouched by the abrasions that had marked the lives of others.

On weekends, Alfie popped out for fresh croissants, knowing that Nizar hated cold mornings but loved warm pastries. On weekdays, he woke him with a kiss and a cup of black coffee, putting Nizar's phone on the bedside table so that he could check the news while still in bed. Even Nizar's catastrophic forecasts charmed him. Whenever he laid out a map of possible disasters, Alfie looked at him with an amused expression, dispersing the storm of catastrophic thinking like the remnants of a bad dream.

In those early years, the question of what was real and what wasn't sometimes lingered in Nizar's mind. Was Alfie's rosy view of the world real, and his own a fiction? Or was it the other way around—was this new relationship a mirage luring Nizar away from confronting the nightmarish reality of existence? Perhaps he could learn something from Alfie. He tried to spend less time ruminating, tried not to agonise over an unchangeable past. And, for a short while, his jaw unclenched.

* * *

When he returned home from his visits to Ishtar, Nizar would shed his clothes and sit in the dark living room of the apartment he was renting. The sublet had been a fluke. He'd received an email in late December from Lola, a Spanish aid worker he had met in Beirut several years earlier. She'd explained that while working in Darfur the previous summer, she found herself tiring quickly, her breasts tender and strange. When she returned to London, the doctors informed her it was stress and hormones. By the time the lump appeared, the cancer was in its fourth stage.

"I've been in Spain for the last two months," Lola had said in a voice note. "Chemical warfare on my body. I'm subletting my flat in Hackney if you know anyone."

After he had offered to rent her place, she sent him a video in which she slowly pulled out handfuls of her hair while Bjork played in the background. Underneath the video she wrote: My body is a war zone.

When Nizar met Lola to get the keys, she'd hugged him for

a long time. They shared a bottle of wine and home-made ceviche, and she told him how the nausea had been immobilising. The disease had estranged her from her own body. She said that when her hair first fell out she wore a hijab "just to fuck with people."

After dinner, they shared a joint. Clouds of smoke hung in the air like ethereal Christmas ornaments.

"Since I've been sick, I've been thinking of what could have been."

Sitting alone in Lola's apartment, he contemplated the decorations she proudly displayed from her travels: Afghan rugs, Sri Lankan masks, bronze statues, strange jewellery. Souvenirs from war zones interspersed with Buddhist iconography. A framed print of an O'Keeffe painting hung on the wall above the bed—an animal skull suspended over a desert landscape, its bleached bone stark against the sky. He had been there for seven months and still every item looked strange and unfamiliar, a far cry from the home he had built with Alfie. He'd tried not to think of what could have been, but the conversations with his aunt brought the past back to him. Now, ensconced in his loneliness, he sought to depose the tyranny of nostalgia.

Alfie's baths? Every night it looked like a sea monster had crawled out of the depths of the ocean and plodded through the apartment. Puddles of water on old Persian carpets. Drenched sofa pillows. Used floss on the edge of the bathtub containing morsels of chewed-up food. How forgetful Alfie was, how he rushed things to save time. The Palestinian side of Nizar was appalled at how Alfie haphazardly flung his passport on the bed after returning from a trip, how he never followed recipes but simply improvised.

"You can't just throw all the ingredients together," Nizar snapped one evening after Alfie had tossed a handful of tomatoes into a pan of onions he was sautéing. "You need to let the onions caramelise."

Alfie had grabbed the arm Nizar was using to stir the onions, forcing him to look in his eyes.

"Don't turn me into another thing to be anxious about."

Perhaps he had been nothing more than a pursuit for Alfie, a quest for him to show that through perseverance he could crack even the toughest nut, heal the deepest of wounds.

* * *

He was sitting at the table transcribing Ishtar's words when his mother rang. She wanted to know how it was going.

"I'm getting some good stuff," he said, describing a few pieces of history he had gleaned, yet withholding any information about Ishtar's boat project. "I'll have something for you by the end of September."

He was about to hang up when she said, almost lightly, "Do you remember, when we were living in Kuwait, the time we took a boat trip in Khiran? You must have been about five. When the engine stopped—I think some people wanted to go snorkelling—you and I peered over the edge and down into the turquoise waters. I pointed to a school of fish under the surface, and as I did a bangle slipped off my wrist. I tried to grab the bangle, but my hand only caught air and it tumbled into the water. We watched it splash, scattering the fish before it quickly disappeared below the surface. You turned to me and asked if we could retrieve it. I explained that it was gone. 'Forever?' you asked. And I nodded."

She described the way Nizar's face had darkened, his brown eyes bottomless pits of grief. How he had that darkness in him, even then.

"What made you think of this?"

"I had a dream last night," she said. "Of losing things in water. In my dream, it pooled around my ankles, shallow and stagnant. I watched as objects—rings, coins, lockets—fell from my hands. One by one they disappeared beneath the surface. My stomach dropped as they fell. Sometimes the loss was slower, more corrosive. Important pieces of paper—passports, birth certificates, old letters, one of your childhood paintings—drank in the moisture and began to disintegrate. I could do nothing but watch the decay."

"Mama, I think you should see a therapist."

He thought of how Alfie's mother called him every Sunday, their own weekly ritual. Lying beside him on the bed, Nizar would pretend to read while he eavesdropped. Alfie would tell his mother about his week and she'd listen to him patiently, extolling advice that he would then bring to Nizar for discussion. His own mother called rarely and without warning, when the mood struck her or when she had a quick request. Often, the calls were just an excuse to complain about her sisters.

Nizar returned to the job at hand. He paused the recording, backed up, threaded his own sentences through the gaps in Ishtar's voice, stitching his own line to hers. When he finished, he flicked off the lights and got into bed. He turned to the emptiness beside him and imagined Alfie there. He had become so familiar with the unique contours of Alfie's body: the gentle slopes of his shoulders, the tattooed topography that mapped his arms, the square plateaus of his fingernails and the soft island of hair that sprouted from the centre of his chest and trailed down his abdomen. He'd often watched Alfie sleep, enjoying his lover's soft snores and the way his top lip vibrated gently as the air escaped through one side of his mouth. He had a particular way of sleeping: on his back, his balled fists resting on his chest, as if shielding himself from a lurking threat. Nizar sometimes wondered whether *he* was the threat Alfie was protecting himself from. Asleep, Alfie drifted beyond his reach. Only then could the full force of Nizar's love flow. He could open himself completely and know there was no way Alfie could hurt him. On those nights, tears would fill Nizar's eyes as he mourned the inevitability of losing him.

Zainab

September 2014

Zainab was already on the road when her phone rang. An unfamiliar voice came through the car's speakers.

"Hi, Zainab. This is Nina. I'm Sheikh Mansour's assistant. Unfortunately, he is held up in a meeting and won't be able to make it today."

"Oh . . ." Zainab took a right turn, following the route towards the coffee shop in al-Quoz where they had agreed to meet. "Can we reschedule for tomorrow maybe?"

There was a long pause. "Let me get back to you."

At a traffic light, Zainab called Mansour directly. The phone rang for a long time. On the street, south Asian workers in fluorescent orange jumpsuits swept sand from the pavement. The line disconnected.

With the sudden absence of a destination, Zainab rerouted to the mall. She drove down the quiet streets of Jumeirah and merged with the highway, the wide, ever-expanding roads that coiled around each other like a basket of snakes.

In the parking lot, Zainab pulled out her phone and found a text from Nizar.

You might want to check Facebook . . .

The algorithm had pushed Ishtar's now-viral post to the top of her feed. A long rant written the night before, in response to an essay by Sheikh Mansour published in one of the national Emirati newspapers, in which he declared the Gulf as the new cultural hub of the region. Pointing to the destruction and deterioration of Baghdad, Beirut, and Cairo,

Mansour argued that 'newer' cities like Doha, Dubai, and Abu Dhabi had taken the reigns as the new capitals of Arab culture.

In response, Ishtar had unleashed the full force of her ire, accusing Mansour of 'undertaking a PR campaign with the blood of South Asian labourers on whose ruptured muscles and pulverised bones these air-conditioned hellholes were built.'

Zainab read the rest of her sister's post, growing angrier by the minute:

> Abu Dhabi, Dubai, Doha. Let's call these cities what they truly are: soulless monstrosities of urban planning devoid of roots, where any creativity poured in will simply run along its surface like grains of sand. They are miscarriages of culture, a Frankenstein's monster of the most distasteful elements of both the West and the Arab world. Their understanding of art and culture is not just regressive, but a bastardisation of patronage and market capitalism taken to gaudy extremes. Al-Qubaiti has the audacity to claim that the turmoil in Cairo, Beirut, and Baghdad is a sign of these cities' regression. Does he not realise that it is within this turmoil that the biggest and most existential questions relating to the future of Arab society, culture, and politics are being fought? The enforced 'serenity' and 'security' of Arab Gulf states is nothing to be proud of. It is a sterile corpse. Nothing will grow out of this barren desert. Far from being the saviour of Arab culture, the gun-to-your-head capitalism, ego-driven and morally bankrupt leadership, and police-state-society fuelled by oil and petrodollars have only corroded, shackled, and prostituted Arab cultures and societies.

"Talk to me," Ishtar said, upon answering Zainab's call.

"Are you out of your mind? What the hell was with that post?"

"The al-Qubaiti post?"

"Yes the al-Qubaiti post. You know, you hold yourself up as a critic of Western influence but you've swallowed so many of their stereotypes . . ."

"What I wrote is true, though."

"Is this because al-Qubaiti never championed your work?"

Ishtar scoffed. "I'm sorry but what kind of self-appointed cultural critic decides that *now*—two months after ISIS announced that Iraq and Syria are dead—is the time to write a tone-deaf essay about how the future of the Arab world is in the Gulf?"

"You might need his support someday." Even as Zainab said this, she knew Ishtar didn't think like that. Her sister's actions were driven by ideology rather than strategy. "He's raised the profile of so many Arab artists in the global art market."

"The art market has corrupted the very concept of art. You know that, Zainab. Art is not a consumable product but a lived practice."

Zainab had heard this lecture before, not long after she had last wired Ishtar money.

"I'm not going to gag myself to appease some rich sheikh in the Gulf."

"Actually, we *do* need to appease him. How else are we going to get Baba's paintings exhibited?"

Ishtar laughed. "So that's what this is about. Your ego."

"What ego? I'm talking about Baba's legacy."

"Exactly. And what does legacy signify? The start of some redemption tour for yourself? You left Iraq with your tail between your legs and now you're hoping that by reminding people of what your parents accomplished, you can gain favour and redeem yourself. That's what you want me to do, isn't it? Write some hagiography of the family story, exalting the genius of Baba like some sort of demigod—"

Zainab hung up and walked into the mall. The blast of the

air conditioning unleashed a wave of goosebumps down her neck. She walked around aimlessly, trying to regain her composure. Perhaps her son was right and she should talk to someone. Then again, Mediha had been in therapy for decades and look how she turned out.

Zainab took an escalator to the next level and looked around at the familiar terrain of gold and glass. She knew the place by heart, every floor and wing of this labyrinthine centre for consumption. It was the second-largest mall in the world. Most things in Dubai seemed to be the biggest or the tallest or the longest or the most expensive.

A group of Khaleeji women walked by, the smell of oud lingering behind them like a memory. What had she been thinking about?

Therapy.

Yes, she must find herself a therapist. For her nerves, for her ADHD—self-diagnosed. She had no idea what it even stood for, but she had heard about it on the radio and decided the affliction sounded familiar: nervous energy, difficulty focusing, the twitching and tapping and shaking legs, the overwhelming feeling of dread.

Until she found a therapist, the mall would have to do. Being here soothed her nerves. She joined the crowds circling the marble and glass building like pilgrims around a sparkling ka'aba. The ritualistic wandering dulled her emotions. There was solace here.

She passed an electronics shop, which stirred the memory of when they pulled Saddam from the hole in 2003. She had been in the mall, and his face appeared across the sea of display televisions: his hair a scraggly, knotty mess, his face smeared with sand and dirt, dark bags under his eyes as a doctor examined his hair and mouth, forcing him to bare his tonsils like a child. Nothing like the powerful man she was raised to fear. Beside her, a woman had burst into tears.

"Allahu Akbar," the woman whispered to herself.

"Why are you crying?" Zainab had asked.

"Is this the way Iraq ends?" She had a Baghdadi accent.

"But he was a monster." Zainab emphasised her own accent to let the woman know they were of the same ilk.

"Of course he was a monster," the woman wiped the tears from her face. "But he was our monster. If this is the fate of the most powerful man in Iraq, what is the fate of people like us?"

Operation Iraqi Freedom.

She is nineteen, and the voice of her favourite singer is blasting from the cassette player, tearing through her dreams. The raw ache of Joplin's raspy voice floods the room. Zainab wakes like a diver gasping for breath.

Bloody Ishtar. She has been doing this all summer. Staying up all night—painting and reading and listening to records—and creeping into Zainab's room at dawn, where she places the cassette player next to her ear, turns up the volume and lets it rip.

The summer of '79.

The summer of Saddam.

The summer Zainab receives the call—

No, no, no. Zainab dragged happier memories to the surface of her mind. The ballet school in Baghdad. The outdoor cinema. The Mansour club. Teenage summers in London, swimming at Hampstead Heath. Spring afternoons under the fig trees in Amma Rajiha's garden in the old family home. Browsing for silver and copper at Souq al-Safafeer. People and places and parties of a long-gone past.

How dare Ishtar say she had left Iraq with her tail between her legs? She knew better than anyone what had happened. Zainab stopped and took a deep breath. She was approaching the feeling that signalled she should leave the mall. The dizzying craving for a cigarette, the scratch in the back of the throat from the chilled, recycled air.

FREEDOM'S JUST ANOTHER WORD FOR NOTHING LEFT TO LOSE

"Ishtar!" Zainab shouts, fumbling blindly for the cassette cord and yanking it from the socket. Joplin's voice cuts off mid-scream. Down the hall, Ishtar has already vanished into her bedroom, the door locked, her laughter echoing like a spell.

Bleary-eyed, Zainab drags herself to the bathroom, the tiles beneath her feet already warming in the summer heat. She is young. She is beautiful. And, for a brief moment, she feels utterly, impossibly free.

But she isn't just a pretty face, no matter what their mother says. Zainab works hard. Mediha's the baby, and Ishtar's the wild creative who can't hold down a job without finding some irreparable fault in it and quitting in a puff of moral indignation. Ammo Kuteiba is his own brand of useless. After their father died, he had moved in with them—it was between that and leaving Baghdad, their mother explained. In the beginning, he helps with costs. Then the Ba'athists come to power and, when he refuses to join the party, they force him into retirement. After that he spends his days in the garden, singing old patriotic songs as he drinks himself into a stupor.

They are all patient with him, except for Ishtar. She and Kuteiba are like two feral cats, always at each other's throats. Stripped of his power and authority, he tries to enforce a kind of order over the house, over how a young woman must behave, but Ishtar refuses to be tamed. The arguments are endless—about the electricity bill she runs up with her late-night bursts of creativity, the friends she brings home at all hours, the fact she walks barefoot in the garden and insists on eating her food with her hands. Ishtar, meanwhile, takes a cruel joy in politically antagonising him. She reads banned novels in the garden and recites political speeches she knows will get under his skin. Their mother, between teaching and travel, is hardly ever around, but when she is she keeps a safe distance from the warfare, an expert gambler waiting to see which horse has the stronger legs. It is up to Zainab to keep the peace, to hold the centre together. At least until—

She couldn't think about Andre now.

She had to focus on making this exhibition happen.

Zainab walked into a stationery store and purchased cardboard poster tubes, rubber bands, and some bubble wrap. Things she'd need for her heist.

How was she ever going to pull off this crazy idea?

A sudden panic overcame her as she left the store. She stopped at the railing and looked down onto the crowds, the shoppers appearing to move in slow, synchronised patterns. Across from her a giant waterfall cascaded down the length of the mall. The roar of the water gave her vertigo. She had a sudden impulse to throw herself over the railing.

"This is the Japanese Embassy calling. I'm pleased to formally extend an offer for the secretarial position."

The call that triggered the troubles.

Ishtar secures a government scholarship to study art in London. That leaves Zainab and Mediha to squabble over what money is left, and then Mediha has to go and . . . oh but she can't even commit to the act! Even the doctors say the pills she swallowed wouldn't have been enough. But they pump her stomach anyway and that seals the deal. Mediha is to go to Edinburgh to study, where she can stay with one of their mother's old university friends.

"You don't need to leave, Bulbul. You're beautiful and you'll find yourself a good husband here, a nice doctor maybe. Mediha is smarter. And look how miserable she is! The poor girl needs to get out."

Zainab wants to be an artist but is too ashamed to say it, can't bear to see how her mother might respond. Perhaps this is all her fault, the consequence of playing her mother's game, of indulging in being the 'beautiful' one. All her life she enjoyed the way her mother paraded her in front of guests, how she always asked her to model for her art students. Mediha was the one who could fix the television or help calculate the bills. One day, Mediha—she must have been thirteen at the time—asked their mother if she could model for the students and Bridget just laughed and laughed.

That was that, then. Mediha will go to Edinburgh to sort her head out. Zainab will stay in Baghdad and get a job to help pay for her baby sister's sanity and education. Gone is the possibility of a British summer, of scones and tea and country walks and smoking in cinemas. No sneaking out to meet boys in Portobello Road, trawling the market for clothes and records, drinking cider in the park and swimming in the ice-cold ponds on the Heath. All Zainab has to look forward to is a long, hot summer in a plaid skirt and white shirt, filing papers and answering phone calls in the stifling offices of the Japanese Embassy of Baghdad, with her monthly salary going to support her sister. But the embassy job pays more than she is expecting, a tiny cherry on a steaming pile of camel shit. Perhaps there is hope, she thinks, if she can save some money—after contributing to the bills and Mediha's education, and, and, and—then maybe she can find a way out of Baghdad and go to London. Who knows, maybe she could even be an artist.

Zainab turned away from the railing and faced a gleaming sea of red. Virgin Megastores. The store had everything you didn't need and never even knew existed. A young person's store, she thought.

She would never be young again.

The thought came to her with surprising violence. She had always held onto the possibility that a wiser youthfulness, where she would not repeat the same mistakes, was just around the corner. But that would never happen. Just like her aunt Rajiha, Zainab would grow old and die.

As if to affirm her youthfulness, Zainab walked into the store. A row of televisions aired the same channel: CNN. Grey buildings and bombs, protests, maiming, killing. Daesh nonsense. Enough of all that. She turned away from the screens. She needed to buy something to soothe her nerves. A lucky charm. She picked up a doughy stress ball.

'Thinking putty', the sign read.

A video installation showed how to use the stress ball. Why would anyone need a video display for a stress ball, she wondered, watching it to see if it provided any other instructions beyond simply squeezing it.

'Proudly made in the U.S.A.' the packaging boasted. You knew it was serious when they put in a period after each letter. U.S.A. Each period added an extra dollop of patriotism.

"A patriotic duty."

That's what the officer tells her.

Zainab isn't nervous as she makes her way to the Ministry of Interior. It's just a routine security clearance for those employed by international entities. She has nothing to hide, nothing to lose. She struts into the Ministry and sits in the smoky waiting area. The halls are full of men who all look the same, their large moustaches framing the cigarettes that hang from their thin lips. The hallmarks of the new government. Zainab watches with quiet amusement as they march around like gorillas. It is true what Ammo Kuteiba says about the Ba'athists: they are nothing more than a gang of adolescent boys driven by testosterone, ego, and violence.

An officer calls her in. She follows him through the door and into a plain room with a large desk in the centre, on top of which rests the largest stapler she has ever seen. A framed portrait of Saddam hangs on the wall. Zainab takes a seat and places her hands in her lap.

"I am a big admirer of your father's work, may God have mercy on his soul."

"Thank you."

"Is this your first job? There's a lot to learn from the Japanese, the way they do things . . . and for you to also do your patriotic duty, of course."

She is impatient. "What do I need to do?"

"You're not married?"

"No."

"We have immense respect for your father; may God rest his soul . . ."

Impatience turns to annoyance. She shifts in her chair, resisting the urge to touch the giant stapler. When the officer circles back to the subject of the patriotic duty, Zainab interrupts him.

"Just tell me what you want me to do."

He chuckles, calls her European for being so straight-forward.

"We ask all citizens working for foreign entities to regularly check in with the Ministry. Who is going to the embassy, who is applying for visas, for asylum . . ."

"That's all?"

The officer hands her a card. "If there's anything suspicious you can give me a call. And if you're able to keep an eye on things in your neighbourhood, you could be rewarded for keeping us informed about anything that might affect . . . social cohesion."

Zainab nods and places the card in her purse.

The man smiles, revealing a row of tar-stained teeth. He reaches into his drawer and pulls out a piece of paper. He signs it, stamps it, and hands it to her. In turn, she signs and stamps her own written commitment, a promise to guard the principles of the party. She thanks him and leaves the room.

"Can I help you?"

Zainab turned around, startled. A Filipino man wearing the Virgin Megastore uniform was behind her.

How long had she been standing there, watching the video display?

"I want that," she pointed at the video.

"What colour would you like ma'am?"

"I—I don't know . . ."

He talked her through the options. The red thinking putty was called 'Chernobyl' and looked like pig's blood. The

'Melting Glacier' was glow in the dark—too garish. A purple and blue one was called 'Nebula' and made her sad. The one called 'Oil Slick' looked like a black hole into nothingness. She imagined what the colours would look like in her palm, each holding the promise of becoming a different person. The existential enormity of the selection overwhelmed her. Her future self, the person she would become, the person she would be when she confronted Mediha and took back the paintings, was now contingent and dictated by the colour of the thinking putty she chose.

She turned to the assistant. "Which colour would *you* choose?"

The man was pleasantly surprised to be asked his opinion. He looked at the different colours, considering his decision carefully. Finally, he pointed to the red box. "I like this colour, ma'am. Chernobyl."

Zainab took a deep breath. She wanted to select the red option, if only to affirm the store assistant's choice, but by doing so she would be setting a precedent, relinquishing her agency and condemning herself to being a pushover. No. She absolutely must not return home with the red thinking putty.

"I'll have the silver one. Tsunami."

If the assistant was disappointed with her selection, he didn't show it. But no sooner had he picked up the box of the silver putty than Zainab regretted her choice. It was too late to change her mind, to redirect her course of action, and she followed him to the cash register, mourning the absence of colour in her putty, in her future. She gave him the money, put the box in her handbag, and disappeared amidst the flood of shoppers.

Nizar
September 2014

Ishtar knelt by the water with seven shoe-sized versions of each of the three boats. From the towpath, Nizar watched as she lashed them together into a single structure with some twine.

"Hey," she said glancing backwards. "Don't just stand there. Film this."

Ishtar carefully put the vessel on the surface and gave it a gentle push. The structure wobbled, then settled into a sway. She leaned towards it, blew at it from different angles, then drummed the skin of the water with a fingertip to create waves.

Back in the houseboat, Nizar made them lunch while Ishtar watched the video several times, taking detailed notes. After they had eaten, she pulled out a large map and drew out the path the ark would take along the Tigris.

"But what about ISIS?" Nizar asked.

"ISIS can go fuck themselves. The real challenge will be finding someone to fund this."

This became one of many frenetic requests Ishtar tasked him with. Nizar researched organisations and initiatives in Iraq, ploughed his networks for contacts working on environmental issues, and scoured the web for grants and funding opportunities. One afternoon, he came across a call for proposals by an organisation called the Mesopotamian Restoration Initiative, a DC-based organisation working on environmental restoration in Iraq. Ishtar's expedition seemed a perfect match. Nizar sent in a query. The head of the organisation, an Iraqi American named Nisreen Al-Asadi, responded almost immediately.

> Dear Nizar,
>
> I am an old friend of the family. It would be a pleasure to work with Ishtar. Let's arrange a time to speak.
>
> Yours,
>
> Nisreen

Nizar delivered the news on a sun-drenched afternoon in early September. When he arrived, Ishtar was outside chopping wood. She heaved the axe high above her head before swinging it down, sending a spray of splinters into the air. Behind her, a family of swans glided through the water. Ishtar turned and watched them.

"Those cygnets won't survive the winter," she said matter-of-factly.

"What do you mean?"

"They're too young. Born too late." She gestured to him. "Help me get the kitchen table out on the deck. Let's enjoy the last of the sunshine."

They shared a beer and chatted as they watched the gentle stream of joggers and dog-walkers along the towpath, but as soon as Nizar mentioned Nisreen's name, Ishtar stood with surprising force.

"Absolutely not! I will have nothing to do with that treacherous woman," she snapped, before storming inside.

Nizar followed her, watching as she pulled a packet of chopped liver from the fridge, then slammed the door shut. She grabbed an onion from the pantry.

"Ishtar, they've funded other projects like this before. There's this project they had restoring the marshes—"

"Propaganda . . . imperial propaganda," Ishtar said as she chopped up the onion. She turned and pointed the knife in his direction. "I want no part in this native informant green-washing malarky. Funded by the US State Department, no less. Do you know that in 2006 the US government spent more on the war in Iraq than the entire world spent on renewable energy investments? Millions—*millions*—of metric tonnes of carbon dioxide have been unleashed into the environment from the gas and oil well fires since the US invasion." She threw the chopped liver and onion into a pan, adding a dollop of pomegranate sauce. Gilgamesh inched towards it, but Ishtar shooed him away. "Oh, but now the US military is *obsessed* with climate change. They talk about it as if it is something to destroy, like an insurgency. They call it a 'threat multiplier'. What kind of language is that? *Threat multiplier.*"

When his mother called that evening, she mentioned her argument with Ishtar over the al-Qubaiti post. Nizar told her that Ishtar had mentioned nothing of it.

"It just means I'll need to figure out a way to do the exhibition myself."

"What exhibition?"

"Oh," Zainab paused guiltily. "I thought I told you. I'm planning to take the paintings from Mediha."

Nizar winced. "Please don't."

"Well what else am I going to do? She'll never sell them to me. I just have to go there and get them." Zainab paused, and when Nizar did not respond she changed the subject. "I was at the mall today and found myself standing in front of the indoor ski slope. I spent twenty minutes watching the Indian and Filipino families sledding down the manmade slopes, throwing snowballs, building snowmen . . ."

Nizar closed his eyes, picturing this. "I suppose it's the closest they'll get to skiing in the Alps."

"Exactly. Most would never be granted a visa to visit Europe anyway. At first it seemed gaudy, the idea of this snowy ecosystem in the middle of a shopping complex in the desert, but the longer I stood there watching the families play, the more meaningful the experience felt."

A memory floated through Nizar's mind like a snowflake: the first time he saw snow in the Troodos mountains, when they'd lived in Cyprus for a year.

"I began thinking," his mother continued, "so what if it's not the Alps? It's still snow. Mediha and Ishtar always say Dubai is fake and use this indoor ski slope as an example of that. But the joy on those children's faces as they raced down the slopes was the most authentic thing I've seen in a long time."

"Perhaps people can root themselves anywhere if they really want," Nizar pondered. "If you use your imagination, you can turn the desert into the Alps."

"I suppose so."

"So then why is your family so obsessed with Iraq?"

"It's not about Iraq." His mother was irritated. "It's about the family legacy."

"It feels more like a family curse. The only thing you and your sisters do with it is use it as a club to bludgeon each other with. And for what? For some imagined idea of a glorious past? Was it even so great, Mama?"

Yet Nizar knew the quiet pull of belonging, and it was Massoud who, three years earlier, had helped him realise that roots were not just an anchor, but an archive.

* * *

Cairo, September 2011. Nizar was attending a conference organised by the British Council's Egypt Bureau, which brought together journalists documenting the Arab Spring. On the first day, Massoud introduced himself to the group as a photographer who had documented the protest squares across Yemen. On the second day, he gave a brief presentation of his photography during the protests in Sana'a and Ta'iz. There was an amateurishness to his pictures, but also a sincerity that Nizar found compelling.

Beyond that, Massoud barely spoke. On the rare occasions he said something, he didn't sound like an activist or a journalist. He wasn't concerned with the minutiae of political manoeuvrings or outraged by flagrant human rights abuses. Instead, his interjections consisted of thoughtful—albeit tangential—quasi-philosophical reflections.

In a small break-out group on the subject of self-care for journalists, he interrupted a conversation to say: "Since we are in Cairo, it is worthwhile to remember what the Egyptian surrealists of the early twentieth century used to say: revolution is condemned by the law of the land, while suicide is condemned by the laws of God. So, where does that leave us? Stuck in some in-between place, neither dead nor alive."

These musings did not impress the British organisers, who nudged the conversation away from his reflections on the paradoxes of freedom towards concrete analysis and policy recommendations.

On the third day, when the session paused for lunch, Massoud turned to Nizar.

"The hotel buffet is disgusting. Let's get some Koshari."

They left the illusory enclave of the five-star hotel for the streets of downtown Cairo, where they found a Koshari stall on the corner of a bustling intersection.

"Where are you boys from?" the stall owner asked.

Massoud said he was Yemeni. Nizar told the server he was half-Iraqi and half-Palestinian.

"Welcome brothers. May all our countries one day be free."

As they ate, Nizar told Massoud that he last visited Yemen during the 2009 war in Sa'ada. Massoud said he was from the south and had little connection to events in the north. His father was from Aden and his mother was half-Eritrean, which explained his dark skin and the angled features of his face. He told Nizar that because of his background he was considered a second-class citizen in Yemen, and confessed that he believed he had been invited to the conference less on the strength of his photographs than on his marginalised status.

Nizar asked what Massoud thought of Cairo. He said it was the most vibrant city in the world but the food was terrible, and that Egyptians had a habit of believing the world revolved around them.

"Doesn't everyone?"

"No," Massoud replied, spooning red-stained macaroni into his mouth. "Yemenis know what it means to be forgotten."

Later, when he re-connected to the hotel Wi-Fi, he accepted Massoud's friend request on Facebook. He scrolled through Massoud's page, which consisted mostly of photographs taken during the protests as well as portraits of street children, many of whom, like Massoud, were dark-skinned.

They met again for an evening shisha on a floating restaurant by the corniche. They sat on uneven wicker chairs as they smoked and looked out over the river, which stretched before them like a sheet of ink, interrupted every so often by a passing felucca or a boat draped in neon lights. Across the water, the city shimmered through a haze of smog.

The conversation turned towards family. Massoud told Nizar about his younger brother, and Nizar told Massoud about his mother. He wasn't sure who else to talk about, and the topic of Alfie seemed—as it always did on such trips—off-limits. He explained that his mother was half-Iraqi and half-British, that they had moved around aimlessly for many years.

"And your father is Palestinian?"

"Was," Nizar pulled on the shisha, inhaling the sweet apple-flavoured molasses. "My parents met in Baghdad, but my father died in the war before I was born."

"Which war?"

"The Lebanese one."

Massoud looked at Nizar with a strange solemnity. "May God rest his soul."

Underneath them the river moved slowly, the deck bobbing lazily in the current. The reflections of the fairy lights strung along the restaurant's railing quivered on the surface of the water.

Massoud asked about the scar on his cheek, and Nizar told him about the first and only time he visited Baghdad for *The Times* in February 2005. He told Massoud about his decision to visit the square which housed his grandfather's monument, how he was proud it had stood firm during decades of sanctions and war. It had been a cold morning. Everything was as it should have been, until the thundering and the furnace of heat. He told Massoud about the fingers on the asphalt, the torn limbs and the headless body, about the man who had been walking around with his eyeball in his palm. How Nizar had placed the eyeball haphazardly back in its socket, had taken off his own bloody shirt and wrapped it around the man's head to keep it in place.

In two years with Alfie he had never been able to find the words to explain the scar's origins, but with Massoud the story unfolded from his tongue with surprising ease, in all its gore and brutality.

"My mother holds all these painful memories of Iraq, I don't even know most of them. I've seen it as this battleground ever since I was young, so I guess it's funny that the one time I visit and go to see my grandfather's monument no less, it nearly kills me."

"These wars . . ." The sentence hung in the air as Massoud drew on the shisha, blowing a cloud of smoke in the air. He opened his mouth to finish his sentence, then changed his mind and grabbed Nizar's hand, interlacing their fingers. A breeze moved over the water, warm and thick with the smell of river-weed and grilled meat. Nizar looked down at Massoud's hands, his fingernails bitten into tiny stubs that seemed painfully embedded in his skin.

They walked back to the hotel in silence. Massoud's room was one floor above his own. When the elevator stopped, Nizar turned to him.

"Come."

On entering Nizar's room, Massoud took off his shoes. The hems of his jeans were slightly torn, like those of a teenager. Nizar watched as he gently removed his socks. There was an intimacy to watching him slowly undress his feet. When he'd finished, Massoud looked up.

"Come," he said, echoing Nizar's earlier command.

Nizar placed a hand on Massoud's cheek. Leathery and sun-exposed, his skin bore the faint scars of teenage acne. He thought of Alfie at home, possibly cooking or sitting in the bath, using his foot to sprinkle some bathwater onto the plant next to the tub. But in the hotel room in Cairo, these scenes of British domesticity felt distant and false. He kissed Massoud's cheek, and Massoud pressed Nizar's body against his with surprising strength. They kissed again, this time on the lips. With a deep breath Massoud inhaled Nizar, then pushed him onto the bed. Nizar gazed at Massoud standing above him. Massoud stared back, not breaking eye contact as he unbuttoned his shirt with trembling fingers, before sinking into Nizar's body.

They spent the next three evenings together. Massoud loved to kiss Nizar, and insisted on pressing their bodies together, hugging him tightly even after they had both come, as if trying to meld their bodies into one. He did not speak during sex, communicating with grunts or vague hand gestures, but he maintained eye contact for long periods of time. It infused the lovemaking with an intensity that felt new to Nizar. Massoud wasn't as seasoned as Alfie; his touch and kisses had the same amateurish quality as his photography, one that was arousing in its sincerity, its boyish charm. But there was solace in kissing a mouth that could also pronounce the guttural Arabic letter *ayn* without reducing the sound to a vulgar gag, to hold close a body that would never remark that Oum Kalthoum's songs 'go on for too long'.

Technically, there was nothing immoral about what he was doing. He and Alfie had never attached value to monogamy. In fact, they often exchanged stories of their erotic exploits with one another, taking pleasure in dissecting the idiosyncratic behaviours of their lovers. But Nizar's time with Massoud felt like a betrayal. In that hotel room in Cairo, Nizar discovered that by loving a foreigner, he had become a prisoner in an exile he was not aware of. The sex with Massoud was a homecoming. It had revealed a hollowness at the core of his relationship with Alfie, one he had been blind to for some time.

It was not until he unlocked the front door of their London flat that the guilt washed over him. The weight of the betrayal was intensified by how much Nizar enjoyed it. He stepped into the apartment gripped by a quiet estrangement, fearful that Alfie would read this on his face or smell it on his skin.

"Hey Niz," Alfie's voice drifted in from the kitchen. The apartment smelled of smoked paprika.

"Hey love." The words felt heavy in his mouth.

He left his suitcase by the door and kicked off his shoes. In the kitchen, Alfie was by the oven in his underwear, stirring a pot of tomato sauce. Nizar walked towards him and wrapped his arms around his thin frame.

"You look tired," Alfie kissed his forehead.

"Yes."

"I'll run you a bath."

A bath. Alfie's solution to the problems in life. Nizar heard the faucet, then the clunk of a bath bomb hitting the bottom of the tub, and the ensuing fizz as it dissolved in the water.

Nizar was scrubbing between his toes when Alfie knocked on the bathroom door. He had a cup of tea in one hand, which he placed on the stool next to the bath before turning to look at his reflection in the mirror.

"How was the conference?"

"Same as usual, a bunch of foreigners trying to put square pegs into round holes. How have things been here?"

"Oh, you know . . ." Alfie stopped, then turned around and ran his fingers down Nizar's back. "You've got scratch marks," he said softly. His face began to break into a knowing smile, and Nizar imagined he was about to say something like 'Seems you still managed to squeeze in some fun'. But something in Nizar's face wiped the shadow of a smile from Alfie's.

"I should get back to the chilli."

Nizar sat in the bath for a long time. He did not remember Massoud scratching him. In fact, he distinctly recalled that Massoud had bitten his nails down to tiny stubs. Yet, when he got out of the bath and turned around in front of the mirror, the scratch marks were unmistakeable. Four jagged lines scrawled down his right shoulder blade.

Zainab
September 2014

Zainab had been enjoying a Frappuccino in the mall when her phone pinged. Mediha's email contained a single image: a photograph of a man in a black balaclava pointing his knife at the camera. She recognised it immediately.

The screenshot, from one of the ISIS beheading videos released that summer, showed Jihadi John—as he had been nicknamed by the British press. Underneath the photograph in large red letters Mediha had typed: *DEAR JOHN*. Below that, the text announced the opening of her new exhibition in late October.

Once the shock ebbed, the opportunity revealed itself. What better way to get back in Mediha's cottage than to indulge her sister's narcissism? Before she could talk herself out of it, Zainab called her younger sister. Surprisingly, Mediha picked up.

"Yes?"

"Middy, I just received your invitation. Thank you."

"I didn't know you were on the mailing list."

Zainab rolled her eyes. "I'd still love to attend."

"The exhibition?" Suspicion edged her voice.

"Yes. It looks . . ." Zainab struggled to find the right word. "Interesting."

"Well, I'll be busy with getting everything set up. I still have some works to complete, and I won't have much time to—"

"You don't need to entertain me. In fact, I can even help take care of Mama while you're working."

"Let me think about it."

Zainab hung up and walked down the mall's outdoor promenade to the manmade lake, which was pumping out golden-hued streams of water into the indigo sky as Whitney Houston's 'I Will Always Love You' blasted from giant speakers. She leaned against the railing and looked out at the lights glistening on the water, which brought to mind the kitschy flashing lights draped across the restaurants that lined the Tigris.

Enough. She couldn't bear to think of it anymore. She no longer belonged there, had not set foot in Iraq in over thirty years. It was barely even a country at this point. And why were all these memories coming now?

Report regularly to the ministry. Inform them of visits to the embassy. Share meetings with dignitaries and requests for asylum. The embassy staff don't suspect her, or perhaps they know the government has informers in every corner of the country. A driver, a secretary, even the pigeons who circle the city—everyone plays their role, fulfills their duty. At least she isn't doing it for free. Every month, the Japanese Embassy gives her one hundred and eighty dinars for filing letters and answering telephone calls—shōshō omachi kudasai, just one moment please, just one moment please—and she sends this money to support Mediha in Edinburgh, and every month the office of General Security sends her eighty dinars which she quietly stores in the bank for her own future escape. And does it make such a difference, really, when brother is suspicious of brother, why should she succumb to any shame about her actions, the tiniest drop in an ocean of violence? All she needs to do is what needs to be done, and then—in just one moment, shōshō omachi kudasai—she'll be free to do what she wants with her life.

July. The early morning sun is already baking the street when Bridget and Mediha get into the taxi with three large suitcases. Her mother tells her she'll be back in a month, "just need to get this one settled in Edinburgh," before the taxi drives off, disappearing in the dusty haze. Ishtar is back home, confident and sexually liberated from her time in London, and quickly shacks up with Nisreen al-Asadi, their next-door neighbour and one of Zainab's most sophisticated friends. Zainab had always been in awe of Nisreen, of how elegant and worldly she appeared despite never having left Baghdad. She read old Russian novels and loved Egyptian cinema, and only ever stirred her drink by twirling the glass slowly in her hands, as if summoning the whole world into motion. Until Ishtar returned, it was Zainab to whom Nisreen was devoted. They spent the hottest part of the afternoon in Zainab's bedroom, talking about boys and music, while through the open window Nisreen's brother Rakan played Bob Dylan records in his bedroom as he clumsily strummed along on his guitar. But now it is Zainab alone in her bedroom on these hot afternoons while Nisreen and Ishtar trade kisses next door, a secret only Zainab knows, and in the evenings it's only Zainab and Ammo Kuteiba at home, her uncle's depression worse than ever. He had been close to Mediha, and her absence intensifies his misery. Disenchanted and thirsty for death, he polishes off a bottle of arak in a single evening. Every night after making dinner, Zainab runs him a bath, prepares him a warm towel, and puts his slippers on the bathmat along with some fresh pyjamas folded neatly on a stool. She helps him disrobe and steadies his drunken body as he steps into the tub, then washes him, dries him, and puts him to bed. On most nights her uncle's drinking quickly sends him to sleep, but on others he is overcome with a deep melancholy. When Mediha was around, Ammo Kuteiba would ask to say goodnight to her, and Zainab would dutifully bring her into his room for what he called their evening chats. "Go up to the roof and gaze at the stars, Zanoobah," Ammo Kuteiba would say, as he took Mediha's hand. "There's a whole universe out there." And Zainab does as she is told. Now Mediha's gone nothing seems to assuage Kuteiba's sadness. Sometimes he comes into Zainab's bedroom in the early hours of the morning. She wakes to the sound of his sobs in her ear and his hot, alcohol-soaked breath on her face, mumbling about past mistakes, regrets. He crawls into her bed and clutches her body, his chest heaving and convulsing with uncontrollable sobs. I'm sorry habibti. I'm a drunk. I'm a failed man. Her body freezes as he pushes up against her, weeping into her hair.

October loosens the heat. The dust settles. The Ministry asks about her neighbours.

Zainab's heart sinks.

"You live beside them, you see them every day. Doesn't their uncle live in Iran now?"

She recalls Nisreen mentioning this once. "So?"

"He's a traitor. Are they in touch with him?"

"I . . . I don't know."

But she does know. Two weeks earlier she had overheard a whispered conversation between Ishtar and Nisreen. Nisreen's mother had been on the phone with her brother, making plans to meet in Paris.

She could just play stupid. But isn't everyone informing on everyone? Why not report the facts, just the simple bare facts, of what the neighbours are up to? She considers how to reveal this information without exposing Ishtar and Nisreen's affair. Most likely they already know, but Ishtar plays the game well and as a respected young artist within the Ministry of Culture, she's protected. The silence widens between her and the man across the table. "The son, Rakan, he used to play Bob Dylan a lot," she hears herself say. Where is she going with this? "Loud rock music, and then the last few months it stopped." There, a harmless fact, revealing nothing about the conversation overheard in Ishtar's bedroom. "It could mean nothing, but it is something I noticed."

It is to Zainab that Nisreen turns when Rakan disappears. Does Nisreen suspect she may have been involved? Or is it because Zainab has always been there for her, the trusted friend, the amiable neighbour, the daughter of the open-minded liberal artists who have an unassuming and non-judgemental air about them? Charming Zainab, the half-foreigner with the alcoholic uncle who crawls into her bed, who each morning puts on her pencil skirt, combs her long dark hair, and takes the bus to the Japanese embassy. Beautiful Zainab, who every last Wednesday of the month makes her way to the windowless government building behind the Hunting Club and walks through the doors, greeting the guards like an old friend. Whatever the reason, Nisreen knocks on Zainab's door when Rakan does not return home from work and is still missing three days later. Her face is a mess of tears. Zainab makes sweet tea and takes it to Nisreen in the backyard. They sit on the porch swing, where Nisreen cries and Zainab consoles, and just as Nisreen is about to leave Zainab turns to her and asks: "Was Rakan speaking to your uncle?" Nisreen looks at her. A wall emerges between them which goes unacknowledged for the year Nisreen remains in Baghdad before she and her family leave the country forever, abandoning their hope of finding Rakan. And anyway, Zainab reasons, she can't be blamed for Rakan. Strange disappearances have become an everyday occurrence. The charges are endless: betraying the nation, colluding with global imperialism, conspiring to overthrow the party that provided people with education and healthcare and worked to unify the Arab world against its enemies. With Nisreen gone it is easy to push thoughts of Rakan aside, at least until three decades later, in 2009, when they will reconnect through Facebook. Nisreen will message Zainab to say she now lives in DC. and works in policy, that she is passing through Dubai on her way to Iraq, and they will meet one evening in a yacht club in the Marina. They will stay up late, talking and drinking wine, and Nisreen will make no mention of Rakan, and it will not be until the second bottle of wine that Nisreen will say "it seems so long ago now, like a dream." And Zainab will nod and smile, and Nisreen will burp softly and ask, in a voice both quiet and confident, "You were an informant, weren't you?"

Nizar

September 2014

When Nizar returned to the houseboat later that week, his aunt was in bad spirits.

"Did you read that article I sent you on the marshes? A five-thousand-year-old civilisation is dying."

"Ishtar, let's send Nisreen an e-mail."

She looked down at her lap, where Gilgamesh purred softly.

"I've seen my father go nuts. I've seen Rajiha go nuts. I've gone nuts . . ." Ishtar turned to Nizar and smiled. "Aren't we lucky with these genes of ours?"

His phone pinged. A message from Massoud, their first contact since Cairo. The message was short and to the point: the situation was getting worse in Yemen, and he was about to take a boat across the Gulf of Aden. He'd head towards Sudan, then through Egypt and Libya before taking a boat to Italy. Did he know anyone at the UK Home Office who could facilitate a visa?

When he returned home, Nizar replied saying he would look into it and gave him the contact details of a friend in Cairo who could house him. It was impossible not to think of Massoud without remembering all that came after. Although the waves of routine had washed over the chasm Massoud opened in their relationship, after Cairo Nizar found he had little patience for Alfie's hopeful naïveté. In their early courtship, his lover's simplicity and light demeanour was a refreshing contrast to Nizar's own. But why should Alfie have the luxury of a carefree life, absolving himself of the crimes of his ancestors, of his own government? Why should Alfie enjoy the spoils of these crimes, the long, lazy brunches of imported avocados and coffee, the guilt-free late-night curries. How did he think these curries made their way to this rainy, miserable island? Alfie's life—in fact, both their lives—were built on exploitation and destruction, and Nizar felt a global responsibility to acknowledge this.

An excavation was needed. He criticised Alfie for the simplest things. He grew impatient and irritable with Alfie's slow and thoughtful way of talking, a monopolisation of Nizar's time. When Alfie interrupted Nizar while he was scrolling through his phone, Nizar sighed and made a show of the disruption.

In response, Alfie demanded more of his attention. While he wrote at the kitchen table, Alfie barged in, erupting into song, his voice uprooting Nizar's thoughts like a settler colony. Sometimes, while Nizar worked, Alfie marched into his line of vision mimicking a soldier, or else pranced around in nothing but a towel he'd draped over his body like a dress. He impersonated people they knew, louder and more obnoxiously, until Nizar was forced to look up and acknowledge Alfie's presence.

"I feel like a nuisance to you," Alfie said one day. "It's horrible."

The flash of pain, of unbridled sincerity, broke through the dam. Nizar apologised. The time had arrived when Nizar's cynicism was no longer charming and Alfie's naïveté no longer endearing. The moment when dating a foreigner felt less like indulging in a world-uniting cosmopolitanism and more like an estrangement from a part of themselves.

As the summer of 2012 gave way to autumn, the flames of global upheaval licked at the edges of their Bethnal Green domesticity. Nizar travelled to Libya to cover the tribal fighting in Bani Walid. When his visa to Yemen didn't come through, he went to Egypt instead, reporting on the election of the Muslim Brotherhood's first president. He entered northern Syria through Turkey and was in Aleppo when Obama articulated his 'red line'. At home, his evenings were spent scrolling through Twitter, battling propagandists and monitoring the latest developments. He worried about friends and contacts in Benghazi, Sana'a, Aleppo, Cairo.

"Enough," Alfie said one evening, grabbing Nizar's phone from his hand.

Nizar looked up at him, incredulous. "Give me my phone back."

"No. Just be present."

"Present? The Syrian government is literally shelling Aleppo right now."

"You've got to try to separate what's out there from what's in here."

"Give me my fucking phone." He lunged for it, but Alfie dodged his grasp.

"You don't have control over what's out there, Niz. Sometimes you have to trust that things will work out for the best."

Alfie's face softened as he touched the scar on Nizar's cheek. Out of the two ways Nizar could have responded, he opted for the familiar route.

"Honestly, you white people and your bullshit belief that everything will work out for the best."

Alfie winced. "Why do you have to make this a racial thing?"

"Because it's such a white person response! What's out there *can't* be separated from what's in here."

"Fine."

"Aleppo is *absolutely* connected to our lives—"

"But—"

"—so when you talk about things working out for the best, do you know how insulting that is to—"

Alfie threw up his arms. "Once again, I am punished for not saying the *exact* right thing . . ."

"Sometimes things *don't* get better, Alfie. Sometimes they get worse and worse and then you die."

"Fine," Alfie tossed the phone on the kitchen table. "Drown in it."

Alfie's disinterest in politics, which Nizar had once found refreshing, was now irksome.

"How can you not be following what's happening in Gaza? It's your government, *your* money that is killing these people. And the apartheid wall, funded by our tax money . . . literally, the money that we earn goes to fund that wall."

But had Alfie wrapped a keffiyah around his shoulders and started taking Arabic lessons, would Nizar not have rolled his eyes and dismissed him? He considered whether there was a part of him that relished the solitude of his pain, that wanted the burden for himself and no one else. After all, was it not Alfie's distance from the global upheaval, a chosen distance certainly, a *respectable* distance, but a distance nonetheless—was this distance not part of what made Alfie attractive all those years ago? The distance that whispered a promise of a world, a life, where the pain of history might not bear down so heavily on his soul?

And yet, Alfie stayed. Nizar wasn't certain whether it was his capacity for optimism that was the source of Alfie's perseverance, or whether he had simply succeeded in dragging the poor man to the depths of his own pessimism.

Or perhaps Alfie had been holding onto the fractures of their relationship within his own body, because—while Nizar brewed some coffee in the kitchen one morning—Alfie let out a sudden cry from the bedroom. Nizar found him shirtless in front of the mirror, itching his right side, his face contorted in pain.

"My skin is burning."

By mid-afternoon, red, blistering welts had spread across Alfie's ribcage and back. At the hospital, he was diagnosed with shingles.

For two weeks he was bedridden, barely able to move. Alfie

had always been the one to care for Nizar. Now, it was Nizar who was thrust into this unfamiliar role. He made food and cups of tea, brought them to the bed where Alfie watched television. He kissed his forehead and gently dabbed oils and balms on the blisters. Nizar wondered to what degree the shingles had bought them more time.

One evening, as Nizar applied tea tree oil onto Alfie's enflamed skin, a gentle rain began to fall. Alfie turned his head to the side.

"I think of you when I meditate every morning," Alfie said, breaking the stillness.

Nizar paused, taken aback. "You do?"

"Of course. I think about all the things I'm grateful for."

"And you're grateful for *me*?"

Alfie laughed at Nizar's surprise, then a seriousness returned to his features. "I've never told anyone this, but I think to myself: I hope Nizar can get through this. I hope he can feel okay."

Nizar's eyes welled up with unexpected tears. He felt as though he were underwater. He stood up and left the room to wash his hands, hoping the sound of the running water muffled his sobs.

* * *

Ishtar agreed to a call. When Nisreen appeared on the screen, Nizar was surprised to see a softly spoken woman; nothing like the war-mongering demon Ishtar had described. Nisreen listened patiently as Ishtar pitched their idea. At first, Ishtar's tone was antagonistic, but over the course of the conversation her icy demeanour thawed.

"Starting the expedition in Hasankeyf is a brilliant idea," Nisreen said when Ishtar had finished speaking. "The Turkish government is in the process of constructing a massive dam that won't just flood the city but will disrupt the ecosystem all the way down the river. We can bring in some local media to raise awareness about the dam and its impacts. Your expedition can demonstrate how connected the ecosystem along the river is." Nisreen consulted her notes. "Timeline wise, we're looking at about eighteen months to put together a team that can build the boats and navigate them along the river."

Ishtar shook her head. "We don't have that kind of time. Let's aim for early October, the boats can be built in two weeks."

"Even if we manage that, the security situation—"

"Let's get one thing straight: this is *my* project."

"Ishtar, there are US air strikes—"

"*My* project. *My* narrative. I'm the one in charge."

Ishtar put down an ultimatum. If they couldn't agree to start the expedition by mid-October, Ishtar would look for another funder.

Nizar expected Nisreen to reject Ishtar's timeline, but instead her eyes softened.

"Let me see what I can do." Whatever the history between them, it was deeper than his aunt had let on.

When the call ended, Ishtar turned to him.

"We're going to Iraq."

Nizar's stomach dropped. The explosion. The blood. The eyeball.

"I've got stuff to do here," he said quickly, looking down at his papers. "Commitments . . ."

Ishtar snapped her fingers. He looked up. "We're going to Iraq," she said, staring into his eyes.

ZAINAB

September 2014

Zainab pushed herself from the railing. The water was bringing so much back. She hurried towards the parking lot, past a knot of tourists angling their phones for the best view of the gushing fountain. The Whitney Houston song ended, the fountain thinned to a dribble, then cut. Another song began.

In the parking lot, she couldn't find her car. Where had she parked? Why was she struggling to remember this small detail, while all those years returned so vividly?

She had just been doing her best. Besides, the country had so much to lose. Unlike Zainab herself, of course. In 1979 she had nothing to lose.

"You're Ishtar's sister, right?"

Zainab is at a New Year's Eve party, thrown by a group of Lebanese boys who share an apartment in Karradah. The war in Lebanon has brought waves of Lebanese to Baghdad. The seventies are tipping into a new decade, and Ishtar and Zainab are not supposed to be here. They lied to their mother and Ammo Kuteiba, saying they would make a brief appearance at the Mansour Club and then come straight home, just after midnight.

She turns around. A slight man with a mop of brown curls, a thick gold chain, and a tobacco brown satin shirt that catches the light like oiled wood. The shirt is unbuttoned all the way down to his stomach, the chain carrying a gold crucifix that nestles in his chest hair. He's dressed as if in disguise: a broom-bristle moustache on his top lip, thick-rimmed eyeglasses, and a purple woollen hat to keep out the cold. She's about to laugh and then his eyes catch her, moonlit water she could drown in if she's not careful.

Spotting her car in the distance, Zainab quickened her pace. She reached into her bag to pull out her keys and tripped over a bump on the ground. Her bag fell, the contents spilling across the dirty concrete. A couple—the man older, white, the young woman Asian, probably Thai—stopped to look at her. Cursing under breath, she picked up her belongings. She had to keep moving, though everything had caught up to her now. The flood was here, licking at her heels.

"I'm Andre," he extends a delicate hand with thin, hairy knuckles, his R rolling in a French Lebanese drawl. Lebanese men are all players, charming and unreliable, and this guy isn't even her type. She prefers the Hollywood look, tall, muscly, and smooth.

"Nice to meet you. I'm Zainab. Your accent—Lebanese?"

"I grew up in Beirut," he says, pushing his glasses up the bridge of his nose. "But I'm originally Palestinian."

The clarification casts him in another light. It is like catching a painting from a different angle and suddenly appreciating a new aspect of its complex beauty. Zainab steps back and examines him.

Keys in the ignition, the engine roared to life. Zainab pressed on the pedal and the car jolted, speeding through the concrete maze and into the warm, humid night. She raced down the highway and sped through a red light, vaguely heard the beeping of a car on the other side of the intersection, but the music in her mind drowned almost everything else.

Donna Summer's 'I Feel Love'. She doesn't like disco, but the song is good. The breathy vocals thaw her.

"Your hat's a bit naff."

"Naff?"

Zainab giggles. "It's not a compliment."

"I'm not used to the dry cold," he says defensively. "Beirut is more humid. Anyway, I'm just coming down to the party for an hour. I have to get back to my room and study, my pre-med exams are next week."

Compelled by the idea of corrupting him, she takes him by the hand and pulls him into the kitchen. She makes him a strong drink and asks about his family. He is an only child, and his mother and father are firmly middle-class.

"I know you come from a family of artists," he says self-consciously. "Though I don't know much about art."

"That's a good thing. Medicine will make you money, art only makes you insane."

He talks about the war in Lebanon and explains the different political factions. She doesn't follow, though she finds his knowledge enticing. As he talks, she nods her head and feigns comprehension. She has never been interested in those kinds of politics, a distraction from the politics of human behaviour, of the politics that play out within the dynamics of a family, a group of friends, and which can shed more light on the world than understanding whoever Gemayel or Arafat are.

"It's nearly midnight," Zainab hears herself say. She must behave, she knows she must not pursue this. But Andre's appearance makes the party more enjoyable, and it is a cloudless winter evening in Baghdad. She takes him up to the roof so they can gaze at the constellations. As the clock strikes midnight, Andre pulls her close and plants a kiss on her lips. Pink Floyd floats up from the party below.

Andre's moustache scratches against the top of her lip and reveals a strange new sensation. Hope.

She pulls herself from his grip.

"I should go home."

"Will I see you again?"

Zainab laughs and heads towards the door that leads down the stairs. She needs to find Ishtar. He follows her.

"Please?" His voice is tentative, searching.

She turns around.

"You think all Iraqi girls will just fall for your superficial Beiruti charm . . ."

"I'm not like that. I'm a good guy."

On the staircase he pulls her back into his arms.

"See me again," he whispers into her ear. She melts as his breath touches her skin.

"I like being free."

"Freedom is overrated."

They get back from the party to an unlit house. Ishtar unlocks the front door. Ammo Kuteiba's shadow stands in the living room.

"You're late," he says quietly.

"Sorry Ammo," Zainab says. "Time did not do what we planned."

Ishtar chuckles, and Ammo Kuteiba charges towards them like a bull. He slaps Ishtar across the face, a blow so powerful the crack reverberates throughout the neighbourhood and sends Ishtar flying backwards until she hits the ground with a thud.

Burning with rage, Ishtar looks up at Kuteiba.

"When are you going to die and relieve us of your misery you old fucking pervert!"

Blood and saliva fly from her mouth.

Zainab runs to put her body between her sister and their uncle. Kuteiba's demeanour changes, he looks down at his hand, as if surprised by its actions.

"Fuck you!" Ishtar screams, as she stands and runs down the street.

Zainab and Kuteiba stand in silence. Bathed in the bluish light of dawn, Zainab waits for her mother to come down, but there is no movement from upstairs. She looks at her uncle. The veins in his neck bulge, and beads of sweat cling to the hairs of his thick moustache. She starts to move around him, to go to her room, but he grabs her arm. With his other hand, he grips her chin.

"How could you do that?" she whispers.

"I'm sorry. I made a mistake."

He begins to cry. He holds Zainab tightly, sobbing into her neck. His breath is rancid, like garbage. She feels his lips behind her ear. She thinks of the giant stapler in the office of the Ministry of Interior, how she wishes she had it in her hands now . . .

"Don't touch me."

This is enough, she knows. Kuteiba pulls away. His face looks like a child, and the darkness that shadowed his features only moments ago is gone, revealing an insatiable grief. He turns and goes upstairs.

Zainab stands alone in her party dress, staring at her feet. From her bag she pulls out a cigarette and lights it. She inhales deeply and blows out a thick cloud of smoke. Ishtar will return, she consoles herself. As the smoke clears, she glimpses her mother's slender shadow near the kitchen, watching her.

Nizar

October 2014

The day before their flight, Ishtar asked to meet at the British Museum.

"To pay our respect to the ancient gods," she joked over the phone.

Nizar spotted her leaning against the gate at the entrance on Great Russell Street. She was dressed in black and wore a long necklace with a gold replica of a Babylonian incantation bowl. A leather messenger bag rested by her feet.

"You look nice," Nizar said.

Ishtar ignored this. "Did you know that in the 2003 war alone, nearly fifteen thousand items were pillaged from the Iraqi Museum? Most have never been found."

In the foyer, an attendant asked if they would like to donate money to support the upkeep of the museum.

"Have you not looted enough from our people already?" Ishtar asked.

They headed straight to the Mesopotamian rooms. Shuffling past tourists and schoolchildren, they stopped at a glass casing. Inside rested a fragment of a baked clay tablet the colour of river silt. They stood in silence in the controlled and sterile air, examining the cracked artefact, their faces ghosts on the glass. Nizar thought of his grandfather, working in the Iraqi Museum while Europe burned. The work had filled his grandfather with a melancholic hope. Everything would end, the death of the Sumerians and Babylonians were proof of that. But the kernels of life in his hands were an assurance that not all would be lost.

Perhaps the only way to create a viable future was to rebuild one's relationship with history. But if that were true, why did history feel so unbearably heavy?

"One thing that's been lost is how queer the epic of Gilgamesh actually is," Ishtar said. "Translators throughout history—nearly always white heterosexual men—have downplayed the queerness of the love between Gilgamesh and Enkidu. Before meeting Enkidu, Gilgamesh had a prophetic dream, where his mother tells him that a strong partner will come to him. 'You will take him in your arms, embrace and caress him the way a man caresses his wife'." Ishtar turned to Nizar. "Is that not the gayest thing you've ever heard? It's all there, etched on this tablet all the way back in the seventh century BC."

Nizar thought of the rituals and jokes he and Alfie had cultivated, how over time they had begun to seem incomprehensible to the both of them, a language they had once been fluent in now heavy and strange on their tongues. How a missing sock became a metaphor for the world's injustices and a witch-hunt that Nizar would hang over his lover's head for days.

"Who gives a shit, it's just a sock. Let it go!"

"Trust the white man to just want to let things go. Baghdad's destroyed and Blair still prances around on television, but let's forget the invasion of Iraq, shall we? Oh, just let it go. No point holding onto the past."

As the bodies piled up in Homs, Baghdad, Aden, Cairo, Tripoli, and Gaza, each carcass was an affirmation. Mentioning the massacres to Alfie and his friends during nights out had resulted in awkward silences or tuts of pity, as if the bodies were only Nizar's to bury and mourn. How could he make them understand that this pain belonged to them, too? In private, Alfie had made heartfelt appeals for Nizar to see a therapist. When he dismissed these attempts to personalise his political rage, Alfie called him 'difficult'.

Perhaps his Iraqi genes were responsible, the genes that understood how a small blip centuries ago could reverberate in the present, the genes that recognised history is not a river that runs clear, but a mountain range built on centuries of tiny moments which shape a person irrevocably.

No. He would not let the fucking sock go.

"I'd like to grab the tablet and take it to Iraq," Ishtar said, cutting through his thoughts. "Can you imagine? We'd build an ark to house all these stolen pieces and return them to their rightful place."

"It's infuriating," Nizar looked around, taking in the hall of vitrines containing thousands of stolen artefacts. "How our past sits in the museums of empires."

"It's like walking into a hunter's home and seeing your mother's head above the fireplace." She set her palm flat on the cool glass case. "We've lost so much. The missing tablets, which carry the story forward, are also gone forever."

"On the positive side," Nizar replied, "think of the potential spaces opened up in their absence. We can fill the missing lines with new stories. The lost fragments are like cracks in a stone that allow fresh growths to take root."

Ishtar considered this. "Perhaps."

They walked through the remaining rooms in silence, taking in the monumental gate slabs, carved guardians, and amputated statues. Nizar looked at the faces cut into the stone, the missing lips and noses lost to history. He kept his hands at his sides, resisting the urge to touch, to feel the weight of their history on his skin. His chest tightened as he considered the years passing, the deep stretches of time, how it had only been ten months, though it felt like a lifetime, since he had heard himself say the words:

"This isn't working."

They had argued about something, and though Nizar could not remember what it was about, he recalled with perfect clarity how the hours of tense sparring had left them in the familiar state of sickly, all-encompassing exhaustion.

"What do you mean?" Alfie's eyes were red and swollen.

"We need some time apart . . . I've already found a sublet."

"Of course you have."

He'd waited for Alfie to say something else, but as the minutes passed he felt the last five years of their lives setting like a dying sun. When Alfie grabbed his keys and walked out of the house, Nizar could only sit at the kitchen table, staring at Alfie's half-empty glass of orange juice.

The threat of their rupture had been hanging over him for so long that when Nizar heard the faint click of the front door closing, relief washed over him. He felt like some sort of order had been restored in the world.

Since that day, Nizar had operated as if history did not matter, as if the present was the only thing that existed. He recalled the first night in his new apartment, how he had slept alone in a bed that belonged to a dying woman, and dreamt about water. Putrid and yellow, flowing from the crack under the door and the tiny slit between the windows, seeping through the walls and slowly darkening the carpet. The water came towards him and he felt helpless as it licked his toes, crept up his knees and chest and seeped into his mouth. Now, surrounded by Assyrian and Sumerian relics, he felt himself drowning in this room of stolen artefacts, carrying the crushing weight of thousands of years of loss.

"I need some air. I'll see you outside."

He turned, quickly escaping down the hall and into the sun-drenched foyer where he could breathe. He ordered a coffee at the cafe next to the gift shop. Through the glass ceiling, rays of sunlight danced against the white marble.

Suddenly, his aunt was beside him.

"The plaque on the stone sculpture from the Easter Islands claims it was a gift from Queen Victoria," Ishtar said. "Can you believe the cheek of it?" She saw Nizar's face and her voice softened. "Are you okay?"

"Yeah. It's just . . . there's no escaping the past."

He expected Ishtar to laugh at this sudden display of emotion, but her eyes contained no judgement.

"For me the past is a source of sad comfort. I suppose that's where we differ."

Nizar finished the rest of his coffee and crushed the paper cup in his fist. Alfie had never understood how history illuminated contemporary pain, and this contributed to the fissures that had torn them apart. History was a prison, but if you had the key there was much inside to be learned.

Zainab

October 2014

The early departure time revealed itself in the dark bags under the flight attendant's eyes. Zainab settled into her seat. She felt a kinship with the anxious energy that suffused airports, the transience and limbo, the possibility of missed connections. The plane took off, thrusting her into the back of her seat. Out the window, Dubai was a glimmer of glass amidst the endless sand.

She pulled out the document Nizar had sent the previous evening and glanced through the pages: the family history. It began with a story about her grandmother, Fatima, on a wintry night in Turkey. She read the first paragraph three times, but her mind would not focus. Admitting defeat, she nestled her head against the leather seat and closed her eyes.

August 1980.

They ask about the Lebanese students. She and Andre have been dating for seven months.

"What about them?"

They see through her defensiveness. "Do they talk about politics?"

"I've told you, I don't know politics."

Veiled threats are made. Her family will be informed about her romantic dalliances, it is suggested, but Zainab is unmoved. Ammo Kuteiba had retreated into the shadows of their lives ever since he laid hands on Ishtar.

The next day she is let go from her job at the Embassy. A decision from higher up, she is told. She will be poorer now, but she feels lighter, freed from the moral dilemma gnawing at her conscience.

When she tells Andre she lost her job, he suggests a short break.

"How about Cyprus? We can find a nice hotel by the sea."

"My mother will not approve."

"We'll come up with a lie!"

They stay in a low-budget hotel in Limassol, a few minutes' walk from the beach. They buy tacky beach towels and a frisbee from a nearby stand and eat ice-cream and peanuts. They drink ice-cold beer and smoke endless cigarettes on the sand. When they make love, it's with the windows open, and without the moral quandary that burdened the sex they had in Baghdad. Free of shame, of negotiating privacy, they follow their lovemaking with long, indulgent naps, with the curtains pulled back and the windows open, allowing the hot breeze of sea and exhaust fumes to envelop their naked bodies.

In the evenings they eat fish. Andre knows how to select the freshest ones. His father taught him what to look for; the cloudiness of the eye, the redness of the tissue behind the gills. As Andre points this out, Zainab is struck by the realisation that Andre will be the father of her child. She pictures a scene in the not-so-distant future: Andre will take their child to a local fish market, and together they will pick out the freshest catch of the day. They will bring the fish home and she will roast it for them. They will raise the child well, teach them how to live and how to love and how to enjoy both to the fullest. It is a scene so vivid in her mind that in seven years, when she is alone with Nizar in Kuwait, she will take her son to the fish market to explain how to identify the freshest fish, but when she begins to speak her mind will go blank.

"The bloodier the gills, the fresher—no, wait, is it the opposite?"

They return home to news of the full-scale invasion of Iran.

Zainab seems to be the only person in Baghdad who remains hopeful about the future. She has Andre, life is good, and not even the scud missiles that shake the houses can convince her otherwise.

Saddam begins sending the buses in the autumn. A gesture of solidarity to the Palestinian cause, he says, as busloads of Palestinians living in Iraq are rounded up and sent to fight in the Lebanese civil war.

She returns to the Ministry. A giant mural now decorates the central hall, showing Iraqis fighting against invaders throughout history: the battles against the Mongols, the Turks, the British imperialists, and now the brave leader Saddam fighting the evil Iranians in his familiar combat uniform.

She is taken inside the room with the giant stapler.

"To what do we owe the incredible honour of your visit?"

"My fiancé . . ."

"You're engaged?"

"Soon, inshallah . . ."

"Congratulations . . ."

"Yes, but . . . my fiancé is Palestinian . . ."

They smile. Now they understand why she is here.

"Orders are from higher up."

"But he is just one person, a student of no importance or threat."

"The government has given these students a free education. They should also do their part for the Arab cause."

She begs. Tears flow from her eyes, but they do not relent. Would they have exempted him had she continued fulfilling her patriotic duties?

Instead of returning home she visits Rajiha. They sit on the old swing with cups of tea.

"Amma, is it better to tell the truth even if it may destroy your reputation?"

Rajiha is startled by this question. She gazes deeply into her niece's eyes, as if trying to uproot a secret. When she finds nothing, she turns and stares at the large palm tree in the garden.

"Did you ask your mother this question?"

Zainab is confused. "No. She's in London for an exhibition of Baba's work."

"Appropriate," Rajiha chuckles bitterly. "Your mother and I will likely have different answers."

"What do you mean?"

"Never mind, Zanoobti . . ."

"So what would your answer be?"

Rajiha chews a date slowly in her mouth, then washes it down with some tea. "Unlike your mother, I believe the truth is the only thing that will set you free."

That night in Andre's room, Zainab confesses everything. She tells him of Rakan's disappearance, of the monthly meetings and the phone calls, of her last meeting before her authorisation was revoked, and her meeting with them that day, how she had shamelessly begged at their feet. She tells him this softly, in whispers. She is furious and terrified and helpless, convinced that the room—that every room in the whole city—is bugged with listening equipment, wires and microphones running behind walls, through closets and beds and under the ground, which broadcasts every whisper and thought to the heart of the General Directorate of Intelligence.

Andre holds her as she confesses her sins. When she is finished, he suggests Kuwait.

It seems like a good idea. He will drop out of medical school and she will find a job. They will build a new life. It won't be the life they imagined; she will lose London, he will forgo medicine, and his parents will be furious at his running off with a Muslim girl. Still, it will be a life of love, away from paranoia and fear.

Andre is not granted an exit visa. A week later he is formally given the date and time for his bus's departure for Lebanon.

Andre's roommates vacate the apartment for their last evening together. Normally, they play music while they cook and argue over the selection, but tonight they eat in silence. The war has moved to Basra in the south and the Kurdish villages in the north. Baghdad is unusually still.

After dinner they retreat to the bedroom, where they quietly undress. They hold one another for a long time, breathing in the scent of each other's bodies, imprinting a memory that they will store for as long as they can. Outside, the moon casts a warm glow across the sky, bathing the buildings in shades of blue. They make love. He releases himself inside her, a keepsake, a promise. She feels him like a breath of life.

"I will come back."

Zainab sits up. A sudden panic comes over her. There is no certainty about anything, she realises. She is twenty and completely powerless, inhabiting a world that is not hers to shape. The only thing she can do is to run and keep running.

Andre sits across from her on the bed, and she looks at his moustache and round cheeks. He is just a boy. The thought comes to her, swift and sad. He is just a boy.

The next morning a sandstorm descends on the city. Everything a sickly yellow. Breathing is difficult, and people on the streets are irritable and short-tempered, eager to get indoors. Zainab can only squeeze Andre's hands and kiss him on both cheeks, as if the sandstorm itself is spying on them. Andre puts his bag in the hold and walks up the steps of the bus, down the aisle, past the rows of young men just like him, until he finds a window seat. He turns to her and winks.

See you in Kuwait, he mouths.

Two days later, Zainab is ironing clothes when a large mirror behind her shatters. Shards of glass rain down on her. She knows then, instantly, that something terrible has happened. She picks up the shards of glass which taunt her with her own reflection as they dig into her fingers and draw blood.

Later, they will blame the shattering of the mirror on a rocket that fell in a nearby neighbourhood, which caused the subtle shaking of the house. Later still, she will learn that Andre is dead. The bus was stopped twenty minutes after crossing into Lebanon. She cannot remember the name of the militia, but they board the bus and demand to see everyone's identification cards. Upon discovering the bus is filled with Palestinians the armed men walk up and down the aisle, working from both ends as they put bullets into the heads of each of the passengers. The driver, an Iraqi, is allowed to escape unharmed.

In his irreverence and innocence, Andre was not a creature of death. Zainab wonders if she is being punished. Wonders if Andre was pushed further up the line to teach Zainab a lesson about what happens to those who stand in the way of Saddam and his demands.

With our spirit and our blood, we will sacrifice ourselves for you, Saddam!

But even he, the Great Historic Leader, God's gift to Iraq, the Beloved of the People, the Consciousness of the Nation, the Father of all Iraqis and the Tent of all the Arabs, even he could not have predicted the violence that awaited those men in Lebanon. Two days after the bus massacre, Saddam calls off the policy. All buses on their way to Lebanon are ordered to return to Baghdad.

The nights are dark and stifling. She wakes often and weeps for Andre's truncated life. She weeps for the man he could have become, for their lost future, for the cruelty and injustice of it all. But most of all, she weeps because, in the simplest of terms, she misses his laughter, the way he smells after a long day, the touch of his skin. She misses who she was in his presence.

Spring brings major infantry offensives; thousands of young men are sent to their deaths. Channel One plays endless footage of trenches with mangled corpses, the charred limbs and rotting flesh of enemy soldiers a premonition of imminent victory. Through the fog of grief, there is a job offer in Kuwait. Zainab makes plans to leave, failing to notice the life growing inside her.

It isn't until she misses her second period that she realises what is happening.

The pregnancy is a glimmer of hope.

The family cannot understand her decision.

"I'm pregnant," she tells Ishtar.

Ishtar looks up from her sketchbook, surprised that her younger sister has said something that remotely piques her interest.

"Shut up! Who is the father?"

"Andre."

Ishtar pauses, puts her pen down. "What are you going to do?"

"What do you mean what am I going to do? I'm going to have the baby."

Ishtar looks at her with incredulity. "You can't just have the kid."

"Why not?"

"It will ruin your career!"

"What career?"

"Zainab, be realistic. You're not married. You know how people are here."

"Let them lose their minds." Zainab lights a cigarette. "I'm not killing this baby."

"If that's what you want," Ishtar says, her voice softening, "Then I'll support you."

Their mother's response is more practical.

"Does the company in Kuwait know?"

"No."

"Well . . . how will you hide it?"

"I'll figure it out when I'm there. I just need to get out."

"We will make it happen." A phone call is made.

Zainab is four months pregnant when the family is invited to attend a celebration in one of Saddam's palaces, awarding Medals of Courage to military generals. After the procession, the family give their congratulations to the leader. Saddam shakes Bridget's hand, heaping praise on her dead husband for his contribution to art and culture. Bridget, in her perfect Baghdadi dialect, introduces her two present daughters. She tells him Ishtar is also an artist, working with the Ministry of Culture.

"Good," Saddam replies. "An artist, much like a politician, serves to advance life."

Zainab's mouth is dry, her head pounds.

Saddam reaches into his pocket and pulls out his pistol. He hands the pistol to Ishtar.

"A gift for your service."

"No," Bridget says.

"Sometimes a paintbrush doesn't quite do the job."

Saddam winks, then turns to Zainab. She averts her gaze as his eyes take her in. For the first time in her life, she longs to be hideous.

"Shall we dance?"

She cannot refuse.

He takes her hand and leads her through the large hall. He smells of gunpowder, sweat, and cologne. She holds back the vomit rising in her throat as she dances with the man responsible for Andre's death, for the death of thousands. But he is a great leader, she reminds herself. He has built schools, hospitals, roads. He has taken Iraq out of foreign control. These thoughts feel hollow. She looks over his shoulder, trying to imagine she is dancing with someone else. Her gaze lands on a painting of him hanging against the wall. There is no escape.

Long live Saddam.

Our leader, our father, our friend.

President of the people of Iraq.

Protector of the nation.

On the way home, Bridget confiscates the pistol and gives it to Ammo Kuteiba. The next day, Zainab receives her exit visa.

She has not been in Kuwait a week when Ammo Kuteiba calls. It is past midnight. He begs her to return, his voice full of sorrow. She hangs up.

On Zainab's due date, Ishtar flies to Kuwait. Days later her water breaks. Thirty-six hours of labour. She never swears so much in her life.

"You've shat yourself," Ishtar says, holding her hand.

"Fuck you!"

She screams. Ishtar screams.

She curses. Ishtar curses.

She roars. Ishtar roars alongside her, squeezing her hand.

The baby refuses to come out. Finally, the doctors use forceps, the head emerging purple and misshapen.

"That's the ugliest kid I've ever seen," Ishtar says.

While Zainab holds her baby in a delivery room, Kuteiba leaves a note on his bedroom door.

A simple note, for his sister-in-law, in English.

"Do not come in. Call the police."

He wraps his lips around the pistol that Saddam gifted Ishtar. The pistol Bridget did not want in the house.

"It's a boy," she hears a nurse whisper in her ear.

He pulls the trigger.

A boy. She has a boy. Suddenly, Zainab has everything to lose. She holds the boy in her arms and realises that for as long as he is alive, she will never be free.

Part II

Prisons of Hope

"I am continually having pain of heartbreak, fright, fear, chills,
I am constantly anxious, I am continually afraid,
I continually talk with myself, I have fearful dreams . . ."
—*Corpus of Mesopotamian Anti-Witchcraft Rituals*

Bridget

October 2014

The not-child was crying again. It had been fifty years since she'd last heard its howls, but she recognised in its folds the harrow and mourning, spiteful and full of sorrow.

The paintbrush shook in her hands. She gazed out of her studio's large windows. Looking through the drops of water that clung to the glass, the landscape appeared born from the brushstrokes of an impressionist painting.

Bridget turned back to the empty canvas. She usually worked from real life, was always meticulous about planning and sketching out ideas before even considering paint. But for her final painting, she wanted to try something new. She would work from memory.

She had never given much thought to memories, had never kept a diary. She tried once, many years ago, but found herself lingering on the tedious and accentuating the tragic. But what else could she do when the present was so lonely and the future too minuscule?

Bridget closed her eyes and tried to conjure a memory of the old Baghdadi building. The same street as the Mackenzie bookstore, one of those side-streets that branched off Rashid. She pictured the clean lines and geometry, the wooden bays and latticed windows. The memory began to breathe. The faint pulse of her heartbeat brought the sounds of voices and traffic, the smell of coffee, the sharp stench of horse manure simmering under a hot sun. And of course, the smell of mud.

Bridget opened her eyes. The not-child's cries had disappeared, and in celebration she made contact with the canvas. The brushstroke glistened: a burnt sienna.

She hesitated. She had always been fearful of colour, something she had admitted to Haydar long ago when they were students at the Slade. When she confessed this, he'd rummaged through one of his drawers, pulling out an old, yellowed copy of *L'Illustration* dated December 1938. A dog-eared page titled 'Le Miroir de Bagdad', a series of al-Wasiti illustrations. He pointed to a painting of a line of camels.

"Each of them is a different shade of soil. When impressionism first arrived in Baghdad, local artists complained that the style would never work because the landscape was devoid of colour, the sun too harsh and unforgiving. But al-Wasiti showed us, centuries ago, that there are endless colours for soil."

She had examined the other al-Wasiti paintings, each showing a slice of Abbasid-era Baghdadi life. One depicted the delivery of a sermon in front of a dignitary and his harem. Another showed a gathering of men sitting around a fountain in a garden, listening as a musician played the oud. The paintings filled her with a sudden longing to visit Baghdad, to glimpse Haydar's world beyond London.

"Something about these reminds me of Matisse," she said changing the subject, fearful that Haydar had read her thoughts. "This crescent here, it's so similar to the way Matisse renders the curves of a body . . ."

"Exactly!" Haydar's eyes lit up. "I came across this magazine when I was studying in Paris, it was one of the few things I took back to Baghdad when the war began. It was the first time I came face-to-face with this artistic history, one I hadn't even known existed. My father's generation obsessed over capturing the most accurate representation of the world, but coming across al-Wasiti I realised there was a missing connection to *my* history. So, when I had to flee Europe I began working at the Iraqi museum."

Bridget's shaky hand returned to the canvas now. Another stroke joined the first. She was about to make a third when the door swung open behind her.

"Mama, this place is a mess."

Mediha's voice tore through her memories, eviscerating the image of the building.

"She lets herself in . . ."

"Where did these crumbs come from? Have you been eating biscuits?"

Bridget detected a whiff of something.

"Is that chicken?"

"Yes. I'm cooking chicken. For dinner." Mediha enunciated each word as if speaking to a child.

The smell took her back to a train carriage in 1950, the excitement and fear that had run through her body as the train raced through the Balkans. She had packed some food for the train: sausage with gravy on brown bread, butter and marmalade on white bread, a few oranges, and a mince pie. The sandwiches were wrapped in discarded Christmas paper. She had eaten both on the way from London to Bonn, where she spent a night with a fellow graduate of the Slade, talking endlessly of the adventures waiting for her in Baghdad. And of Haydar, too. How much she looked forward to seeing him again.

"Mum, did you hear me?" Mediha swept through the room, pouncing on dirty clothes, discarded paper, empty mugs with teabags. Her movements, forceful and frantic, rendered Bridget helpless. Taunted by her daughter's power, she could only sit on her stool and gaze at the two strokes on the canvas. Though Haydar had wanted her to fly to Baghdad directly, she had insisted on taking the train. She had wanted to see Europe.

Mediha gripped her shoulder. "This room is a mess. I'm going to do a quick clean, and then you need a bath."

"I don't want a bath."

"You haven't bathed in two days . . . my God, how can one

person use so many different mugs? Look at these crumbs! Zainab's coming tomorrow and she'll be looking for anything to criticise me."

The smell of the chicken drew her back to the train. She'd noticed some spotting in her underwear that morning, but she brushed any concerns aside. Racing to Istanbul, the journey was fine. Until the chicken arrived. In the studio, Mediha droned on, but her voice was drowned out by the thudding of the tracks.

Bridget remembered how her lower back had ached, how impossible it had been to get comfortable on the wooden benches in the second-class carriage. As the train shot through the Balkans, she closed her eyes and imagined her arrival. She thought of al-Wasiti's paintings, picturing herself inside them, and recalled Haydar's warnings about Baghdad.

"It's a dusty oven."

"I spent a good part of my childhood in bomb shelters," she'd replied briskly. "I can handle a bit of dust."

Was it between Thessaloniki and Istanbul when she began to feel hot and clammy, a queasy tide rising? Yes, because it was in Thessaloniki that the men came in. Three burly men, stinking of alcohol and sweat, carrying an oil-stained paper bag. They sat beside her and pulled out a whole chicken, the skin crisp and brown. The pungent smell suffused the carriage. Metal at the back of her tongue. The low ache in her back cinched round to her front, and her stomach twisted. The three men huddled around the chicken, talking loudly as they tore at it with their fingers, shovelling strips of dull, grey meat into their mouths, their lips glistening with oil and fat, morsels of flesh in the spaces between their teeth. The pain intensified. The cramps came in bands now, tearing through her body. She clutched her stomach as the train raced through the countryside, the trees blurring into one long, endless smudge of umber.

Across from her sat a kind Turkish man, an architect who

worked in Berlin. His voice was soothing, his company pleasant, and this helped take her mind off the cramps. What was it they talked about? Architecture? Yes, the politics of architecture in post-war Germany, a battle of control between the Allies and the Soviet bloc. She clung to the conversation, his voice a lighthouse in the sea of pain. *It's just chicken*, she reminded herself as a sheen of sweat gathered at her hairline.

"It's just chicken . . ."

"Yes, just chicken," Mediha's voice came to her now. "What, you want a feast?"

"Winning the war is only a fraction of the battle. It's how you rebuild that matters."

"Mum, what on earth are you on about?"

Another cramp, harder, lower, as if the men were tearing at the soft flesh of her stomach. A sudden warm rush between her thighs. She stood up and the carriage tilted, black stars floating in her vision. She couldn't faint, not here in front of everyone. The rumble of the carriage created tremors that reverberated through her body.

The Turkish man looked up at her. "Miss, are you okay?"

She shuffled down the carriageway to the bathroom and locked the door, her fingers slipping on the latch. She knelt by the toilet and the retching began. When there was nothing left, she leant back against the dirty walls. She looked at the space between her legs, the stain on the back of her pale blue dress. Her legs were smeared with blood, and further down . . . It was not large enough to be a child, no more than four inches in length on the dirty toilet floor. The not-child, skin translucent, eyelids nothing more than gentle creases in the skin, like the early stages of a sculpture. A bluish cord trailed from the small belly, resting against her thigh.

She cut the cord with the small pocketknife she carried with her and tried to wipe the mess on the floor with the paper by the sink, holding the not-child in her palm. Clean enough. And the sick from her face, yes, the blood from her legs too. She had to return to the carriage before they came looking. She held the foetus over the toilet bowl, but couldn't release her fist. A body, no matter how small, demands rites. She returned to the carriage and sat down, the moist softness of the not-child in her palm, its delicate, half-formed body resting against her clammy skin. Another cramp, lower this time. Something loosened inside her. Busy yourself, Bridget. The mince pie. The orange. She reached into the bag and pulled them out, turning to the Turkish architect. Would you like these? Really? Thank you, I don't think I've ever had this before. Mince pie, you say? Is it sweet? Oh. As he bit into the pastry she slipped the not-child, tucked in old Christmas wrapping, into her bag and leaned back against the wooden seat. Her body felt battered, pulverised. She fought the urge to writhe on the floor and scream in pain. Clench your jaw, fight it, she told herself. Crumbs lined the mouth of the architect as he peeled the skin of the orange, releasing the fresh scent through the carriage. It masked the oily smell of grilled poultry, the rustic smell of her own blood. Only a few more hours until Istanbul. The construction of every street in Berlin, every brick, is an intensely political act, the architect was saying, chewing on the last slice of orange. We are in the midst of profound global change. It's a most exciting time to be alive.

"A most exciting time to be alive."

"Are you listening to me?" Mediha's question dissolved the architect's voice, like acid through flesh. "I am running you a bath and you are going to get in it."

"But—"

"No buts." Mediha opened the cupboard and pulled out a fresh towel. "Now you sit here for ten minutes until the bath is ready."

And then Bridget was alone. How had she become so old, so helpless? She had lived through wars for goodness' sake. She had sat for hours on that train, carrying the not-child in a bag, not shedding a single tear.

Now, a confrontation over a bath had nearly broken her.

* * *

Mediha poured a jug of soapy water over Bridget's head. It flooded the creases of her skin, cooling as it trickled down the nape of her neck. Drops of water broke the surface of the bath, like the not-child as she dropped it into the Bosphorus during the stopover in Istanbul, the black waters swallowing her offering as she said a few words of prayer. After that she must have collapsed, as her next memory involved waking up in a hospital bed.

"I need the telephone," she had croaked, and, telephoning Haydar, explained she had fallen ill and would stay an extra night in Istanbul, maybe two. Nothing to worry about, just some bad chicken. An embellishment for the sake of a clean narrative, a legacy untarnished by grief, was that where it all began? The days passed in a stupor of blood, the doctors exploring inside of her until the miscarriage was announced 'completed'. The remainder of the journey she barely ate, her body gripped in shudders of pain, her sleep shallow and fleeting. She felt helpless. She thought she might die.

"What are you thinking about, Mum?" Mediha asked, scrubbing the back of her neck.

"I'm thinking about why you insist on bathing me when I can very well do it myself."

And that was a thought, yes, lamenting her waning independence, but it was joined by the memory of seeing Haydar on the platform all those years ago, his eyes scanning the passengers as he nervously massaged his hands. Bridget waved and he ran to her, pushing through the crowds. She collapsed into his embrace, melting into his familiar scent: cigarettes, and the cologne he used to wear in London, spicy and autumnal. But he also smelt of Baghdad, of hot sun on cotton, the nuttiness of soil, the sweetness of fresh sweat.

"Remember the last time you washed yourself? You slipped and nearly cracked your head open . . ."

"Nudging me towards senility, that's what you're doing."

In Haydar's arms, Bridget decided she could never tell him of the not-child. He would grieve viciously, ruminate on all the ways the tragedy could have been averted, and ultimately find a way to blame himself. The memory of the not-child would live inside her, alone, until she died.

He had grown a beard. He'd always been particular about his appearance, aware of his physical presence in the world—the aesthetics of his existence—though driven by creativity rather than narcissism. The beard, Bridget would later discover, was uncommon in the intellectual circles of Baghdad, and that was precisely why he wore it—his way of quietly challenging urban codes of class privilege among the intellectuals. "My mother says I look like an Afghan pilgrim on my way to Karbala," he joked as they settled into his small red Fiat and sped off towards the family home. Bridget had forgotten how much she loved the way he spoke English, holding each word in his mouth, pronouncing every letter, refusing to overlook a single sound.

"Honestly darling," he said, holding the steering wheel with one hand while massaging her neck with the other. "I don't know why I asked you to come. This city is like a giant oven in a perpetual sandstorm. Sand everywhere, pooling in pockets and around the edge of every window, swimming in our underwear and caked around our eyes . . ."

"A little sand never hurt anyone," she replied.

"It's not sand, Mum. It's biscuit crumbs."

Mediha scrubbed the loofa hard against Bridget's back. She wished she could feel Haydar's fingers again, gently caressing her skin. Everything might feel resolved somehow.

"Please keep the room clean until Zainab arrives. No painting either, because I won't be able to help you tidy up. I'll be in Edinburgh for the exhibition."

"Exhibition?" Bridget stared at her pale skin under the water. Along the rivulets of the surface she saw a London-style double decker bus and several fashionable Volkswagens, Cadillacs, and Chevys, nothing like she expected Baghdad to be.

"The collection about ISIS I've been working on for the past three months."

Thinking back, it was embarrassing to admit that she'd had in mind magic carpets and harems and palaces, had thought the city would be something from the Arabian Nights. Policemen wearing pristine white gloves directed the sleepy traffic with their hands and a series of shrilling blows on their whistles. The buildings were low. Many disappeared behind palm trees, with only the slim minarets of mosques poking out of the horizon. And everywhere, just as Haydar had shown her in London, shades of sienna bled into one another.

The colour of soil.

"I've moved the paintings into my bedroom," Mediha said, massaging shampoo into Bridget's hair. "Just in case she goes snooping."

"You should have just sold them already. I do wish you weren't in Edinburgh while your sister is here. I'd like you two to talk."

"Maybe *you* can talk to her, explain your reasoning. I understand your decision, Mum, but Zainab's not logical . . . she doesn't think things through."

"It's important to me, Mediha. I don't like these wars between the three of you."

"And who is responsible for these wars, Mama? Who drew the battle lines?"

Bridget sighed. "I just wish I could see you all get along before I die."

Mediha poured a jug of water over Bridget's head. Bridget spluttered and coughed.

"Oh, sorry. What were you saying?"

"I'm not scared of death you know. Like I've always said, you just become worm food."

Worm food. Bridget thought of the half-formed thing she dropped into the Bosphorus. Rivers had taken so much from her, but they had given her something too. Like that cold dreary evening in 1947. She had been walking along Tower Bridge, the November wind blowing fiercely across the river. She'd just started at the Slade, finally away from her mother's grip. She was five when her father died of tuberculosis. Bridget recalled the day of the funeral clearly because she had a large boil on her inner thigh, and as she watched her father's coffin descend into the earth she was aware only of the pain as it rubbed in that awful black dress her mother insisted she wear. Her mother remarried six months later, an older man, a vicar, religious and unforgiving. She quickly shirked her maternal responsibilities, and when her mother gave birth to Bridget's half-sister, Bridget was relegated to the role of carer. During the war she spent countless hours in bomb shelters with the family, trying to study while her mother lamented her own misfortune at being alive in such a dire time.

"Keep that nose in your books, Bridget," her mother would say. "The world needs more nurses."

Caring for people was the last thing she wanted to do. When she secretly applied to the Slade and got in on a scholarship no less, there had been a massive row. The city shook as her mother cursed her selfishness. *An artist*. The words were spat at her. Yet there she was, on that cold November evening, pursuing an art degree in London against her mother's wishes. As she walked across the bridge, a single scream cut through the force of the wind. She turned to see a woman hanging onto the railing. Beside her was a short man with a dark complexion.

Bridget ran towards them. The young man was talking to the woman, his voice calm and his accent strange. The woman turned to Bridget, looked her in the eye, her red face twisted in agony. Then she let go and dropped into the river, disappearing with a splash.

The young man turned to her, his face drawn in despair.

"I tried. I didn't know her—she wouldn't share her name."

They gave statements to the police, and afterwards Bridget and the young man—Haydar, an artist from Iraq—walked the city for hours. They walked through the night, their hands and faces aching from the cold, hoping that through each other's company they could somehow reconcile themselves with what they had seen.

Haydar was also a student at the Slade. He had come from Baghdad, to continue an education interrupted by the war. He was cosmopolitan yet distinctly Iraqi, dedicated not just to his art but his country too. He told her he had not always been this way. "I was miserable when I first returned to Baghdad" he admitted, but she found it impossible to believe that he had not held Iraq in such reverence all his life.

The river had given her Haydar. But it had taken him away, too.

"Mum, you're shaking," Mediha said. "Is the water too cold? Let's get you out . . ."

Mediha helped Bridget to her feet and grabbed the towel from the rack, rubbing her body to bring the warmth back. Bridget always thought it would be Zainab who would take her in when she aged. Her middle daughter was the more natural carer, the only one of her girls who became a mother. Of Ishtar, Bridget learned to expect nothing. Ishtar had condemned herself to a life where her art trumped everything else. But Zainab was off in the desert and Bridget could not live with that heat, not at her age, though she was happy for her middle daughter, beautiful and romantic, the one who got it right and married rich. It's what Zainab always wanted: leisurely morning coffees, shopping, exercise classes. In the end it was Mediha—her youngest, practical and exacting—who opened her home, though not without resentment. In her old age, Bridget was much less able to fold herself into someone else's life.

But that's exactly what she had done upon moving to Baghdad. She was only twenty and it had been easy to reinvent herself, to toss England away and jump headfirst into Haydar's world. Stepping inside his family home, she remembered the first words she said to his mother—in English, how foolish of her—"Mama Fatima, it is a pleasure to finally meet you." The old woman smiled without saying a word. Haydar's brother Kuteiba was stationed somewhere with the military, so it was just Haydar and the women in the house: his sister Rajiha, their mother Fatima, and Sumaya, a young girl from Mosul who helped with the cleaning. Mama Fatima took Bridget by the hand and sat her in front of a heaving plate of rice and meat, and though she still felt unwell she ate the entire plate, as well as the second helping Fatima insisted on putting in front of her. Haydar's sister Rajiha watched her with a scowl.

The next day she and Haydar went to the sheikh to sign their marriage papers. Mama Fatima insisted this be done as soon as possible, she feared the neighbours would talk. The ceremony was brief and practical, neither of them fans of a spectacle, and before she had time to process it, she was his wife. Afterwards, Haydar bought her a ring from the jewellery market, a deep-blue lapis lazuli set in silver. He told her that the stone was prized by Mesopotamian kings, mined from faraway mountains and carried across deserts. They walked down Al-Mutannabi Street, weaving through the rows of books piled high on wooden tables, the air thick with dust and ink. To celebrate, they took a small boat across the Tigris, the water a murky jade, swirling with silt and flecks of light. On the river the air was bitterly cold. Haydar held her hands in his and she felt giddy, the low buildings on either side of the banks seeming to sway with the current, the sky so immense it threatened to swallow them whole.

Other than her wedding day she spent most of that first week in bed, vague sounds of the outside world floating through the window. At night she struggled to sleep, was often awake for the dawn call to prayer. What sleep she did get was fitful and frantic, plagued with dreams of the not-child. She dreamed the half-formed thing was alive, its eyelids slowly opening, revealing large black eyes that bore into her soul, its tiny mouth enlarged in a shriek.

"I'll heat up the chicken, Mama," Mediha said, leaving the bathroom. "Come to the kitchen when you're dressed."

"I'd like to do more painting."

"You need to rest."

"But I won't be doing much painting when Zainab's here."

"Just half an hour after dinner, then."

To ask permission now, as back then. A houseguest in one's own life. Haydar's world had been in full swing. He had been working on a series of paintings to accompany a new translation of *One Thousand and One Nights*. He was drawn to the character of Sinbad, what he represented about bringing the world together, making differences smaller and more digestible. He'd also recently been promoted to the head of sculpture at the Institute of Fine Arts. In the mornings he taught and lectured, and in the afternoons he painted and sculpted.

Bridget's life was barren in comparison. In the beginning, Mama Fatima had been too fearful to let her leave the house alone. If Bridget so much as suggested taking a walk in the neighbourhood, Mama Fatima's face lost its colour and her head shook vigorously. Instead, she helped her mother-in-law with the cooking. Communicating in a hodgepodge of words and hand gestures, Bridget learned to cook a few Iraqi staples: beans, meat, dolma, pickled carrots, turnips, and cucumbers, or else lazily read a novel as Sumaya cleaned the house around her. The house girl was just sixteen but she was a hard worker, and Bridget watched in awe as she easily lifted furniture with one hand while sweeping underneath with the other. Sumaya and Rajiha spent the afternoons together, joking and laughing in a language Bridget did not yet understand. She suspected they were talking about her.

Yet despite her alienation, Bridget had carried a sense of hope. If there was one thing she was certain of, it was that she and Haydar were on the cusp of a new and important period in their lives, one that would irrevocably change them both. She had not a single regret at having tossed that sorry old life in England away.

"Baghdad was about as far away as I could get from that horrible woman," Bridget muttered to herself as she looked at her reflection in the mirror.

"Which horrible woman?" Mediha called out.

"My mother," Bridget said, walking into the kitchen where Mediha stood watching the chicken rotate under the light of the microwave. "You know, when my stepfather died of a heart attack after I moved to Baghdad, I refused to return for the funeral. My mother's death was more gradual. I returned home for that, of course. I still have a clear memory of her lying on her deathbed, her skin dry and thin like old wallpaper. It was the late seventies, and you know what's funny, Middy? My first thought upon seeing her was that I could probably carve a painting onto her skin using only my fingernails."

"Oh, I thought you were talking about Zainab when you said 'horrible woman'."

"Don't start," Bridget snapped as she took a seat at the table. "This is not what I want, for your father's paintings to be another weapon in the family arsenal. The past is dead. When I moved to Baghdad, I never looked back. My encounters with the British in Iraq reminded me why I had left."

"And you didn't regret leaving?"

"Not once." She studied her daughter's face. Mediha had dark bags under her eyes, and the edges of her hair were frayed and unkempt. Her daughter looked so British, Bridget realised, as if she had removed any shred of her Iraqi DNA.

The microwave beeped. Mediha took out the chicken and placed it in front of her, steam rising from the puckered skin. "I'm not very hungry, Middy. I'll just have some tea."

"A bite won't kill you."

"If you had just sold the paintings years ago like I told you to . . ."

Mediha sighed and leaned against the counter. "I was *organising* them. When I took them out of Baghdad they were a mess! So disorganised, no information, and every time I looked at those paintings awful childhood memories returned."

Bridget scoffed. "You make your childhood out to be so terrible."

"Mum, don't open a door you're not willing to walk through."

Bridget pushed her plate away. "Ishtar could have helped you organise everything."

"If Ishtar found out I was in Baghdad with the British government when I took the paintings out—"

"It's not like you were on the front lines, you were a Gender Advisor for the Foreign Office for God's sake."

"In Ishtar's mind I might as well have been rounding Iraqis up for slaughter. The work I was doing was good, those women needed help. You know as well as I how the Iraqi woman suffers . . ." Mediha cleared the food away and began to wash the dishes. "Besides, reckoning with the paintings was something I had to do for *myself*, to process my trauma." She worked the sponge hard at a rim of grease. "And it's been healing. My exhibition speaks to this, tracing a line between the false glories of the past and the present nightmares. An excavation of sorts, to root out the deep-seated rot at the core of the country, the core of our family." Mediha turned around and stared at Bridget, as if expecting a reaction, but Bridget only sighed and looked away. "One of us must tell the truth in our art, and God knows Zainab's little trinkets and Ishtar's reification of the past aren't going to do it. This worship of legacy is how we got into this mess in the first place . . ."

Bridget studied her daughter's face for signs. Could she have known? They had sworn to keep the secret, even though Rajiha had not been happy about it.

"Enough with all this," Bridget stood up.

"In any case, *I* was the one who sacrificed my life to get those paintings out . . ."

"Oh how dramatic—"

"I could have gone to jail! I could have been slaughtered, Mummy!"

"I suppose that's what we get for trusting Rajiha to take care of the paintings . . . I should have known she would be handing them out willy nilly as soon as I left the country."

Mediha turned off the tap and dried her hands on her trousers. "What is it with you and Amma Rajiha?"

"That woman was simply awful to me from the moment I arrived," Bridget said, relieved the conversation had taken a turn. "That first summer in Baghdad was a killer, and I was glued to this rickety old fan that blew hot air in my face. Rajiha would laugh at me as I dragged it from one room to the next. But one thing I *will* give her is that when I first arrived, she taught me how to prioritise my art. She was home with us all day but refused to help with the chores. She insisted *she* was an artist too, that her time was just as valuable as your father's. She'd spend all day painting."

"Painting what?"

"Painting Sumaya, the house girl. She was working on these mythological portraits of modern Iraqi women as Mesopotamian goddesses. Sumaya would model for her. They'd spend hours in Rajiha's bedroom."

Mediha left the kitchen to set up Bridget's paints, and Bridget returned to the past. It was true that Rajiha had been terrible at times, but she had also shown Bridget that to exist in Baghdad, a woman must fight for her independence. And it was with that in mind that Bridget asked Haydar for a map of the city, one month after she had set foot there. Haydar explained that there were no city maps of Baghdad, as the government had banned their creation to prohibit the organising of riots and protests. So she asked him to draw one for her, with routes she could take on her own. The next day, armed with her make-shift map, Bridget had packed a small bag of things, taken a deep breath, and—ignoring Mama Fatima's frantic cries—walked out into the blazing light.

* * *

Back at her easel, Bridget closed her eyes and tried to re-imagine the building. She had been walking by the river with Mama Fatima the first time she saw one of the traditional buildings with the teakwood structure.

"What is that?" She asked in her broken Arabic.

"An old qasr," her mother-in-law replied. "They'll tear it down soon."

Bridget pointed to the building's ornamented wooden balconies, engraved with geometric shapes and calligraphy. "What are those?"

"Shanasheel," Mama Fatima said. Later, Haydar explained how they worked. The protruding wooden structures on the frontal facade of the buildings was an ancient technique to facilitate sunlight and airflow, keeping the rooms cold while also maintaining privacy and natural lighting.

Bridget opened her eyes. Slowly, she brought her hand

towards the canvas. She made a few rough strokes, then a few more to denote the geometric shanasheel on the windows. How many of the old buildings remained today? When she'd first arrived they had already begun to be demolished. That had always been part of Baghdad's charm, Haydar once told her, how routinely the city shed its skin in endless cycles of destruction and reconstruction. But through this, much had been lost. She saw it with her own eyes. Westernised architecture had become more popular, teakwood no longer as cheap to import, and no records were kept of the ingenious architecture that incorporated functionality within their design. That was why, not long after arriving in Baghdad, she began to paint these old buildings.

The heat demanded an early start. When she heard of buildings that were scheduled to be demolished, Bridget rushed to the site at dawn and quickly sketched, anxious to record what she could before the wrecking ball obliterated them. Many were already in disrepair, their wooden frameworks rotten and sagging, and she maintained this in her sketches, rendering the weight of history and the phantom lives that had been lived inside the building's walls. Like Henry Moore, she found inspiration in timelessness—weathered buildings, chipped artefacts, whitened bones. She'd believed she was inscribing the buildings into history, maintaining a record of them long after they were gone. By mid-morning she would return to the studio she shared with Haydar in the family home, and would work all afternoon to refine her sketches, drawing and redrawing the same lines to perfect the dimensions and angles, stopping only when Haydar returned from work.

Now here she was, decades later, painting alone. Her wrist ached with a small tremor that had lately set in.

"So foolish," Bridget said out loud, adding more brushstrokes to her canvas, roughing the forms, steadying her arm against the easel. "Believing I was travelling through history.

Excavating the past, preserving its lessons, uniting it with the present in some transcendental bloody union . . ."

"You weren't foolish." Haydar's voice was in her ear. A cool ripple crossed the back of her neck, and her brush stopped midair. "You showed me how to see my world through fresh eyes."

On her canvas, the old building came to life. Heat rose off the brick, traffic pressed at the windows. Out of her strokes the voices gathered—first muffled, then clear. The angular voice of Ibrahim, Haydar's closest friend, a sensitive Palestinian painter whose existentialism was both a cause and consequence of his depression. He had been one of Palestine's countless poets and painters exiled and unmoored after the Nakba, drifting between rooms as if the ground were provisional. Haydar and he were inseparable, hosting soirées in Ibrahim's room or else talking for hours in smoke-filled cafés about classical poetry and modern painting. Aisha's throaty laugh rung in her ears. Aisha, the Kurdish poet, who always wore a thick coat of red lipstick and was never without a cigarette in her mouth. She brought it to her ruby lips as she prepared to recite a poem. The air smelled of arak, sour and sharp. Haydar had told Bridget it was lion's milk, and she took a big gulp and the world spun. Never again. The sharp smell of aniseed mixed with the thick smoke from Ihsan's pipe. He was always with a pipe in his hand, thought it made him an intellectual. He tapped it on a saucer and produced grey petals of ash. He called himself a communist, though his ideology was nothing more than an outlet for his misanthropy.

The image of Ihsan fizzled. "That horrible man," she muttered to herself, rubbing her forehead. He would go on to become Haydar's biggest public critic, something Haydar could not understand and would spend too much of his time trying to appease.

Should she warn them of their fates as she sat among them

now, in Ibrahim's room off Rashid Street? How Aisha would die of lung cancer around the time of Abdel Qasim's assassination, how Ibrahim would last until the nineties. Bridget recalled their last conversation. She had called after hearing about his ill health, and Ibrahim had lamented the misguided optimism of the Palestinian leadership and the Oslo Accords from his home in Amman. And Haydar, how could she warn him of his fate? Should she interrupt their conversations in that small and dusty room, their debates about the past and future, their explorations of deep and meaningful questions about the world and their purpose in it, just to tell them they would die? No, better to stay silent as the existentialists argued that art was about exposing the individual's path to freedom, while the communists claimed that artists had an obligation to take art out of the private sphere and put it back in the realm of the people. Those more classically trained made the case for art as a reflection of the beauty of the world. They all spoke in Arabic and the language washed over her. She had only been in Baghdad a year and Haydar translated some of the conversations, but inevitably he was sucked into the discussion. One night she had interrupted the conversation out of curiosity, and Rajiha scolded her on their way home.

"If you want to be part of our life, you must learn Arabic. Don't allow yourself to just be the British wife."

Bridget took those words to heart. She began spending her afternoons studying Arabic, and insisted others only spoke to her in the language. By the end of her first year in Baghdad she could follow conversations, and they were impressed when she joined the conversation. While Haydar was a big-picture thinker, Bridget had an eye for precision.

They were all so earnest, Bridget thought as she dipped the paintbrush in some turpentine, correcting an uneven line on the building's latticed windows. So filled with the optimism of youth.

Why were these memories returning? Why was the past coming to life now, intruding into her ever-diminishing present?

"You must know where you come from to know where you are going," she heard Haydar whisper in her ear. She looked around, but she was alone. She smiled to herself, and remembered how, in that small hotel room off Rashid Street, he showed the group of artists al-Wasiti's paintings, reminding them of the Mongol's destruction that ushered in centuries of darkness.

"As Arab artists, we should not fear European modernity," Haydar told the group. "But it is incumbent on us to dig into our past, to rebuild the link that was broken centuries ago, and develop a balance between past and present, ancient and modern."

"Why must we always look to Europe for answers?" Ihsan derided him.

"Haydar is right," Ibrahim replied. "We shouldn't reject European modernity for the sake of some imagined authenticity. Such a thing doesn't exist and never did. We have to find a way to embrace all techniques and styles while remaining rooted in our own history."

Bridget decided to speak up, in Arabic, for the first time.

"If Matisse can utilise elements of al-Wasiti, if Picasso can draw on primitive Iberian art, African art, and Post-Impressionism, and in the process take the first steps towards the development of what we now call Cubism, why can't Iraqi artists also draw inspiration from wherever they desire?"

Perhaps she should not have spoken, not given Ihsan the ammunition he so desperately sought, but she was blinded by cosmopolitan idealism, and her brief interjection spun the conversation into other examples of Europeans—from Moore to Pollock—who had utilised ancient works from around the world.

The group talked well into the night, drunk on arak and the possibilities of the future, planting the seeds of the movement: a new direction for Iraqi art that embraced modernity, while also rooting itself in Mesopotamia's past.

When they returned home that night, Bridget only managed two hours of sleep. The moon was full and bright, illuminating the entire room. Haydar was not beside her. Softly, she called out his name. When there was no response she left the bedroom, feeling herself drawn to their shared studio. The door was shut. No light emerged from beneath the crack.

She opened the door. Haydar was sitting on a stool in the dark. He was naked, his elbows resting on his thighs as he observed the empty canvas across from him. His genitals hung limply between his legs. His pose would have been comical were it not for the severity of his expression.

"Is everything okay?"

"Go to bed, my darling. I'll be there soon."

Bridget was suddenly aware that she too was naked. She looked down. A trickle of Haydar's semen had dried along her inner thigh. At any moment Fatima or Rajiha might catch her standing naked in the hallway, without even a sheet to protect her modesty.

The tremor in her wrist brought her back, and she looked up from the canvas. Haydar was standing by the window, looking out at the silhouette of the hedges Mediha had trimmed the week before. In his reflection, the spotlight she used to illuminate her canvas drew shadows across his face, deepening the lines between his brows that appeared whenever he was lost in thought.

"You mustn't put too much thought into what Ihsan says," she told him now.

Haydar turned to her. "This anti-European stuff is just . . ."

"He will use anything to criticise you."

Haydar sighed. "I feel lost in a world of unforgiving duality," he said, turning back to the window. "It's like I've fallen through the cracks between al-Wasiti and Picasso, between sculpture and painting, between Iraq and Europe. I wish I could forget everything I have read and learned, so I can begin to understand my true self . . . to connect with the emotions in my soul rather than the ideologies in my head."

Bridget longed to walk over to him, to hold his face between her hands and touch the rough hairs of his beard which had begun to curl. But she had grown old, and he was as young as the night she had seen him in their studio. She recalled how vulnerable he had looked, sitting naked in the darkness, and how she watched him silently from the darkened corridor feeling a sudden, powerful urge to protect him.

She turned back to her painting and examined the brushstrokes. Were the tremors noticeable? Her brushstrokes had once been so precise, so thoughtful and planned. When she was younger, she had taken for granted how easily she could move and breathe and talk, how powerful her body was.

But more powerful than their youth was their conviction. In the early fifties, flames could be felt in the tone of conversations. The British impact in Baghdad was deeply felt and the war had left Europe in ruin, but artists everywhere searched through the devastation, looking for answers, for hope.

Where was this hope now? Where was this belief in the power of the past?

As she inspected her paints, she thought she heard the not-child's cries. She mixed a shade of okra for the window frames and crimson for the doors, the only splashes of colour in a painting she wanted to keep a ghostly sienna. She mixed the paste together with a splash of turpentine and linseed oil to beat the paint, to keep the not-child away. What had triggered its cries, this harbinger of lost hopes, this soul whose existence was known only to her? Why were the dead returning now, when the living couldn't stand to be around her? Mediha treated her with contemptuous obligation, Zainab hardly visited, Ishtar never called. The last time they were all together had been an unmitigated disaster. After Zainab had stormed off, Ishtar spent the rest of her stay distracted and on edge. She spent most of her time reading news about ISIS on her phone, and after three days abruptly announced that she had to return to London. Something in Ishtar reminded her of the darker side of Haydar in the last years of his life, in the late fifties, when everything fell apart.

She recalled waking early one morning during her second summer in Baghdad. The room was imbued with the bluish tint of dawn. Though her body was tired her mind was wide awake. She knew that if she got up she could make her way to the riverbank and work solidly for several hours, powered by solitude and the coolness of early morning. She listened as Haydar's gentle snores marked the passing of time.

She pulled herself out of bed and tiptoed down the stairs. The door to their shared studio was ajar, and rustling sounds came from inside. Bridget poked her head around the door.

Rajiha and Sumaya were in a passionate embrace. Rajiha was kissing Sumaya's neck, and Sumaya sighed as her fingers ran down Rajiha's bare arm. They held each other with a familiar tenderness that made it clear this was not the first time. What to do with this knowledge? She wished she had never seen it.

She turned to Haydar now, who was staring out at the gentle rain with a quiet smile on his face.

"Did you know Rajiha's secret?" she asked. "I never told you. I wasn't sure if I should have."

Haydar shrugged. "Perhaps I never really knew my sister. She was blissfully happy during that time, was she not?"

The door swung open.

"Painting time is finished!" Mediha announced. "Time for bed."

"For God's sake Middy, knock before you come in."

"Who were you talking to just now?"

Bridget turned to the window, but Haydar was gone. Mediha drew the curtains then picked up the stack of brushes.

"I'm not finished!"

"You can finish when Zainab is here."

Bridget stood up and snatched the dirty brushes from her daughter. She turned on the tap to rinse them, and as the water gushed forth, a flood of memories washed over her. Working side-by-side with Haydar, consulting the works of Matisse and Moore, photographs of Assyrian and Babylonian artefacts that Haydar came across in the museum. Their conviction in showing the world the works of their new movement, a public exhibition, yes. They had worked hard all year, Bridget and Haydar in the lower studio, Rajiha in the upstairs bedroom—the music of Dinah Shore and Farid al Atrash seeping through the floorboards. The exhibition would be a watershed moment, a turning point for the country's state of the arts and an opportunity to introduce a marriage of modern schools—from Cubism to Expressionism and even Surrealism—with local styles and subjects.

"We're the civilisation of Gilgamesh, the world's first story," Haydar coached the group. "Our art should tell a story too."

A phone rang. Bridget turned off the tap. Behind her, Mediha cursed under her breath. "Hello? Yes . . . she said she would bring . . . oh that's ridiculous. Well, I'll be there first thing tomorrow . . . hang on—Mum, I'll be back in a minute."

Bridget turned around. Sand everywhere. The room was engulfed in a storm of yellow dust. She felt herself choking. Who had opened the window in the middle of a sandstorm? Bloody Rajiha . . . Bridget had long suspected her sister-in-law of entering their studio and stealing paints and brushes without asking. But a sandstorm in Scotland? Bridget was getting confused. And the paintings, oh dear, just a week from the exhibition and they were covered in sand . . .

"Rajiha! Did you go inside our studio?" She had yelled up the staircase.

"I ran out of white," Rajiha's voice floated down through the house.

"But why did you open the window?"

"The smell of turpentine was too strong."

"Well the bloody sand has ruined my painting."

The sound of footsteps, sharp and angry. Then Rajiha's round frame at the top of the stairs, her hair pulled back, her apron stained with paint.

"You think you can just come into my house and tell me what to do?" Her sister-in-law shook her finger at her. "You really are so British, aren't you?"

The fissures between Bridget and Rajiha grew. Also twenty-one, Rajiha was coddled and over-protected. She always had a long list of demands for Haydar as soon as he walked through the front door. Did you buy me the cherries I asked for? Can you take me to the supermarket in an hour? We've been locked in this house all day, can't you take us for a stroll along Abu Nawas? Haydar agreed to these demands with patience and a sense of unquestioning duty. When Bridget tried to speak to him about it, he simply shrugged.

"She copies your style too," Bridget had once said. "The series she has for the exhibition, the Mesopotamian goddesses, those lines and curves are straight from your pieces."

"She's my sister. She learned painting through me."

A palpable excitement had charged the exhibition hall in Bab al-Sharqi. Journalists and writers were present, as well as other artists, members of the diplomatic corps, and a few politicians. Haydar's beard was trimmed for the occasion. When he took the stage he delivered his speech in an Iraqi dialect. It was a purposeful performance. Though he looked confident as he approached the microphone, Bridget noticed the subtle shaking of his hands. She did not understand everything he said, but she knew the beats, recognised the important words and phrases: new school of painting in Iraq, combining western techniques with the unique character of Mesopotamian civilisation, rebuilding the broken link with history, celebrating life's joy and sorrow, the everyday spirit of the people, reaching the hearts of the masses through the visual image. Afterwards, the guests moved through the works. An older man approached Bridget.

"Are you the artist of the architectural works?"

Bridget pointed to the four paintings of the old Baghdadi buildings that hung beside a work of Ibrahim's. "These? Yes."

"I'm the dean at the architecture department at the university. Your work is very evocative. You have an eye for structure, for detail."

Haydar came up beside her, and she introduced the two men.

"Have you ever thought of teaching?" the dean asked.

She agreed to visit him the following week. As the dean walked away, she turned to Haydar. A large smile was drawn on his face, his eyes sparkling with pride.

"Do you think Mama Fatima would—"

Haydar squeezed her hand. "It doesn't matter what she thinks."

The critics were divided. Many celebrated the exhibition's fresh perspective, the marriage of modern styles to ancient techniques. One review described the exhibition as "a portal that brings the ancient civilisation of Mesopotamia into the modern world." Bridget's paintings were praised, with one writer describing her series as "a beautiful and necessary reminder of what is lost in our pursuit of a hastened modernity."

Others were more cutting. One critic faulted Haydar's reliance on al-Wasiti, an artist "far too obscure to be influential or worthy of revival". Another remarked that Surrealism and Cubism were too bourgeois and abstract to be relevant to the realities of everyday Iraqis.

It was Ihsan who launched the most vicious attack. Ihsan, who had been in that dusty hotel room when the group first embarked on their shared journey, penned a scathing three-column piece with the headline: *A New Frontier for Imperialism?* In it, he accused the group of too much abstraction and blasted them for creating an art that was not serious enough, was too vague in its intentions, and thus easily coopted.

"The danger of such art is that it may affect the emotions and safety of the working classes, becoming yet another tool for propaganda and foreign influence." Haydar's voice trembled with anger as he read the article out loud.

Ihsan went on to write that many of the artists had studied in Europe and now saw Iraq through European eyes. Worst of all, the piece questioned whether Haydar—having married a British woman—might have helped this imperialism take root.

"Why are British painters even allowed to present in an Iraqi exhibition? Our politics and economics are controlled by Europeans, must our art be the same? Perhaps it is no surprise then that the weakest works belonged to the artists married to the foreigners."

The article sent Haydar into a state of muted despair. It was clear that Ihsan had been planning this attack long before the exhibition opened its doors.

"I welcomed him into my studio," Haydar said as he stewed in the bath, absent-mindedly scraping the paint from underneath his fingernails. "For the last several months he was by my side, encouraging me . . ."

Later that evening, as they lay in bed, sentences and phrases from Ihsan's hit piece floated in the air above their heads.

"Perhaps I could talk to him," Haydar said softly. "To understand why he was so cruel."

"It's natural for an exhibition to get some criticism."

"That man has absolutely no passion for life. He talks about what it means to be Iraqi as if it is a thing you frame and hang on a wall. That's not what culture is. That's not what history is. Culture and history are ever moving, ever shifting. Something that is lived in rather than worshipped unchanged."

"You aren't a traitor, Haydar. You know that . . ."

"That's easy for you to say. Your works have received universal acclaim . . . they got you a job at the university!"

Bridget sat up in bed and gripped his arm.

"You *cannot* let these critics harden you."

"I'm not hardened—"

"A danger with carving out new paths is that you don't know where you are going or what you may find. There is always the chance the path leads nowhere, that years of work amount to dust. That's the risk of being revolutionary."

That night, they had promised one another to always remain vulnerable, to each other and to their art. Bridget would recall this promise years later, as she watched Haydar pick up mounds of soil and shove them into his mouth, and she would wonder whether the vow they had made that evening was the seed of her husband's future madness.

Two days after the exhibition, Mama Fatima asked to speak to Bridget. Fatima was weaving textiles while sitting on the old swing. Bridget took a seat beside her. They were shaded by a large tree with dates so abundant they could never eat them all, and often had the Hadaqchi scoop them into bags to distribute to the neighbours.

For some time Mama Fatima did not speak. Bridget watched her mother-in-law work, occasionally providing an extra pair of hands to steady the scissors or fabric.

"I've sent Sumaya back to Mosul," Fatima finally said, without looking up from her work. "So, I will need you to help around the house more."

"What happened?"

"The girl has not been working well these last months."

Bridget hesitated. "Is this about Rajiha?"

Fatima pretended not to hear this. She asked Bridget to hold the edge of the piece of cloth she was working on. When Fatima spoke again, the conversation took another turn.

"In the months before he died, my husband lived with a heaviness in his heart."

Bridget was surprised by the mention of Haydar's father. Few topics were off-limits in the family household, but one was the patriarch's sudden and unexpected passing.

"Every time he got up or sat down, he sighed as if heaving a bag of stones. Sometimes he sat in silence, staring into space. He began to smell very badly. I put powders and jasmine on his clothes, but the rotten smell spread through the house, entering rooms before he did and leaving long after. It was as if he had already died and his body was rotting."

A cloud moved past the sun, casting a large shadow over the garden.

"He never spoke to me of what happened during his imprisonment in Istanbul," Fatima said, "but he returned a different man. He was considered a national hero while I was just a seamstress who could not read or write, though he never forgot that I saved his life, that I had thrown myself in front of the carriage. He tried to manage the pain in his heart through his paintings. Some days he made beautiful, swirling colours from the pain. Other times, the empty canvas sparked flashes of terror, and he would abandon it and start to drink."

The cloud passed, the garden once again bathed in sunshine. The rotting dates glistened on the ground.

"It is difficult to love an artist," Fatima continued. "They are selfish creatures. An artist might lie, cheat, and steal with the belief they are creating something more important than a single life. To love an artist, you must have an even stronger belief in the power of art. An artist's lover lives with the heat and smoke of the fire, but the light falls elsewhere."

The sound of rattling lifted her from the garden in Baghdad. Bridget turned to the window. The wind was driving the rain sideways. One of the windows had flung open, the others shook in their frame. Bridget rushed across the room. She could not have sand coming in. The painting was still wet, the dust would cling to the paint, smudging the lines she had painstakingly drawn.

"Rajiha!" Bridget called out. "How many times have I told you about keeping the windows shut!"

Outside, the horizon was a thick haze of yellow fog. But was she in Scotland or Baghdad? She was no longer certain, and as she shut the window she caught a glimpse of her reflection in the glass. White dust was caked around her eyes and mouth. Her hair was blonde, not grey, her skin taut and youthful.

Her legs collapsed underneath her. Her arms reached for something to stop her fall, but her body crashed to the floor.

"Rajiha!" Bridget yelled, or maybe it was a mangled cry. She could not be certain because there was pain now, an orchestra of nerves shooting through her body.

* * *

Had she been painting? Bridget turned her head. The easel had toppled over and her half-finished painting lay face-down on the floor. Yes, she had been painting. Before the storm, before Rajiha opened the window and let the sand in. Now the painting was ruined. This is why they had to move out of the family home. Not to mention Mama Fatima, following her like a shadow and making that awful scraping sound as she dragged her bad leg behind her on the tiled floor, asking questions every time she left the house. Stubbornly wed to tradition, she had set out to find Rajiha a husband after sending Sumaya away, settling on an older man who had lost his wife to tuberculosis, someone desperate enough to overlook Rajiha's unfortunate face so long as she was young enough to bear children.

The marriage took place in the autumn. On the day of the wedding, as Bridget and the other women prepared Rajiha for the ceremony, she turned to her sister-in-law and said: "I wish Sumaya were here to see how beautiful you look."

Rajiha caught Bridget's eye through the mirror and looked away.

Two weeks after the wedding, Mama Fatima passed. It was as if she held on until she'd ensured her daughter had a man to secure her future.

She should have held on a few weeks longer. One morning, less than a month after the wedding, Bridget was startled by a banging on the front door. Rajiha and her husband were on the other side. The old man, incandescent with anger, shoved Rajiha into Bridget's arms.

"She's not working," he spat. "I want a divorce."

Bridget took Rajiha into the living room and made her a cup of tea.

"What happened?"

"He woke up yesterday and asked me to cook dolma. But with Mama gone, I don't have to pretend anymore. I told him that I do not cook, and that I do not clean either. I then told him to go to the store to buy me some paint."

Bridget couldn't help but laugh and Rajiha laughed with her. By mid-morning, Rajiha had set up her canvas and begun work on a series of paintings featuring a husband and a wife, a feverish creative journey that would last six months.

But the laughter that briefly united them that morning did not last long. Without Sumaya and Mama Fatima, there was nobody to blunt the sting of Rajiha's snide comments, her rolling eyes and deep sighs, and, of course, the veiled accusations wielding Bridget's Britishness against her. British this, British that, coming in to tell us how we should run our affairs.

"The Bridget mandate, that's what we live in."

"Oh, shush, you're dead," Bridget was crying now, crying on the floor for poor Rajiha, dying alone and half-insane during the brutal sectarian fighting, the final remaining root in Iraq's soil. "You've been dead for eight years, your body's worm food—"

Had Rajiha ever reunited with Sumaya? Had she fallen in love again?

Had she told Mediha the truth about Haydar?

"Mediha."

The quivering of her voice embarrassed her.

She tried to get up but her legs wouldn't move. Mediha would return and see her on the floor, shake her head, tell her not to get up without assistance. She would finally assign her to the wheelchair she had been threatening her with, and her humiliation would be complete.

"Get up, pick yourself up, don't cry."

That's what she told the girls when they fell. She had been harsh with them, strict but never cruel. Was this why they were all so bloody miserable, estranged from her and each other? No, they knew she always had their best interests in mind. And look how things changed, how the roles were now reversed and Bridget was the stubborn infant, the helpless child. Her lips twisted into an ironic smile as she considered how strongly she now clung to motherhood, a role she fiercely resisted when it had been thrust upon her. Prior to her pregnancy she had wanted to be a mother in the abstract way one might want to one day write a novel or travel the world. But, when a dizzying nausea had overcome her on the bus to work one morning, the dread she felt surprised her. She got off the bus and ran to the nearest store, a bookshop on Rashid Street, where she begged the shop owner to let her use the bathroom.

When she emerged from the toilet, the shop owner looked concerned.

"Would you like some water?" Recognition dawned on his face. "Aren't you the wife of the artist Haydar Mathloum?"

Bridget was overwhelmed with pride. Her husband had become known, not just within artistic circles and those who orbited them, but more widely. But, as this emotion stirred inside of her, another, more insidious one took its place. She had become the artist's wife.

The pregnancy gave them the perfect excuse to move out of the family home and away from Rajiha's demanding ways. Haydar dedicated the summer and early autumn of 1953 to renovating the new home, a two-storey villa on the west bank of the river in the 'New Baghdad' neighbourhood of al-Mansour.

The house was smaller than the old family home but proved to be a cocoon of creativity. Meanwhile, political turmoil churned in the city's streets. Haydar followed the debates closely and was passionate about the need for greater freedoms. He was critical of British hypocrisy, which preached the virtues of democracy on one hand while stifling it with the other. It was impossible to stand in silence while prisoners staged hunger strikes against inhumane conditions, and the government shut down cafes and newspapers where dissenting voices congregated.

Alongside the uproar on the streets, Bridget's body faced its own rebellion. In the first three months she barely left her bed. Was the child staging an insurrection against her, or was Bridget's body rebelling against the unexpected occupation?

"We've got a revolutionary on our hands," Haydar joked when Bridget complained about the nausea. He said this with pride but he was also worried about her health, disquieted by the public rhetoric. He urged the group to keep this in mind as they prepared for their second exhibition.

"Let's connect our work more closely with the lives and concerns of people on the streets," he suggested, Ihsan's criticisms still seared in his mind.

The pregnancy interfered with Bridget's ability to work. She vaguely continued her architectural series, focusing on the intricate geometries of the shanasheel, but her artistic drive disappeared, redirected to another type of creation.

Summer arrived, and the sun grew more oppressive. The

garden stewed with heat and dust. Bridget was so nauseous she could barely move. She thought of the small life inside her, and the one that came before. The not-child was a sacrifice, she realised, a martyr to her creative life. A door banged open and she waited for Mediha's voice, but it wasn't Mediha, no, it was Haydar, he had returned home with a large watermelon under his arm. He split it, and the sickly-sweet smell filled the room as he excitedly relayed the goings-on at the institute where he taught and joyously described the developments of the sculpture he'd been working on. Juice ran down his chin as he talked, and a thought she did not choose touched her; a yearning, shameful and cruel, for the sight of the red juice on her husband's chin to release the child inside of her, much like the chicken had done three years earlier.

Fuelled by the excitement of fatherhood, Haydar's productivity soared. One day in early November, in her fifth month, he took her to the Institute to show her the finished sculpture, which was inspired by the prisoners' protests. The metal work was composed of a series of geometric shapes influenced by the crescents and lines of Islamic art, alongside columns and bows and spheres.

Bridget circled the piece, studying it. The metal spheres were suspended in the air, held in place by wires that connected to the columns, suggesting that their natural state—to be in motion—was itself an illusion. It was a sophisticated work, abstract and complex, bringing to mind feelings of entrenchment and rootlessness, the illusion of freedom, and the shackles—both political and personal—that kept individuals imprisoned.

"I wanted to explore freedom and captivity in a more abstract sense," Haydar explained. "Is freedom our natural state, or is its unattainable struggle the purpose of life?"

Bridget turned her back on the sculpture and looked out the window. The water levels were high after an unexpected week of rain.

'Aren't you the wife of the artist Haydar Mathloum?' she heard the shopkeeper's voice in her mind as she felt Haydar's eyes on her back, awaiting her verdict on his sculpture. That was not the first time she was referred to in this way. She had first come across it in Ihsan's piece years earlier: *The artist and his British wife*.

"I think it's brilliant," she finally said, unable to look her husband in the eye. And the sculpture *was* brilliant. It would remain a favourite of hers, one she would reflect on many times in the decades that followed. But in that moment, she was unable to divorce her appreciation from the resentment she felt with this body of hers, a body that no longer belonged to her, that was now just another of Haydar's sculptures, one he was molding with his calloused hands just like he did to the clay and wood and metal that gathered in his studio.

A few weeks later, in a newspaper article about an exhibition opening they attended, there was a photograph of the two of them standing at the entrance. The caption, in Arabic, read: *Haydar Mathloum and wife, at exhibition, 1953*. Bridget read it twice, then looked at her face in the photograph: the thin smile, the inward-gazing eyes, the face puffy with pregnancy.

Haydar Mathloum and wife.

The roots of her jealousy were deep. She had aspired to be Matisse, had studied his techniques and life closely, but she was not Matisse. She was his unknown wife, Amélie.

While standing in the exhibition room during the opening of the group's second show she fielded questions and remarks from attendees, all of which centred on the creature in her belly, its sex, and the date it was due to be expelled from her. Her melancholic shanasheel paintings hung largely ignored, a fitting testament to their subject. How had this life inside of her inspired her husband, yet left her so bereft? She could barely focus on Haydar's words in his opening speech.

"In our first exhibition, an old friend and dear critic called us enemies of the people. He advised the Iraqi people to resist our dangerous art. Perhaps he is right, and it is our art that is responsible for the hunger on the streets, for the ninety per cent illiteracy rates, for the horrible conditions in the prisons."

Haydar's sculptures were universally praised, winning prizes worldwide. In her final months of pregnancy, his schedule sent him around the world, from biennale to symposium, and though he was hesitant to leave her she urged him to go. The small art movement born in Ibrahim's dusty hotel room three years earlier grew by ten and then fifteen. Even Bridget, swollen and nearing full term, found her inspiration renewed.

In early spring, as Baghdad was threatened by a great flood and the government debated whether to evacuate the city, her water broke. She could feel it now, lying on the cold floor, the water between her legs extending up her back and down her thighs. As the army placed sandbags and a mountain of soil to protect the city from the unpredictable waters, Bridget lay in a hospital room with Haydar by her side. Grunting and screaming she felt feral and alive, and from the destruction of her body and selfhood emerged a radiating, expansive joy.

She never saw it coming.

Ishtar came into the world like a storm, burning with a fury that Bridget struggled to recognise in either herself or her peace-loving husband. Their daughter was dark pink—almost purple—her fists clenched and her body taut, her mouth in a permanent scream of despair.

Motherhood. An oxbow in the river of life. Bridget marvelled at the child. She would never create something as beautiful or complex with her paints.

As a baby, Ishtar was a menace. She wept all the time, barely slept. Bridget was constantly tired. Lying on the floor now, she wondered how much of Ishtar's stormy nature was due to the timing of her birth, or whether she was simply taking after her namesake. One time Bridget left her screaming in the bedroom as she sat in her studio, painting defiantly and stewing in resentment. She hated her baby and suspected the feeling was mutual, that her child was purposefully keeping her from her art. She believed her creative life was over, and the only way she could get it back would be to pick the baby up, take it to the river, and drown it. It was a fleeting thought. Was it the reason Ishtar hardly came to visit, the reason she always complained about the family's debt to her, as if blaming Bridget for bringing life to her in the first place, for birthing her in a country that would later fall apart?

When she gave birth to Zainab three years later, the contrast couldn't have been greater. Zainab was a beacon of serenity. Calm, eager to please, quick to smile.

"Mum? Mama!"

No, she did not want to return. She wanted to stay in that simpler time when Haydar was still alive. She missed him so much, missed how his devotion, unlike her own, presented itself without paradox. She could do nothing but watch as the birth of their second daughter unleashed in her husband another swell of creativity. How quickly he set to work after each of their daughters' births, exploring new ways of understanding this precious link between the past, present, and future. Bridget loved and envied him for it.

"Oh God. What happened? Why are you on the floor? It's okay, just relax. Let me help you up. There you go. Oh, you wet yourself. Shh, Mama, don't cry. It's going to be okay."

* * *

"My water broke! Middy, we need to go to the hospital."

"You just had a little accident."

"Is the baby okay?"

"There is no baby, Mama. It's just pee."

"But I can hear it."

Past and present clarified, if only for a moment. Bridget was not pregnant. She was old and she was dying.

"I'm tired! I'm tired of this prison!"

Those were his words after the heart attack. He had been on his way back from an excavation in Ninewa when it happened. He was sentenced to several months of bedrest. No teaching, no travelling, no sculpting. His life became confined to the bed, the television, the trays of food brought to his room. This new reality obliterated his world.

"I'm tired of this prison," he wept.

Bridget assured him it would get better. She told him that for the time being he would have to explore the world in his dreams. A flippant remark, meant to assuage his claustrophobia, but it stirred something inside him. The next day, when she brought him breakfast, he was in better spirits.

"Modern culture demonises sleep," Haydar said to her. "Wasn't it Lenin who once remarked that revolutionaries are the last to sleep and the first to wake? But living in your dreams is a revolutionary practice of its own. It is more powerful, more hopeful, than living in one's memories."

If the solution to Haydar's disquiet lay in his dreams, then his view of sleep needed to change, he explained. He approached dreaming as an apprenticeship, drinking various teas and potions rumoured to facilitate the potency of dreams, and keeping a journal on the nightstand into which he recorded his dreams every morning.

As the Cold War experienced terrifying shifts, the streets of Baghdad were gripped with repression and fear. But in their two-storey house in Mansour, a humble serenity prevailed. Haydar's dreams had opened a portal to a new dimension, connecting him to the collective subconscious of the whole world.

Mediha squatted beside her, and Bridget felt herself being lifted. She was in the air now, her body levitating through the room.

Waves of riots. Legacies of impunity had caught up to the British, but the Iraqi people would pay the price. The breaking of shackles: Egypt, Algeria, Syria, a new path was possible, one of freedom, of reclamation.

"You should go to London until things calm down," Haydar had said. "I worry for you and the girls."

"I'm not leaving."

Throughout all this, bedridden, Haydar painted his dreams. Scenes of everyday life: street musicians, men toiling in the field, children eating watermelon, women in black abayas carrying jugs of water on their heads, a portrait of a Baghdadi bride and groom. Abandoning three dimensionality for a more abstract and playful two-dimensional vision, he relied on geometric shapes, teardrop faces and triangular necks, each shape in harmony with those surrounding it, an explosion of colour, a series of paintings he referred to as *Qayloulat*—siestas.

She was being lowered now, felt the softness of the armchair on her skin. She turned her head. Mediha was carrying a mop, a fresh pair of clothes, a wet sponge.

"Do you remember how you fell?" Mediha said.

"Rajiha opened the window. I stood up to close it and—"

"Mummy, Rajiha is dead."

"She never agreed with our decision, Middy."

"What decision?"

"And she's *furious* about it."

A month before the revolution, Haydar felt well enough to take short walks in the neighbourhood. His energy was returning, and *Qayloulat* came to a natural end. The final painting in the series, the last of his life, was *Woman Dreams by Water*. Weeks before he had spoken to her about a recurring dream, an image of a woman taking a nap on a rooftop. He had tried sketching it many times, but nothing he produced satisfied him. One afternoon he woke from a deep nap and painted all night at a feverish pace. In the morning, he called Bridget into the studio.

And there she was.

The woman was sunbathing on the roof of a typical Baghdadi home. Her hair curled around her body like a black wave as she lay beside a pool of water, presenting herself to the sky. The woman had just come out of the bath; brushstrokes rendered the rush of blood to her skin. The woman's body twisted towards the viewer, the triangular shape of her breasts juxtaposed with the curve of her hips and the flow of her wild hair. Beside her was a cat, staring at the viewer with a white-hot gaze.

One day, Bridget was sitting with the children in the garden when they heard shouting in the streets. She brought the children inside and called Haydar at the institute. There was no answer. A neighbour knocked on the front door.

"Stay home. There are mobs targeting foreigners."

Dread thickened as she listened to the radio in the living room. The military had seized the airways. An announcement declared the liberation of the Iraqi people from the corrupt government that had been put in power by the imperialists.

Two hours later Haydar arrived home, excited and terrified.

"King Faisal is dead. I saw his body with my own eyes."

He explained how the entire royal family had been rounded up, showered with bullets from a machine gun and dragged through the streets. The body of the Crown Prince dangled from a balcony. The King was strung from a lamppost.

"I believe in General Qasim," Haydar said. "But the way this unfolded . . . I don't know."

"The violence of it . . . it's bloody barbaric."

Ishtar, not yet five, looked up from the piece of paper she was painting on.

"Bloody is a bad word!"

Haydar shook his head. "It's as if in every act of creation, we plant the seeds of our future destruction."

The phone rang. It was Ihsan, the critic from long ago. They hadn't spoken in years.

"Would you like to speak to Haydar?"

"No need," came Ihsan's voice, full of abrasive confidence. "Just pass on a message: all these years he has been talking about the art of the common people. Go out on the streets. This is the art of the common people."

Chaos, conflicting information, unverified news. The British embassy in flames, the ambassador and his family fleeing to a suite at the Grand Hotel. The prime minister shot and buried, an angry mob digging up his body, hacking his corpse, dragging the pieces through the streets while cheering crowds held up pictures of Gamal Abdul Nasser. An obliteration of the old order. But strewn within were glimmers of hope. Feudal lands confiscated and redistributed to peasants. Schools and clinics opening in dilapidated towns and villages. Bridget studied court hearings on the television as the new government put on trial hundreds of people accused of plotting against the country. To survive, she had to understand the logic and language of the new powerholders.

* * *

"We were wrong, Middy," Bridget said as her daughter pulled a clean dressing gown over her head. "We thought the past would guide us, that hope was possible even in the darkest of times. I warned him, you know. I warned him not to do it."

"Warned who?"

"After the revolution, you see, your father got this idea. To create this magnificent piece. He believed in the new republic. He felt that artists had an obligation to imagine a new future into existence. The new government called him in. We knew it was going to happen, by then he had made a name for himself. They wanted a monument to honour the revolution. He didn't hesitate."

Mediha walked to the window and dipped the mop into the bucket of soapy water. Swirling the mop on the floor, she cleaned up the puddle of urine that had begun to soak through the floorboards.

"When your father came back that day and told me, I lost it. I told him 'You're not well, Haydar. You only just returned to work.' I said, 'The children need their father.' Those were my exact words. And you know what he said? He said that his country needed him too, that this project was much bigger than him. He knew even then that he would create something that would outlive us all. But at what cost?"

Bridget wished she had found a way to make Haydar reconsider. She had thought about it many times, desperately searching for the precise arrangement of words that would have stopped him from pursuing the project. But he was persistent. He had in mind a monument that would tell the story of Iraq from the times of ancient Mesopotamia up to the current moment. Just as *Guernica* had captured the horrors and pain of the Spanish Civil War, he sought to create an Iraqi version.

In his first meeting with the General, Haydar explained how the monument's structure would be modelled on a Sumerian cylinder seal made up of bronze sculptures, with a total length of about forty meters and a height of seven. They gave him seven months. An impossible timeline. But Haydar agreed, on two conditions. First, the monument would not be iconoclastic. Second, it would not be hung too high. It was important for people to be able to examine the details up close.

"And if children climb it?" The General said.

"Then that would be a sign the monument was alive," Haydar replied.

The next day, Haydar received a phone call requesting that a statue of the General be placed in the centre. He refused.

When the officers called the next day, Haydar hesitantly agreed to depict the central figure in the monument as a soldier in uniform, breaking free from the chains of history. A compromise that satisfied them for a few weeks, but soon the calls came daily.

"I'm not a politician," he complained to Bridget after another anonymous call threatened him with exile if he did not include an icon of the General. "I don't understand the games they play."

Bridget struggled to pinpoint the moment Haydar's descent began. Some of his colleagues informed her that at a faculty meeting in March 1959 Haydar appeared 'tense', 'nervous' and 'irritable'. His handwriting had changed from long elegant swirls to scratchy and almost unintelligible scribbles. At home, he was quiet and lost in thought. Occasionally, in moments of silence, he suddenly spoke to himself.

"Oh God," he muttered once, the words steam rising from a pressure valve.

"What?"

"Huh? Oh, nothing."

One evening after making love, Haydar trembled in her arms.

"Do you believe that violence is innate to the human spirit?" he whispered.

"I'd like to think not," she replied.

"I was watching Ishtar play with her building blocks," Haydar said. "She built the blocks into a tall tower and then kicked it and laughed as it fell. She did this many times, and each time the tower fell my heart fell with it. She took more glee in the act of destroying the tower than she did in creating it. I asked her, 'Why must you destroy the tower?' but there was not an ounce of guilt nor regret in her eyes."

"Have you decided what you will call the monument?"

"Yes," he said, tracing his thumb over the mole on her left breast, a habit he started years earlier and which seemed to calm his mind. "I think I will call it *The Symphony of Hope*."

Funding delays deepened his despair. The government had provided an initial sum for materials, but Haydar needed more, and the ministry kept assuring him the money was on its way. Throughout April, he called the ministry daily to inquire about the money. He grew resentful and paranoid. By spring's end, he gave up hope that the money would come and was financing the cost of the monument from their savings.

A conspiracy began to take shape in his mind. A global conspiracy, one maintained by the Iraqi government, linked to both the USSR and the CIA, and bound to end in world destruction. He studied the radial distances from central Moscow and Washington DC. He calculated that two bombs sent within minutes of each other would tear the world apart. When he wasn't working, he feverishly followed the news. One hot August evening, Bridget found him tossing their clothes from the wardrobe onto the floor.

"What on earth are you doing?"

"I need your help," he said as he climbed in, the wooden panels creaking under his weight. "Shut the door, please."

"Haydar . . ."

"Darling, just shut the door."

She sighed and pushed the wardrobe doors shut, entombing Haydar inside. She watched the final stream of light disappear from her husband's face. Inside, she heard his breathing, slow and heavy. She sat on the bed and waited. He emerged ten minutes later.

Bridget thought of calling the doctor, the institute where he worked, or even the General himself. But creatively, Haydar was making progress. Though he spent the nights pacing his studio, accusing close friends of being spies or saboteurs and preventing Bridget and the children from leaving the house, she could see the monument being birthed into existence.

Date harvesting season came and went. While Haydar worked, Bridget finished a painting of a group of men—gathering their dishdashas between their legs—as they climbed the trees to gather the sweet fruit, capturing the swiftness and ease with which they ascended the trunk with their bare feet and a wide leather strap around their waist. It was the only painting she had completed that year, and the last she would complete for some time.

By October, the different pieces of the monument were finished and spread out on the ground like a jigsaw puzzle. The date of assessment was at the close of the year, and all that remained was to assemble the pieces together. Haydar's anxieties turned ever more inwards.

"I'm nothing but a charlatan who has recycled old ideas and stolen the techniques of others. That bull over there," he pointed to one of the sculptures on the ground. "That's from *Guernica*. Look, the closer you examine it the more obvious it becomes. And what about that mother and child? Henry Moore."

"That's not true."

"And all these 'nods' to Sumerian civilisation? It's just theft. Nothing original."

"But you've created something new. Isn't that what art is about? We've been saying this for a decade now. Building on what has come before."

"I want to forget everything I've learned!" His scream reverberated through the house. In the living room, Zainab began to cry.

The more Haydar studied the pieces, the more anxious and despondent he became. Nothing Bridget said could change his mind. He begged her to take the kids and leave him. He blamed himself for bringing this darkness into their lives.

"You don't deserve any of this."

Some days he wept in bed. He clawed at the sheets, screamed into the mattress, bit the pillows. Bridget sat by his side, gently stroking his hair. Hot tears streamed down his face as he hugged his body into a ball, wanting to make himself as tiny as possible, to disappear into the earth.

"Maybe you should see someone," she suggested.

He shook his head and wept. The weight of his life felt too much to bear, he told her, the probability of destruction too high.

One morning in November, a thick fog enveloped the city. Looking out the windows, Bridget could see only the faintest silhouette of the palm trees in the garden. The air was warm and wet. Haydar demanded they shut all the windows in the house to keep the fog from coming in.

"The mist will eat at the foundations of the house," he remarked as they stood watching the encroaching greyness.

That night in bed, Haydar spoke of his father. He missed him terribly, he confessed. He then asked if she believed that anxieties could be inherited from previous generations.

"This might explain why Iraq has so much pain inside her."

The next morning, while Bridget prepared some eggs and basterma, Haydar drank his coffee and stared out of the window into the garden. She watched from the corner of her eye as he ran his fingers over the tabletop. He examined the film of dust on his fingertips, brought them to his nose, then his lips.

"The soil," he whispered in Arabic, turning back to the window. He stared at the dark bed of the vegetables she had planted the previous spring. "My father's in the soil."

Haydar placed his cup on the kitchen counter and walked outside in his bare feet. From the window, Bridget watched him take off his pyjamas and sink his bare knees into the wet earth. He grabbed two clumps with his hands and studied them, then brought the soil to his nose. He scratched at the soil so that the dirt embedded itself under his fingernails. He rubbed it on his cheeks and through his beard. He knelt, put one side of his head to the ground as if the earth was whispering to him. It was not until he began eating the soil that she called the hospital.

"Mama, let's get you to bed."

Mediha helped her up. Bridget took a few uneasy steps, her legs faltering.

They sedated him right there in the garden. With Zainab and Ishtar by her side, Bridget watched as they wrapped Haydar in a white straitjacket and put him in an ambulance. Bridget drove behind with the children, crying the entire way. During the psychiatric exam, Haydar was unruly, spouting conspiracies about the end of the world and the coming periods of endless violence.

He had been hospitalised for a week when it happened. She had been looking through the monument's assessment report when she received the call.

"What do you mean you found his body in the river?" She screamed into the phone. "No, it's not him. He's in the hospital."

What was he doing by the river? He was such a good swimmer, how could he have drowned? She hung up, convinced a mistake had been made, and it was this conviction that allowed her to turn off the stove, wash her face, and take the children to the neighbour's house before getting in the car and driving to see him.

"Middy," Bridget said, as Mediha slowly walked her to bed. "Did you know that before your father's body was taken away, his students asked to make a mold of his face. I watched them pour plaster over his head, into the creases of his skin, the crevices of his eyes and nostrils, the thin line between his lips, and I . . . well, I began to scream."

"That must have been so upsetting," Mediha squeezed her arm. "What I still don't understand though—what I never understood, really, was how he could have drowned."

"He drowned. I saw the body."

"Yes, but did he *intend* to drown?"

"What do you mean?" Bridget tried to hide the panic in her voice. Why was Mediha asking this?

"Everyone said that he was such a good swimmer. I remember Rajiha telling me how as a teenager, Baba would often cross the length of the Tigris and back every morning. The more I think about it, the less sense it makes . . ."

Bridget had been sitting with Rajiha in the hospital waiting room, the both of them sedated, when the men arrived. Kuteiba met with them in Haydar's room for forty-five minutes before emerging.

"The government have asked us not to reveal the truth about his death," Kuteiba said.

"What do you mean?" Rajiha asked.

Kuteiba reached into his pocket and pulled out a cigar tube.

"This was in his coat. They found it with his body."

He handed the tube to Bridget. She opened the cap and pulled out a single piece of paper that had been rolled up inside. She glimpsed the first words, immediately recognising Haydar's handwriting. It was his old handwriting, long and elegant, as if his decision had brought him some final clarity and peace of mind.

My darling Bridget, this is the only way we can put an end to the anguish I have put us through. I don't expect that this—

The letter fell from her hands. Beside her, Rajiha screamed.

"It's a question of legacy," Bridget heard Kuteiba say.

"A tragic drowning," Kuteiba said, or was it Bridget saying this now to her youngest daughter, insisting on the myth they had built? "That's the story. If the public were to find out, what would it mean for the monument which is intended to signal a bright future for the country? How can we instil hope in citizens when its creator saw no escape but through death?"

"No," Rajiha cried. "We have to tell the truth."

As Kuteiba and Rajiha fought over Haydar's legacy in the hospital waiting room, Bridget understood, then, that she and Haydar had been following a lie their entire lives. Memories of the past can so easily be changed, misremembered, manipulated. Hope was a road to ruin.

"I'm going to give you something to help you sleep," Mediha said as she pulled her mother's legs up on the bed, positioning a pillow under her feet. "Zainab is coming tomorrow. You need to be well-rested."

Oh, to strip the present of its past.

"Why haven't you sold them yet?" Bridget heard herself cry, and Mediha shushed her gently. "I just want to get rid of those wretched paintings. They've been haunting me for years!"

Hope had destroyed him. In a cruel world, hope was a road to madness.

"Did he tell you what he wanted the monument to be called?" Kuteiba had asked her, after the story of Haydar's death had been settled.

"He called it the Symphony of Fate."

This lie, folded within the creases of others, provided closure to the subject that contained unanswerable questions, questions of why tragedy selects its victims, of what could have been done to prevent the inevitable, of the fate of the fools who trade in hope.

The days passed in a haze of chores that blurred into one another: hanging the laundry outside, collecting the dates that had fallen in the garden, bathing the children, teaching, going to the bank. Bridget took pride in maintaining her stiff upper lip. At certain moments, while cooking for the children or standing in line at the post office, she momentarily forgot her heaviness. But then—just as suddenly—the grief returned, crushing all other emotions until she was choking back tears.

Some afternoons she heard the not-child's cries echo in the empty house, and a sudden panic would tear through her lethargy. She'd jump out of bed and follow the sound of the crying, entering Haydar's studio where the sound appeared to originate, and find nothing. The sound would then come from the kitchen, but there was nothing there either. She'd turn on the radio to drown out the cries and return to bed, but the not-child's cries continued into her dreams, and she woke up in a cold, sickly sweat.

To stifle the cries, she focused on finishing the monument. Without Haydar, she drowned in detail. She stared at the pieces scattered on the floor of the large industrial warehouse, unable to find the sequence of events, the timeline of history. When the monument was erected in the centre of Baghdad amidst a chorus of celebration, Bridget barely recalled a thing beyond the vague warmth of the bodies beside her that held her as they wept for him.

Mediha pulled the blanket up to Bridget's neck and opened the bedside drawer. She took out a bottle and shook two pills into her palm.

"Open your mouth, Mum."

Mediha pressed the pills past Bridget's lips. A glass touched her mouth, and the water carried them down. Again, she heard the not-child's cries, a reminder of what had been hidden, of what had been purposefully unremembered.

In the first two months after Haydar's death, she was so lost in the fog of grief that she hardly noticed the life growing inside her own body.

"Is that why you are so sad Middy?" she said, as Mediha kissed her forehead. "Because I was so grief-stricken when I gave birth to you?"

"We both know why I am sad, Mum."

Coups came and went, wars were declared. Unable to paint, she devoted her time to Haydar's legacy. It was a way to keep him alive. They loved his work in Paris and London, and she took it upon herself to speak about him. Her Britishness came in handy, her fair skin and perfect English bestowing a legitimacy not granted to Rajiha. The children stayed behind and Kuteiba was happy to care for them. He took her and the girls under his wing. Bridget hardly knew him at the time; he had appeared in and out of their lives while he was in the military. When she did meet him, as he passed through the city between postings, she had found him handsome and charming, though underneath there was a darkness she chose not to acknowledge.

One morning in the late seventies, Bridget woke up with a film of dust lining her mouth and was filled with a sudden loathing for Baghdad. She blamed this country, with its arduous politics and stubborn people, for taking her husband away. She blamed the river. But most of all, Bridget blamed herself. She remembered one of the first things Haydar had said to her when she arrived. His voice, soft and playful, in her ear. "This city is like a giant oven in a perpetual sandstorm."

Bridget opened her eyes.

"Haydar, is that you? Are you there?"

"Mama, it's me, Mediha."

"Mediha." Tiredness came over her. "Oh, Middy. You never did meet your father . . ."

To leave Baghdad would be to abandon the canvas she and Haydar had spent their lives painting. But one by one, the girls left. Secretly, Bridget blamed herself. Believed it was her quiet acquiescence that had driven them away. Yet she stubbornly remained. As the war with Iran rolled through the eighties she worked part-time for the Ministry of Culture, going through the films and books coming into the country, reading them and identifying those deemed politically sensitive or insulting to the government. It was cynical work, but she had become cynical.

Mediha turned off the bedside lamp. Bridget heard her footsteps recede as she walked towards the door.

"Middy," she called out.

The footsteps stopped. "Yes?"

"Your childhood wasn't all bad though, right? You had Ammo Kuteiba. You and he were close."

Mediha was quiet for a long time. When she spoke, her voice

shook. "He was a fucking monster. Don't you remember how he beat Ishtar?"

"He beat Ishtar?"

"You certainly have a selective memory. He broke Ishtar's jaw."

"But it was just one time. He was beating the artist out of her, Middy. I couldn't let what happened to your father happen to her . . ."

"Beating the artist? Are you mad?" Mediha slammed the door behind her, the darkness closing over Bridget once more.

"It's the freewheeling, the disobeying. That sort of thing was too dangerous then," Bridget said, though she was now speaking to herself. "That's why I had to get you out so fast when you took those pills. I couldn't let history repeat itself. And so what if the paintings were sold? We had nothing but your father's legacy. Why not sell it to those who could afford it? How else could we eat? And then there was nothing, not a painting, and I just had to leave."

She remembered the day in November 1992, when she had taken a private taxi to the border with Jordan, wearing a black abaya. As she passed through passport control, the officer looked at her papers.

"You're the wife of Haydar Mathloum, right? The Symphony of Fate!"

He stamped her passport. Behind him, a portrait of Saddam caught her eye. He stared straight into her soul.

Part III

Carcasses of Home

The years stretch out in front of us
Blood and fire
I forge bridges with them
But they become a wall.
—Badr Shakir al-Sayyab, *City of Mirages*

Ishtar

October 2014

It was past midnight by the time they arrived at the guesthouse in Hasankeyf. The owner, a Kurdish man named Murat with a mane of curly hair, showed them to their rooms.

"When can we see the boats?" Ishtar asked as Murat handed them their keys. Weeks ago, she had asked him to procure some goatskins to build a kalak. Meanwhile, she had contracted a few fishermen from Baghdad to build the guffa, insisting that it had to be constructed in Iraq with reeds and tar, and be shipped by land to Hasankeyf.

"Tomorrow, when the sun is up."

Despite her tiredness, Ishtar only managed a few hours of sleep. She woke before dawn, nervous and excited. All her past projects had led up to this, rivulets feeding into an expansive sea.

She pulled out a folded piece of cardboard from her bag, the beginnings of a painting inspired by the epic of Gilgamesh. She had started it thirty years earlier, when she was still living in Baghdad and dating Nisreen.

In the centre of the painting she had drawn her namesake, the goddess Ishtar, bare-breasted and covered in jewels. Beside her were Gilgamesh and Enkidu fighting the Bull of Heaven, their locks of hair entangled. Along the borders, Ishtar had wanted to draw miniature scenes documenting various moments in the epic: Gilgamesh's early beginnings and his encounter with Enkidu, their adventures together, Enkidu's sickness and death, and Gilgamesh's quest for eternal life. But not long after Nisreen had left Baghdad, Ishtar abandoned the painting. The unfinished piece had haunted her for decades.

She walked through the guesthouse and made her way outside. The stars were out in force and there was a chill in the air. Ishtar wrapped her shawl around her as she sat at the breakfast table underneath a giant pomegranate tree where large, maturing fruit hung precariously from the branches.

She picked up the book she had brought with her on ancient Mesopotamian civilisations. Turning to the index, she searched for the word 'Dreams'. She read different sections on how dreams were understood in the melancholic world of Mesopotamia. In the Epic of Gilgamesh, dreams held a prophetic power. They were a source of knowledge and foresight, a communication channel for the gods.

The sun began to rise, clearing the mist from the valleys. Ishtar closed her eyes and breathed in the cool air. She could smell traces of the river, the wet earthiness of its bed. The smell of her childhood, of Baghdad. She had spent most of her life grieving Iraq from afar, until she was no longer sure whether she was mourning the country's destruction or her own irreversible estrangement. It was time to face the grief head-on.

A young man appeared with a pot of Turkish coffee, which Ishtar drank as she wrote down a list of what they still had to do. The list helped to siphon off some of the grief in her soul. It was not just exile, but loneliness too. A natural consequence of having devoted herself to her art. It took up all the space in her life and more, spilling over onto those around her.

Lily had said this to her the night she moved out. By then, she bore no resemblance to the fresh-faced twenty-eight-year-old Ishtar had met at the talk she gave at Whitechapel Gallery. Lily had shyly approached her. They shared several drinks at a nearby pub before Lily agreed to come back to the houseboat, where she stayed for the next two years.

The first eight months had been bliss. Lily was enamoured with Ishtar and followed her around like an apostle. She worked for the council three days a week, which gave them enough money to eat and drink and purchase the necessary equipment for Ishtar's work, meaning Ishtar was no longer reliant on family handouts. When Lily was not working, they spent their time on the boat: making love, cooking, talking about the disasters of global politics, and working on Ishtar's mixed media project inspired by US drone footage from Pakistan and Yemen.

Then slowly, Lily withdrew. She smoked more dope, began accusing Ishtar of demanding too much from her. She was spending all her free time running errands, she complained, and barely had time to pursue her own creative work. "Even if I did," Lily added, "your eyes glaze over anytime the conversation drifts away from your own projects."

It wasn't that she held no interest in Lily's work. Lily was talented, though Ishtar questioned whether the world needed another young, white artist with mother issues. It was just that Ishtar was busy, and her drone project was so expansive, so all-encompassing. If Ishtar didn't devote every waking moment to the project, it would collapse. Besides, wasn't Lily learning by observing Ishtar work, by seeing first-hand the way her mind connected different ideas and concepts? It was a privilege, she wanted to tell Lily. It was an *honour* to shadow an artist like herself so closely. People paid for this kind of apprenticeship.

One evening, Lily broke a wine glass against the cabinet and threatened to slash her wrists. A neighbour called the police. Ishtar didn't know how she managed to find these broken creatures, whether there was some magnetic field that drew them to her, or whether she was the cause of their damage somehow.

And then Lily left. She said she needed to get out of London for a while, wanted to be with her mother in Belfast. Ishtar was miserable for weeks, didn't leave the boat, threw herself wholeheartedly into the drone project, mapping out flight paths and gathering information on the victims' lives in obsessive detail. When Lily finally returned it was only to collect her things. She told Ishtar that being around her felt like being sucked into a black hole. "I've lost myself in you," she had said tearfully.

And so what, Ishtar thought as she stared out at the mountains, her eyes drifting down to the river below. Now that the mist had cleared she could see it, a shimmering liquid silver. Why shouldn't Ishtar centre her own creativity? Besides, her art was serious, complex, multi-dimensional. Her art was the zeitgeist that no one even knew was the zeitgeist because most people were idiots. No one had ever shifted Ishtar's immoveable focus on her art. Not Lily, not her sisters, not even her mother. Only Nisreen had done that.

Just after nine, Nizar finally emerged.

"The prince awakens," Ishtar said, looking up from the map of Iraq she was examining.

"Morning," her nephew mumbled, sitting across from her. Large reflective sunglasses covered his eyes.

"You look like some Blackwater schmuck with those shades."

Nizar removed the glasses. By now the sun was bright, but the sky was patchy with clouds.

"I love the smell of freshly cut grass," Nizar remarked, taking a sip of coffee.

"It's the smell of trauma."

"Huh?"

Ishtar turned back to her map. "The smell of freshly cut grass is a chemical distress signal that the plant is injured."

"Right . . . Is Nisreen arriving today?"

"End of the week."

Murat emerged from the house with a tray of food and joined them for breakfast. The guesthouse was built in Murat's family orchard, and as they marvelled at the view he pointed out the caves that had been etched into the mountains centuries ago.

"Do people still live in them?"

"Very few," Murat replied. "The government ordered families to leave the caves in the sixties. They said it was dangerous, though I think the government feels it's barbaric for people to live in caves."

"It's not actually dangerous though, is it?" Ishtar asked. "Living in the caves?"

"When I was a child, a large rock fell in front of the mouth of one of the caves, blocking the entrance. A family was inside, no one could get them out. For days, we heard them screaming." Murat took a sip of coffee. "On the tenth day the screams stopped."

When they finished breakfast, Ishtar asked to see the boats.

"I have good news and bad news," Murat said, leading them down a dirt path along the side of the guesthouse. "The good news is that the boat from Baghdad arrived."

They turned a corner to find a small clearing, where the guffa was laying on its side against a tree. Ishtar inspected the vessel. Murat and Nizar held their breath.

For a few moments, Ishtar said nothing. She circled the guffa, knocked on its side, ran her fingers along its curvature. A single tut emerged from her mouth. More tuts followed, like drops of rain in a gathering storm. Finally, she spoke.

"The curvature is not high enough. The guffa should curve inwards. This is like a giant Easter egg basket. And a traditional guffa should have a very specific layer of material . . . plaited reeds, which are then covered with a layer of liquid tar, two layers of bitumen, then a layer of lime and clay. This one has no lime or clay, and there's only one thin layer of bitumen. This won't be waterproof."

The bad news awaited them in the shed. Murat's large frame appeared shrunken as he led them back towards the garden.

"For the other boat . . . the raft," Murat said as he climbed the hill, "We got the goatskins, like you asked . . ."

"But?"

"There was a problem."

Murat stopped at the shed and opened the door. The smell hit them immediately. Ishtar used her shawl to shield her nose and mouth from the stench. Nizar gagged.

The shed was dark, illuminated only by the slivers of light that peeked through the wooden slats of the walls. Murat flicked a switch, turning on the naked bulb that hung from the ceiling. The goatskins were stacked in a pile in the centre of the shed. Above them circled a swarm of flies, buzzing furiously at having been disturbed by the light.

Ishtar gasped and ran towards the stack. She stuck her arm inside the mess of rot and flesh. Soft and viscous, the skin seemed to melt in her hands.

"Didn't you tan the skins to preserve them?"

Murat shook his head. "We don't have the materials here."

Furious, Ishtar marched outside and pointed a finger covered in blood and slime at the pomegranate tree in the garden. The skin dripped like wax down her arms.

"Pomegranate peel," she snapped. "You tan skin by using pomegranate peel."

"We'll get more goats!" Murat said, sprinting back to the guesthouse.

Ishtar returned to the goatskin. She watched in stunned silence as a single maggot pushed its way through the top layer of skin, writhing until it broke through the rotting flesh.

Six days and seven nights I waited
Until a worm crawled out his nose

Ishtar strode out of the shed, stumbling through the uneven grass until she was safely concealed behind a wall. She crouched down, bit her fist to stop the tears. Perhaps the past really was dead. There would be no regaining what had been lost. Time, in the end, provided the true perspective. They had so little of it left, so little time.

Time did not do what we planned.

Zainab had said that decades ago. New Year's Eve, 1981. Their uncle had asked why they were late, and Zainab had said, softly, "Time did not do what we planned". Ishtar had been taken aback by the strangeness of the phrase. She loved the simplicity of it, imagined time as a companion with them that night, wild and impossible to tame. And it was while she chuckled, imagining this, that her uncle punched her. For the rest of Ishtar's life her jaw would click unpredictably.

"Ishtar . . ." Nizar was by her side.

"Those poor goats . . . killed for some great ideal. Now just a feast for worms!"

Her gaze retreated inwards. She was in the underworld, with no way out. Everything she touched would rot and die.

"We can't build a guffa right, we can't even tan goatskin. We've forgotten everything. There's no salvation for us."

"We'll figure something out . . ."

"Don't you understand?" She grabbed his arm and looked him in the eye. "We're no longer in the cradle of civilisation. We are in its corpse."

Zainab

October 2014

Standing at the front door of the cottage, Zainab felt the drops of rain slide down her neck. It was almost five in the afternoon, the skies had opened on the drive from the airport, but Zainab hesitated to go inside.

Mediha stood at the door, smirking. "Are you just going to stand in the rain all night?"

Zainab stepped inside and took off her coat. She removed her boots, reached inside her bag and pulled out the thinking putty. Kneading it in her palm, she was pleased with her little companion.

"All this darkness and rain. I bet this feels like the underworld compared to Dubai . . ."

"I think that's the nicest thing you've ever said about Dubai."

Mediha ignored Zainab's comment. "I'll be out of your way in a moment, I don't want to eat into your time with Mama."

"I'm here to see you, too, Middy."

Mediha's face, hard and angled, looked up at her. "I actually need to head out in a bit, I'm spending the night in Edinburgh for some last-minute prep. I was waiting for you because I didn't want to leave Mum alone. She . . ." Mediha paused. "Shall we have some tea?"

She led her to the kitchen, making small talk about the changes she had made to the house since Zainab's last visit. Zainab glanced at the closed door to Mediha's bedroom. She was certain the paintings were in there.

As they sat at the kitchen table, Mediha put her mug down

on the table and took a deep breath. “I wanted to tell you about Mum,” she said, her eyes fixed on Zainab. “To prepare you.”

“Prepare me?”

“She had a fall yesterday. Not serious, but . . . she wet herself. And she’s been saying things.”

“What kind of things?”

“I could have sworn she was yelling at Rajiha last night. Her memories of things are all muddied.” Mediha pulled a piece of paper from her back pocket. “Here’s her medication schedule. She insists she can follow it and will get angry if you try to remind her, but just keep an eye out in case she misses anything. Oh, and . . .” Mediha paused. “She wants to feel independent, but she’s not. She has a fridge in her room and she won’t let me clear it out. But there are lots of things in there—cheeses, yoghurts, cold meats—that sometimes go bad. I forgot to check it last night, so if you get the chance to do so without her knowing—”

“Without who knowing?” Bridget appeared at the door wearing a white nightgown.

“Mama!” Zainab stood and embraced her. Bridget had aged rapidly in the four months since Zainab had last seen her. She had lost weight too. Her body felt frail and bony, the muscles in her arms like putty.

“Middy, why’d you let me nap for this long? It’s dark.”

“It’s not that late, Mum. They changed the clocks last weekend. Remember?”

Bridget turned back to Zainab. “How was the flight, habibti?”

“Great, fine.” She kissed her mother on the nose. “Had a good nap, sleepyhead?”

Bridget smiled and nodded.

“I’ve prepared the guest bedroom for you,” Mediha said.

“There’s no need. I’ll sleep with Mama.”

“Are you sure?”

"Absolutely. If she lets me."

"It would be a pleasure," Bridget said, beaming.

"That's settled then," Mediha stood up. "Alright, I'll leave you both to it."

As Zainab watched Mediha's car drive down the cobbled path, a sudden euphoria rose inside her. Alone in her sister's house, she felt like a child trespassing. The feeling reminded her of being young in Baghdad, when she and Ishtar would sneak into construction sites at dusk, after all the workers had gone home for the day. They crawled up pieces of concrete and makeshift ladders to explore the half-finished rooms, careful not to get caught on the mangled metal rods that coiled out of the walls. She'd often collect materials from these sites, nails in funny shapes, old pieces of wood and tile which she sometimes turned into collages.

"What are you smiling about Zainab?"

"Oh, I'm just happy to be here again."

"I'm glad you arrived safely, I was worried about you. There are mobs targeting foreigners out there."

"Mobs?" Zainab had heard about the rising xenophobia but hadn't realised it had gotten this bad. "Are you sure?"

"That's what the neighbours—" Her mother stopped herself. She seemed disturbed by something. "Never mind."

In the living room, Zainab's eyes were drawn to a photograph on the bookcase: her parents standing by the shores of the Tigris. Her mother had a cigarette in her hand, baby Ishtar on her hip. Their father stood with a leg on a circular-shaped boat. It looked like it had been taken in the mid-fifties. Everyone looked young and happy.

"Do you ever think much about Iraq?" Zainab asked, turning away from the photograph. She grabbed her bag and curled up on the sofa beside her mother.

"I have a few memories."

"What kind of memories?" Zainab fished through her bag.

In Dubai airport she had purchased a slim, clip-on digital recorder to ensure that any conversation with Mediha would be recorded. She would not allow her sister to manipulate things further. She also wanted to record her mother's memories, and as Bridget began to speak Zainab pulled the recorder out of the bag, turned it on, and placed it discreetly in the space between them. All her life, Bridget had cherished her stories, tending to them like flowers in a garden. Now, Zainab would ensure they survived long after her mother was gone.

"Just memories," Bridget said. "What's funny is that my memories have been returning lately. Sometimes they feel more real than life." Her mother paused. "Do you remember much about your father?"

How could she admit that her lasting memory of her father was of him being held down, restrained in the garden by three men in white coats? How she distinctly recalled the sound of him grinding his teeth, how the men had to squeeze the bridge of his nose to stop him from breaking his own jaw.

"I have some memories of Baba, but only from the months before he died."

"You can't have your image of him sullied by that period."

"Tell me more, then."

Her mother began to speak. The memories flowed organically, linked together by a particular smell, a specific person, a common emotion. Zainab listened as her mother spoke of a time long before she was born, a time when her parents first met in London, of her mother's first few years in Baghdad. Bridget spoke until she began falling asleep in her chair, at which point Zainab stopped the recorder and took them both to bed. In the corner of her mother's studio, Zainab saw an unfinished painting, one which filled her with an unexpected sense of hope. As she slipped under the sheets beside her mother, she pulled the duvet to her chin, and felt, in some uncertain way, that she had arrived home.

Zainab woke to her mother's warm body nestled beside her and carefully slid out of bed. In the kitchen she made coffee and opened the door, flooding the room with a bluish light. Bracing herself against the cold, she lit a cigarette and inhaled deeply. She burned through the cigarette, careful to blow the smoke out the door. When she finished, she dropped the butt into the sludgy remains of her coffee and turned around. Her mother was standing behind her.

"Mama! You scared me."

"I was wondering who was rustling about the kitchen in the middle of the night."

"It's nearly eight in the morning."

"I suppose that's not a bad time to get up."

Zainab made more coffee. While it brewed, she looked through the fridge and pulled out a selection of cold meats, tomatoes, cheeses, and bread, which she laid out on the kitchen table where her mother sat.

"We don't need to eat *her* food," Bridget said, standing up. "I've got some wonderful stuff we can eat."

Zainab recalled Mediha's words about the mouldy items in their mother's fridge. "Maybe tomorrow," she said, making a mental note to go through the fridge at some point in the afternoon.

After breakfast, there was a pause in the rain. Zainab suggested they go for a short walk. She wasn't sure how well her mother would be able to manage, but Bridget seemed excited by the idea. At the front door, they followed the cobbled path and made their way towards the woods. She took in a deep breath, inhaling the intoxicating aroma of damp earth that she so deeply missed in Dubai.

They walked in silence for some time. Bridget's breathing became heavy. Zainab was about to suggest they return when her mother suddenly said, "I'd like to be buried in these woods."

"Mama, I don't like talking about these things . . ."

"I don't want a coffin or anything of the sort, just plop me into the ground."

"I don't suppose Health and Safety regulations would allow that."

"Sod them."

"Wouldn't you like to be buried in Baghdad? Beside Baba?"

"Of course. But with all this stuff on the news, one has to be realistic . . ."

The forest was cloaked in silence, broken only by the sounds of birds in the trees above, and her mother's heavy breathing.

"Shall we turn back? You seem tired."

"Don't project, Zainab. I'm fine."

They continued walking under the canopy of pine. Silver droplets clung to the leaves, occasionally hitting them as they walked. The path was a glistening mosaic of green and brown stones, and in the air mist threaded through the dappled sunlight that filtered through the trees. Zainab felt she was in a dream.

"What I would really like," Bridget said suddenly, "is for you and your sisters to get along."

"I try Mama, but Mediha is not easy . . ."

Bridget laughed. "She's more British than the British, that one. I always say to people: I have one Arab daughter, one British daughter, and one daughter lost in between. That's how it works with genes. You can't control them."

"We *are* very different . . ."

"It's like trying to herd cats with you girls," Bridget said. "I made sure all three of you got what you wanted. Mediha got the UK, you got a rich husband, Ishtar got her art. I mean, you all got what you wanted, didn't you?"

Zainab said nothing.

Bridget stopped walking and turned to her. Her eyes were sharp and cutting. "Didn't you?"

"Yes," Zainab said quietly.

"Then why are you all so *bloody* unhappy?"

At home, as they took off their coats, Zainab put in motion the first part of her plan.

"Mama, do you have a hair dryer? I'm thinking of washing my hair today and I can't let it air dry in this weather."

"What do I need a hairdryer for with my stringy British hair? You're lucky you got the Arab hair."

"Maybe Mediha has one. Do you have a key to her room?"

Her mother hesitated.

"Are you scared of her?"

"Bullshit."

Bridget went into her bedroom and returned with a set of keys. She handed them to Zainab, who carefully opened Mediha's bedroom door. The room smelt of incense. Her eyes scanned the space, landing on the closet that she suspected held the paintings. She felt her mother's eyes on her as she walked to Mediha's bathroom and rummaged through the drawers. She found a hairdryer and waved it at her mother as proof.

"Good," her mother said cautiously. "Now come out and lock the door."

Zainab locked the door and handed the set of keys to her mother. Visibly relieved, Bridget pocketed them. She seemed not to notice that one of the keys was missing.

Ishtar

October 2014

The next morning, Ishtar was able to appreciate the irony. How fitting that her homecoming began with decay. The rotting goatskins held an important lesson. Things had changed. Things always changed. It was incumbent on her to adapt.

"We have three days before Nisreen arrives," Ishtar announced to Murat and Nizar over breakfast. "That should be enough time to fix the boats."

The news that emerged from Iraq filled her with a helpless, choking sensation. ISIS was advancing towards Baghdad. Military bases had been taken over, hundreds of thousands of people had fled western Iraq. Thousands of Yazidi men had been executed, and thousands more women had been enslaved. The Australians authorised air strikes. So too did the Danes. Even the Canadians were getting in on it, and the Americans gave the war a name: Operation Inherent Resolve.

The work proved a good distraction. Instead of goatskins, they tied together some old rubber tires onto which they mounted the raft. Ishtar watched as Murat and Nizar tested its buoyancy in the guesthouse pool. When the vessel floated, Murat jumped on the raft and did the Macarena. For the first time on their journey, Ishtar cracked a smile.

While the men worked on the raft, Ishtar focused on reconstituting the guffa. As she pleated and sawed, sandpapered and molded, the calamity unfolding across the border took on a soothingly abstract nature. Dismantling what she could from the existing vessel until just the skeleton remained, she revisited her sketches to understand how to fix the structure. With no palm in the vicinity, Ishtar used pomegranate wands from the guesthouse garden. Then, with the help of Murat's son, she selected long, slender wands for the guffa's body, and thicker, more robust ones for the skeletal structure. Arranging the reeds in the shape of a semicircle like the ribs of a giant fish, she lashed them together with cords, adjusting the tension to ensure the frame was symmetrical and sturdy.

Once the skeleton was complete, Ishtar began the process of weaving. She wet the wands to make them more pliable, then manipulated them through the vessel's ribs. The task was long and repetitive, but her hands moved with a graceful flow, her fingers guiding each reed into place; a meditative act that allowed her mind to drift, her memories entwining into a narrative that promised buoyancy and resilience.

It was odd to think she'd only dated Nisreen for six months. Returning from London at twenty-four and armed with a respected family name, a prestigious British degree in fine arts, and a reputable job with the Ministry of Culture, Ishtar was treated with reverence. This went some way towards confirming what she desperately tried to believe about herself: that she was brilliant and invincible.

Nisreen was the only one who saw through it all. She had a way of looking at her, peering into the inner workings of her psyche to understand not just what Ishtar was saying but *why* she was saying it. It was a talent that spoke of Nisreen's perceptiveness, her ability to detect bullshit. Ishtar was instantly enamoured.

They disagreed, fundamentally, on politics. Nisreen had little time for nostalgia, was always forward-looking, a liberal cosmopolitan. Ishtar should have known Nisreen would become one of those bootlicking Arabs of the American Empire. At the time, the intellectual sparring turned her on. They argued in heated whispers in Ishtar's bedroom, on topics ranging from the Iranian revolution to the pan-Arab project, finding solace in each other's quick wits as their passionate debates became foreplay. Political debates and sex were their points of intimacy and trust—in Saddam's Iraq, it was impossible to detect which was more subversive.

Their time together had been both a sanctuary and a rebellion. Nisreen raised questions about Ishtar's involvement with the government. Ishtar argued that she was continuing in her father's footsteps, utilising Mesopotamian mythology to help conceive of state-sanctioned sculptures and monuments. 'Don't let your creativity be manipulated,' Nisreen warned her vaguely one afternoon, as their soft lips brushed against each other, Nisreen's fingers delicately weaving through Ishtar's hair. Ishtar believed Nisreen was paranoid, which was only natural given her uncle's forced exile.

Then, after her brother vanished, Nisreen began avoiding Ishtar as if blaming her for Rakan's disappearance. Tormented by her inability to confide in anyone about the true depth of their relations, Ishtar had no one to help her understand what happened.

Bridget casually broke the news over dinner one evening.

"Did you hear the al-Asadis have moved to Paris?"

Ishtar was too shocked to say anything. For months, Ishtar mined her memories of their conversations, searching for reasons for this sudden abandonment. In the end, Ishtar concluded she had done nothing wrong. Nisreen had simply betrayed her.

That had been the last Ishtar heard of her until the mid-nineties, when an old friend mentioned that Nisreen had married an American man and was now working as a policy advisor in DC. Probably drumming up an anti-Saddam agenda under the guise of freedom, women's rights, and the restoration of the environment, Ishtar thought, the nice shiny wrappings that concealed murderous US sanctions and bombings. The moral indignation that rose up in her served as a useful reservoir for Ishtar's heartbreak, fuelling her own activism and art for the next decade.

In the winter of 2002, twenty years since they'd last spoken, Ishtar woke up to an email. Nisreen would be in London for some meetings and wanted to know if Ishtar would be happy to meet. Ishtar said yes. She was curious to see how the years had shaped her former lover. But there was something else Ishtar desired; a longing for a lost time and place, for the version of herself—young, in love, full of hope—that had been lost to time, and that only Nisreen could help her find.

They met at the rooftop bar of Nisreen's Knightsbridge hotel. Nisreen was sitting by the window, a glass of wine and a near empty bowl of olives on the table. Ishtar had hoped to catch her unaware, to have a moment to observe her before contact, but Nisreen turned her head as soon as Ishtar walked in. She smiled broadly and stood up to embrace her.

She was just as beautiful and quick-witted as she had been twenty years ago, and possibly even more charming. She had darkened her shoulder-length hair, which framed a smooth face that betrayed a lengthy skin care routine or a good doctor. She wore a white silk shirt, unbuttoned to the curves of her breasts, and navy-blue trousers. Everything about her signalled wealth.

Nisreen leaned back and crossed her arms in front of her chest. "It's been a minute," she said, a smile breaking across her face. The gap between her front teeth was still there, and Ishtar felt a pang of longing at the sight of it.

"You vanished," Ishtar grabbed an olive from the bowl and tossed it in her mouth. "I thought I would at least get a postcard."

"It was a difficult time," Nisreen said, shifting in her seat. "I see you left too. Finally got bored with preserving the spirit of victory?"

Ishtar bit down hard, the olive bursting in her mouth. "What brings you to London?"

"Some meetings."

"What kind of meetings?"

Nisreen caught her eye. "Let's talk about that later. I want to hear about you. I've been following your work."

She inquired about Ishtar's projects and listened attentively as Ishtar described the series of sculptures she had been working on. Nisreen asked to see some of her work, expressed interest in purchasing something.

"You don't need to buy anything."

"I know, but I want to. You're talented, Ishtar. You've always been talented."

"I see you're married now," Ishtar said, gesturing to the ring on Nisreen's finger.

"I am. My husband's American."

"So not a lesbian, then."

"I don't like labels."

Ishtar leant over and took a sip of Nisreen's wine. "Does that mean I'm in with a chance?"

Nisreen did not bring up her proposal until they were sat naked in her hotel bed. She rested on her side, gazing at Ishtar while turning her ring with her finger, the metal catching the dimmed overhead lights. Beside her, Ishtar sat propped against the headboard, one knee tented, the sheet to her waist. Her hand lay flat on the bed, palm open, preserving the deliberate inch of space between them.

Nisreen reached across and, with one finger, traced the curve of Ishtar's rib. "The Americans are itching for a war."

"So I've heard."

"It's not a question of if, it's a question of when. And for you, the question is whether you want to be a part of this *when,* to have a say in Iraq's future."

Ishtar stared at the clutter of Nisreen's policy papers and toiletries on the desk. "What are you suggesting?"

Nisreen got out of the bed, and Ishtar watched her naked

body cross the length of the room. She opened the minibar, pulled out a bottle of white wine and poured them each a glass before returning.

"The State Department are going to bring together Iraqis from different sectors," Nisreen said, handing Ishtar a glass. "An advisory council of sorts, for after liberation. You would make a great cultural advisor."

Ishtar lit a cigarette and looked out the window. The suite overlooked a line of expensive storefronts. A sports car sped down the road, the revving of the engine recalling two words: oil money.

"Is this why you're here?"

"I'm not in town just for you, if that's what you're asking," Nisreen said. "And I didn't just fuck you to get you to agree. But yes, I've been meeting different opposition figures here, and I thought of you."

Ishtar contemplated throwing her drink in Nisreen's face, announcing that she would rather die than accept Nisreen's offer. But to her surprise, she found herself considering not the proposal itself, but what it might open. It was not just her estrangement from Iraq that had brought Ishtar so much pain over the last twenty years. It was the estrangement from people too. Her relationships had weakened over time, falling away like leaves from a tree. Though she would never, could never accept it, she mourned the possibilities the offer held: a chance to shrink the distance between herself and Iraq, to reconnect with her countrymen on something deeper than nostalgia.

"There's good money involved. Not that this should factor into your—"

"It doesn't."

"Consider it a way to have a say in the country."

"By colluding with invaders?" Ishtar set the wineglass down too hard. The stem snapped, and wine flooded the top of the bedside table. "Oh fuck—"

"Please don't get angry, Ishtar. It's just a proposal."

"I'm not angry," she tried to mop up the wine now dripping on the carpet.

"You are a ferocious talent—"

"I know that."

Nisreen grabbed Ishtar's arm. "You have to set this moral indignation and righteousness aside. The Americans are amassing a huge coalition. Don't you want Saddam gone?"

Ishtar turned to her. "I'm not naïve enough to believe that invading and bombing a country will bring democracy and human rights."

"Well regardless of what you believe, it's happening."

Hers was a Faustian deal: accept a foreign invasion in exchange for the possibility of return. She imagined herself in a studio overlooking the Tigris, teaching young Iraqis about their country's art, liaising with a reformed Ministry of Culture to erect monuments of freedom. The daughter of Haydar and Bridget Mathloum, continuing her family's long legacy. But as the image clarified in her mind, she saw the river's black waters, littered with chemical spills and charred bodies. She pictured herself struggling to teach amidst the roar of jet planes in the sky, the militarised walls emerging across the city, the students in her class with missing limbs, her father's monument reduced to rubble—

She loosened Nisreen's grip. "I should go," she said, picking up the clothes which hours earlier had been passionately thrown about the room.

"I'm curious," Nisreen began, as Ishtar retrieved her bra from the shade of a standing lamp. "Why did you leave? What was the final straw?"

Ishtar considered this question. Was it the breaking of her jaw that New Year's Eve? Zainab's departure? Kuteiba's suicide? It was the culmination of these things and more, she realised. But if she were to pinpoint the single incident that propelled her to book a flight to London in 1986, it was the day she was called into the Ministry of Interior and reprimanded for one of her paintings, a rendering of the mythological tale of the goddess Ishtar's descent to the underworld. In the piece, Ishtar had painted a starry night. But why did the stars have six points, she was interrogated by a man who had probably never seen a painting in his life. Was Ishtar secretly inserting the Star of David in her artwork, subliminally infecting the populace with Zionist propaganda?

Ishtar did not trust this story in Nisreen's hands. She wanted Nisreen to have no part in using her memories to construct a narrative, not just about her but about Iraq as a whole. She wouldn't let her memories, her life, be misconstrued for nefarious agendas.

"There wasn't a final straw, Nisreen. I loved Baghdad. I still love Baghdad. I just left."

Over the next few months, as she marched and leafletted against the vicious invasion, the more she thought about Nisreen's proposal the angrier she felt. When Baghdad fell and television screens pulsed with footage of its skyline exploding, the memory of that evening in Nisreen's hotel suite rotted in her soul. She was furious with Nisreen, the heartless traitor, the snake, but she was also filled with rage at herself. At her own powerlessness as she helplessly shouted and protested in the streets.

A few months later, Nisreen got back in touch. She was working with a Dutch production company on a documentary about Iraq, she wrote in her email. The objective was to uncover what *real* Iraqis thought about the war. She wondered whether Ishtar was interested in being part of the film, to 'help the production team move beyond binary notions of pro- or anti-war.' Would Ishtar be interested in joining them in Baghdad?

Ishtar surprised herself by how quickly she agreed. She was

desperate to get back into Iraq, needed to see with her own eyes what she had only gleaned from media footage.

Returning would also mean seeing her aunt again. When Ishtar asked her mother for Rajiha's whereabouts, Bridget warned that their aunt was not in a good state of mind.

"Last I heard, she sold the family home and is living in a smaller place. I think she's being cared for by a family who live in the neighbourhood. Bear in mind the country is falling apart, so I don't imagine your aunt is doing any better."

They landed in Baghdad in July 2003, the day the post-Saddạm 'Governing Council' was announced. Each name was marked by the member's sect and ethnicity, a classification that suddenly shackled every Iraqi to rigid identities and divided loyalties. Nisreen and Ishtar had boarded the plane as Iraqis, but landed to find themselves as something different: Ishtar a Sunni, and Nisreen a Shi'a.

Baghdad had fallen, and the Americans were everywhere. Soldiers crawled through the streets like steroid-pumped cockroaches, a brutish weight on the city. Tanks and Humvees lurked at intersections, suffocating the streets and blocking traffic. Devastation was burned onto the faces of the people like scar tissue from an oil-fire. Jan, the Dutch filmmaker shooting the documentary, kept his camera focused on Nisreen and Ishtar as they made their way through the city.

From the very first day, Nisreen was talking shit. On camera, she pontificated about the freedom that was coming, about how Iraq was finally in the hands of its people. On the second day, she bought a dove from the market and had Jan film her releasing the bird in the centre of Tahrir Square. The dove flew into the sky and Nisreen cheered, tears in her eyes.

"I feel like this dove," Nisreen said, looking at the camera before turning her head dramatically to watch the bird's flight.

"And you?" Jan asked, turning the lens to Ishtar.

Ishtar refused to be coaxed into a fight.

"How do you feel, Ishtar?" Nisreen urged her.

She gestured vaguely to a group of men. "Ask someone who lives here."

The next day at breakfast, Nisreen told Ishtar they had a problem.

"We need you to cooperate."

"What do you mean?"

"We're shooting a documentary. We need to express ourselves. Even if we disagree—"

"We do disagree. We disagree on a lot."

"That's good. That's healthy. That's democracy."

Ishtar stood up from the breakfast table and returned to her room. She packed her things and left the hotel, then got in a taxi which drove across town to the address her mother had given her. The driver dropped Ishtar off in front of a villa in Qadisiya. At the address, she introduced herself to a young woman who explained that she was the daughter of the family caring for Rajiha.

"She won't let us clean the house," the young woman warned. "But we make food for her every day, and make sure she visits the doctor every few months."

Ishtar was taken to a shed enclosed by unkempt vegetation and weeds. A scrawny orange cat was sleeping on a rusty swing by the door. Beside it was a dying narenj tree, its brown leaves caked with a white fungus.

Ishtar gently knocked. There was no answer, so she let herself in. The shed was dark and stank of shit. Paint was strewn across the floor, as were plates with scraps of food so old they had crusted to stone. Rajiha sat hunched on a wooden chair in the corner.

"Amma," Ishtar said, walking towards her. "It's me. Ishtar."

"Who?" Rajiha was draped in an old shower curtain, the plastic sheet decorated with yellow and pink flowers.

"Your niece. Haydar's daughter."

"Ishtar?" Rajiha looked up, her face creased with wrinkles. "Did you see what they did?"

"I did, Amma. I saw."

"They've destroyed us."

"I know, Amma."

Ishtar touched her shoulders. Rajiha sank into her. A powerful smell assaulted Ishtar's senses.

"Amma, I'm just going to clean a little, okay?"

"No. I like things the way they are."

Ishtar ignored her. She cleared away the plates and old newspapers, swept the dust from the floors, and cleaned up the paint with a jar of turpentine she found on a sagging shelf. When Ishtar finished, she turned to her aunt and cleaned her, too.

"Amma, why are you wearing a shower curtain?"

"Protects against the burning. The chemicals," Rajiha whispered in her ear.

"Let me take you back with me, to England."

Rajiha smiled. "But everything I have is here."

They sat in silence for some time. Ishtar did not know what to do. Bringing her aunt against her will was impossible. Rajiha didn't have a foreign passport, and even then, how to go about pulling a tree—no matter how sick—from its roots?

"Has she forgotten the truth?" Rajiha whispered, breaking the silence.

"Who?"

"Your mother. I hope, for her sake, that she now believes the lie."

"What lie, Amma?"

"Tell her I understand. I still don't agree, but I understand."

"What do you mean?"

"I kept his letter." Rajiha pointed towards a cardboard box on a shelf. Ishtar pulled it down and opened it. Inside was a stack of letters, yellowed with age. On top was a rolled-up piece of paper.

My darling Bridget, this is the only way we can put an end to the anguish I have put us through. I don't expect this to be clear to you now, but in time you will see this is the only way for you and the girls to live again. You have been so patient, so loving, so inspiring to me. When you came into my life that cold November evening, we began a journey I could never have dreamed of. Everything in my life I have because of you. Madness has muddied everything, but this I know with perfect clarity. This end does not negate the memories we have had. In fact, it is a desperate attempt to preserve them.

Yours always and forever,
Haydar

The grime-streaked walls closed in around her as the letter slipped from her fingers. Her father, the towering figure who had shaped her entire world, who she only remembered as this gentle, brilliant spirit, had taken his own life. And her mother . . . Her mother had hidden this from them, from the world. She'd locked this dirty secret away, made up a lie, and spent decades travelling the world with it.

Ishtar's chest tightened with grief. She wanted to scream, but all that escaped was a pathetic choking sound. Rajiha re-adjusted the shower curtain on her shoulders. Ishtar's grief turned into tears, unstoppable waves. She wept for Rajiha, cloaked in her makeshift armour. She wept for the land they'd tried so hard to save. She wept for her father, for his genius, tortured soul. Finally, she wept for herself. The daughter who had built her entire life upon a carefully constructed lie.

In the hotel lobby, Nisreen and Jan were having coffee.

"Reception said you checked out," Nisreen said. She registered the vacant look in Ishtar's eyes. "Is everything okay?"

All the pride and bravado Ishtar carried with her to Iraq turned to dust. Nisreen took her hand and led her up the elevator and into her room. Ishtar told her everything. About Rajiha, her father's letter. She wanted to be near Nisreen then, near to the familiar past, away from the soldiers and the thudding boots on the ground, from George Bush and his apish ears, the southern drawl in the word 'freedom' echoing in her mind. Nisreen kissed her neck, and this helped her to forget many things: the suffering, the smoke blooms, the firecrackers in the night sky. "It's okay, Ishtar, lay down." Those words brought to her mind a rough American voice, "Lay down. Lay the fuck down," as they kicked open doors, women screaming in dark living rooms, sunlight pouring in from behind the large shadows of soldiers armed to the teeth. She was soothed by the softness of Nisreen's lips, but it broke her to feel so weak, as easily toppled as Saddam's statue, the rope around the statue's neck like a noose, the pulling, the tumbling, his arm frozen in salute as the crowds descended, as she too descended, engulfed in the smell of Nisreen's perfume. This was what had to be done, she knew, as she kissed Nisreen back, as Nisreen's soft hands roamed her body. This was what had to be done.

The next morning as she met Nisreen and Jan in the breakfast area, Jan's eyes burned with excitement.

"Nisreen told me what happened at your aunt's house. Can we go back and film it?"

Three years after that trip, Rajiha died from natural causes in her small shed in Qadisiya. Ishtar decided she would never forgive her mother for leaving Rajiha behind, for withholding the truth about their father. Any part of her that might begin to understand her mother's reasons was swiftly banished to the darkest recesses of her mind. Beyond her moment of weakness with Nisreen, Ishtar never revealed to anyone that she knew about her father's suicide—the truth that Zainab's quest for the paintings now threatened to uncover.

What was it that George Bush Jr., that imbecile, that butcher, had said? *Fool me once, shame on you. Fool me . . . you can't get fooled again.*

Nisreen had fooled her once already, and yet here Ishtar was, over a decade later, agreeing to work with her again.

She stepped back and observed the day's work. The boat had taken shape, a piece of art, a labour of love. Its proportions were correct. It would hold water. It would take her home.

"Perfect," she whispered.

She would not be fooled again.

Zainab

October 2014

Zainab stood by the kitchen window watching the strong winds whip the grass until the whole field looked as if it were running from something. Her phone buzzed. Mediha's name flashed on the screen.

"Have you been enjoying your time with Mama?" Mediha asked.

"It's been lovely. I should tell you though, last night she stole a cigarette from my bag and smoked some of it in the living room, just in case you notice a smell . . ."

Mediha was irritated. "You shouldn't have brought cigarettes with you."

"What am I supposed to do, just quit before I come?"

"You should take better care of your body. It's not just the outside that matters."

"Mediha . . ."

"I worry about you."

"Please don't."

"Is she still talking to dead people?"

"No." Zainab stopped to look back. Her mother was still in her bedroom. "But she mentioned something about mobs outside. Mobs that target foreigners. Does that ring a bell?"

"I don't think so . . ."

"I was wondering if, maybe when she fell, she might have had a concussion?"

"She doesn't have a concussion, Zainab. She's just old."

"You put her to bed straight after, didn't you? I've heard that's not—"

"Seriously?"

"I was just wondering, that's all." Why were conversations with Mediha so fraught? "Your exhibition's at seven, right? When should I leave?"

"The carer is coming around four-thirty. You should leave as soon as she arrives, you may need to change trains."

"Okay."

"The carer is staying until midnight, so that gives us time to have dinner after."

Zainab grabbed her sketchbook and went to the living room. She sat on the sofa by the fire and began to sketch an image that appeared in her mind, of two children playing around the legs of a female figure. She sketched for some time until her mother's voice startled her.

"It's derivative."

"Huh?" Zainab turned around. Her mother was dressed in a red and gold Chinese robe. Her hair was dishevelled.

"Your work. The shapes are similar to your father's. Too much so."

Embarrassed, Zainab shut her sketchbook. "Nice nap?"

"Hamdulillah," Bridget sat beside her. "This might be the last time you visit me here."

"Don't say that, Mama."

They stared at the fire for some time, watching as the flames consumed the wood.

"Have you spoken to Ishtar?" Her mother's question was unexpected. "I don't know what to do about her. She never calls. She's always so angry with me."

"Shall we call her?" Zainab suggested.

"She won't pick up."

"Let's try."

The call rang through to voicemail. Bridget took a deep breath and put on a perky tone as she left a message: "Hallo habibti, it's me. Your mother. I'm with Zainab. Okay. Love you. Bye-bye."

* * *

The trip from Dunkeld to Edinburgh should have been easy, but Zainab's nervousness disoriented her. She arrived at the station and couldn't figure out which platform she needed. When she tried to buy a ticket, the machine ate her fifty-pound note. In the end, she ordered a taxi to drive her straight there.

As the taxi approached the gallery, Zainab spotted Mediha standing outside. She lit a cigarette and walked towards the exhibition hall. Mediha was chatting to a tall, spindly man dressed in black. She smiled as Zainab approached.

"This is my sister," Mediha said to the man. "Zainab, this is Gary, a *wonderful* local artist."

Gary wore a large, feathered coat that made him seem like a bird. In fact, in their coats and hats, everyone on the street appeared dark and bird-like.

"I was just telling Gary that—" Mediha paused, studying Zainab's mouth as she finished her cigarette. "You shouldn't smoke it all the way down to the filter, it's not good for you."

"Nice to meet you, Gary," Zainab said, stubbing the cigarette against the red brick wall and pocketing the butt. She didn't dare toss it on the ground in front of her sister. "How's the exhibition going?"

"Good, I think. People are connecting to the work . . . I'm curious to know what you think, too. What you *really* think."

Mediha's face was tentative and searching. The idea that her baby sister cared about her opinion sent a brief warmth through Zainab. But this came with trepidation, too. Zainab recalled the image of Jihadi John in Mediha's email.

"I promise I'll be honest."

The exhibition was spread across two rooms, the main hall and a small alcove in the corner. The four walls in the larger room were filled with prints of various sizes. On one wall, screenshots of several text message chains. A white plaque above the prints read 'Grooming'.

"These are actual messages between ISIS and the British teenagers they recruited," Mediha said, watching Zainab closely as she read the texts. "It's surprising what you can find on the Internet."

"All of them?"

"Well, some are messages that have come from my various romantic entanglements, long ago. And then these are excerpts from my diary when I first moved to Edinburgh. I manipulated them into a patchwork of sorts." Mediha swept an arm across the space. "You see how they're in conversation with one another?"

Zainab scanned the collage of texts. A sentence caught her eye.

Last night I dreamt Ammo Kuteiba followed me here.

"I found myself obsessed with these young Muslim Brits who grew up here their entire lives but were so easily lured into the madness of fundamentalism." Mediha's voice seemed far away. In fact, everything seemed far away, as if Zainab were sinking into a cave that held memories she had long buried. Her sister's voice echoed from above. "It made me think of myself—when I was their age—leaving Baghdad to start a new life in the UK. Essentially, this exhibition is about these two opposite journeys. It's a reckoning with our present moment, cutting across political divides to find solace in a shared desire to escape."

Mediha touched her arm. She felt herself return to her body.

"Are you okay?" Mediha's expression had changed from pride to concern.

Zainab moved to the next wall. The frames held enlarged family photographs she recognised at once—the three of them as girls, their mother either behind the camera or in the shot. She stopped at a garden photo taken on the first day of the school year. She must have been around eight, Ishtar twelve, Mediha six. They wore matching pinafores, knee socks. Zainab's long hair in plaits. Ishtar and Zainab smiling, Mediha on the verge of tears. In the kitchen window behind them, a ghostly figure stood watching.

"Is that—"

"Jihadi John," Mediha said. "Yes."

Another photograph was at a birthday party: all three sisters standing on chairs, a cake between them. Except it wasn't a cake. Mediha had altered the image so that the girls were standing above a table of headless bodies and severed limbs. Another of their mother—young, a paintbrush poised—stood before a background that, on second look, resolved into a ruined street. A living room snapshot overprinted with a checkpoint still. A swan-boat picture from Al-Zawra Park—the three girls crammed into a yellow paddle boat. But Mediha had sheeted all three of them under niqabs and abayas, their laughing faces swallowed under the black. In the background, at the water's edge, the masked figure watched on, a knife in his hand.

Zainab felt unsteady on her feet.

"Zainab?" Mediha's voice seemed far away again. "What do you think? Be honest."

What could she say? There was no way she could tell Mediha that she loathed the artworks, that she thought it was the same tired Western bullshit, shockingly vulgar and terribly predictable. That everything felt designed to provoke not just the family, but *her* specifically. More than that, Zainab did not want to tell Mediha that this work threatened to destroy the very family legacy they had spent decades building. She knew that if a single word of truth emerged from her lips, it would shatter any hope of reconciliation. But maybe that was exactly what Mediha wanted . . . Yes, of course, it was all by design. She intended to rip the family apart! It had been her project for so long now, why would this exhibition be any different? Mediha watched her, searching, curious. No, Zainab thought. Now was not the time for this. There were too many others present.

Zainab tugged at her earring. "Why focus on the horror?"

Her sister frowned. "What do you mean?"

"You've turned Iraq into this monstrosity . . . it's so dark."

"The darkness is the point. Whenever I read up about the Islamic State, I feel sick to my stomach. Watching the violent videos, I felt myself becoming so . . . aggressive."

The word 'aggressive' escaped from Mediha's mouth like a snake. Zainab stepped away from her.

"I don't watch the videos."

"It's easy to avert your eyes, but we're all complicit. I choose to stare the horror in the face, to channel my anger into something constructive."

Zainab turned to a set of black and white photos in one corner of the room. The images were of a nude woman in a variety of explicit poses: open legs, nipples clamped, masturbating. Surrounding her were headless corpses. With dawning horror, Zainab recognised the woman in the photographs.

"Mediha," Zainab gasped. She lowered her voice, whispering in Arabic. "You're naked. This is pornography! What if Mama sees this?"

"Why speak in Arabic? I don't have secrets. I don't like this very Iraqi thing of," Mediha mimicked brushing something under the carpet, "sweeping secrets away. How we always want to hide things rather than confront them head on."

"I need a cigarette," Zainab said.

Outside, the wind had picked up. A police car raced down the road, sirens blaring. A couple walking down the other side of the street stopped and stared as the car flew past. Zainab thought of her mother's warnings. *There are mobs attacking foreigners*. She turned to the poster of Jihadi John plastered on the glass front of the gallery.

A hand on her waist now. She turned. Mediha was beside her. "It's okay to feel overwhelmed. It's part of acceptance."

"Acceptance of what?"

"We lived in a bubble in Baghdad. The bubble has now

burst, and that," Mediha pointed to Jihadi John, "that is the pus seeping out."

"Is that really how you see our lives in Iraq? Our childhoods?"

A young man raced down the street on a skateboard, scaring a flock of pigeons who were pecking a half-eaten kebab left on the ground. One of the pigeons shot up and flew past Zainab's head, brushing her ear and causing her to scream.

"It's just a pigeon! Are you okay? You're very pale."

"I'm fine. I'm just jet lagged."

Mediha rubbed Zainab's arm, but the gesture lacked affection. "Let's grab a drink."

The pub was dark and crowded. Inside, a large poster of Muhammad Ali hung on the wall above the bar.

"Do you remember that fight?" Zainab asked, pointing at the poster as she discreetly pressed the button on the recording device she had clipped to her bag.

Mediha nodded. "Rumble in the Jungle. We watched it in Baghdad together."

"Do you remember the food fight after? Ishtar started it, and you were furious when we stained your favourite pyjamas."

"Was I?"

"You were always so serious."

"Not as a child. I became more serious later."

"You were *always* serious. Even as a child. Always scolding us for being too loud, for not following orders. You were too young to remember."

Mediha rolled her eyes. "I swear, every single member of our family has a disordered relationship to memory." She rested against the bar. "We are all mini-Saddams, rewriting history to suit our agendas. I'm going to order us both the roast beef, it's the best thing on the menu."

They found an empty table in the corner of the pub, and when they sat down Mediha asked if Zainab had been in touch with Ishtar.

"I've tried, but she hasn't been taking my calls," Zainab said carefully. "Are you?"

"Occasionally."

Pangs of fear shot through Zainab. What if Ishtar had found out that Nizar was visiting her to write down the family story? And what if she had told Mediha? Perhaps this was all a ruse, the exhibition, Mediha's sudden tenderness. Could all of this be a trap?

"She sometimes calls. At times manic about a project, other times wracked by paranoia. She asks if I still like her, if I believe she has wasted her life with nothing to show for it. Sometimes she calls to apologise for being a terrible older sister. She's a bit like Baba in that way . . . I mean I never met him, but it seemed that Baba's whole life was a struggle to keep the cracks from bursting."

Zainab pulled the thinking putty out of her bag and massaged it in her palm. The fear she felt moments ago gave way to jealousy. Ishtar had never confided to her in this way. She had always considered herself the sister who had stayed behind, who didn't run off to Britain when she had the chance. But perhaps it was she who had been estranged all this time?

"She's in Iraq now, actually," Mediha said.

"What?"

"I didn't tell Mama. I didn't want to worry her. She's there for some boat project." Mediha sipped her pint. "I sometimes think about what it would be like to return to Iraq."

"What are you talking about? You returned to get the paintings out."

"The bar is too noisy for that conversation."

"But—"

"Not now," Mediha's voice fought against the chatter in the pub. "We can speak about this tomorrow when I'm back home. I'll cook for you, and we'll have all the time and space to discuss the past."

Their food arrived, clay-like slabs of beef on a plate with a side of chips and greens. Neither of them spoke. Mediha cut at her meat, moving it around her plate. Zainab too had lost her appetite.

"How did you find Mama?"

"You were right, she's lost weight—"

"Why would I lie to you?"

"—but other than ageing . . . wait, I'm not saying you'd lie."

Mediha nodded, finally putting a piece of beef in her mouth. Her eyes narrowed in concentration as she chewed. Finally, she asked: "What have you been talking to her about?"

"Baghdad, the old times."

"Take what she says with a grain of salt. Her memories are not as good as they used to be. Especially around Baba . . ."

"Does it matter how accurate her memories are?"

Mediha looked up from her plate. "Memories matter . . . how things are remembered *matters*. And the one thing I've learned about our dear mother is that she has a masterful ability to reshape her memories to absolve herself of complicity."

Zainab was quiet for some time. She did not understand what Mediha was referring to, and perhaps, she was coming to realise, she did not want to.

"Why not just let Mama live in whatever narrative she chooses?" Zainab finally said. "I think it's sweet that she's talking to people—"

"That's easy for you to say. It's one thing to come and visit once a year, it's another to be there every day, to find your mother in a pool of her own *piss* . . ." Mediha rubbed her temples. "I'm sorry, I'm tired. This exhibition has brought up a lot. Working on my trauma feels like a full-time job these days . . ."

Mediha said the word 'trauma' as if it were a family treasure that had been entrusted to her, but also as a weapon, a gilded knife she could cut them with at any moment.

Ishtar

October 2014

On the day of the launch, Nizar, Ishtar, and Murat woke before sunrise and congregated in the garden. They followed the footpath through the orchard, which slowly merged into a wilder path that snaked along the canyon. As they walked through the darkness, guided by the light of their phone torches, Murat spoke about the Ilisu mega-dam. Constructed by the Turkish government, the dam was expected to flood two hundred villages in the area.

"Twelve thousand years of civilisation will soon be under water."

In her mind, Ishtar rehearsed the speech she had prepared for the launch. A quiet confidence grew inside her. The dissonance she had felt between the expedition and the ongoing violence had clarified over the last two days. In fact, her goal of reconstituting the link between culture and nature, symbolically uniting the people and ecosystems along the river, seemed ever more pertinent as Iraq was fragmenting.

By the time they reached the canyon's mouth the sun had emerged, drenching the valley in a golden light. Old bridges rose from the water like the bones of prehistoric beasts. Along the sides of the cliff, an intricate series of caves were etched into the rocks. The caves had a superstructure protruding from them, but the foundations were embedded in the mountain. A few of the caves were still inhabited by families, evidenced by empty pots and the hanging clothes left out to dry.

Murat pointed to a series of ridges that ran between the

man-made caves along the slopes of the plateau. "Traditional water purification system. Ancient, but very sophisticated. No home is more than five meters from a water source. And see that spot there? That's where they threw the Armenians in the river. My grandmother watched their bodies float down like a procession of rafts."

"The effects of the dam will be felt all the way downstream," Ishtar said. "The marshes in southern Iraq will dry up, livelihoods will be destroyed, plant and animal species will go extinct . . ."

The bleating of goats echoed through the mountains. Nizar turned to Ishtar. "The dam will break the link between the people and the land. That's what you've been saying, right?"

She nodded. "Cutting people from their land and centring resources into the hands of an out-of-touch government. All the way down the river."

Murat pointed to a clearing in the horizon. "My parents are buried in that cemetery there. Their graves will be submerged, the streets where I grew up will be under the water. All my history, drowned."

"Do people support this?" Nizar asked.

"What can they do? Erdogan promises the dam will make Turkey more powerful, that it will bring jobs. But the government has neglected this region for so long. A lot of the workers building the dam will see their houses destroyed by the flood. The new houses the government built are in a desert. Very dry. No life. But, if we stay, we will drown in our homes."

Ishtar sighed. She watched a lone woman washing clothes in the river. "A population starved begs its rulers to unleash the flood to quench their thirst."

Nizar turned to her. "Isn't that what you said about the myths we tell ourselves? That they contain within them a warning, a premonition?"

Ishtar thought of her mother then, an intrusive and unexpected thought. By concealing the truth about his death, their mother had crafted a myth of their father. Perhaps the lie was a crucial element of the story. But then, what was the lesson hidden within the folds?

Her eyes rested on a flock of birds perched on one of the ruins, a crumbling arch of ancient stone. Their dark forms, tightly packed, made the ruins seem as though they had been dipped in tar.

"The birds are always there before sunrise," Murat said, following her line of sight. "It's their resting place. After the flood, where will they sleep?"

Without warning the birds erupted into motion, their wings beating furiously as they dispersed into the sky, black specks in an ocean of blue.

* * *

They returned to find Nisreen under the pomegranate tree. Ishtar had been apprehensive about their reunion, and even the brightening of Nisreen's face when she saw her failed to assuage her dread. A bald bull of a man sat across from her in mirrored aviators, his neck brick-red, his jaw squared and razor burned.

"Ishtar," Nisreen stood up. She tentatively opened her arms for an embrace. Ishtar gave it to her, coldly. "I was just telling Dave you've done a great job with the boats."

"And who is this Dave?"

The bald man stood up—a tall, imposing presence—and shook Ishtar's hand.

"Dave is our security guy," Nisreen said. "He knows Iraq like the back of his hand."

"Does he now."

Nisreen glanced at her phone. "We've told everyone the launch is at midday. Local media are coming. That gives us a couple of hours to do a quick security briefing and then head down to the river."

Ishtar introduced Nizar and Murat, and the five of them sat around the table. Dave pulled out a map, and with a red pen drew large circles to show areas of ISIS control, followed by arrows darting outwards to indicate their advancements. He spoke in practical, military language, and with a strong American accent that made Ishtar's skin crawl.

"We have authorisation to cross the northern border," he said, tapping the map with a knuckle, "but we're gonna cut the trip short at Erbil, and re-start south of Baghdad."

"But that means we aren't following the river's path," Ishtar said. "Mosul, Baghdad. These are key elements of the journey."

"I get the poetry, lady. But Mosul is a no-go." Dave tapped the map again, harder. "Unless you want to walk around in a burka for the rest of your life."

Ishtar drew in a breath. "We can negotiate access. If you just *talk* to people—"

"The situation is too dangerous, even for locals."

"But we *are* locals."

"They'll take one look at you and—"

"What are you implying?"

"Ishtar," Nisreen said gently. "Iraq's changed."

"What about Baghdad?" Nizar asked. "Can we at least hold an event there?"

"We weren't able to get authorisation," Dave said.

Ishtar chuckled. "We need authorisation to put a raft in the water?"

"You need authorisation to take a shit in Iraq these days. I don't think you understand the situation. ISIS are knocking on the doors of Baghdad as we speak."

Ishtar resisted the urge to argue further. She did not want this American telling her what she could and could not do in her own country, but she felt the noose of the conversation tighten around her neck. So she sat quietly as Dave continued his briefing, talking about risk matrices and evacuation plans and threat assessment forms, bureaucratic nonsense that constructed Iraq as a hostile nation. And it was a hostile nation, she thought. To someone like Dave, perhaps. But not to her. She would not allow that to happen.

The boats were waiting for them on the shore, along with two marsh Arab sheikhs Nisreen had invited from southern Iraq. The men wore elegant thawbs, gold-rimmed black cloaks and chequered keffiyehs. The sheikhs were here as a symbolic gesture, Nisreen had explained, uniting the northern tip of the river to its conclusion in the Iraqi marshes.

Soon, a small group of journalists arrived. A photographer took pictures of the sheikhs as they stood by the boats, while the reporters interviewed Nisreen and Ishtar.

Nisreen said a few words about the reasons her organisation funded the expedition, and Ishtar stood beside her, staring at the ground until Nisreen introduced her as the brains behind the project. Ishtar told the journalists about her inspiration, about the search for modern day solutions in ancient myths, about the need to look to the past to understand how to solve the problems of the present, and how this had led her to the story of the Flood.

"We're living in an inverse of the myth of the Flood. Whereas before, Utnapishtim built an ark to save the world's animals, our current way of life is slowly killing off countless species of flora and fauna from across the river."

She talked about the role climate vulnerability played in the collapse of the Assyrian empire, which was brought to its knees by a decades-long megadrought, and how the destruction the region was now experiencing had echoes of those past calamities. Her voice was clear and assured, the words came to her with ease, ideas that had stewed in her mind for years emerged coherent and whole. She was proud of herself. She had been so broken when Nizar first visited her, and through drawing out the family story he had helped pull her out of her despair, and he had returned, again and again, helping to make of her misery something creative and even hopeful. She turned to her nephew, who was closely following her words. It suddenly occurred to her that in the past two months she had not once inquired about his life. Why was it that Nizar had first paid her a visit, and why had he insisted on returning, week after week, agreeing to follow her all the way here?

Ishtar suddenly realised she had gone silent. The journalists looked at her, waiting.

"The impact of this dam will extend far beyond Hasankeyf's destruction," Nisreen said, stepping in. "We've been working out the expected reduction of water levels and we're looking at a reduction of about half the current level, which is pretty devastating as it is. Combined with the increasing salination of the soil, there is a real risk that the ecosystem as we know it will die forever."

Afterwards, Ishtar turned to her.

"Thanks for stepping in, I lost my train of thought."

"You did great."

A silence fell between them. "I should probably get the boats in the water," Ishtar said. She took a few steps before Nisreen called her name.

"It's good to see you again, Ishtar." Nisreen was smiling softly. "You're looking well."

"Thank you." Ishtar hesitated, careful not to reveal that underneath the pain of their shared history she still desired Nisreen. "You too."

Before the boats could be put in the water, there was the question of sacrifice.

The sheikhs were insistent. Blood had to be spilt to protect the boats. Murat called for his son to bring a goat from the market.

Ishtar threw her hands up. "We haven't got time. Besides, we've already slaughtered twenty-five goats."

She grabbed a knife from the waistcoat of one of the sheikhs and made a deep, diagonal cut across her palm. The line turned white, then pink, and then a deep red. She squeezed her palm until blood dripped down her arm. She ran her hand across the boats, marking each with a bloody handprint.

"Let's go."

There were discussions over who would ride which boat. Nisreen suggested she and the two sheikhs ride the meshouf, the sturdiest of the boats, bestowing a sense of authority to the vessel that irritated Ishtar. Nizar and Murat rode the kalak, the raft-like vessel common in the northern parts of the Tigris. That left Ishtar to navigate the guffa, the more complicated boat to steer.

She got inside the coracle, placing her feet on either side to gain balance. The vessel spun in circles in the water. She tried out different positions, finally finding some steadiness by perching on the side of the guffa and pushing her feet against the bottom, wedging her legs diametrically across the circular frame. She turned to the sheikhs, who watched her from the safety of their canoe.

"Why don't one of you join me? This boat is made for transporting people, it'll be more stable with an extra person."

Tentatively, the older of the sheikhs agreed. She helped him into the coracle, and he sat down cross-legged in the centre. Ishtar grabbed an oar and tested different rowing techniques. At first the guffa spun in circles in the rushing waters, but when Ishtar used the oar as a punt, balancing her weight against that of the sheikh, she was able to gain forward momentum.

Green and brown shrubs lined the banks of the river as they made their way downstream. The guffa moved like a rabbit in quick forward jerks. The meshouf, long and elegant, glided through the waters while the kalak trailed behind, floating with the speed of the current as Murat and Nizar used their oars to navigate.

The river braided as they neared Hasankeyf, parting around a stony bar. The meshouf and guffa slipped into the left channel, the kalak drifted to the right. White water lifted over jagged rocks along one side of the riverbank. Ishtar dug her oar, but the guffa lurched towards it, defying her.

"Rocks!" The sheikh white-knuckled the guffa's rim.

Ishtar felt excited and terrified. "Grab hold of that plank and row."

They navigated the guffa away from the rocks, and the current began working in their favour, steering them towards the other side. Up ahead, the meshouf was better able to ride the rapids. By the time the two boats made their way to calmer waters, the split stitched itself back into a single run. The kalak—floating lazily on its makeshift rubber tires—had already arrived in Hasankeyf.

"We win!" Murat cheered as the other two boats came into view. Ishtar grinned. Of course the kalak had won—after all, it was a boat designed to navigate the stronger currents this far upstream.

They docked the boats and got out. She turned to the crew. "Shall we keep going? To the dam?"

No one was listening. Nisreen's staff were packing up the gear and discussing plans for lunch. Some put on jackets, others lit cigarettes. The photographer took photos as Nizar and Murat cheered and hugged one another. The sheikh in Ishtar's coracle rested against a rock, trembling hands clasped at his knees. There was a sense of accomplishment in the air, one that made Ishtar wary.

"Fuck it," Ishtar said under her breath. She waded through the shallows and jumped back into the guffa. She stood up, found her balance, and punted the boat away from the bank.

"Where are you going?" Dave called out.

Ishtar did not respond, even when Nisreen called her name. She rowed until the rushing waters drowned out their voices, until they were nothing more than a thicket of waving arms. Downstream, the river was silent. The land felt wild and uncontainable, but a stillness enveloped her. She shipped the oar across her knees and closed her eyes, taking in the landscape's sounds and smells: the faint rasp of water on stone, wet metal and river weed in the air, the steady chirr of crickets. She could almost feel the place speak, a language she knew she had it in her to understand. Her breath slowed, falling in line with the gentle ticking of the reeds.

A car horn sheared through the hush. Ishtar opened her eyes. A white minivan bumped onto the bank, Dave's face, jutting from the window, slick with sweat and misplaced authority. He barked at her to get back in the van. He looked like a thumb, she thought, a small laugh rising and falling as she turned to the horizon. If she kept going, she could ride this water all the way to Baghdad. An older woman in a coracle would hardly read as a threat. An Iraqi woman, no less. Ishtar lived within the confines of this plan for some time as she rowed downstream, but the quick calculus asserted itself: permits, checkpoints, money most of all. She would need him for a while longer. She pocketed the thought, set the oar back in the water, and angled the coracle towards the bank.

* * *

They set off the next morning. The boats went in one van, and in the other the five of them squeezed in: Nisreen and Dave up front, Ishtar, Murat and Nizar in the back. They arrived at the border by lunchtime, a militarised zone drenched in Kurdish patriotism. As their van pulled up behind a long line of trucks, Ishtar noted the absence of Iraqi flags.

"I'd have thought they'd at least fly the two flags side-by-side."

"Things have changed . . ." Nisreen said from the passenger seat.

"I suppose you must be happy with these changes then?"

"What is Iraq, really? Just a colonial creation . . ."

"Oh, don't Sykes-Picot me."

"Kurds, Shi'a and Sunni all put together under a brutal dictator."

"That is a convenient American narrative. Iraq as a unified region existed well before colonial powers came in."

The line of trucks was not moving. Ishtar rolled a cigarette and opened the door.

"Stay inside," Dave ordered from the driver's seat.

Ishtar ignored him, hopping out of the van. Dave's approach to security—his insistence on bending and molding the world into some false sense of structure and control—fundamentally clashed with Ishtar's distaste for authority, her preference for malleability. The fact she'd so openly welcomed Murat's impromptu decision to join the expedition had only stoked Dave's resentment.

She stretched her legs and tried to light her cigarette, but the flame was too weak for the wind. She looked out at the line of cars and trucks extending to the horizon, their metallic structures shimmering under the sun. Ishtar had crossed many borders in her life. Some were invisible and she had traversed them unaware, on a bicycle, a boat, a car. Others were disputed, drawn and re-drawn as battles created new frontiers and configurations. How quickly porous borders could harden, calcifying suddenly and without warning, mobilising thousands of men on either side to fight to the death for these imaginary lines.

Permeable or hard, whatever the crossing, Ishtar felt a queasy dread. Borders were a space of transience, a man-made in-betweenness where the threat of violence was most acute. It was at borders where the force of collective power—a tribe, a people, a state—could most freely be unleashed. The threat of falling through the abyss of a no-man's land imbued these lines with a symbolic power. The disquiet she felt at borders only increased over time. How much of this unease was rooted in sadness, the grief over the arbitrary termination that borders demanded of her? And where did she fall along this new Iraqi border—was she inside of it, or out?

The traffic started moving. Ishtar returned to the van.

The patriotic display continued past the border as they drove towards Faysh Khabur, a town near the perimeters of Syria and Turkey and the closest they could come to the battle line between the Peshmerga and the Islamic State. Kurdish flags danced on either side of the highway. They had been in Iraq for nearly an hour, and Ishtar had yet to see a single Iraqi flag.

Perhaps Nisreen was right. Perhaps things *had* changed. But how powerful were these imaginary borders anyway? Once the Ilisu Dam was finished, the land of Iraqi Kurdistan would face its own water shortages. Already the Kurdish Federal government was building its own system of dams across the rivers, which would serve to further choke off the supply of water to the south of the country. The stratification of the world intensified.

They stopped at one of the restaurants dotting the highway and bought some food, and later found a supermarket. Ishtar, Murat, and Nizar got out to buy some essentials, while Nisreen and Dave took the van in search of a safe place to camp. They bought some bread, a few gallons of water, three cartons of eggs, some canned tuna, rice, a large packet of Nescafe sachets, and some biscuits. They waited in a teahouse until the others returned, and when the car pulled up half an hour later, Dave was in better spirits.

"The Peshmerga have authorised us a place to camp for the night that is safe," he said. "It's a short drive from here, just out of town along the bank of the river. The van made it through customs and is on its way there with the boats."

The campsite was on a stony riverbank, beside one of the

pillars of a bridge that emerged from the water like the leg of a bathing giant.

"These guys are happy to keep watch over us," Dave explained, pointing to a Peshmerga checkpoint on the bridge where another Kurdish flag was erected.

"And tomorrow we make it further down?"

"Tomorrow we can talk."

"What does that mean?"

"It means you aren't in charge of security decisions."

"I was just asking a question."

"Leave the questions for tomorrow. It'll be dark in an hour."

Ishtar mockingly raised her hand in a military salute. "Aye aye sir."

The roar of an engine announced the arrival of the boats. Dave, Nizar, and Murat unloaded them, while Ishtar and Nisreen set up camp. As they erected the tents, frustrated groans rose from the van behind them.

"What's going on?" Ishtar asked, walking towards the men.

"They've fucked the boats," Dave muttered. "Must have been while they were loading and unloading at customs . . ."

Ishtar examined the boats in the dying light. It was difficult to gauge the extent of the damage, but it was clear the meshouf had several large holes. The guffa was chipped, the bitumen at the base grated to a thin veneer. It had struggled to keep out water at the start of the expedition. It certainly wouldn't now. And the kalak . . . well, the kalak was just planks of wood tied to old rubber tyres.

"Is it bad?" Nisreen asked, resting a hand on Ishtar's shoulder.

Ishtar moved away. "No." She had to keep the team's morale up. Dave would look for any opportunity to cut the trip short. "First thing tomorrow, we'll fix the boats."

While the others prepared the camp, Ishtar worked on a fire. The sky had turned the trees and shrubs to shadow, the air settled into a cool breeze. She made a nest of twigs and dried leaves, then placed a white paraffin fire starter in the centre and struck a match. The first match blew out in the wind, but the second took and the paraffin lit up. Feeding the fire twigs and branches, she watched as the flames crawled over the dead wood.

She was relishing the satisfying crackle of the fire when Nisreen came up beside her.

"How does it feel to be back?" She began to gently massage Ishtar's shoulders, which were stiff from a week's worth of work.

"I don't know." Ishtar busied herself with the fire, watching the flames rise in the growing darkness. She considered shifting from Nisreen's touch, but under her fingers the knots in her muscles began to loosen and relax. "Is it even home anymore?"

Nisreen sat down beside her, their legs touching. "Iraq's changed. But it's still home."

"How does it feel for you?" Ishtar turned to look at Nisreen, whose skin glowed in the light of the fire. "To see Iraq in this way."

"It's terrible. The environmental impact alone . . ."

Ishtar recalled what she had told Nizar back in London, when her nephew had first floated Nisreen's name as a potential funder for the expedition: proponents of war now masquerading as protectors of heritage.

"Does that mean you regret supporting the invasion?"

Shadows danced across Nisreen's face as her expression hardened. She had not expected the ambush. "I don't think it's useful to flatten our narratives like this. You're acting as if I singlehandedly opened the door."

"You certainly didn't help pull up the drawbridge."

"And what if I did? Can you tell me that things would have been any better?"

They were silent for some time. Finally, Ishtar spoke.

"I'm terrified of going to Baghdad. Terrified of coming face to face with the reality that I won't be able to walk down the streets of the city I grew up in without fearing for my life. I foolishly thought Baghdad would always be there, waiting for me."

"I did too. I didn't expect Baghdad to take my family away from me, the way it did all those years ago. I think about my brother every day."

Ishtar rummaged through her bag. She pulled out the half-finished painting of The Epic of Gilgamesh that she had brought with her.

"Do you remember this?" She asked, handing Nisreen the painting.

Nisreen traced her fingers around the sketch of Enkidu and Gilgamesh wrestling the Bull of Heaven. A smile appeared on her lips. "You were working on this a long time ago . . ."

"I started it when we were together in Baghdad. I've tried returning to it many times over the last thirty years, but I've never been able to complete it. It's like a block. Even though I know how the rest of the story goes, I feel incapable of imagining it."

Nisreen placed her hand on Ishtar's knee. "Have you ever considered that it's not Gilgamesh's journey you need to paint, but your own?"

Zainab

October 2014

Bridget was asleep by the time Zainab returned home. She saw the carer off in a taxi, then sat in the living room and played back the recordings of her mother from the first night. Her mother's voice sounded frail. The stories and recollections appeared disjointed and incomplete, nothing like the string of solid memories Zainab remembered them to be. She paused the tape and went to the bathroom, staring at herself in the mirror as she brushed her teeth. If Mediha was right and her mother's memories were nothing more than myths, when did the fictionalisation begin?

When she'd finished in the bathroom, Zainab took the key from her pocket and unlocked Mediha's room. She walked through the darkness to the closet. To her surprise the door was unlocked, and stacked between sheets of protective paper were at least twenty of the family paintings. She was so close to rescuing the artworks from obscurity, from under Mediha's iron grip. She wanted to grab them then and there and take the first flight back to Dubai.

But she had to be patient. She could not leave just yet.

Back in the living room, she replayed her conversation with Mediha at the pub. Their voices were mostly drowned out, but Zainab could make out the contours of their conversation. She heard Mediha mention Ishtar's name. If Ishtar was not willing to come to Bridget, perhaps Zainab should bring Bridget to her. As soon as this thought occurred to her, Zainab smiled. Of all her grand and unfeasible ideas, taking her mother all the way to Baghdad was surely the most deranged.

The thought must have followed her into sleep because she dreamt of Baghdad. She was on the roof of the family home. A yolk-yellow moon shimmered in the sky. She heard footsteps rising on the staircase, and thought of Jihadi John, the glistening knife in his hand. She knew the door standing between them would give.

Zainab woke with a start and looked around the bedroom. It was late morning; her mother was not beside her. In the kitchen, Bridget was already up and dressed. The dull rays of the sun streamed across the breakfast table she had set.

"Isn't it wonderful to sleep in?" her mother chirped.

"What time is it?" Zainab said, her eyes taking in the plates of cheese and cured meats.

"Nearly ten. I've prepared breakfast."

Zainab brewed some coffee and sat down.

"How are you feeling today?" she asked her mother.

"Huh?"

"How are you feeling?" Zainab repeated, louder now.

"A bit shaky," her mother said, picking up a slice of bread.

Zainab buttered her toast and grabbed some of the turkey breast. It felt slimy in her hands, and when she turned it over green mould dotted the meat. She had forgotten to clear out her mother's fridge. She looked at the pâté in her mother's trembling hand with horror.

"Mum, wait—" she began, then stopped herself. *One thing I have learned about our dear mother is that she has a masterful ability to reshape her memories to absolve herself of complicity.* Mediha's words returned to her like a key, unlocking a truth she had known for some time but had buried inside of her. *Let her poison herself*, a spiteful voice said. Zainab was not sure whose voice this was, whether it was her own or someone else's, but it was too late. Bridget had taken a large bite.

"I'll take a nap after breakfast," her mother was saying now. "That's the beauty of being old, isn't it? You are free to do whatever you want. I can take a nap when I want, I can make some pancakes right now if I want. But really, Zainab, all I want is to die in peace, surrounded by my daughters."

Zainab felt sick to her stomach. Not at the mouldy food, nor at the fact she had let her mother consume it, but at something else. She turned to Bridget, empowered by a long-simmering resentment only now rising to the surface, and in the same spiteful voice that had instructed her to poison her mother, Zainab finally spoke.

"I'm surprised you don't have more of Baba's paintings on the walls."

"I don't even know where most of them are . . ."

"You do know, Mama," Zainab said. "You do know where the paintings are."

"It was a chaotic time, the eighties. Rajiha stole many things . . ."

Zainab recalled how in the late seventies her mother had been so convinced Rajiha was stealing their father's paintings that she asked Zainab to go to Rajiha's house to snoop among her belongings. At the time, Zainab assuaged her mother's paranoia by visiting her aunt almost daily. Rajiha's house was filled with strange junk and hidden treasures that she collected from the streets or markets or other people's homes, and which she would magically transform into complex and beautiful art pieces that no one ever bought. Zainab admired the strange, eccentric woman. One afternoon, Zainab asked her aunt whether she suffered from kleptomania.

I just like to collect things, her aunt said, seemingly unbothered by Zainab's question. *It's like a piece speaks to me, asks me to take it. Sometimes something just feels like it should be mine.*

Why do you think that is? Do you think maybe something was stolen from you?

Her aunt considered this question for some time.

Yes, Rajiha finally said. *Someone was stolen from me.*

"That woman never stole anything more valuable than a

piece of chalk. I feel sad, honestly. At first, I couldn't believe you would just let Mediha sell the paintings, but I get it now."

"I do wish you and her would be nicer to one another," Bridget said as she picked up some mouldy turkey breast.

"I feel sad for Baba. More than anyone else."

"You know I loved your father. I stood by him."

"Yes, but you also let him be forgotten."

"Forgotten? What on earth are you talking about? I spent the sixties and seventies making sure his legacy survived. He was the most famous artist in Iraq. *Is* the most famous artist in Iraq."

"But ever since you left Baghdad it's as if you've purposefully kept his art hidden. Is there anything else you've lied about, Mama? Any other convenient truths you've forgotten?"

Bridget was now visibly upset. "I don't understand why you are bringing up the past now. Mediha is doing it too, saying horrible things about your uncle Kuteiba. He wasn't perfect but he cared for us when your father died. You were too young to remember, he was like a father for you girls!"

"Don't you remember New Year's Eve? You were watching that night, when he broke her jaw."

"What? No. I wasn't there."

"But I saw you."

Her mother looked up at her, an animal trapped in a snare. "We've all made mistakes, Zainab."

* * *

After breakfast, Zainab threw the remaining food in the trash. She heard her mother's voice drift through the house.

"It just plopped into the Bosporus. Just like that. Plop."

"Mama?" Zainab called out.

"I should have told you then, darling. But I knew it would break your heart."

Zainab stepped outside and lit a cigarette. Feeling strange and disoriented, she called Nizar. Her son answered on the third ring.

"Where are you?"

Nizar hesitated. "I'm . . . in Iraq."

"What do you mean you're in Iraq?"

"Don't worry. I'm fine."

"Are you with Ishtar?"

"Yes. Did she tell you about the boats?"

"What boats?" A gentle rain began to fall.

"We built them and we're sailing down the Tigris . . . well, not right now, we've had some difficulties."

Zainab felt the worlds of dream and waking life converge in an unstoppable nightmare.

"No, no . . . you have to be careful." The line seemed to cut. "Nizar, are you still there?"

"Yes . . ." He hesitated. "I wanted to tell you. This trip has made me realise some things. And one of them is that for our family, art has always been our map home."

The rain came down harder. Zainab was soaked. The connection was weak.

"Nizar?"

"And this whole squabble . . . family paintings . . ." the connection was very bad now, "you are all reckoning with the . . . and the paintings . . . way to bring you all together."

"Nizar? I can't hear you!"

The line died. She called him back, but the call went straight to voicemail. She was about to try again when she received a message.

—Bad connection. All is fine here. I love you.

In the bathroom, Zainab stepped under the shower. The water pressure was weak, the shower was old, nothing like her large rainforest shower in Dubai. As she massaged the rose-scented bar of soap on her body she felt hollowed out and helpless, and she despised this about herself, despised the cage she had put herself in.

She tried to cry but nothing came, only a few forced sobs. She thought of Nizar's frustrations with her, how he said she never listened, how she worried too much and was quick to spiral. Yesterday she had briefly entertained the idea of taking her mother to Iraq to be with Ishtar. A preposterous idea. But if Nizar was there too—

The bathroom door opened. She heard footsteps.

"Mama?" Zainab poked her head around the edge of the shower curtain. Her mother was standing in the bathroom, her nightgown pulled up to her waist, revealing her pale thighs and the sparse hair covering her crotch.

"Mama! I'm showering . . ."

Bridget didn't hear her. She sat down on the toilet and stared straight ahead at the beige and yellow tiles on the wall. There was the unmistakeable sound of her mother relieving herself.

"Mama!" Zainab shouted.

Her mother turned to her and smiled. "Bulbul . . . you're here."

"I'm showering, Mama!"

"How lovely you're here."

Her mother stood up and took small, shaky steps towards her. Zainab's eyes moved down her mother's body. Smears of shit, soft and green, ran down her legs.

"Mama, you're not finished!"

The greenish smear was growing, dripping onto the floor.

Zainab stepped out of the shower, forgetting her own nakedness, and sat Bridget back on the toilet. She wiped the excrement from her mother's legs.

"Oh Mama . . ."

Zainab retched as the stench hit her nose. She recalled how much she had dry heaved when she heard about Ammo Kuteiba's suicide, a mixture of remorse and relief. She had been estranged from her family for thirty years. Yes, there were phone calls and yearly visits, but Zainab had not really been present. She had failed her mother. But her mother had failed her too.

Bridget looked down at Zainab, at the dirty toilet paper that now covered the floor.

"Oh, this is embarrassing."

"The mouldy food made you sick."

"Mouldy?"

"It's why you had diarrhoea. You ate rotten food. I'm sorry."

"But why?"

"Allah kareem, Mama. Allah kareem."

And, as if by calling out to God, the tears finally came.

Ishtar

October 2014

The next morning, Ishtar crept out of her tent and perched on a log by the dead fire, watching the slow glide of the river. As her eyes followed a piece of driftwood, a glistening whiteness in some shrubs caught her eye. She got up and walked towards it. A human skull. Every bit of skin and muscle had been consumed by parasites and bacteria until nothing but the porcelain whiteness of death remained.

She picked up the skull and moved it further away, burying it under some soil. If anyone came across it, the future of their expedition would be called into question.

Would things be different had Mama not hidden Baba's suicide?

The thought came to her suddenly, and with surprising force. A more complicated legacy, certainly, but a necessary complexity, one that could have opened new and important conversations about her parents and the political changes of their times.

Slowly, people emerged from their tents. They mumbled greetings, discussed coffee. Dave kept checking his phone.

"There's been a series of car bombs and mortar attacks in Shi'a areas of Baghdad."

"Will this affect the trip?" Murat asked.

Dave stared at Murat for a moment, then snorted condescendingly.

Ishtar inspected the boats. In the morning light, the damage was worse than she'd feared.

"It's going to take a full day of work," she announced. She rummaged through her bag and pulled out a knife and some rope. Kneeling over the guffa, she cut at the strands of straw that had uncoiled from the sides. She turned to Nizar. "Can you go and find some more wood—reed preferably, or something similar?"

Nizar stood up, but Dave blocked his path.

"No one is going anywhere."

Ishtar looked at him. "Excuse me?"

"We are in an active conflict zone. I understand wanting to put the boats in the water, but it's too risky to stay here."

"That's not your decision."

"I'm the security focal point. You're just a consultant."

"Consultant?" Ishtar gasped.

Dave turned to Nisreen.

"We should head to Erbil. It's not safe to go to Baghdad now, ISIS are at the outskirts of the city. We may be able to restart the expedition in the south, but—"

Ishtar turned to the others. "Don't listen to this guy."

"*This guy* served in the US military for five years," Dave barked, getting in her face. "*This guy* was a private contractor for another five years after that. *This guy* knows a thing or two about this country."

Ishtar looked at Nisreen, who had still not said a word. "You hired a colonial mercenary? Why am I not surprised? *Of course* you did."

"Let's start loading the boats onto the van," Nisreen said quietly.

Dave walked towards the guffa.

"Wait," Ishtar pleaded. "If you want to go—"

"It's not about what anyone wants," Nisreen said.

"But I'm not going anywhere."

"Ishtar, it's a liability problem," Nisreen said. "Did I not get you the sheikhs from the south? Did I not get media coverage in Hasankeyf? We've done what we can. You've made your point."

"My *point*?" Ishtar was so angry she could barely see. "No, you're not taking this away from me, Nisreen. You, Dave, and whoever else wants can fuck off. I'm staying."

Nisreen turned to Dave. "Let's get our stuff."

Dave nodded and began to pack his gear.

Ishtar turned to Murat. "Are you going with them?"

Murat shook his head.

Dave returned with his duffle bag and turned to Ishtar. "If you get your head chopped off sweetheart—"

"Call me sweetheart again and I'll be the one chopping heads," she spat, waving the knife in her hand.

"We're taking the boats. Nisreen paid for them."

"Over my dead body."

Dave pushed past Ishtar to get to the guffa. She pointed her knife in his face. "I'm not joking. I'll kill you before I let you take them."

He charged like a tank and she was thrown backwards, her body thudding against the inside of the guffa. Nizar leapt towards Dave, jumping on his back and throwing him to the floor.

"Don't you *ever* point a weapon at me," Dave yelled. He got up from the ground and grabbed the knife that had fallen.

"Khala are you okay?" Nizar helped her to her feet. Ishtar brushed herself off, stunned. She caught the look in Nisreen's eye—one of pity, concern, protection—and this sent her into a spiral of humiliated rage.

"I'll fucking kill you. Occupier!" There were tears in her eyes and her breath was sour as she flung curses at the American. Murat held her back while Nisreen wrestled Dave towards the van. Within minutes, they had thrown their belongings inside. Nisreen got in the passenger seat, refusing to make eye contact. Dave took the knife and slashed the tires tied to the kalak. With each slash the raft sank further and further into the soil. When he'd finished, he got into the van and sped off.

"Thanks for the plane ticket," Ishtar called out to the dust swirling in the air.

When the van disappeared, Ishtar turned to the destroyed boats. Nothing could be done to fix the punctured tires. They would have to find new ones. The guffa was salvageable, but the work would take at least a day. The expedition would continue regardless. She turned to Murat and Nizar.

"If we start now, we can fix the boats before sundown."

Ishtar gathered her tools from the ground. She turned to the guffa, trying to ignore the shaking of her hands as she touched the inside of the coracle.

"The job doesn't need to be perfect," she said, glancing up at the men who stood watching her, unmoving. She turned back to the guffa, sat on its edge, and pulled her tobacco from the pocket of her dusty shirt. "Can one of you scout the area for—"

"How are we getting out of here?" Nizar interrupted her.

"We'll fix the boats and sail down," she said, pinching some tobacco and laying it on the rolling paper.

"What do you mean 'sail down'? We're in a war zone."

As if to confirm this, the deafening roar of a jet tore through the sky.

"We'll be fine," Ishtar said once the noise subsided. She continued rolling her cigarette but her hands shook violently, spilling the tobacco on the ground.

"I don't want to fucking die!" Nizar launched his water bottle, which clanged against a rock and tumbled towards the river. "You're not on some expedition to bring Iraq together, you're on a suicide mission." Nizar paused, as if considering something, and then began to laugh. "You know, I should actually thank you. When my mother asked me to visit you, I was about to kill myself. But here I am, four months later, and I don't know what's changed but I don't want to die anymore. So thank you, because in some weird fucked up Ishtar-like way, you kind of saved my life."

Ishtar froze. She looked up at her nephew. "Your mother told you to visit me?"

"Yes," Nizar was unapologetic. "She asked me to do what you couldn't—write down the family story. In a way, that story saved me. For the first time I felt rooted in something. What you told me about your parents, how they believed in being open to the world, that through holding on to hope, even if it left them vulnerable—"

"Fuck you, Nizar." Her words seethed with acidic rage. "You used this expedition as a Trojan Horse to extract information from me."

Nizar looked incredulous. "That's what you took from what I said?"

"This expedition is bigger than our family. It's—"

"Yes, I know, the climate, the myth of the ark, the quest to reconnect people to the land . . . we've heard it already. But all that won't bring you any closer to the country you abandoned thirty years ago."

He turned around and went inside his tent. She heard noises that indicated he was packing. Murat, who had been quietly watching them spar, finally spoke up.

"I'm going to walk into town. It's safest for me as a Kurd. It's a thirty-minute walk, if I remember. I'll find us a car."

"I'm not leaving without the boats."

"We'll find a way to take them with us."

Ishtar watched Murat's solitary frame disappear in the direction of the town. When she could no longer see him, she walked to the bank and sat down.

She felt heavy, trapped and helpless amidst the brokenness. The brokenness of the boats, of Iraq, of her trust in Nizar. She fought her instincts to discard him, as she had many before. She had lost so many friends in her life. Time and space played a role, certainly, childhood friends from Baghdad now scattered across the world. But many friendships had been lost due to her own ego, to petty political differences, to a single judgement made and uttered in the heat of a moment. It was true that Zainab had lived her life in sanitised and safe memories of Iraq, ones that refused to deal with the ugliness under the surface, and that Mediha had created of Iraq a monster to justify her own estrangement. But she too had run away from her grief, channelling her personal pain into political outrage until she'd incinerated every single relationship in her fury. Now, here she was: a failed artist, and a lonely one too.

Without knowing it, Nizar's secret mission—to extract the family story—had clarified something for her, too. The suffusion of the family history within the folds of the expedition had brought her back to the seed of her own pain. She considered the three boats that made up the mythological ark. In a way, each was like a sister: Ishtar the guffa, innovative and headstrong; Mediha the kalak, sturdy and practical; and Zainab the meshouf, beautiful and grand.

A lizard crawled onto a rock beside her. It paused for a few moments, bathing in the new sun. Its small head twitched as it sensed its environment.

She heard the unzipping of a flap behind her. Nizar crawled out of his tent. He sat cross-legged on the ground beside her and took in a deep breath.

"For the last few days, I've been thinking of what compelled me to come with you. Part of me believed that by seeing all this first-hand, I might understand the brokenness inside of me. That I would understand the part I played in destroying my relationship with Alfie."

"Nizar, I'm sorry." The words felt like marbles in her mouth.

Nizar waved a hand in the air. They stared into the river. Dark blue ripples cut across the water, making their way towards them. Tilapia fish, swimming in circles just under the surface.

"What you were saying about my parents living with an openness to the world . . . that's not true. At least not later."

"What do you mean?" Nizar asked, tracing his thumb along the dent in his water bottle.

"My father didn't accidentally drown in the Tigris. That's a myth. He drowned himself. My mother and aunt hid his suicide to protect his legacy."

Nizar was quiet for some time. "Does my mother know this?"

"No," Ishtar replied. "Your grandmother kept it from all of us. She doesn't even know that I know the truth."

"So this is why my mother's plan to find the paintings and hold an exhibition . . ."

"Bringing attention back on my father worried my mother. People might ask questions, look into things a bit deeper." Ishtar pulled out her tobacco pouch and began rolling another cigarette. The wind off the river worried the delicate paper. "My point is that in his final act, my father gave a middle finger to the very concept of hope, turning his entire life's work to dust. And my mother . . . well, hope can never be built on a lie."

"Do you think you can ever forgive her?"

Ishtar sealed the cigarette with her tongue and lit it up, protecting the flame from the breeze. Somewhere in the distance, a generator droned.

"I don't know," she said, blowing out a cloud of smoke.

They were interrupted by the sound of engines. Ishtar stood up. Two vans pulled up at their camp, sunlight flashing on their windscreens. Murat hopped out, smiling.

"I found someone who can drive us, and the boats, to Erbil. From there we can get a flight to Baghdad." He pointed to a young man in his twenties, who was behind the steering wheel of the first van. "From Erbil, our friend here can help ship the boats to wherever we need them to go."

They loaded their belongings into the vans. Ishtar felt both relief and sadness at the idea of leaving the river. As they strapped the guffa to the roof, she turned to Nizar.

"I've been thinking about what you said. About me abandoning Iraq all those years ago."

"I was angry . . ."

"But it's true. Somewhere along the way I deluded myself into thinking that if I knew everything about this country, that if I held on to all this anger, it would somehow reduce the estrangement in my heart."

Nizar nodded. "I understand," he said quietly.

"But all of this is not just a metaphor. The ecosystem really *is* dying. The rivers of Iraq have always been the spinal cord of the country, and now they're dying from within like severed nerve endings . . ."

"Of course," Nizar said. "But—and I say this from personal experience—just because you are angry about imperialism, war, and climate destruction doesn't mean you also don't have a problem with your mother."

Zainab

October 2014

Zainab woke in the dark, her mother asleep beside her. It was nearly eight thirty in the evening. She had taken a nap, she remembered now, shortly after her mother walked in on her in the shower. Careful not to wake her mother, she got up slowly and left the bedroom. Mediha was in the kitchen, stirring a blood-red sauce.

"I thought you'd never wake up. I'm making bolognese."

Mediha walked over and embraced her. The hug was powerful and long, a show of domination.

Zainab pulled herself from her sister's grip. She had a sudden urge to abandon her plan, to return to Dubai and get as far from her sister as she could. Mediha poured each of them a large glass of red wine. Zainab took a big gulp.

"I've turned the sauna on. We can have a session after dinner."

Mediha walked out of the kitchen and returned a moment later with an embroidered pouch, which she placed on the table between them. She pulled out some marijuana and began to roll a joint.

"You're smoking marijuana?" Zainab asked.

"Don't be a prude."

Zainab took another gulp of the wine.

The bolognese was served with polenta. Zainab complimented her sister on the meal and listened as she spoke about her exhibition. People were impressed, Mediha said. The exhibition had made people think.

The wine and the meal calmed the nervous energy between them, and they settled into an easy rhythm. Zainab even took a puff of Mediha's joint and felt herself drift into a cloud of contentment.

"Did you say you were returning to Edinburgh tomorrow?"

"Yes," Mediha said, watching her. Did she know, Zainab wondered? She suddenly regretted not taking the paintings that afternoon when she had the chance. "I'll be staying two more nights there, but I'll be back on Thursday. That's the day you leave, right?"

"Yes. Quite early. We'll miss each other."

"Right," Mediha took a sip of wine. "Well, I'm glad we have this evening together."

"Me too. You know . . . all this stuff you say about Dubai . . . you have such strong feelings about a place you've never even seen. I'd like you to come visit, meet some people—"

"I don't want to visit. I've heard about the slave labour. I'm well aware of the laws around homosexuality. I've read the stories about British couples jailed for kissing in public."

"That's nonsense."

"It was in *The Guardian*, Zainab. It's not nonsense."

"Come on—"

"Why are you getting upset?"

"I'm not upset." Zainab stood up and put on her coat. "I'm heading out for a cigarette."

Outside she smoked a cigarette, then another. When she returned, Mediha was standing by the kitchen door with two white towels folded in her arms.

"The sauna is ready. It's out in the shed."

"But I didn't bring a swimming suit."

"It's best to be naked."

Zainab laughed, then saw that Mediha was serious.

"We're not going in naked . . . Middy, don't give me that look. It's weird . . . just give me one of your bathing suits."

"Does it bother you to be naked in front of your sister?"

"Yes, actually, it does."

"Why?"

"It's a modesty thing . . ."

"Don't give me this Arab modesty nonsense," Mediha muttered, taking off her t-shirt and slipping out of her yoga pants. She stood in the kitchen in her bra and underwear. "There's nothing wrong with nudity. It's completely natural."

"And there's nothing wrong with modesty . . . to be modest over one's body—"

"It's not modesty." Mediha unfastened her bra. "It's shame. I know because I used to be ashamed of my body. My body was the depository of different people. It felt dirty. I did not own it, did not feel connected to it. It was a reminder of all the horrors inflicted on it, all the shame I was made to feel."

Mediha pulled down her underwear and stood naked in the kitchen. Zainab tried not to look at her sister's body, but something inside her felt Mediha *wanted* Zainab to look. She lifted her gaze. Mediha's body was firm and toned—years of yoga and weightlifting had left her with the figure of a woman half her age. The strong, wiry frame of a European, Zainab thought, not the soft, rounded body of an Arab. It was the first time she had seen another woman fully naked.

Mediha met Zainab's gaze, and her eyes narrowed. "Perhaps if you had not been taught to feel shame over your body, you might not have been so complacent about him touching us as children."

Zainab froze. *Last night I dreamt Ammo Kuteiba followed me here.* "What did you say?"

Mediha handed Zainab a towel. "If it bothers you, you can wear this when you're inside." Then she opened the door and walked out into the cold.

Zainab stared at the pile of clothes where her sister once stood. She called Mediha's name. There was no response. She took off her clothes and wrapped the towel around herself. If she wanted to have a real conversation, it would have to be in the sauna.

She was about to leave when she remembered her recorder. She grabbed it from the pocket of her bag and clipped it to the hem of her towel so the mic faced out. For good luck, she grabbed her thinking putty, then stepped outside into the cold air.

Her body broke out in shivers. Through the darkness, she could see the warm glow of the sauna in the shed. She sprinted across the backyard and opened the door.

A wave of hot air smacked her face. It took time for her eyes to adjust to the heat. Mediha was a silhouette in the dim orange light, naked, sitting on her towel, her hands resting on her knees. She looked like a queen on her throne.

Zainab tightened the towel around her body and sat down beside her sister. Mediha turned to face her. Sweat glistened off her skin.

"In a strange way, I feel a sort of kinship with Jihadi John."

"What are you talking about?"

"The idea of holding something hostage so the truth can be revealed, so that the violence of the past can be shared with those complicit . . . with those who choose to turn a blind eye. I mean, he's a monster. But maybe we're all monsters."

"Middy, what did you just say to me in the kitchen?"

"We'll get to that," Mediha said. She took in a deep breath, rubbed her temple. "Do you have any idea of the memories those paintings bring back for me?"

"The paintings?" Zainab was confused. "But we could have helped. I was happy to help with whatever—"

"Oh, please," Mediha snapped. "I saw the way you dealt with the paintings you had. You were rolling them outwards. Who rolls paintings outwards? Oil paintings must be rolled *in*, not *out*."

"Don't talk to me like I'm stupid."

"You really don't get it, do you?"

The hot air burned her lungs. She looked at the sweat pooling in the crevice of her sister's collarbone.

"It's too hot. Can we have this conversation outside?"

"You haven't been here five minutes. You must stay for at least fifteen, otherwise you get no benefit."

The recorder Zainab had clipped to her towel was heating up. She felt it burning into her skin, imagined it melting into her flesh, becoming a part of her body forever, the memories recorded inside of it seeping through her bloodstream.

Mediha pointed a finger at her. "Our mother and that *monster* . . . I can't even say his name . . . sold so much of Baba's work during the Baathist years. You didn't know that did you? I had to run around the houses of former politicians to find those paintings. Do you know how hard it was for me to go back to Baghdad? But I had to. I knew it was the only way any of you would ever listen, would ever pay attention."

The back of Zainab's throat tightened. She rolled the thinking putty along the side of her leg.

"You and Ishtar were out all the time with your friends. Mum told you to take me with you, but no one wants their awkward baby sister with them."

"We brought you with us sometimes . . ."

"You were out there in your bubble, living your lives, while I was at home in the *real* Iraq. And these patterns continue! Who was left saddled with Mum while you both went off to live your lives?"

Mediha rose, stepping off the lower slat. She took up the ladle and flung a thin arc of water onto the stones. The stones hissed. The air wavered as a surge of heat hit Zainab's face. She felt lightheaded.

"Why didn't you tell me about the paintings?" Cedar and sweat stung the back of her throat. "I wouldn't have told anyone how you got them out. You could have trusted me."

"Trust you?" Mediha spat. A drop of sweat snaked down her forehead as she walked back towards Zainab. "Trust the sister who sold people out to the government, the sister who sold me to our uncle—"

"Don't you dare!" Zainab snapped. Mediha towered over her.

"What, all this time in the Gulf and you can't take a bit of heat?"

"That's it." Zainab stood up, adjusting her towel around her. "I've been so patient with you. I wanted to talk to you in the pub the other night, but you didn't want to speak. Now I've followed you into a sauna and you're sitting here making these horrible accusations."

Mediha stepped towards her, their faces inches apart. She stared at her with a look of icy hatred.

"Why the fuck did you think I swallowed all those pills?"

Something inside Zainab buckled. She shook her head. "Why are you bringing this up now?"

"Us Iraqis, we always want to sweep things under the carpet. Eib this, eib that. It's what got us into this terrible mess. Look at what's happened to our country. I won't live like that." Mediha's voice broke. She took a deep breath and rubbed her temples. "I told Mum by the way," she continued. "When she took me to Edinburgh after I swallowed those pills. And you know what she said? She said, 'Why you and not Zainab?' That was it. Why *you* and not Zainab?" Mediha looked at her with tears in her eyes. "Did he touch you too, after I was gone? Did he not then move on to you?"

Steam pressed at Zainab's throat. She set a palm on the wall to steady herself. She had to get out of there. The sauna was too small, and she was choking, oh God, she was choking and there was no way out.

"Don't do this," Zainab whispered. "I'm begging you."

"Do you remember how he would send you to the rooftop to watch the stars? Did you know? One night I looked you straight in the eyes, Zainab, and you turned around and left me there."

There were tears now, hot tears of shame and remorse. She retched and gasped for air, covered in sweat, as in those hot summer nights in Baghdad, those nights when Ishtar was studying in London and their mother was travelling, when Zainab was instructed to go up to the roof to gaze at the stars, leaving Mediha alone with . . .

Habibti, the stars are very bright tonight. You should go up to the roof and watch them . . . there's a whole world out there.

She heard his voice, soft and coaxing, as if he were sitting beside them in the sauna.

Zainab stumbled to the door. It was raining, and the memories chased her as she tried to run but they were inside her now, flooding her veins like ice-water. The thinking putty she'd been kneading slipped from her fist and rolled down the path. She smelt the whiskey on her uncle's breath as he nuzzled up beside her. *Soooorryy habibti*, he whispered as her wet feet slapped against the stone. She could feel his kisses, his hot breath on her cheeks. *Soooorryy habibti*, his tears, so many of them wetting her hair. Was it bad? Was it really that bad? The constellations of memories crystallised in her mind, and her heel struck the putty. She rolled over it and slipped, falling to the floor. She came down hard on the recorder, which gave a sharp crack, the casing splitting, its parts strewn about like entrails. She covered her face and wept.

Somehow, she found her way to the side door. She ran through the house, leaving puddles in her wake, and locked herself in the bathroom. She dropped to the tiled floor, hugged her knees and began to rock, a move that only made her feel more unhinged.

She was not sure how much time had passed when there was a knock on the door.

"Zainab, can you let me in?"

"Leave me alone."

"You can take the paintings. That's what you're here for, right? I'll be gone tomorrow. Take the stupid paintings. I don't need them anymore."

It occurred to Zainab then, as she lay on the bathroom floor, that Mediha had planned this all along. She had wanted Zainab to find the letter from Sotheby's. It had all been part of the trap to lure her here, so she could finally say her piece.

"I used to think that time would heal all wounds, but that's not true. Time only makes them fester."

"Go away!" Zainab screamed.

There was silence. The ringing in Zainab's ears subsided. She stood up, covering what she could of her modesty with the hand towel by the sink, and unlocked the door. Mediha was not in the hall. Zainab's clothes were folded neatly on the ground beside the bathroom door. She got dressed and walked towards her mother's bedroom.

"Bulbul?"

"Yes, Mama," she replied weakly.

Her mother sat up in bed and turned on the lamp. She studied Zainab's face. "Is everything okay?"

Her mother was to blame for all of this, for sowing division and mistrust, for selling the paintings, for banishing their father to obscurity, for bringing Ammo Kuteiba into their lives. She wanted to yell and scream at her for not protecting them, for allowing everything to fall apart.

But in the glow of the bedside lamp, it was as if her mother was no longer there. The person across from her was just a ghost of a memory.

Zainab undressed and got under the blankets beside Bridget. They were silent for some time. Finally, her mother spoke.

"I've been remembering this concert from many years ago. Your uncle had not yet moved in, this was before he was let go from the military, and he'd invited us on a trip to Stockholm.

Do you remember? Maybe you were too young. It was springtime, and Harry Belafonte was singing in the city. Martin Luther King was there. We debated whether to go. In the end we thought, if we go then we won't be able to record it, so will only enjoy it once, and then it will be just a memory. But if we watch it on the television, we could record it and listen to it again and again. And we did, you know, for the longest time we listened to it repeatedly. I've lost the recording now . . . it's gone forever."

"What year was this?"

"What?"

"What year was the concert?" Zainab asked, louder now.

She fiddled with her mother's hearing aid. "Can you hear me now?"

"It doesn't matter."

"What do you mean it doesn't matter? It does matter if you can't hear me . . . what year was the concert?"

"1966. Five years after your father died. So that would have made you seven?"

"Seven or eight, yes."

Zainab got up and grabbed her iPad, then returned to bed. She went to YouTube and typed in 'Harry Belafonte concert Stockholm 1966'. She played the video. Her mother's eyes widened.

"How did you find it?"

"The Internet has everything that has ever happened."

"He was such a charming man," Bridget said as Belafonte encouraged the audience to sing along. "He really knew how to work a crowd."

Belafonte began to sing 'Where have all the flowers gone?'.

"This song came out soon after your father died."

Bridget began to sing along softly. And as she did, tears pooled in her eyes.

"Your uncle was a good man, Bulbul. He took care of us.

But he drank. What could I do? I wanted to stay in Baghdad. I was doing my best."

Zainab recalled what Nisreen had told her the night she was visiting in Dubai, after Zainab had desperately tried to explain away Nisreen's accusation. *But you were the daughter of artists. You were protected*, her old friend had said. *And you had a British passport. You could have just left. You didn't have to inform on anyone.* Zainab had made many mistakes, and though she had tried to bury them, the guilt had been there all along. But they had all made mistakes. Zainab could only offer herself—and others—compassion.

She stroked her mother's hair. "You did your best, Mama. We all did our best."

Her mother began to weep.

"I feel the weight of your resentments, all three of you. They burn and boil in different ways. All you girls left, and there was nothing I could do. The situation got so bad, Zanoobti, I had no choice but to sell them off to survive. I destroyed his legacy."

"We all did what we could to survive," Zainab said, and the truth of this statement extended like a river through the core of her.

Zainab thought of Nizar, in Iraq with Ishtar. She thought of the man her son had become, the mixture of pride and fear that burned in her whenever he came to mind. She wanted to be near him now.

"Mama, is your Iraqi passport still valid?"

"Yes. Won't ever give it up. You know they gave it to me after your father died, as a gift for helping them finish the monument."

"Would you go back to Iraq?"

Her mother was quiet for a long time. Zainab thought that perhaps she did not hear her, but just as she was about to let the question fall into the dark abyss between them, her mother spoke.

"Why would I? To see that the Baghdad I know no longer exists? What would happen to all my memories then?"

They watched the concert for a few more minutes before her mother spoke again.

"He would act so silly when he drank, Bulbul. He could not control himself."

"I know Mamati."

"And I left him with you. Is that terrible, Zainab? That I left him with you girls?"

"Yes."

"But you were always such a responsible girl! I knew I could rely on you. So beautiful and responsible. One beautiful daughter, one smart daughter, one creative daughter . . ."

"You have to stop saying that."

"Just because I don't talk about things doesn't mean I don't know. I just believe some memories shouldn't be shared around the table like a mezze . . ."

"Mmhmm . . ."

"I don't know what to do Bulbul, I'm scared."

"I know, Mama. Me too."

"Have I made too many mistakes?"

"We all make mistakes, Mamati."

"I mean he just could not control himself."

Ishtar

October 2014

The roads crawled with patrolling militiamen in civilian cars. Most had big beards; all were armed. Ishtar felt herself back in the days of the Iran-Iraq war. It had rained that morning and the smell of fresh earth suffused the air, mixing with the smell of petrol and sewage. The scent of young mud, complex and earthy, transported her to childhood summer afternoons sitting in their back garden, when they would douse the ground with water to clear the dust. She clung to this memory, tenuous and small as it was.

The route to their hotel was a labyrinth of checkpoints, each with its own culture and ecosystem yet all drenched in the same paradoxical feelings: danger and safety, reassurance and threat. Strokes of fear, boredom, and shallow authority were painted on the faces of the young men guarding the structures. Ishtar stared at them, at the cars, at the hands shuffling papers through open windows, at the children and older women who approached each vehicle to beg. Many of the checkpoints were painted in camouflage. Some had slogans on their barriers: *Respect and you shall be respected*, said one. *Everyone is subjected to the same law*, said another. At one, blue doves were painted in diagonal lines against the white background. Even in the most mundane of military structures, art found a way to seep in.

Nizar booked the Babylon, a luxury hotel tucked in a crook of the Tigris on the Jadiriya peninsula—expensive, but they needed a safe landing spot, somewhere to take stock.

Ziggurat-shaped, it was enormous and unapologetically gaudy. The gilt lobby, meant to signal wealth and power, was largely empty: a handful of foreign UN officials held meetings around stacks of papers, and one or two businessmen sat wide-legged in the lounge, scrolling their phones.

In her room, Ishtar flicked through the television channels. Government stations broadcast a stream of patriotic songs alongside images of soldiers running through obstacle courses, marching in uniform, and shooting at unknown targets. She switched to CNN which played the day's news in long loops. She took a long, hot shower, and put on the hotel's white cotton robe.

Pulling back the curtains, she stepped out onto the small balcony. The terrace looked onto the pool and, beyond that, the waters of the river, which appeared grey and murky under the cloudy sky. The stone riverbanks were empty, save for a large, docked boat with a neon sign that read 'Floating Restaurant'.

She returned inside and got dressed, selecting a long-sleeved t-shirt and baggy cotton trousers, over which she wore an abaya. She pulled her hair into a ponytail and used her scarf as a makeshift hijab, then made her way down to the lobby. At reception, she ordered a taxi.

"To the Hunting Club," Ishtar directed the driver when the car arrived. The old family home had been a two-storey villa in the Mansour neighbourhood, several blocks over from the Club. Though Kuteiba had forbidden them from going there, formerly the breeding ground for Baathists and their supporters, it had always been the marker of their neighbourhood, a reference point to which everything else was situated.

Outside of the hotel barricades, the streets were quiet. Traffic picked up as they approached the suspension bridge. Despite the war, Karrada bustled with life. The jungle of concrete was marked with palm trees, but the trees seemed fewer than she remembered, and those that remained were unkempt and thirsty. As they drove further, Ishtar grew disoriented. Roads had been closed, neighbourhoods divided, cement blasts erected, and the route they were taking was unfamiliar, the city an impenetrable maze.

"Where do you live?" the driver asked, clocking her foreignness. He was a slim man in his sixties, with kind eyes and a scruffy beard.

"London. But I grew up here. In Mansour actually. I'm trying to find my family home."

"Do you remember where it was?"

"Not exactly, but I can find my way if you drop me off at the Hunting Club."

"You should be careful. Baghdad isn't like it once was."

As a child, Ishtar and her sisters often played in the streets with no concern beyond a scraped knee or twisted ankle. They had long picnics on farms and grassy lawns and moved through the city without a care. In the new Baghdad, a terrain that's hospitable to one person could be deadly to another. Her movements would need to be calculated.

The Hunting Club came into view, and behind it, the unfinished mosque Saddam had been building on the site of the old racetrack. Construction had halted when the US invaded, and the concrete shell had dominated the neighbourhood ever since, a monument to the country's post-war divisions. She gazed at the ring of domes shouldering the sky, the centre open like the crater left behind by a pulled tooth.

Out of the taxi, she walked down the main road that paralleled the suburban row of houses in Al-Mansour, adjusting her scarf in the breeze. Traffic was heavy and men on motorbikes whizzed by, splashing through puddles that mirrored the wires cross-hatching the sky. The rain had left the rubbish slick and clotted in the gutters. Soldiers cradling rifles scrolled their phones, torn posters of martyrs peeled from the concrete. She took a left and stopped in her tracks.

Nineveh Kebab.

The glowing letters brought forth a flood of memories: late-night kebabs in fresh samoon bread, onions dusted with sumac and lemon halves cupped like small suns, served in pink plastic baskets. She paused at the door and peered in. How had this restaurant survived all these years? Inside, it looked unchanged and dilapidated. Hope rose inside her. She had a marker, she could orient herself.

With her back to the restaurant, she reached into her memory. "Seventh road from Ninevah," she whispered to herself. It was how they had always described their street. She counted each road as she passed. They were largely empty, the neighbourhood's grid system more or less unchanged. The villas and town houses, no more than one or two storeys each, resembled those of her memory. But something felt unfamiliar. It was as if a new neighbourhood had risen, and she struggled to map past to present. She had spent all her childhood here, she reminded herself. Even after their father had died, their mother remained in the home they had built together. It had been Kuteiba who had moved into their life, not the other way around.

She counted the fifth, then sixth, and turned onto the seventh. The street was unrecognisable. The family home had been about halfway down the left-hand side of the street, but as Ishtar walked the length of it, she was at a loss. Could it have been torn down? Perhaps she hadn't counted correctly. Perhaps she had walked a street too far. She walked back to the main road and retraced her steps. No, she had been right. She returned to the seventh street.

She looked for recognisable faces, familiar signs, abandoning Ninevah Kebab for the reliability of the Hunting Club. She tried to situate the Club behind her, picturing where her house would be. Opening her eyes, she headed back down the same street, hoping that she would stop at a point of memory, that something inside her would tell her when she had arrived. If she could find a way back to the Hunting Club, she'd be able to ask someone. But ask them what? How to find your home in a city torn apart by a brutal invasion and civil war? The city had been excavated, and whatever had been constructed on its ruins bore little trace to the city in her memories.

Palm fronds rustled in the wind. Ishtar did not know where she was going, had no clear direction or point of return. She stopped and adjusted her hijab, her forehead sweating under the intensifying sun.

The family home had been demolished.

And it was as if, upon accepting this, she suddenly felt reoriented. She walked to the end of the seventh road, which connected to 14 Ramadan Street. Comfortingly busy, she passed a bakery setting out samoon, steam fogging the glass. On the street, a woman in a black abaya was selling roses. She offered one to Ishtar with a warm smile. Ishtar smiled back, took the rose, and paid the woman what she asked. She spotted a large coffee shop that looked hip and modern and, dare she say it, comfortingly Western. Ishtar stepped inside. Most of the patrons were teenagers; they must have been no older than seven when the coalition forces invaded. Everyone in the cafe had only ever known a destroyed city.

"Can I help you?" The server behind the counter asked, a young man in his mid-twenties.

She felt old and helpless. She cleared her throat, tried to bring authority to her presence. "I need a taxi," she said, her voice steadier now, more assured. "I need a taxi to the Babylon Hotel."

* * *

Despite the threat of bombs, they dined outside of the hotel. In a waterfront restaurant at the end of Haifa Street, a young man moulded raw meat onto skewers. A tattoo down the side of his neck read: *My Mother, queen of all humans, is the candle of my life.*

They were led to a table along the bustling riverbank. They ordered masgouf and selected their fish, a slimy grey carp with long, feline whiskers. A man with a thick moustache stunned it with a short club, then plunged his knife into the back of the head and butterflied the carp open.

"Is the fish from the river?" Ishtar asked, as the man removed the carp's guts and gills, before rinsing the cavity clean.

"You'll only be eating trash and human remains from this river," the man laughed, scoring the thick meat with a flick of his wrist. He massaged in rock salt and oil, a dusting of turmeric and a sour swipe of tamarind, then fixed the fish to a metal rack and propped it in a crescent around a low fire. "The safest fish are bred in freshwater pools."

Ishtar had hoped the food would relieve her of her disquiet, but even the fish's familiar smokiness could not stifle her despair. It grew inside her like a fog and consumed the hope that had fuelled her over the last two weeks. As the waiter cleared their plates, she wiped her mouth with a napkin.

"I think we should call it a day."

"What do you mean?" Nizar asked.

"The expedition's over."

Murat and Nizar were silent for some time. She had prepared for the possibility that a return to Baghdad would not be a reconciliation. What she had not prepared for was that the return would not be a return at all. Her eyes drifted to the napkin on her lap, which contained lines from an al-Jawahiri poem in elegant gold lettering: *I greeted your banks from afar, so greet me. O blessed Tigris, mother of orchards.*

"There can be liberation in failure," she said, though the words felt hollow. "Murat, we will purchase your ticket back to Hasankeyf, of course."

"We can fix the boats," Murat said. "It's safer now that we are heading south."

"We don't have the money . . ."

"I can use my mother's credit card."

"Nizar, it's over."

They paid for their meal and hailed a taxi. Murat and Ishtar got in, but Nizar held back.

"You go on ahead without me."

Ishtar blinked. "What do you mean?"

"I need to see it."

A car behind them honked.

"See what?"

"The square. I almost died there. I need to see it again . . ."

She searched his face, confused. Then she understood. She couldn't leave him to go off on his own, but she felt unprepared to face her father and reckon with the monument that effectively killed him.

"It's late," she reasoned. "We'll go tomorrow when it's safer."

Nizar shook his head. "I'll only be half an hour. Go on ahead. I'll text when I'm back."

Ishtar got out of the taxi. "Murat, we'll be back soon."

Murat nodded and the car sped off, swallowed by the ribbon of lights heading south. Ishtar and Nizar hailed a Sapia taxi. Inside, Ishtar stared out the window at men of various ages who sat along the trash-littered banks in the moonlight, taking selfies and laughing. Some had brought their own shisha and were smoking it on the bank. Despite the threat of death, there remained an insistence on life. How many of these men would draw their last breath in the next six months? How many would still be standing in the next twelve?

They got off at the neck of the bridge and walked the rest of the way in silence. The mood had darkened, the night felt dangerous. Still, they kept a steady pace. They dodged potholes and puddles of lingering rainwater and ignored the few men staring at them.

When the monument came into view, they stopped in their tracks and took it in. Illuminated with golden lights, the stonework stretched out against the starless night like an ancient scroll. Ishtar was surprised by the size of it. It had been larger and more imposing in her memory.

Though smaller than she remembered, the monument was infinitely more beautiful, both awe-inspiring and totally ordinary amidst its surroundings, backdropped by the palm and eucalyptus trees. The square, larger than when Haydar was alive, had fallen into disrepair. Trash accumulated on corners, the once ornate buildings now encrusted with grime.

As she approached, the top of the structure rose further away as if stretching into the dark sky. She felt its imposing shadow falling not just on her but inside of her, as if she had been carrying it within her all these years.

There is no permanence, do we build a house to stand forever, do we seal a contract to hold for all time?

The line from the Epic appeared in her mind, Gilgamesh's reflections on the nature of life following his futile quest for immortality. Over the past decade, one of her foremost creative obsessions revolved around the violence unleashed by modernity, how its unwavering pursuit of progress, its emphasis on science and rationality, enforced a violent separation between the present and the past.

Life, which you look for, you will never find. For when the gods created man, they let death be his share.

Had she never discovered the truth of her father's death, so much at the hands of his most ambitious creation, would modernity still have tormented her so relentlessly?

"The life of man is but a wind," she spoke aloud, though as the words emerged from her mouth it was as if her father were speaking to her. As if, with these ancient words, he was guiding her through her sorrow, reminding her to cherish the moments in her possession. She didn't need to find a grand meaning in this journey.

But she wanted to. She wanted to find hope.

Beside her, Nizar began to cry.

"I've lived my entire life feeling that everything was on the verge of being taken from me."

She wrapped an arm around his shoulder, feeling the force of his tears. She held him until his sobs quieted, and he grew still in her arms. After a while, he pulled away and wiped his face.

Ishtar drew in a breath. "All my life, I had sought out unattainable perfection. In my work, my relationships, my politics. It was only in endings that I felt safe enough to appreciate what had been there all along, and by then it was only in mourning."

She turned her back to the monument and walked away, guided by a presence. Whether it was her father or something else she could not say, she only felt suddenly and wholly understood, and this propelled her towards the river. Nizar followed. They took a right down a dark and dirty road lined with half-destroyed buildings, facades half-gutted, floors held up by short-through pillars, rusted rebar combing the night sky. Generators throbbed behind shuttered shops. The bottom of the street opened onto Abu Nuwas, which ran alongside the black river. The once grand boulevard had been home to restaurants, galleries, and cafes, but now only a few dance clubs peppered the street, which was largely empty save for a few drunk men sitting alone in darkened cars. Each time the door to one of the clubs opened, ear-splitting pop music spilled out onto the road.

They crossed the road to be closer to the water. They tried various gates down to the river, but all were locked. They walked on until Ishtar found a shorter gate, low enough to climb. She scanned the promenade: a guard hut near the stairwell.

"Keep watch," she whispered to Nizar, then slipped over the gate.

She walked until she found a gap down to the sandy bank, slick from the rain. She slipped off her shoes, watching for glass, and let her toes sink into wet sand. A cool wind came off

the river, carrying the smell of algae. Even after the previous night's rain, the water ran low. Plastic bottles nuzzled at the edge, taken a little by the current and then brought back. Her feet in the shallows, she cupped a palmful of sand and let it seep through her fingers. She wiped her hand on her calf and stood up. Her desire to sail down the Tigris now felt like someone going back to the ruins of their home following a terrible fire.

A strong gust of wind blew across the river, lifting swirls of dust in the air. She closed her eyes. When she opened them again, a silhouette emerged across the black water. The shadow drifted closer until she could make out a guffa, the first she had seen on their journey. For a moment she thought she was dreaming, but there it was, bitumen-dark wicker, palm-fibre seams, manned by a tall man with long, thin legs and a broad V-shaped back. He was dressed in a long, oversized dishdasheh, a black and white keffiyeh on his head.

Ishtar raised an arm in greeting, and the man smiled and said hello. Deep leathery creases were carved into his face, the lines like a language Ishtar recognised but could not understand.

"Where are you returning from?" the man asked.

How had he known that Ishtar was a returnee?

"London."

He nodded. "Thanks to God for your safe return."

Ishtar pointed to the boat. "This is the first guffa I've seen on the river."

"The new generation prefers speedboats."

The man manoeuvred the guffa towards the sandy bank with two clean strokes. He docked, lifted his dishdasheh elegantly, and hopped ashore.

"Abu Rashid," the man introduced himself.

"Ishtar. Where are you from?"

"Down south. The marshes."

"I've been travelling down the river, starting from Hasankeyf in Turkey."

"By boat?"

"Yes. I built my own guffa, though it needs some work. It holds too much water."

"One third of the depth should be below the river surface. No more than that. What materials did you use?"

Ishtar told him of the rotting goat skins, and how she'd resorted to using materials from further north. She told him about her now abandoned goal of connecting the different boats together.

"An ark," Abu Rashid said with a knowing smile, drawing his long fingers through his white beard. "I can help."

When they returned to the hotel, Ishtar sat on her balcony and smoked. She looked out across the black waters, glimpsing The Green Zone across the river. The epicentre of the brutality of the last fifteen years. What should have been prime riverfront real estate was now walled off and restricted, the breeding ground for the worst the country had suffered and continued to suffer.

She stood up and went inside the room, rummaging through her belongings until she found her unfinished painting of the Epic of Gilgamesh tucked inside her backpack. She examined the empty space bordering the central image. Without too much thought she sat on the bed and began to sketch Dave's face. She drew his thick neck and square jaw, his large reflective sunglasses, the deep dimple in his cheek.

"He really does look like a thumb," she said to herself.

Then, she began to sketch the fight. She drew herself falling into the guffa as Dave towered over her. She drew the shadows of the others around them.

She returned to the balcony and continued to sketch. She drew one of the checkpoints they had crossed on their journey from the airport to the hotel. She drew the blue doves painted across the concrete walls, the armed men with dirty hands exchanging identification cards. She drew herself lost in the labyrinth of her childhood neighbourhood. The images poured out of her so fast she could barely keep up, her hands moving furiously about the page until a knock on the door pulled her from her trance. When she opened it, Nizar was standing on the other side.

"What is it?" She asked.

"They're coming."

Part IV

Where the Rivers Meet

"The river rises, flows over its banks
and carries us all away, like mayflies
floating downstream: they stare at the sun,
then all at once there is nothing."
—Utanapishtim, *The Epic of Gilgamesh*

November 2014

I see my father in his workroom. Rather, I smell him, cigarettes and turpentine and a strange, sweet cologne. I am six years old, and I am watching my father sketch the boat he has promised to build for me. I lean over his shoulder as he writes down the dimensions of the vessel: fifty centimetres from bow to stern, a sail measuring thirty by twenty, and a width of fifteen. I tell him I want it painted in the colours of the Iraqi flag, and he says that we will call the vessel 'Ishtar', after my own name. I smell wood shavings and glue as I listen to him describe the mechanics of ensuring the boat stays afloat.

We will place a small hook on the boat, he says, which will allow us to attach a long piece of rope. This way you can run alongside the boat and stop it from drifting too far downstream.

My mother's voice. Ishtar! I told you to get in the bath thirty minutes ago.

I am peeled away from my father, from his smell and the sounds of his anxious pencil scratchings, and my mother takes my place behind him, laying a hand on his shoulder and bending over to kiss his neck.

My father will die in two weeks, suddenly and without warning, and in time we will leave the country, one after the other, and I will produce many works of art, but none will match the grandeur of my father's final creation, and the boat will remain a sketch on paper. His promise to sail the boat down the river will be broken.

I turn around. Zainab is wheeling Mama through the doors

of our hotel in Baghdad. Behind them, a taxi driver struggles with three heavy cases. My mother looks frail, but her eyes remain alert. I run towards them, towering over my mother's slight frame, and kiss her forehead. The smell of turpentine rises from her paper-thin skin as she closes her eyes and accepts my offering.

I turn to Zainab.

She's too old to be here, I whisper.

She's not going to get any younger, Zainab replies.

I'm right here you know.

I look at the three suitcases and tell Zainab that she won't be able to take all her baggage on this journey.

This entire family has so much baggage, she laughs.

I point to the cases and say, no, literally, your bags. We don't have space.

Zainab frowns. But these are the family paintings, she says.

* * *

The hours after the sauna are a blur. When Mama is asleep, I buy two first-class tickets to Baghdad. If Ishtar is not willing to come to us, then I must bring Mama to her.

The next morning, when Mediha's taxi disappears, I sneak out of Mama's room. Mediha's bedroom is heavy with the previous night's revelations. I realise that I have always known, deep down, the secrets that plagued our childhood. For so long I had sanitised my memories of Baghdad, like the pretty trinkets of Iraqi heritage I create and sell.

I open the door to the closet. The paintings are there, on top of one another, unframed, protected by large sheets of paper. Was Mediha holding the paintings hostage until she could speak her truth?

It was never about the paintings.

The works are categorised by artist and date, and I sit cross-legged on the floor, selecting several of Baba's works from different periods of his life: the early years, when Matisse and Picasso dominated his shapes and colours, and some from later, from the final series he painted when he was bed-ridden following his heart attack. I select my favourite painting of his, of a woman sunbathing on the roof of a typical Baghdadi home. Beside the woman, a cat with large, almond-shaped eyes stands guard.

I also take two works done by Amma Rajiha. One is of a woman standing in front of a mosque—the look on the woman's face is one of uncertain defiance, the other is of a group of women drinking tea by a river. Like all her works, the paintings are untitled.

Finally, I take a few of my mother's paintings and even something of Mediha's, a collage of photographs of dismembered body parts arranged in the form of a dancing body, entitled 'Self-Portrait in Exile'.

Before leaving, I write a long letter to Mediha. I explain that I am taking Mama with me to Baghdad, and that I have borrowed some paintings for the trip. I ask her to join us and tell her that I have transferred five thousand pounds to her account to purchase a round-trip ticket. *I hope to see you there*, I write.

During our layover in Dubai, I pick up an old painting Nizar made when he was twelve, along with a small metal embossment of a bull I made the year before.

Now, I am here in Baghdad, smoking a cigarette with Ishtar, and I tell her all of this.

I know it sounds crazy, I say, and maybe I am crazy for bringing Mama all the way here . . .

Ishtar is quiet as she drags on her cigarette. I am waiting for her to scold me, to tell me that I am irresponsible and reckless.

I'm glad you're both here, she finally says. *We* are glad.

Something inside me awakens, and I touch her arm.

Where is he? I ask. Where is my son?

* * *

My mother unzips her suitcase, her brow knitted as she carefully unrolls the paintings on the carpeted hotel room floor.

You've done it, I laugh. You've taken the paintings.

Am I stupid for doing this? My mother asks, suddenly self-conscious.

No, I assure her. I'm laughing because I'm impressed, and because I'm happy you're here.

I'm sorry I roped you into all this, she says.

It's the best thing you've ever done.

I've always dreamt of exhibiting the family's work in Baghdad. It makes sense, somehow, to bring them on this expedition. In some ways, Ishtar's ark is like a home, isn't it?

From the very beginning, it's been our art that has saved us.

It is the first time I include myself within the family. For years, it has always been 'they' and 'them', and as this 'our' spills from my lips, my mother's anguish over the paintings clarifies. Watching her face as she looks at them, I realise it is her own home she's looking at, a home she has been estranged from for decades.

My mother unrolls one painting, hands it to me, and asks if I remember it. It's a painting from an art class many years ago when we were living in Kuwait. I must have been twelve, maybe thirteen. The art teacher had taken us outside to paint landscapes, and my eyes settled on two minarets in the horizon, visible between the branches of a large tree. I began to paint, meticulously trying to stay true to the image I was seeing, but by the time I had finished the painting looked nothing like the reality. The blue skies and green leaves of the tree blended into a dark purple colour, and the minarets bled into the branches. Two ghostly shapes emerging from behind the leaves.

You brought this painting? It's terrible!

I love it. It looks like two lovers meeting in an enchanted forest.

I re-examine the painting from this perspective, and a distinct memory rises to the surface. Alfie and I skipping down the street laughing at ourselves. What would it take for me to break old patterns, to stop myself from picking up and leaving?

* * *

We contact several fishermen and explain our project. They help us collect boats: guffas, kalaks, and meshoufs. We arrange the boats together in an expanding, circular pattern, with the guffa at the centre surrounded by petals of mashoufs. We buy a large white cloth to which we pin the paintings, as well as some protective plastic to preserve them. We create two long bundles of reed to hold the cloth up, a makeshift sail to the ark. We plan to hold the event in Dora, on the outskirts of Baghdad just south of Jadiriya. There we will be able to sail the ark along a stretch of the river unobstructed by river police. When we visit Dora the next day, the factories along the riverbank blow out thick clouds of industrial fog. The surface of the water is a soup of black oil, with clusters of white froth and floating refuse. We return to the car and head back into town. That afternoon, we decide to brave the threat of bombs and militias and hold the event in the old city centre.

* * *

On the day of the launch Ishtar warns me that I will have to speak to the crowds, if only on Haydar's behalf.

Just imagine you are talking to us in your living room, she says. Tell them some of your stories.

The weather is hotter than anything I have experienced in decades. My body tires before the speeches even begin. I'm reminded of my first year in Baghdad, how wedded I was to that rickety fan. The memory materialises in my mind as I watch the curious crowd gather, larger than expected, surrounding a floating water taxi stand that has been transformed into a makeshift stage on the river.

I am seated beside my grandson in the front row. The crowd turns towards the stage as Ishtar makes her way to the podium. She is dressed in white. Her black hair is woven in a single braid that runs down her back like rope. Her eyes are large, and her brow is furrowed. Beside her are two men. One is large and burly, with a mane of curly shoulder-length hair, while the other is tall and thin, with leathery skin and a white beard. Ishtar holds a microphone in one trembling hand and a piece of paper in the other, and I recall Haydar's trembling hand as he took the stage the day of our first exhibition sixty years ago. The chatter of the crowd reduces to a whisper.

Ishtar begins to speak.

I left Baghdad twenty-eight years ago, in 1986. For most of my life, I have been estranged from the city of my birth. And yet, I always bristled at the idea that I was in exile. How could I be in exile when I felt so intimately connected to this country, when the soil and the water felt one and the same with my own flesh and blood? As much as I wanted to believe otherwise, the truth is that my link with this country and its people has been broken, shattered by decades of violence and pain. But this brokenness is felt not just by those who have left. Even those who remained have had their connection to the land broken. Today, on this river, physical barriers and security restrictions prevent fishermen from travelling through these waters. Up north, an enormous dam will soon flood one of the oldest cities in the world, displacing its inhabitants and suffocating the livelihoods of those who use this river to survive. Slowly, river by river, blast by blast, our tether to the land is severed.

A few days ago, I visited the Iraqi Museum and asked the curator whether there were plans to create a museum to commemorate the recent wars and occupations. She laughed in my face. 'Who needs a museum when you're living amid the destruction? What we need is a museum of forgetting.' Her words stayed with me. After decades of destruction, our city cannot look to the future. We have become a culture of memories. Memories can prevent us from being, even as they remain indispensable to being. It is easy to live in the past. What is more difficult is to use the past to imagine a future. In many ways, the crises we now face are crises of creativity. Not just in our failure to imagine how bad things could become, but also in our inability to imagine a way forward.

In time, the river will become saltier, the southern marshes will dry up, the northern villages will drown. To prepare for this we must remember what came before. This knowledge will serve as our ark. Beside me on this stage is a man from the north of the river and a man from the south of the river. Before this journey, they had never met. They come from different walks of life. And yet their lives are interwoven, because a stir upstream will cloud the water hundreds of kilometres away.

Ishtar lowers the microphone and turns around. Behind her, three young men pull away the blue tarp behind the stage, revealing a giant ark composed of three different boats. On the water, the ark does not so much float as roll in stride with the gentle waves. Across the diameter of the circular structure, a large white tarp flutters in the wind with several encased paintings carefully fastened to the cloth. My eyes fall on Haydar's painting almost immediately: *Woman Dreaming by Water*. From the *Qayloulat* collection, his daydreams, his final series. I look down at the painting below it. My breath catches in my throat.

After Haydar's death, all his friends and admirers needed to be beside me. I did not know whether they were driven by an obligation to help, or whether they were hoping to find traces of Haydar in my presence. I felt less like a grieving widow and more like a medium to a higher being. I retreated to the shadows. I no longer painted. The smell of turpentine made me retch, the touch of paper like a knife against my skin. I remained this way for eighteen months. I thought I would never paint again.

One morning, I woke up with a gentle gnawing in my soul. I packed my pencils and some paper and drove down to the river. I sat by the riverbank and observed the buildings on the other side, admiring the old architecture that had enchanted me when I first arrived. I realised that for many years I had stopped seeing them. The quaint buildings had grown familiar over time, melting into the background. Through Haydar's death, I had once again become a foreigner—to the city, but also to myself—and because of this I saw the horizon with new eyes. I began to sketch, recalling a piece of advice Haydar told me when we were students in London.

In art as in life, we do not draw the light, we leave room for it.

The lightest point is the page itself. From there, one builds gradients towards the darkest point, where the pencil pushes down the hardest, filling every possible pigment, every crevice of paper, with lead. It is the simplest of illusions, a trick of perspective allowing the untouched page to become light. That morning, I felt as though Haydar's hands were holding my own, guiding and steadying me as I drew the shadows of the old Baghdadi house across the river.

Fifty years later, I am face-to-face with that same painting. I look past the crowds, past Ishtar and her ark, and I see, across the river, the old Baghdadi building. I am sitting at the exact point I had been standing when I painted it all those years ago. The past and the present are one. Memories flood back, of Haydar, of sanding tables and painting chairs and building a life and talking, yes, those nights spent talking, our minds and hearts bursting with ideas and dreams. These memories are mine and only mine, and when I am gone, they will be gone too, floating away like specks of dust in the expanse of the universe.

My eyes take in the remaining paintings. Some I thought had

been lost forever, but they are here. My daughters have brought them back from the dead.

Bibi, my grandson says as he grabs hold of my arm. Bibi, it's your turn to speak.

I shake my head and try to move my mouth to say 'no', that simple word, but I cannot speak. And now a pair of strong arms grab my own, helping me to my feet, and I am staring into my eldest daughter's face.

Come on Mama, Ishtar says. Just a few words. Hundreds of eyes follow my journey to the stage. Someone brings me a chair, another holds the microphone to my mouth. I look out across the sea of faces and wonder whether the crowd contains people I taught many years ago, or perhaps children of my former students. So many students passed through those art classes in Baghdad. Where are they now? I clear my throat. It has been so long since I have spoken Arabic.

I am the widow of Haydar Mathloum. Most of you know him as the creator of the *Symphony of Hope.*

Traces of confusion flicker across the faces of the crowd, and I realise that I have referred to the monument in its original name, the name Haydar intended it to be. Everyone here, my daughters too, know the monument only as the *Symphony of Fate*, the name I cynically changed it to after his death all those years ago.

I did not misspeak, I assure the crowds. That is the true name of the monument, and it is time for this name to usher a new dawn.

A murmur ripples through the crowds.

One of the first things my husband told me when we met was that light can only exist in the presence of darkness. The rule applies to art as well as life: to create light, one must cast a shadow. My late husband brought so much light to the world, but, like all light, he cast a shadow. This shadow was a product of many things: anger at authority, fear of betrayal, a creative unease with the march towards an ill-defined progress that never looked back, and whose costs were borne by ordinary people, in Iraq and beyond. It was the shadow of a generation.

I ask for some water. It is brought to me. I feel like a queen, I tell whoever hands me the water, and the crowd laughs. I open my mouth to speak again, but a loud gasp in the audience stops me. I hear Zainab's voice cry out in surprise:

Mediha! You came!

My youngest daughter is standing by the front of the stage. She is wearing large, dark sunglasses. Zainab reaches out to her, and they hold each other in a deep, turbulent embrace. Ishtar is beside them. I want to run to them, to hold them and apologise for all I was unable to protect them from, but I cannot move, and tears gather in my eyes. Mediha turns to me and smiles. It is a smile she has never given me before, soft and gentle and full of grace.

Come on, Mama, she says. Keep going.

I do as she says.

It is true that our paths, our myths, our histories can give us clues to find our way back home. But how to look back, to construct meaning from fragments and broken mirrors? We try to organise our memories into a portrait of something or archive them like artefacts in a museum. Perhaps we should instead embrace the uncertainty of memory. And to embrace uncertainty, one can only be armed with hope.

* * *

Baghdad is behind us and the landscape begins to change, imprinting in our minds new visions, new memories. The walls of the riverbank give way to shrubs and reeds, which shimmer in golden hues under the sun. The stink of urban decay fades, the gentle aroma of wet earth remains. Concrete blocks of houses dot the landscape. An endless stretch of palm trees unfolds towards the horizon, discarded plastic bags dancing on their fronds. We see smaller settlements—sprinklings of huts carved with mud, straw, and reed—emerging from foliage. The river flows unimpeded along an alluvial plane. The topography is composed of flatlands, pockets of glistening light collect on the surface of the river and shoot up towards the sky. The early burst of youthfulness in the gushing waters up north make way, allowing us to bide our time, to reflect, to breathe. The expanse of the water disorients, but the flow is constant, indistinguishable, dissolving memory and eroding identity. Our boats are heavy with drinking water, with canned food and rice, but everywhere we go the people provide us with everything we may need. We exchange stories and ideas, our voices are jovial and loud. We form a new type of closeness, one centred on our bodies, the aches and pains of the journey, the challenges of going to the bathroom, a familiarity created by sleeping side-by-side, under the stars.

In the weakened flow, debris gathers and swells. At the edges of the river, sludge collects with plastic bottles and bags, cartons and tyres, dead fish. We glide through the weaponised waters, and we imagine the city-state of Umma and Lagash battling for centuries over irrigation canals, the waters siphoned off, withheld, diverted, and poisoned. We see the United States drop bombs on sewage plants, we watch the waste leak into the waters. We watch hydro-treatment facilities break down in the sanction years, and we see Saddam build enormous earthworks that divert the flow of the waters from the marshes, cutting off the nerve-endings to the river's essential organs, suffocating the complex ecosystem and turning wetlands to desert. We watch thousands die and more be displaced. We feel war chemicals seep into soil, killing animals and plants. We watch the Islamic State advance down the river, poisoning water supplies with oil toxins, capturing strategic dams and waterways, cutting supplies to villages downstream. Across the landscape are millions of words written by thousands of UN bureaucrats. Sentence fragments float along the surface of the water, outlining 'environmental destruction', calling on the 'international community', expressing 'concern' and 'outrage', releasing 'warning calls' that drown in the torrents. The words disperse as our oars break the surface in rhythmic strokes.

When we reach Kut, we decide to break. Entry through the Kut barrage will be difficult, we are told. Authorisation is needed, and these things take time. We set up camp in a crater by the riverbank, a few kilometres upstream. We start a fire and watch the flames spit in the darkness. We cook a stew of beans and rice and drink sweet red tea. We dream of battlefields, of powerful armies both ancient and modern, charging against one another, using technologies of warfare that stretch and transform through history. We toss and turn as soldiers crawl through the mud around us, as corpses float along the waters, and in the clear light of day we notice the marks on the ground, deep crevices of tank tracks cut into the muddy banks of the river. We come across the remains of a destroyed military tank further downstream, the treads half-submerged in the water like a snake slithering out of the shallows. In the heat of the midday sun, we wash ourselves. We rinse our hair and beat our clothes dry against rocks, and we wait.

* * *

I do not know whether we will wait for days or weeks, but I know that we need to repair the boats. Zainab and Mediha make food and care for Mama, while I help Murat, Nizar and Abu Rashid reconstruct the vessel. We must make it limber enough to pass through the barrage, and easier to navigate in the weaker currents this far downstream. Mama spends most of the days resting. She is happy to be among us, and this gives her strength.

On the second sunset, I sit alone on the riverbank. Our camp is in the centre of an old bomb crater, which is hardly a surprise given that Kut has been a battleground for a long time.

In the First World War, fierce battles between the two empires were fought in this part of the country. After months of sieges, Ottoman troops defeated the British, but not before the entire town of Kut was levelled to the ground. Months later, British forces recaptured the town, but thousands of British soldiers were killed in battle.

I can feel the ghosts of the dead around me, and I reach down and stick my hand in the slick water. I bring a palmful to my tongue. The water tastes brackish, of soil and debris.

Behind me there is rustling. Zainab comes and sits next to me, looking out at the water and the reddish sun that has begun its descent. She seems, for the first time, unburdened.

Everything feels alive, she says. But it's sick. This ecosystem, it's not well.

I grab a handful of soil from between my legs. Zainab reaches over and traces shapes in the soil in my palm. I tell her what I know about Kut. If this is the site of a battle, I say, then there must be depleted uranium in the soil. I ask her if she has seen the scrap metal strewn across the banks. She nods. She tells me she's been picking some of them up, those with interesting shapes and colours.

I want to use them in my art, she says. A sadness falls upon her. Being here makes me realise how much my art is just a polished version of the past. My handiworks are nothing more than an exploitation of the rose-tinted nostalgia of my customers.

That's not true. Your work is a reminder of all that is beautiful about us.

I can't keep doing that. I have to accept the dark stuff, too.

* * *

Ishtar and Zainab are perched on a large stone by the river. My sisters' closeness has always made me feel like an outsider, a status I've carried with me my whole life. In the past, I would have silently watched them from afar, grown resentful and angry in my loneliness. But now I make my way towards them.

Middy come sit with us, Zainab calls out to me. She pats the space beside her. The three of us sit in silence as the colours of the sky change, from soft violets to shades of ever-darkening blue. Over the river the mist slowly clears, revealing the flies and insects buzzing along the stiller parts of the water. A butterfly flits across the periphery of my vision.

I haven't seen Mama this coherent in a long time, I tell them.

I think being back here has oriented her somehow, Zainab agrees. She places a hand on my leg, says, I'm glad you're here.

I almost didn't come, I say. I cried the entire way. I wanted everything about this country to be in the past.

I'm sorry, Middy.

Ishtar brings her palm up and holds a handful of soil under my nose. I breathe in deeply. The stink is intoxicating, taking me back to my childhood. I smell him again, vividly. The soil brings him back.

* * *

A day is spent fixing the boats. In the afternoon we are visited by men from a nearby village. That evening, a group of women bring hot food, tea, and offer to shelter us in their homes. We accept the food but politely refuse the shelter. Word spreads further downstream. The next morning people come on foot, on bicycles or in cars. They are in awe that anyone would travel down the length of the river. Free movement in Iraq is a luxury, afforded only to those with power.

* * *

I try to make my grandmother comfortable. I prop her up with some cushions that have been brought by women from a nearby village, and together we watch Ishtar negotiate with some officials. By the looks on their faces, my aunt is charming them. They appear interested in her project. Everything I wear, everything I own, smells of river water and mud.

My grandmother points to a packet of cigarettes on the ground, and I pull one out and help her light it. She brings the cigarette to her lips, her hands like the claws of a bird. She inhales deeply and with surprising power, then looks out to the river.

Your grandfather would be proud of you, she says.

Why?

Because you have devoted your life to tell the stories of those whose voices are unheard.

I tell her that I no longer do that work, that I don't do much of anything anymore.

And why is that, she asks. Her skeletal face glistens with sweat, a waxy appearance against the light of the fire.

I guess I just lost hope.

Hope for what?

I suppose I was hoping to find my way home somehow.

And do you still feel hopeless?

I believe we are all doomed.

Of course we are. And accepting this is fertile ground from which hope can sprout.

She stubs out her cigarette and turns back to the river, her gaze moving further downstream where Abu Rashid is performing his ablutions in the algae-filled water. He splashes water on his forearms, his legs, his face.

You should have more compassion, my grandmother says.

For whom?

For yourself. You need to forgive the world. You need to forgive yourself.

The world is not a forgiving place.

Not with you in it, she says, laughing gently. As a child, you used to paint.

I don't paint anymore.

Oh, but you must. It's the key.

To what?

Your grandfather always believed that everything you are searching for is already inside of you. You just need a vessel to bring it to the surface.

There are tears in my grandmother's eyes. In all the years I have known her, I have never seen her cry. She turns back to the river.

The world is a more forgiving place than you think, she says.

* * *

On the third day, we receive permission to cross the Kut barrage. Five hundred metres in length, the barrage has over fifty gates. The passage that allows vessels to pass through is eighty metres wide and seventeen metres deep. Authorities agree to block the flow of water for ten minutes. The minutes pass as we negotiate the locks, before finally navigating the boats to the other side. We cheer and whoop as the barrage closes behind us.

A silence flows along the river. There is nothing more in our way, no bridges, dams, or police. The soil and the sky stretch endlessly before us, mirroring one another. The rhythm of the rowing takes over our bodies and our minds. The boundaries between sky and river, our bodies and the water, dissolves. When the sun drops in the sky, we dock the boats in a clearing and set up camp.

* * *

I wake before dawn, my body feverish, my stomach convulsing in vicious cramps. I leave the tent and vomit in some shrubs, then empty my bowels. I return to the camp and sit by the dead fire. I gaze out at the algae waters, at the film of oily liquid resting on the surface.

What has made me so sick?

The water.

It is the river water I tasted, days earlier. The battle in my body has begun.

Why do you prolong grief, Gilgamesh?

I take my blanket and curl up in the guffa, gazing at the brightening sky. I fall in and out of a feverish sleep.

The others are awake now, I can hear their rustling, their quiet chatter. Their bodies loom over mine, casting a shadow on my feverish frame. Mediha crouches down and puts a hand to my forehead. Shall we take you to a doctor? I tell her no, we should continue. I stand up, fighting the nausea. I will get better.

Curled up in the belly of the guffa, I am back on the water. Above me Abu Rashid is paddling, his long, wiry arms never tiring. I am too weak to pick up an oar. I feel my body twisting in the currents as I drift in and out of consciousness, hot and then cold, cold and then hot. The sun falls and the moon returns, but the sound of the river continues. Abu Rashid's gravelly voice echoes along the water as he sings the blues.

Your name is so beautiful
How did your father come to name you that?
Would he know the destruction you would bring to me?
Oh, oh, who dares to fall into the river of desire
The river of love

On the third day, I pick up the oar and row. Abu Rashid nods approvingly.

* * *

We are in the final days of autumn, but the sun intensifies. We stop to take shade when we can, under bridges, palm trees, enclaves created by the riverbed. We wrap our faces with scarves and pull our hats low against the sun. We develop a rhythm. The waters—green and muddy and clear all at once—gurgle as we dip our oars. We grow accustomed to the pain, to the stiffness in our arms and backs. We pass clusters of houses and fields, we picnic along the river, boiled eggs, biscuits, dates. We laugh. We eat in the houses nearby, grilled fish, rice, spicy tomato sauce, bread. We pass remnants of Ottoman bridges, discarded boats, water extraction stations. We pass a herd of water buffalos, hamlets, an agricultural farmland. We watch two teenagers do backflips off a rusty boat half-submerged in the water. We exchange greetings with strangers, in Arabic and in English.

We stop in Amarah, a city of highways and overpasses, of cranes and aluminium and plastic cladding. We stock up on cigarettes and food. We visit a Sabaean-Mandaean temple, where an elder gives us a tour and explains their community's strong attachment to the dualistic interplay between light and dark, the centrality of water in their rituals and practices. Most have left Iraq for Sweden or Australia, lands where flowing waters are plentiful and the shallows are free from trash and broken glass which cut their feet, allowing disease into their bodies.

After Amarah, palm trees and foliage emerge from the soil on either side of the river, which narrows as farmlands grace the riverbanks, dense orchards with trees bearing oranges and pomegranates. Thin metal wires criss-cross the length of the river just above water level, erected by villagers to ferry themselves across from one bank to another. We are on the river for longer and longer stretches of time. We take turns rowing, singing songs, smoking. Sometimes, we sit in silence and let the boats drift in the water. We lay back and shield our eyes from the glaring sun.

* * *

A fake clementine tree stands at the entrance to Ezra's Tomb. The plastic leaves are brittle and covered in dust. On one of the walls an arrow points towards Mecca. The courtyard opens out into small, cave-like dwellings, rooms for pilgrims to take shelter during their travels. Small lizards dart across the walls as we unroll our sleeping bags onto the concrete floor. The skies open and large, heavy raindrops fall. We huddle together in one of the rooms, eating the bread and dates left by nearby villagers, and watch the torrential rain pour down.

I fall asleep quickly and dream I am standing by the Thames, the water a thin ochre skin over an unyielding blackness. The man I am waiting for is a creature of routine. I recall his ritualistic Sunday afternoon calls with his mother, the evening baths, the way he preserves his Tuesday afternoons for grocery shopping. I am here because I remember how he likes to cycle along the South Bank, his route to his favourite supermarket.

I turn away from the river and catch a glimpse of a handsome man cycling past. I raise my arm and the man glances at me, then stops, hesitates, and smiles. He makes a long, seamless loop with his bicycle until he stops right next to me. My heart swells.

How are you?

I'm good, I respond, and a memory returns to me, of lying next to him in a hotel bed along the Amalfi coast, his heavy leg draped over my body, anchoring me to the world when I had wanted nothing more than to disappear.

I'm just on my way back from Waitrose.

I ask about his family. He asks about mine. The pleasantries feel like a deflating balloon. A desperate frustration rises in the air as we try to return to that place where even the most mundane conversations possessed an easy depth.

He looks down at his feet, nods. Right, he says, I should probably go. It was nice to see you Nizar.

Before I can say anything he turns and walks away, his bicycle by his side. There is a newfound heaviness in his step. I call out his name, half-expecting my voice to be swallowed by the wind, half-expecting him to keep on walking, for the dream to end.

But he turns around. His face, a portrait of hope.

* * *

Nizar snores gently beside me as I lie awake. I think about how betrayed I have felt since finding out the truth about my father's death. I've been carrying this resentment towards my mother for over a decade.

I crawl out from my sleeping bag and walk to the entrance of the cave. I kneel to the ground and pray. It is an urgent, hysterical prayer. I pray for grace and also for time, not just for more of it, but for its reversal. I do not know my mother, really, will never understand all parts of her, but for so long my own anger has made it impossible to see her pain.

I turn to see my mother watching me from one of the caves.

I walk towards her, help her sit so she is leaning against the ancient walls. Above her head, the stone is engraved in Hebrew script. She asks for a cigarette, and I tell her no, that it will wake the others up.

Roll me a cigarette you tyrant.

She lights the cigarette, blows out a cloud of smoke.

Can't sleep?

I tell her that I am thinking about Baba's death.

To lie awake in a tomb thinking about death is a strange irony, she says.

Do you remember the boat Baba was building for me before he died?

She thinks for a moment, then says she does not remember.

He had planned to build me a sailboat, I say, from some wood he found in the garden. He had drawn the dimensions and structure, had even started on the vessel. We were going to sail it down the river, but then he died. It felt like the world collapsed.

I pause.

Do Mediha and Zainab know the truth about his death, or is it just me?

If my question comes as a shock, my mother hides her surprise well. She takes a drag of her cigarette and smiles to herself.

Why are you still living in the past?

Because I need to destroy the myth you created. I won't keep up the lie any longer.

Are you angry at me, or are you angry at your father?

I don't know. Both, maybe.

I did the best I could at the time. I wish you could see that.

Do you want my forgiveness?

Not your forgiveness. Your understanding.

I shake my head. That's not how the world works. We don't have to accept all the wrongs that have been done to us.

I know. But I'm giving you that option.

A distant light breaks through the darkness.

* * *

We can think only of the journey's end, in Qurna, the point where the rivers meet.

We arrive just as the sun dips behind a belt of palm trees, turning the waters the colour of blood.

Once upon a time, the river here was strong and plentiful, the land thick with palm trees and foliage, buffalos and cows lazing in the waters. Now, there is only parched land. The long stalks of reed are frail and dry, the cattle dead or sold. The river's flow is weak, seawater backs up and creeps upstream. We recall a passage in the Quran which says that one of the signs of the end times is when the Euphrates recedes. We hold this passage in our minds.

And yet, the marshes are magical. Kingfishers dot the landscape with splashes of colour among the brown and yellow reeds. Bats swoop over our heads, catching insects mid-air. Green bee-eaters skim the surface of the river. A single water buffalo stands along the manmade causeways, looking at us curiously in between sips of the tepid water, its black body shining under the sun. Young men on boats with engines fixed to the back zoom past us. They smile and ask us where we are from, before slipping past the high walls of brush and into the maze of water passages.

Along the passageways, reeds are tied in elaborate knots. Some signal directions: turn right, dead-end, turn back. Others are existential, messages to strangers or friends: I was here. Openings that were used to place machine guns during the war are now submerged, consumed by the landscape. What were once marsh villages are now hamlets, nests on the embankments. We see a family shovelling buffalo manure into patties to start their fire. We hear a pack of dogs barking as we approach. We see an elderly woman weave a basket using multi-coloured fluorescent wrappers of American and British chocolate.

We arrive at our guesthouse in Shat al-Arab and climb out of the boats. Our feet touch the land where the two rivers meet after their long estrangement.

* * *

I am helping my mother pack. Tomorrow we will return to Baghdad and fly back to our respective homes—me to London, she to Dubai. I am not sure what I am returning to. Since walking out on Alfie, I have spent the last eleven months drifting.

Did I ever tell you the story of the fishermen? My mother asks, looking up from the rusted piece of metal in her hand, one of the many trinkets she has collected from the river.

I was in the old port of Dubai one afternoon, and took a water taxi from one side of the river to the other. On the way, I saw a group of South Asian fishermen in a boat. As our boats crossed paths, I asked them where they were from. They gestured vaguely towards the sea and said: ‘From everywhere’. I think about that often.

Why are you thinking of this now?

It reminded me of us, my mother says. Don't you remember how much we wandered? We are the same, belonging everywhere and nowhere.

I help my mother pack the last of her trinkets. Her face strains as she struggles to fit her newfound treasures into the suitcase. She is wearing a white cotton nightgown and has wrapped her freshly washed hair in a pink towel. She complains about her knees and her back, and has a cough from all the cigarettes she smokes. Watching her, I am overcome with a sudden urge to hold and cradle her in my arms.

Why are you looking at me like that? She asks.

Like what?

Like, I don't know. So serious. You were always so serious. Your first word was 'no'.

My mother sits down on the bed. She has always been so invested in my well-being, has made her happiness contingent on my own. I resented her for this for most of my life, for placing such a burden on me, for dragging me along in her escape from the past, for sowing the seeds of rootlessness and rage inside me.

I take a seat beside her on the bed.

You don't have to return to Dubai, I tell her.

* * *

It is the final night. I lean out of the small window to light a cigarette. The stars are large and bright without the smog of the city. I hear the bats darting across the river, and I am aware that I will treasure this moment for the rest of my life. A memory is already constructing itself inside me, of the time I built an ark and sailed it down the Tigris with my family. I feel an intimate connection with a force much larger than myself. I can hear my father's voice, telling me I have fulfilled his promise. I have sailed the boat.

I stub my cigarette against the edge of the window and return to bed. My body drifts in and out of a gentle sleep. I dream of Murat and his village, soon to be flooded. I dream of Abu Rashid, living in a dying ecosystem. I dream of my family of artists, shot across the world like pellets from a gun.

Hasankeyf will drown, the marshes will dry out, and my mother will soon die. The absences in the trip, the absences in history, confirm the impossibility of a perfect restoration. This acceptance, I realise, carries its own type of radical hope.

There is a rustling by the window. I open my eyes. A black-feathered bird is resting on the ledge. It looks at me curiously. The Sumerians believed that when someone died, they transformed into a bird. It spreads its wings, pushes itself off the window ledge and takes flight, its sleek, black body soaring.

You have my understanding, I whisper to the darkness.

* * *

I have not told my daughters of the large, black feathers that have appeared in my sleeping bag over the last several nights. I hid them away, tossed them in the water or buried them in the soil. They inspire a hope that my decaying body will one day transform. I feel a wildness return inside me that I stifled many years ago, a wildness I've only felt at two other moments in my life: the day I lost my child on the train, and the day Haydar died.

Through the walls of the guesthouse I hear Ishtar get out of bed. She opens the window, and I hear the flick of a lighter.

How quickly life slips past, like a river deposited into a vast sea.

Even decay is a type of transformation.

I try to lift my arms, but it is all too heavy, everything is heavy. I feel him by my side. He grabs my hand, I feel his breath against my ear, can sense him smile mischievously. He pulls me out of bed and we run through the busy street. My body no longer aches. The music and sounds and smells swirl around our bodies.

Where are we going?

To the river, he calls back, laughing, and I am pulled down the narrow streets of Karradah until we are on Abu Nuwas Street, along the eastern bank. Hundreds of people are there. Children play with balls, music blares, celebrations echo around us. Above, the full moon lights up the sky, glistening over the river as guffas glide along the still waters.

He stops, turns to me. He looks so young, like the day we first met on the Thames.

I sometimes come here in the early evening, he says, to watch the sun set on the banks of the river. It's in this chaos of colours and sounds that I find serenity. Am I mad for finding this city so peaceful?

I don't know, I respond. I've only just arrived.

You'll see what I mean soon enough. This soil under our feet is where the whole world began.

Selected Historical Timeline

1917 British occupation of Baghdad
1920 Iraq mandated to the United Kingdom
1921 Enthronement of King Faisal in Baghdad
1931 End of Mandate and Iraqi independence
1933 King Faisal dies; King Ghazi succeeds
1939 King Ghazi killed in car accident; succeeded by son, Faisal II, under regency of Prince Abd al-Ilah
1941 Military coup d'etat; regent flees Baghdad
British troops march on Baghdad
Regent returns to Baghdad
1948 Mass protests in Baghdad against Anglo-Iraqi Treaty
1951 Strikes in schools and prisons
1955 Formation of Baghdad Pact
1958 Military coup d'etat; British-backed monarchy overthrown
Brigadier Abd al-Karim Qasim becomes prime minister
1959 Iraq withdraws from Baghdad Pact
1963 Military coup d'etat by Ba'athist and Arab nationalist officers
Qasim and colleagues killed
Ba'athists ejected from power
1965 War erupts in Kurdistan
1968 Military coup d'etat by Ba'athist officers
1969 Saddam Hussein appointed to ruling Revolutionary Command Council
1971 Relations between Iraq and Iran severed

1979 Saddam Hussein sworn in as president
1980 Over 40,000 Shi'a expelled to Iran
Iraqi forces invade Iran
1984 Escalation of war between Iraq and Iran
1987 Iraqi government campaign against KDP and PUK in Kurdistan
1988 War with Iran ends
Iraq attacks Kurdish town of Halabjah with poison gas, killing thousands
1990 Iraq invades and annexes Kuwait
UN imposes total trade embargo and sanctions on Iraq
1991 United States-led military campaign forces Iraq to withdraw
Southern Shi'a and northern Kurdish uprisings; brutal crackdown enforced
1998 US and British Operation Desert Fox bombing campaign on Iraq
2003 US-led invasion topples Saddam Hussein's government
US-appointed Governing Council
Saddam Hussein captured in Tikrit
2004 Photographic evidence emerges of abuse and torture of Iraqi prisoners by US troops
2006 Sectarian violence erupts; hundreds are killed
Saddam Hussein executed for crimes against humanity
2011 US troops pull-out from Iraq
2013 Sunni insurgency intensifies
The Islamic State emerges in Iraq
2014 The Islamic State seizes Mosul; declares the establishment of a caliphate in Iraq and Syria

Author's Note

At a bustling intersection in the heart of Baghdad stands *Nasb al-Hurriyah*—the Freedom Monument. Commissioned in 1959 to commemorate the 14th of July Revolution, the project was designed by the architect Rifat Chadirji and was brought to life through the sculptural vision of Jewad Selim, widely regarded as one of the most influential Arab artists of the 20th century. Both men envisioned the monument as a timeless emblem of freedom, rather than as a tribute to a specific event. Weaving Iraq's history into a sweeping frieze of bronze figures, the monument's centrepiece—a man breaking through prison bars—evokes the struggle to take control of history and imagine a freer future. It is a marker as iconic to Baghdad as the Statue of Liberty is to New York City. A blend of the ancient and the modern, of rupture and continuity, the monument captures a tension that I've long wrestled with in my own writing: between memory and imagination, the past and the present, resistance and hope.

Jewad died of a heart attack before the monument's completion, on the 23rd of January 1961. Following his death, the monument was finished and erected by Chadirji with the help of Jewad's wife, Lorna Selim, a British artist who moved to Baghdad in 1950. Lorna passed away on the 23rd of January 2021, sixty years to the day after her husband's passing.

Alongside the artist and sociologist Shakir Hassan Al Said, Jewad founded the Baghdad Modern Art Group, a movement that emerged in mid-20th century Baghdad (and which included

Lorna), whose artistic styles and creative visions were markedly postcolonial yet cosmopolitan, celebrating a harmonious mixing of tradition and modernism and of east and west, blending Mesopotamian history with modern European techniques.

Those familiar with the history of modern Arab art will recognise that the characters of Bridget and Haydar are inspired by Lorna and Jewad. Certain biographical details and creative works are drawn from their lives, serving both as a source of inspiration and a practical anchor to tether the novel to the real world.

Ultimately, however, I have written a work of fiction. The personal and inner lives of Haydar, Bridget, and their daughters bear no resemblance to Jewad, Lorna, or their children. I wanted to maintain echoes, not fashion replicas. As such, I approached the creative legacies of Jewad and Lorna Selim not as blueprints for biography, but as wells of artistic inquiry—drawing from their shared preoccupations with identity, heritage, hybridity, and the role of art in times of rupture—to shape the novel's central questions around memory, grief, and the possibilities and limits of creative hope. I hope that admirers of their work recognise that the decision to fictionalise and dramatize their lives was not made lightly, nor with the intention of disrespecting their legacies. Rather, it was a way to honour their creative spirit while protecting their privacy and preserving my own literary freedom.

For their support and guidance in navigating this dynamic, I am especially grateful to Miriam and Zaineb Selim, Jewad and Lorna's daughters, who read countless drafts, advised me on sensitive elements, and corrected historical inaccuracies. Their thoughtful engagement with the manuscript exemplifies not only their generosity, but also a deep commitment to understanding the role of art in navigating history, life, and the dizzying prism of truth. Any remaining errors, historical liberties, or interpretive choices in this novel are entirely my own.

Saleem Haddad

Acknowledgements

This novel was first conceived over a decade ago, the long river from which countless other creative and professional projects branched out. A comforting, challenging, yet necessary companion, one I returned to in moments of despair and hope alike.

I owe deep thanks to the many people who supported this project in ways large and small. My family—Sami and Nadeem; Amal and Mona; my principled, honest and hard-working father; my generous, creative and free-spirited mother, who accompanied me on an unforgettable research trip to Baghdad and was always on hand to answer my questions. My agent, Anjali Singh, for her faith, kindness and persistence. The Europa Editions family for their ongoing support: Eva Ferri and Daniela Petracco, as well as my UK editor Millie Guille and my US editor Michael Reynolds, who embraced this novel and provided thoughtful, clarifying edits. Tareq Baconi, who tenderly coaxed the first draft out of me many years ago, I feel blessed to have gone through that creative journey alongside you. Nabil Salih, who served as a virtual guide to Baghdad from afar and was always on hand to answer my frantic questions ranging from political and cultural analysis of Iraqi history to the direction and flow of traffic on specific Baghdadi roads and bridges.

Illuminating conversations and correspondence with Saleem Al-Bahloly and Moudhy Al-Rashid deepened my knowledge and appreciation for Iraqi modern art and Mesopotamian mythology, respectively. The work of the archaeologist Uzma Z.

Rizvi was also clarifying in understanding the different ways we think of land, history, and belonging. Ishtar's ark project was partly inspired by the artist Rashad Selim's work reviving traditional Mesopotamian boat crafts. His generous conversations with me about the purpose and history of his work revealed a complex and inspirational artistic philosophy rooted in history, cultural continuity, and the preservation of heritage from the violence of empire. These conversations planted seeds that grew into many of the novel's key questions and themes, fusing its artistic spirit with its literary ambition, and I appreciate his time, scholarship, and openness.

I also drew knowledge and inspiration from various resources, including (but not limited to) Irving Finkel's 'The Ark Before Noah'; Ghaith Abdul Ahad's 'A Stranger in Your Own City: Travels in the Middle East's Long War'; Andrew George's translation of 'The Epic of Gilgamesh'; Nima Sagharchi and Zaineb Jewad Selim's 'Jewad Selim: Catalogue Raisonné of Paintings and Sculptures'; In'am Kachachi's 'Lorna, Her Years with Jewad Selim' (Arabic); Jenny Lewis' 'Gilgamesh Retold'; Jabra Ibrahim Jabra's 'Princesses' Street: Baghdad Memories' and 'Contemporary Art in Iraq: The Painting Movement' (Arabic); Nada Shabout's 'In Between, Fragmented and Disoriented: Art Making in Iraq'; Justin Marozzi's 'Baghdad: City of Peace, City of Blood'; Adil Kamil's 'Contemporary Painting in Iraq: Stages of Establishment and Diversity of Discourse' (Arabic); Shams C. Inati's 'Iraq: It's History, People, and Politics'; Abbas al-Sarraf's 'Jewad Selim' (Arabic); and Tommaso Vitali's documentary 'This Was Hasankeyf'.

Thanks as well to Ashleigh Allen; Bridget Guzek; Kate Nevens; Mo Fakhro; Sarah Martin; Alyssa Songsiridej; Adrienne Eiser Treeby; Jatinder Padda; Hannah Wright; Sarah Nasar; Kifah Hanna; Alison Wittenberg; Ahmad Azzawi; Nur Turkmani; Tony Nakhle; Tania Tabar; Jack Casey; Eliane Mazzawi; Raya Hamdan; Chloe Benoist; Joud Abdelmajeid; Sara

Yasin; Hector Santiago Perez; Yasmeen Tabaa; and the Selim family. Gabriel Avila—amorzinho, obrigado pelo seu amor e amizade, e por abrir uma nova porta no meu coração. I am also grateful for the time and space provided by the Corporation of Yaddo and the Literarisches Colloquium Berlin.

And finally, Adam: my home. Thank you for believing in me; for standing beside me at every turn; for living inside this story with me; for celebrating the peaks and holding me in the pits; for waking up every day for the past seventeen years and showing me how to love.

About the Author

Saleem Haddad was born in Kuwait City to a Palestinian-Lebanese father and an Iraqi-German mother, and educated in Jordan, Canada, and the United Kingdom. He has worked as an aid worker with Doctors Without Borders in Yemen, Syria, and Iraq, and has advised on humanitarian and peacebuilding issues throughout West Asia and North Africa. He is the author of the acclaimed debut *Guapa*, a 2017 Stonewall Honor Book and the winner of the 2017 Polari Prize. His 2019 directorial debut, *Marco*, was nominated for the 2019 Iris Prize for "Best British Short Film" and is available to watch on YouTube. He is currently based in Lisbon.